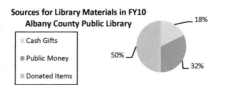

Sources for Library Materials in FY10
Albany County Public Library

- Cash Gifts
- Public Money
- Donated Items

18%

50%

32%

# JASPER
# JONES

THIS IS A BORZOI BOOK PUBLISHED BY ALFRED A. KNOPF

All rights reserved. Published in the United States by Alfred A. Knopf, an imprint of Random House Children's Books, a division of Random House, Inc., New York. Originally published in paperback in Australia by Allen & Unwin, Crows Nest, NSW, in 2009.

Knopf, Borzoi Books, and the colophon are registered trademarks of Random House, Inc.

www.randomhouse.com/teens

Educators and librarians, for a variety of teaching tools, visit us at www.randomhouse.com/teachers

Library of Congress Cataloging-in-Publication Data
Silvey, Craig.
Jasper Jones / Craig Silvey. — 1st American ed.
p.   cm.
Summary: In small-town Australia, teens Jasper and Charlie form an unlikely friendship when one asks the other to help him cover up a murder until they can prove who is responsible.
ISBN 978-0-375-86666-1 (trade) — ISBN 978-0-375-96666-8 (lib. bdg.) —
ISBN 978-0-375-89678-1 (ebook)
[1. Interpersonal relations—Fiction. 2. Secrets—Fiction. 3. Murder—Fiction. 4. Family problems—Fiction. 5. Recluses—Fiction. 6. Australia—Fiction. 7. Mystery and detective stories.]
I. Title.
PZ7.S58846Jas 2011
[Fic]—dc22
2010009364

The text of this book is set in 11-point Goudy Old Style.

Printed in the United States of America
April 2011
10 9 8 7 6 5 4 3 2 1

First American Edition

# JASPER JONES

a

novel

by

# Craig Silvey

alfred a. knopf
new york

# 1

Jasper Jones has come to my window.

I don't know why, but he has. Maybe he's in trouble. Maybe he doesn't have anywhere else to go.

Either way, he's just frightened the living shit out of me.

This is the hottest summer I can remember, and the thick heat seems to seep in and keep in my sleepout. It's like the earth's core in here. The only relief comes from the cooler air that creeps in between the slim slats of my single window. It's near impossible to sleep, so I've spent most of my nights reading by the light of my kerosene lamp.

Tonight was no different. And when Jasper Jones rapped my louvres abruptly with his knuckle and hissed my name, I leapt from my bed, spilling my copy of *Pudd'nhead Wilson*.

"Charlie! *Charlie!*"

I knelt like a sprinter, anxious and alert.

"Who is it?"

"Charlie! Come out here!"

"Who *is* it?"

"It's Jasper!"

"What? *Who?*"

"Jasper. *Jasper!*"—and he pressed his face right up into the light. His eyes green and wild. I squinted.

"What? *Really?* What is it?"

"I need your help. Just come out here and I'll explain," he whispered.

"What? Why?"

"Jesus *Christ*, Charlie! Just hurry up! Get out here."

And so, he's here.

Jasper Jones is at my window.

Shaken, I clamber onto the bed and remove the dusty slats of glass, piling them on my pillow. I quickly kick into a pair of jeans and blow out my lamp. As I squeeze headfirst out of the sleepout, something invisible tugs at my legs. This is the first time I've ever dared to sneak away from home. The thrill of this, coupled with the fact that Jasper Jones needs *my* help, already fills the moment with something portentous.

My exit from the window is a little like a foal being born. It's a graceless and gangly drop, directly onto my mother's gerbera bed. I emerge quickly and pretend it didn't hurt.

It's a full moon tonight, and very quiet. Neighborhood dogs are probably too hot to bark their alarm. Jasper Jones is standing in the middle of our backyard. He shifts his feet from right to left as though the ground were smoldering.

2

Jasper is tall. He's only a year older than me, but looks a lot more. He has a wiry body, but it's defined. His shape and his muscles have already sorted themselves out. His hair is a scruff of rough tufts. It's pretty clear he hacks at it himself.

Jasper Jones has outgrown his clothes. His button-up shirt is dirty and fit to burst, and his short pants are cut just past the knee. He wears no shoes. He looks like an island castaway.

He takes a step toward me. I take one back.

"Okay. Are you ready?"

"What? Ready for what?"

"I tole you. I need your help, Charlie. Come on." His eyes are darting, his weight presses back.

I'm excited but afraid. I long to turn and wedge myself through the horse's arse from which I've just fallen, to sit safe in the hot womb of my room. But this is Jasper Jones, and *he* has come to *me*.

"Okay. Wait," I say, noticing my feet are bare. I head toward the back steps, where my sandals sit, scrubbed clean and perfectly aligned.

As I strap them on, I realize that this, the application of pansy footwear, is my first display of girlishness and has taken me mere moments. So I jog back with as much masculinity as I can muster, which even in the moonlight must resemble something of an arthritic chicken.

I spit and sniff and saw at my nose. "Okay, you roit? You ready?"

Jasper doesn't respond. He just turns and sets off.

I follow.

After climbing my back fence, we head downhill into Corrigan. Houses huddle and cluster closer together, and then stop abruptly as we reach the middle of town. This late, the architecture is desolate and leached of color. It feels like we're traipsing through a postcard. Toward the eastern fringe, past the railway station, the houses bloom again and we pass quietly under streetlights which light up lawns and gardens. I have no idea where we're going. The further we move, the keener my apprehension grows. Still, there is something emboldening about being awake when the rest of the world is sleeping. Like I know something they don't.

3

We walk for an age, but I don't ask questions. Some way out of town, past the bridge and the broad part of the Corrigan River and into the farm district, Jasper pauses to feed a cigarette into his mouth. Wordlessly, he shakes the battered pack my way. I've never smoked before. I've certainly never been offered one. I feel a surge of panic. Wanting both to decline and impress, for some reason I decide to press my palms to my stomach and puff my cheeks when I wag my head at his offer, as if to suggest that I've smoked so many already this evening that I'm simply too full to take another.

Jasper Jones raises an eyebrow and shrugs.

He turns, rests his hip on a gatepost. As Jasper sucks at his smoke, I look past him and recognize where we are. I step back. Here, ghostly in the moonlight, slumps the weatherworn cottage of Mad Jack Lionel. I quickly look back at Jasper. I hope this isn't our destination. Mad Jack is a character of much speculation and intrigue for the kids of Corrigan. No child has actually laid eyes on him. There are full-chested claimants of sightings and encounters, but they're quickly exposed as liars. But the tall stories and rumors all weave wispily around one single irrefutable fact: that Jack Lionel killed a young woman some years ago and he's never been seen outside his house since. Nobody among us knows the real circumstances of the event, but fresh theories are offered regularly. Of course, the extent and nature of his crimes have grown worse over time, which only adds more hay to the stack and buries the pin ever deeper. But as the myth grows in girth, so too does our fear of the mad killer hidden in his home.

A popular test of courage in Corrigan is to steal something from the property of Mad Jack Lionel. Rocks and flowers and assorted debris are all rushed back proudly from the high drygrass sprawl of his front yard to be examined with wonder. But the rarest and most revered feat is to snatch a peach from the large tree that grows by the flank of the cottage like a zombie's hand bursting from a grave. To pilfer and eat a peach from the property of Mad Jack Lionel assures you instant royalty. The stone of the peach is kept as a souvenir of heroics, and is universally admired and envied.

I wonder if we're here to steal a peach each. I hope not. As much as I like the idea of raising my station, I was born without speed or courage, which are both essential to the operation. Besides, even if I miraculously managed to acquire one, I'm certain that no one, not even Jeffrey Lu, would ever believe me anyway.

Still, I notice that Jasper is staring intently at the house. He flicks and grinds his cigarette.

"Is this it? Is this where we're going?" I ask.

Jasper turns.

"What? No. No, Charlie, just stoppin for a smoke."

I try to conceal my relief as we both survey Lionel's property.

"D'you reckon it's all true?" I ask.

"Yeah, I reckon. It's all bullshit what people say mostly, but I reckon he's mad, all right."

"Fersure," I say, and sniff and spit again. "Completely."

"I seen him, you know. A bunch of times." Jasper states it so plainly that I believe him. I beam at him.

"Really? What does he look like? Is he tall? Does he really have a long scar down his face?"

But Jasper just kicks dirt over his smoke and swivels as though he doesn't hear me. We are moving again.

"C'mon," he says.

I shuffle on.

\*\*\*

We link back with the river. We walk east along its worn banks for some time. Neither of us speaks. The paperbarks and floodgums that shroud us look eerie and ethereal in the silver light, and I find myself matching Jasper's step.

I begin to recognize the landscape less and less. The banks become more littered and cluttered as the river thins, and small shrubs frost its edge. Soon we're confined to filing along the narrow kangaroo tracks further from the water.

Jasper's stride is long and strong. I walk behind, watching his calves clench in the gloom. His sureness and his presence make him easy to follow. I'm still afraid, of course, but something about being in his bubble is reassuring. I trust him straight up, though I have no reason to, and that makes me one of few.

Jasper Jones has a terrible reputation in Corrigan. He's a Thief, a Liar, a Thug, a Truant. He's lazy and unreliable. He's a feral and an orphan, or as good as. His mother is dead and his father is no good. He's the rotten model that parents hold aloft as a warning: *This is how you'll end up if you're disobedient.* Jasper Jones is the example of where poor aptitude and attitude will lead.

In families throughout Corrigan, he's the first name to be blamed for all manner of trouble. Whatever the misdemeanor, and no matter how clear their own child's guilt, parents ask immediately: Were you with Jasper Jones? And of course, more often than not, their kids will lie. They nod, because Jasper's involvement instantly absolves them.

5

It means they've been led astray. They've been waylaid by the devil. And so, as the cases are closed, the message is simple: *Stay away from Jasper Jones.*

I'd heard Jasper Jones described as a half-caste, which I'd never really understood until I mentioned it one night at the dinner table. My father is a serene and reasonable man, but those words had him snapping his cutlery down and glaring at me through his thick black-rimmed glasses. He asked me if I understood what I'd just said. I didn't. Then he softened and explained that it was rude to discuss somebody's racial heritage.

Later that night, he came into my room with a stack of books and quietly offered me the very thing I'd wanted all my life: permission to read whatever I liked from his library. My father's rows and stacks of novels had awed me since he taught me to read, but he always chose the volumes he thought were appropriate. So it felt important, and it was clear to me that he thought it was significant too. But I wondered if it came about because he thought I was growing up, or if he worried that Corrigan might be luring me toward things that troubled him.

Either way, something forbidden had been lifted. He gave me a leather-bound stack of Southern writers to start with. Welty, Faulkner, Harper Lee, Flannery O'Connor. But the biggest portion of the stack was Mark Twain. There must have been a dozen of his books in there.

As he laid them gently on my desk, my father told me Twain was the single reason he taught literature. He said there was nothing he couldn't teach you, and nothing he didn't have an opinion about. He said that Twain was as wise a counsel as any, and that if every man read at least one of his books at some time in his life, it would be a far better world for it.

He pressed his thumb on my cowlick, as he sometimes did, and ran his hand through my hair and smiled.

That was winter. By now, I'm halfway through that bundle. I understand why he chose them. I enjoyed the Harper Lee book the best, but I told my father that *Huckleberry Finn* was my favorite. I started

*The Sound and the Fury*, but had to abandon it. To be honest, I had no idea what the hell was going on. I refused to ask my father, though. I didn't want him thinking I wasn't smart enough.

Because that's all I've ever had, really. Corrigan is a town whose social currency is sports. That's where most kids find and hold their own. The mine employs most people and the power station herds in the rest, which means there isn't much class divide. And so kids have established a hierarchy based on their skill with a ball, rather than their clothes or their family car. I'm lousy at sports and better than most at school, which garners me only ire in the classroom and resentment when report cards are issued. But at least I have something over them, even though it's a lonely celebration.

Of course, it also means I'm mostly ignored. It's worse for Jeffrey Lu, my best and only friend, who is younger and smaller and, if I'm honest, smarter than me. Jeffrey has been moved up a year, and he's my main competitor for primacy other than Eliza Wishart, who I mainly blush at from the other side of the classroom. But I don't mind either of them in the race. Least of all Eliza.

Jeffrey's parents are Vietnamese, so he's ruthlessly bullied and belted about. He probably cops it worse than Jasper. But he takes it all astonishingly well, which has always eased my guilt, given that I'm never brave enough to intervene. Jeffrey is unflappable. He has a smile that you can't wipe or slap or goad off his face. And unlike me, he never stoops to sycophancy or spite. In a way, he's more assured than any of those vindictive bastards with peach pits in their pockets. But I'd never tell him that.

*** 

When Jasper Jones stops and grabs my shoulder, I jolt like he's shot volts through my body. I point the bridge of my glasses further up my nose and wait. Jasper pushes through a bush and ushers me through. We're moving off the path. I hesitate.

"Where are we going? What do you need me for?"

"S'not far now, Charlie. You'll find out."

I trust him. I have to. I've come too far. If he were to leave me here and now, I'd never make it back.

I can't hear the river anymore, and the canopy overhead has stolen the moonlight. As we press further, I'm finding it harder to imagine what kind of help Jasper needs. I don't understand what particular unique skill I bring to the table. It's a strange coalition, me and Jasper Jones. We've never really even spoken before. I'm surprised he knew my name, let alone where I lived. He's rarely at school, just long enough to qualify for football. I've only ever caught glimpses of him from a distance, so I can't help but thrill in this sense of inclusion. In my head, I'm already composing my recount to Jeffrey.

We are in fairly thick bush now. It's unearthly quiet. Jasper still hasn't said a word without my prompting, and his replies have been nothing but brusque bursts. Despite the absence of any landmarks, he seems to know exactly where he's going, and I'm grateful. I stick close behind, like a loyal and leashless dog. My anticipation is growing. I wonder if my parents heard me leave. I'm not sure what they'd do if they found my room empty. Sheets bunched, bed pared bare, louvres stacked. They'd have to assume I'd been snatched. Kidnapped. They'd never believe I had slipped out of my own accord. This is, by far, my worst-ever transgression. Probably my only-ever transgression. And if I am caught out, I'd probably be the only kid in Corrigan who could truthfully argue that they'd been led astray by Jasper Jones.

He's starting to walk faster. Branches and shrubs snap back at me with more force. My arm has been scratched by bracken. I don't complain. I just adjust my speed to match. Our feet share the same crisp military rhythm. I'm sweating.

Then Jasper Jones stops.

Right here. At the foot of an enormous old-growth jarrah tree. It has an astonishing girth. I can't help but stare straight up to see how far it reaches into the sky. I can feel my pulse thrumming my temples. I'm panting. I need to clean my glasses. When I glance back down, I notice Jasper Jones is staring at me. I can't place his expression. It's as though he's about to leap from something very high. I tilt my head to the side and I'm suddenly very fearful. My anticipation is usurped by a sense of dreadful foreboding. Something is wrong. Something has happened. My weight is on my heel. I don't want to be here anymore.

He motions toward a wattlebush to the left of the giant jarrah.

"It's through here," he says.

"What? *What* is?"

"You'll see it, Charlie. Shit. You'll've wished you dint, but you'll see it. It's not too late but. Are you sure you're gonna help me?"

"Can't you just *tell* me? What is it? What's through there?"

"I can't. I can't, mate. But I can trust you, Charlie. I reckon I can trust you."

It isn't a question, but it seems like one.

And I believe if it were anyone else, I would choose to step back and turn away right now. I would never bow my head and push through that bush, and its golden flowers would never shake loose and nestle in my hair like confetti. I would never grab at its rough trunk to save me from tripping. I would never part its locks of foliage. And I would never lift my head to see this neat clearing of land. I would never look past Jasper Jones to reveal his secret.

But I don't turn back. I stay. I follow Jasper Jones.

And I see it.

And everything changes.

The world breaks and spins and shakes.

I'm screaming, but they are muffled screams. I can't breathe in. I feel like I'm underwater. Deaf and drowning. Jasper Jones has a hand pressed over my mouth; another across my shoulder, pulling me in toward him. My hips lurch back, back, back out of here, but my feet are rooted to the clearing. Blessedly, my eyes cloud over with tears and obscure it all until they are blinked away. And it's there before me again. Jasper has me hard. He covers my thin frame easily. It's horrible. Too horrible for words.

It is a girl.

9

It is a girl and she is in a dirty cream lace nightdress. She is pale. In the silver light I can see she bears scratches down her arms. And her calves. And her face is smudged and bruised and bloody. And she is hanging by the neck from a thick rope tied to the bough of a silver eucalyptus tree. She is still. She is limp. Her feet are bare and turned in. Her long hair is trapped tight under the noose. Her head is to the side, like a piece of biblical art. She looks disappointed and sad. Surrendered.

I can't look away. Jasper can't look. He holds me like that, his back to the girl, absorbing my movements until I fall quiet. I am breathing very quickly. And quaking. I don't understand. He *knew* this. He knew and he brought me here. To see a girl hanging from a tree. She's dead. She has died. Jasper drops his arm from my shoulder as I speak. I can barely stand.

"Who is it?"

Jasper Jones takes some time to answer.

"Laura Wishart. It's Laura."

It takes me a moment.

"Oh my God. Oh my God. It is. It *is* her."

"Yeah," Jasper says softly. He's observing her now. Out of the corner of my eye, I see his head shake softly. He looks so skinny now. And slouched. Like a boy. I am completely lost. Everything seems slow and dreamlike. It really does. Like I'm not really here and it isn't happening. It is all apparition. I am removed from it. Spectating from beyond my body, watching it all on a screen.

"I'm sorry, Charlie. I'm sorry about this, mate. I dunno what to do."

I am hugging my elbows. I turn to Jasper Jones.

"Why would you bring me here? I shouldn't be here. I have to go back home. You have to tell someone about this."

"Wait. Charlie, not yet, mate. Not yet." It's a firm plea. We fall silent.

"Why did she do this? What is . . . ? I mean, *what*? I don't understand. What *happened*?" I am almost whispering.

"She dint do it. Herself, I mean. It weren't her."

"What do you mean?"

"I mean she can't have, Charlie."

"What? Why?"

"She can't have. For starters, look. Look at that rope. See? That's mine. That's my rope. Use it to swing into the dam there. Look. See? But I always hide it after. I wrap it way up there on that branch so you can't see it."

Jasper speaks fast. Too fast to absorb. And for the first time, I observe the surrounds. Behind the eucalypt, which is broad and hollow at the base, like an open tent, there is a small water hole. In front of that, the space we are standing in is perfectly cleared and ringed by high shrubs and trees. It's a strange little enclave. I imagine it might be something rare and amazing during the day. A quiet bush oasis. But right now it just seems sinister and suffocating. I need to leave. I can't be here. Laura Wishart has died. And she's right here. I can't look.

The eucalypt rises bare for over fifteen feet before it extends the thick arm the rope is tied to. Save for a fat black burr about halfway between, there are no footholds or grips.

11

"And it's fuckin hard to get up there," Jasper goes on. "You got to almost sort of shinny up. Like those coconut trees or whatever. See? No way Laura could have got up there and brought it down herself. No way."

"What about with a stick or something? Or it might have just come loose. With the wind. I don't know."

"I don't see any sticks about, Charlie, d'you? Or wind. And it can't have come loose, cause I wrap it up and tie it. Cause I don't want anyone to know about this place."

I nod, dazed. I can't think properly.

Everything falls silent again.

"So what are you saying? What does this *mean*?"

"Charlie. Listen. I'm saying *she dint do it*."

"So who *did*?" I ask, before a cold feeling of terror and dread suddenly has me backing away from him. I gag on the word:

"You?"

He turns to me. He looks baffled and disdainful. He shakes his head impatiently. His chin kicks.

"What? Shit, Charlie. I thought you were smart, mate. You reckon this was *me*? You reckon *I* did this? Is that what you think?"

"I don't *know*. I don't know what I think."

And it's true. I don't. I just feel ill and very tired. I want to leave.

But Jasper turns and shakes his head again. He spits.

"Listen, Charlie. I got to explain. This spot here, this space, it's sort of mine. See, I'm not the only one who's bin here, but I'm the only one who knows how to get here. No one has bin here without me. Ever. Well, till now. Till tonight. But this is sort of where I stay. I sleep here and eat here when I'm not at home. It kind of *is* my home. You unnerstand?"

He pauses to scratch the back of his hair and slide his arm across his forehead. He clears his throat.

"Anyway, I come here tonight. And first thing . . ." Jasper pauses and shuffles, his voice gets thick. "Fuckin hell, first thing, I saw her up there. I saw it was Laura straight up. And I run over there and grab her legs and I try to hold her up. I try to stop her. But she was gone already, Charlie. I could feel that she was gone, right?"

It is all coming at me in a dim rush. My mouth is ajar.

"So what did you do?" I ask.

"Well, I dint know what to do. I just sort of backed away and looked at her. But I couldn't stay here. I just couldn't. I got out. And that's when I come to your place."

"And you think somebody did this? Somebody hanged her?"

"I do, Charlie. Look at her face. It's all beat up. She dint do that to herself, did she? Someone's done this to her."

"Who?"

"I don't know."

At this point I shrink away and scan the trees. My knees actually tremble. This is a nightmare. It has to be. I'm not living it.

"Christ, Jasper! What if they're still out there? What if he's watching us right now? What were you thinking? Why would you bring me here?"

I keep scanning. It feels as though the trees are closing in.

"Easy, *easy*. It's orright. Charlie, it's orright. There's nobody around now."

"How? How do you know that?" I'm shrieking. Like a girl.

"I dunno. I just do. I can tell," he says calmly.

But my fear is itching me. A sickly buzz on my skin. I feel as though somebody is watching us. Listening intently. The body of Laura Wishart is haunting and surreal. It is so *close*. The fact of her death still hasn't entirely occurred to me. That it isn't Laura Wishart anymore. It's an empty bag. A wax doll. A sloughed shell. It is so strange. I can't muster any tenderness for it. It's as though there's a part of me up there, limp and unfeeling.

But it's clear that something very violent has happened in this still place. And we are here in its wake, in its passing. Bucked by its ripples. Laura Wishart is dead. Look. Dead. She is right there, hanging from that tree. Right there. In the center of Jasper Jones's part of the world. Hovering above his piece of earth.

Two boys and a body.

There are drums in my head. *Doom doom doom*. It's so difficult to breathe in this little clearing. Something has shifted. A bubble has burst. I want out. I feel faint. I've got to be away from this. I want to be back at home, but that seems very far away. And I'm so threatened by the fact that even if I broke out of here, I couldn't get back there if I tried.

No, it's too late. Like Jasper Jones, I have seen what I have seen. I am involved.

"Jasper, I don't know what to do. I don't know why I'm here," I say, observing Laura Wishart's bare, grubby feet. "This is horrible. We've got to go tell somebody."

Jasper looks at me with unnerving intensity.

"No, we can't. We can't tell anybody. We can't tell *anybody*, Charlie." Jasper presses his lips firm, his eyes wide and white.

13

"We have to find out, Charlie."

"What do you mean, *find out?*"

"We have to find out who did this. Who killed Laura. We have to find out who come here and done this to her."

I shake my head briefly before I reply.

"What are you *talking* about? No we don't! We go to the police! That's what we do. We go to the sarge and we tell him what happened and where she is, and *they* find out. That's their job. We can't keep this a secret. Her family have to know. It's got nothing to do with us."

"Shit, Charlie. You got no idea, do you?"

"What? Why?"

"Open your eyes, mate."

"What does that *mean?* They *are* open! What are you trying to tell me?"

Jasper sighs heavily.

"Bloody hell. Listen, Charlie, we can't tell *anyone*. No way. *Specially* the police. Because they are gonna say it was me. Straight up. Unnerstand? They're gonna come here, see that it's my place; they'll see her face, they'll see she's bin knocked around, they'll see that it's my rope. And they're gonna say it was me that lynched her up. They'll charge me and put me away, mate. No questions."

"What? *Why?* That's bullshit, Jasper. That's not going to happen."

"Really?" And Jasper points at me now, rising like a snake. "Who was the first person *you* thought of? Who was the first person who come out of *your* mouth?"

And it happens like that. Like when you first realize that there is no such thing as magic. Or that nothing actually answers your prayers, or really even listens. That cold moment of dismay where your feet are kicked from under you, where you're disarmed by a shard of knowing. He's right. Jasper Jones is right. He's really in trouble.

Of course this town will blame him. Of course Corrigan is going to accuse him of this. And it doesn't matter what he says. His word isn't worth shit. All that matters is the fact of this girl's death and this town's imagination. He'll be cuffed and led away. The outcast that killed the shire president's daughter. He doesn't stand a chance.

"Then what do we do? And what about Laura?" I ask. "They'll start looking as soon as they notice she's gone. They're going to find her here anyway."

Jasper shakes his head shortly as he pinches out a cigarette. I notice he is quivering slightly. He doesn't answer my question. Instead he pulls at another thread of thought. "That's what I don't get, Charlie. Why *here*? How did it happen *here*? Someone must've follered me. Someone else knows about this place. I don't think it's chance. It can't be."

"What, you think someone is trying to set you up?" I ask. Jasper offers me a smoke, and again, for some reason, I gesture to suggest I'm too full to accept.

"Yeah. I reckon they might be, Charlie."

I narrow my eyes.

"But you said earlier that people had been here before. With you. Like me, tonight."

"Sure. I know. But you're the only bloke who's bin here, and I can count on my hand the girls who have."

"Did you ever bring Laura Wishart here?"

Jasper Jones pockets his hands and looks at the ground.

"Yeah. Yeah, I did. A few times, Charlie. A lot, actually. But I always took her a different way through the bush, so she'd never know how to get here on her own."

"Why would you do that?"

"Well, why d'you reckon? I don't want anybody knowing how to get here. It's hard to explain. It's orright to share it sometimes, but I also want to keep it to meself."

I nod.

"But it wasn't like how you're thinking with Laura," he goes on quickly, though I have no idea what he's presuming. "She weren't the same as other girls round town. She was smart, Charlie. Not smart like you. Different. Sort of *wise*. We got on real good. She always wanted to come here. She was always on at me. But I liked to let her. You know how you meet someone and you feel like you've known them all your life? That's how it was. Real easy. It wasn't like those other girls that come here. We never really fooled around much, even though she were older. She was strange about all that stuff. But I never cared, really. It's not why I brang her here anyways."

None of this clears my confusion. Jasper's shoulders have eroded. He looks defeated and sad.

"Who would do this, then? Who? You knew her—is there anybody who could do this? Who would want to?"

"I have a suspicion," he says, and lights another cigarette. Despite the stillness of this place, he shields the tip with his curved palm. He doesn't offer me one, though this time I almost wish he had. "I think I know who could have done it. It came to me straightaway, and I can't shake it off. I keep thinking about it. And I reckon I might be right."

"Who?" I lean forward.

He taps his cigarette, holds it by his thigh, and turns to me.

"Jack Lionel. I reckon it was Jack Lionel."

My eyes widen.

"See, Charlie, when I say I seen him a bunch of times, it's because he's got it in for me, more than anyone else in this town. For certain. He's a bloody madman. Every time I pass his house on the way to here, and I mean *every* single time, he comes out on his porch wavin and yellin, callin out my name. Real strange. He knows my *name*, Charlie. I reckon he's out to get me. Got to be. For sure."

This is all too much. It's all too fast. I'm hopelessly lost. And afraid. I really feel like that cigarette now. I watch its amber ember rise and fall with each toke. It looks comforting. I feel tired. I want to sit. Or to lie down on this soft bit of earth. But I can't. I'm involved. That's what I don't understand: that somehow I've become enmeshed in this.

"But what has this got to do with Laura? If Mad Jack Lionel is out for *you*, why would he do this?"

"Because he were out on his veranda hollerin every time I walked past with Laura. So he's seen her. He knew we were together a lot. And she's seen him too. She got really afraid of him. He got her all worked up and tense. So maybe *he* followed us. He's the only one I can think of who might've. Or maybe he knew somehow where we were going. Maybe he knows about this place. Maybe it was him, Charlie."

Jasper anticipates my next question.

"Every night he sees me, he runs out and screams and yells and carries on. Every single night. Every night except *tonight*, Charlie. Remember that? Not even a light on. Nuthin. And we were out there *waiting*. Not a word."

I frown. I don't feel so removed anymore. I bite at the inside of my cheeks. Sudden tears sting my eyes. I really don't want to cry, but I'm angry. And stunned. And I'm very afraid. I don't know. I feel betrayed. Or something. But mostly just scared. My voice cracks and breaks.

"Wait, after you had a suspicion that Mad Jack Lionel had just *killed* someone, you came to get me, and then you took me straight to his house? Without telling me *why*? And then you bring me here, to see this! And there's a chance this crazy bastard is still around here, waiting for you or for the both of us? Why? Why would you do that to me? Piss off. And . . . fuck *you*. I'm going. I'm fucking *going*."

17

I grind my teeth hard to stop the tears from coming. My nostrils flare and my tongue grows fat and my mouth tastes sour. I've never really sworn like this before. It feels strange. And of course, I'm not going anywhere. I'm trapped here. There's no avenue for escape. From anything. This place, this mess. Jasper Jones is my return fare.

And he walks tall toward me, his smoke resting between his lips. He extends a hand to my shoulder and it is immediately calming.

"Don't go yet, Charlie. Please, mate? I need you to help me. I dunno what else to do. I really don't. I'm real sorry. I really am."

I blink hard. I sniff and spit and readjust my glasses. Jasper's hand stays on my shoulder.

"Listen. You're safe here with me, Charlie. Trust me. You got to trust me. Like I trust you. I know you're a good sort. I know it. We're gonna do the right thing. We are."

I shake my head.

"But *what*? What are we going to do? Don't you see how hopeless all this is? We're not detectives! This isn't Nancy Drew! This is serious. We can't conduct interviews. We can't *talk* to people about it. We can't *do* anything."

"But we can still try. And that's more than the Corrigan police are gonna do if I go walk in there right now and tell them what's happened. It'll be 'case closed' before it's even opened, Charlie. There'll be a fuckin court date before there's a funeral. You know it. You *know* this town. I don't have to do nothing to get into trouble here. So we got to find out who done this. We *got* to."

And as much as this is absurd and illogical, there is something in Jasper's reasoning that is irresistible. It's easy to accept that he really could be right. That he *will* go to prison for something he didn't do. That this town *is* that crooked and low. That Mad Jack Lionel *could* really be responsible for this. That it *is* up to us. That the curse over Jasper's head *is* that thick and evil. And maybe we *can* solve this and set things right. Maybe I am the only person in Corrigan who would ever believe Jasper Jones. Maybe that's why he came to me. Maybe that's why he sought me out. Which means that, for some reason, he had trust in me from the moment he vaulted our back fence and approached my weatherboard sleepout. He must have presumed me to be genuine and fair. Like Atticus Finch: dignified and reasonable and wise. Or the closest thing to it in this town. Or maybe he just knows that I don't have it in me to ever betray his confidence. Maybe it was a mix of both. Safety and trust. Though I prefer the thought of me sitting up late at night, poring over Mark Twain, while Jasper Jones rushed to me for my poise and wisdom. As though I were Solomon himself. The person you come to when it all goes horribly awry.

But it's far from the truth. I don't know what help I can possibly offer. I'm lost. I can't look to my left. I've blocked Laura's body from my sight and my mind, but she keeps pressing, keeps insisting. She's so close. It is too much to think about. Too much for one sitting. It's too fast. Too, too fast. We seem to be willfully ignoring Laura Wishart. Hanged. Hanging. Just meters away. If we don't look, if we talk around her, she'll dissolve into the night. And this won't have happened. And I can go back home, sleep, and wake without the weight of knowing.

After a considerable silence, I turn to Jasper and sigh a shaft of air through my nostrils. I speak quietly.

"Okay. What if *I* report it? Just me. Without you. What if I go to the police, or my parents, right now, and tell them what I've seen. I never mention your name. Ever."

Jasper Jones pinches his chin. Then abruptly shakes his head.

"Never work, Charlie. First off, why would you be here all by yourself? Makes no sense."

I shrug. "I could say I've been sneaking out all summer. Just fishing and that. Exploring. Whatever. Stuff. It's no big deal."

"All due respect, Charlie, I don't think anyone will believe that, least of all your folks, and specially not the sarge."

"They could," I say, indignant.

"And second, soon as they find out where she is, half a dozen girls in town are gonna recognize this place and come forward, start telling the police who brang them here. They'll see a pattern, right? And then they'll know you covered for me. They'll find out, don't you worry. And you'll be an accessory after the fact, Charlie. For certain. And then I got no chance."

I wipe the sweat from my brow. Palm the back of my head.

"Well. Okay. Suppose we move her, then. If it is mostly the fact that Laura is *here* that will get you into trouble, suppose we move her someplace else, someplace closer to town so that someone else finds her. Discovers her. You know, for the first time. That way, you've got a chance, right? That way you're nowhere near her."

I can scarcely believe that this is what I am saying. I can't honestly be proposing this. Surely. But by the way Jasper is rubbing his cheek, he seems to be considering it. My belly roils. I want to retract it immediately.

"I see what you're saying, Charlie. But it's too risky, mate. If someone sees us, if we're caught, we're done then and there. No questions asked, we're good as guilty. Even if we're not caught, the police aren't idiots. They'll know. They'll know she bin moved. We might leave prints or whatever. Shit, they might even trace our steps back to here."

"Too risky," I agree readily.

"I like your thinking but. I hadden thought of that."

I turn.

"Okay, Jasper. So, what if we do find out who did this. Suppose we somehow find evidence that can convict Mad Jack. What then? What do we do? Tell him to confess? Send an anonymous letter?"

Jasper Jones picks at the hairs on his arm and sniffs. "I guess we cross that bridge when we make it to the river. I mean, we don't know the circumstances or nuthin yet, right? Who knows? It might not even be a decision we have to make. But we got to *try*, Charlie. We got to do that. We owe her the truth, right?"

I shake my head softly and sigh. This makes no sense: to cover this with lies to uncover the truth. I try to reason with him, like Atticus might.

"Jasper, there's still a chance that they won't blame you for this. There's a *chance*, isn't there? Listen, we can still do this properly. Tell the right people. The authorities. Do it by the book. I mean, you're still protected by *law*, by . . ."

"Christ, Charlie! I ain't protected by shit. See, that's you bein afraid. That's you washin your hands. You know that's not honest. You *know* what'll happen. This town, they think I'm a bloody animal. They think I belong in a cage, and this here is just an excuse to lock me up in one. They don't need any more than what they see right here. All that matters is how this looks. I'm in *trouble*, Charlie. Real trouble. And I can't run, because they'll find Laura, then they'll find me. I got to tough it out. We got to do this."

I cradle my head in my hands, lifting my glasses and rubbing my eyes with my palms.

"*Do? Do what?* What the hell do we *do?*"

"Only one thing I can think of. Only one thing that's going to save me for the time being."

I look up. Bleary and weary.

"What?"

"We got to bury her. Hide her. Here. Ourselves."

"*What?*" I look at Jasper, horrified.

"It's the only way, Charlie."

"It's not the only way! That's *you* being afraid!"

"Yair, I *know*. But I got somethink real to be afraid of. This is the only way I can keep myself out of trouble for now. Don't you see?"

I shake my head. Incredulous. I try desperately to conceive of alternatives, ways of escape.

"Well, no. We can't. We can't bury her here and now. Okay? I don't know. We don't have any shovels. Or anything. Either way, it'll take hours. The sun will be up before we're finished. And it is going to look real bloody suspicious if I arrive home after sneaking out, dirty as shit from digging a *grave*, and then suddenly everyone knows that Laura Wishart is missing." 21

"Not in the ground, Charlie. In there."

And Jasper Jones motions toward the dam, its surface still as a sheet. My stomach knots.

We are going to drown the dead.

"The dam?"

"Yeah."

I'm caught in a rip, being dragged out further and deeper against my will.

"But what about her family? Don't they have the right to bury their own daughter? To say goodbye? What about Eliza? What about last rites and sacrament and all that? What about their beliefs?"

"Do *you* believe in that?"

"It doesn't matter what *I* believe! That's not the point."

"Listen. I know for a fact that her old man is no good. He's worthless, and he drinks worse than mine. And her mum is near enough to the walking dead. Strangest woman I ever seen. For certain. And I know that doesn't come into it. But, end of the day, I reckon they'll be more concerned with the real truth than how she's bin buried. And that's all we're doing, Charlie. We're making time so we can find out who done this. And I don't know, after this is all over, when Mad Jack is put away, we might still be able to do things right. We'll know where she'll be, right?"

I can't believe any of this. I'm being pulled further down. I glance across at Laura Wishart's hanging frame and feel a fresh sluice of sickness and fear. She's a gossamer ghost. She's not real. Neither is this place.

"I don't know, Jasper. What if we *don't* find out? Ever? What if the Wisharts never find out *any* part of the truth? What if you're wrong, what if we're wrong about Corrigan? About Mad Jack? About everything?"

Jasper suddenly leaps to his feet, shaking his head and looming large. He swats the air, like he's trying to catch a passing insect.

"What would you rather, mate? You want me to go to prison for nothing just so the Wisharts can say goodbye properly? I didn't *plan* this, did I? I'm just tryin to do the right thing without seeing myself strung up like that." And he points at Laura, his eyes bearing in at me wildly. "Because that *is* what will bloody happen. And you *know* that. And I *swear* to you, again, on my mother, that I knew nuthin about this. That I come here tonight and found her here, and I don't know what to do except to save my own arse and then maybe try to work it all out. And that's why I need your help. Because you're smart, and you're different to the others, and I thought you'd understand for sure. I mean, *shit*, I took a big risk when I come to you, Charlie."

I cast my eyes down and keep quiet.

"It's a big thing for me to trust you, Charlie. It's dangerous. And

I'm askin you to do the same. I can't force you to do nuthin. But I hoped you might see things from my end. That's what you do, right? When you're readin. You're seeing what it's like for other people."

I nod.

"Well, Charlie, you think about this space here, and you think about what this means for me. And think about what I've got to do. What the right thing is."

I feel grimly resigned. How could things be so messy and complex outside this quiet bubble of land? Laura Wishart, her hanging body—this shouldn't be our responsibility. It shouldn't be our hideous problem to solve. We should be able to pass this to the right people. We should be able to run like frightened kids, to point and pant and cower someplace safe. The real truth shouldn't be for us to discover. Laura Wishart has been hanged, and Jasper Jones is in serious trouble. Somehow I am here among it.

Jasper softens. He squats and roughly ruffles his own hair.

"But, Charlie, just so you know. I mean, if you stick with me here, if you help me, nuthin is going to happen to you. At all. I mean that. If something happens, I'll do everything it takes to keep you clear, orright? You don't have to worry about that. And that's a promise."

I nod again.

"You got to get brave, Charlie. It's all it is. I know you unnerstand what I bin saying and why I'm in so much trouble. Me, I had to get brave in a hurry. Since I can remember. I had to do it all real quick, Charlie. Some days I feel so *old*, you know?"

"Yeah, I know it," I say.

"See, everyone here's afraid of something and nuthin. This town, that's how they live, and they don't even know it. They stick to what they know, what they bin told. They don't unnerstand that it's just a choice you make."

I raise my head and look Jasper in the eye.

"I mean, I know people have always bin afraid of me. Kids specially, but old people too. Wary. They reckon I'm just half an animal with half a vote. That I'm no good. And I always used to think, *why?* They don't even *know* me. Nobody does. It never made sense. But then I realized, that's exactly why. That's all it is. It's so stupid, Charlie. But it means I don't hate them anymore."

How eerie and distilled this night is. How strange and abandoned and unsettled I am. Like a snow-dome paperweight that's been shaken. There's a blizzard in my bubble. Everything in my world that was steady and sure and sturdy has been shaken out of place, and it's now drifting and swirling back down in a confetti of debris. A book I knew by heart, torn up and thrown into the air. Everything has been rocked with such rigor and tumult. Everything has been uprooted and broken. A dozen disasters at once. I can't begin to collect the pieces and try to set them as they were. It's like I've got to crawl out of my own eggshell and emerge. And, a little like Jasper Jones, I no longer have the luxury of choosing the right time. I can't unfurl from my cocoon when I'm good and ready. I've been pulled out early and left in the cold.

We nurse this strange, empty silence for a while. Our heads turned away from the tree.

Jasper finally suggests that we have one last look around. One final survey of the surrounds before we disrupt them forever. I don't object, but I stick right by him, shrinking when we approach Laura's body.

I'm too distracted to really concentrate on details. I don't even really know what I'm supposed to be looking for. Footprints, I guess. Evidence. A scrawled confession. Anything. But everything is so unfamiliar anyway that I have no idea what's inconsistent. It just reaffirms how hopeless this mess is. How firmly the odds are stacked against us. Jasper frowns and bends slightly as he walks.

We scour the whole area by moonlight. It doesn't take too long. When Jasper finishes inspecting the last of the surrounding shrubs, running his hands across their skeletal branches, he nods, satisfied.

"Well, they must have come in the same way I always do. Same way we come in before," he says finally, motioning toward the wattle-bush, deep in thought. He points. "But look, there's some grass up till this bottlebrush which looks like it's bin trampled. Not much, though. I dunno. It could mean anythin. Maybe she tried to escape. Maybe not. We don't know. We don't know anythin. We don't even know if they hanged her. Proper, I mean."

"What do you mean?"

"I mean, anythin could have happened here, Charlie. They might've killed her and then strung her up to make it look like she did it herself. We just don't know."

I nod absently, distantly. It's too much for me to think about. I wonder how Jasper Jones remains so straight and level. How he can make these kinds of considerations, right here and now. I just follow him in a mute daze.

I glance up and Jasper is looking at me. Patiently. The world is spinning.

"You ready, Charlie?"

I stare back blankly.

Jasper Jones regards me for another moment. Then he tells me to wait where I'm standing, for which I'm relieved. My feet, my pansy sandals, are rooted to the earth.

I watch Jasper walk toward the eucalypt. He ducks into the cavernous hollow at its base. As soon as he is out of my sight, I'm beset by anxiety. My arse tries to crawl into itself and my head is a white whorl. He emerges, holding a broad knife by the handle.

I watch him fasten it to his long shorts through his belt loops. He is so close to Laura's body, so close he could touch her, but he keeps his head bowed from it.

Jasper begins climbing. In spite of my proximity to this scene, in spite of the cloying press of this little plot and its stifling air, I feel almost completely detached as I spectate. As though I'm watching a spider crawl a wall. Jasper grips and pulls himself up to the sturdy burr, and I'm thinking about Jeffrey Lu. I remember that tomorrow is the Test Match debut of his favorite cricketer, Doug Walters. I'll wager that Jeffrey can barely sleep tonight with anticipation. I wonder if Doug Walters is as breathless and nervous as I am at the moment. I wonder if he can sleep tonight. I wonder if he's ever seen a dead person.

Jasper's climb has slowed as he nears the branch. He's shunting up by degrees. It's true: it looks like a hard climb. You'd need to be strong and nimble.

Looking at the stress and strain in Jasper's arms and calves, I wonder how Jack Lionel could have done the same. It seems an unlikely feat. I wouldn't ever make it anywhere near that branch, or even the burr, so how could an old man? But I don't ask Jasper. I stand here and I wait.

Nearing the wrinkled elbow of the branch, Jasper twists his body and hoists himself high, releasing his legs in an act of faith I could never summon. He looks fearless. Like a circus acrobat, practiced and sure. He swings, levering himself up and straddling the limb. He scoots his body toward the rope knot.

My heart is rattling. And I'm suddenly a little less detached, unbearably anxious now as he reaches for that knife. I'm tired and on edge. I'm afraid and bestilled. I guess I feel everything at once: every bell is ringing. But I'm not thinking about Jeffrey anymore. And I'm not thinking about the Wisharts. My head is just that drumbeat pulse as I watch Jasper carefully saw at the thick tie that suspends Laura. I can hear my breathing. My fingers are in fists, but I can't let them go.

And it is sudden when she falls. Fast. Like a white kite spearing the ground, its tail lolling lazily behind. She folds and crumples. Like a doll. Like a bag of wet bones. With a soft, horrible thud when she meets the earth. A sound that reminds me that she's just loose meat. And I guess I shouldn't be, but I am shocked by her lifelessness. She looks so heavy. So helpless. My body is fizzing. It feels like there are ants crawling all over me. Jasper tosses the knife; its blade slots easily into the ground. He starts to slip back down the trunk.

When he alights, he crouches and approaches her very cautiously. I have not moved. I hope he doesn't wish me to.

26

Jasper kneels. And he straightens her limbs tenderly, aligns her body. As though she's just sleeping deeply and he's being careful not to wake her. I think I see him brush her cheek with the back of his hand, but I can't be sure. His movements are slow and deliberate. Respectful. I feel awkward, as though I am witnessing something very private. Like I've come creeping to Jasper's bedroom window and I'm peering at something intimate inside. I should turn my face and look away. It's not for me to share. But I'm eerily adhered. Jasper Jones is carefully unpicking the knot round her neck. This is torrid to watch. My ears are pinned back. I think Jasper is getting frustrated. He pulls at it, but it won't give.

Then my feet move. I don't know how. I find myself kneeling cautiously.

Jasper glances up briefly.

"Hey, Charlie," he says, as though I were just passing by.

I don't respond. I am transfixed. And terrified. The color of her face. The swell of it. The glaze in her gaze. I feel ill. Her right eye is dark and puffed. There is a small cut on her jaw, another on her eyebrow. She's been hit. Beaten badly. It's true. My stomach seizes. I am shaking as I push my glasses back.

"I don't want this round her neck," Jasper says under his breath, his head bowed. "But I can't get this knot. It's not even a noose. Look. It's just a knot. It's all for show. Maybe she really weren't hanged until after. Maybe she died before. I'm gonna have to cut it, Charlie. Got to be careful but."

I nod.

Jasper rises to retrieve the knife. I immediately want him to come back.

He slices at the rope with a surgeon's care, as though he might hurt her. All I can hear are those slight slices. *Shick. Shick. Shick.* Eventually it comes away. I jump slightly. It feels like we've accomplished something purposeful. And Jasper removes the rope slowly. Like he's unclasping a precious necklace.

27

I don't think either of us is prepared for the dark ridges pressed into her neck. I feel a rash of goose bumps. My hands go numb. We both take in a sharp breath and hold it. Jasper makes a noise like he has something caught in his throat. He is clenching his jaw.

Jasper lightly inspects Laura's body. Touches the thin scratches on her cheekbone and her shoulder. Runs his fingers down her smooth alabaster arms. It's a strange and silent examination. I hope he's not expecting me to do the same. He looks at her legs, her ankles, her feet. He is frowning. Then he lifts the hem of her nightdress. I immediately shy away. I turn and stare at the ground. I think I know what he is looking at. And I think I know what he is looking for.

When I glance back up, Jasper is gone. He's vanished.

Of course, I panic. Frantic, I slew my head side to side, then behind. Another flush of goose bumps covers my back like a cape. I can't see him anywhere. I am alone in this clearing. The walls of leaves loom. They push in at me. I shrink into myself, crouching. Eyes wide. I hold out my hand for balance and I touch Laura on the shoulder and she is warm and I flinch like I've touched something burning. I yell in fright. She is *warm*. I could faint again. Right here. Right next to her. That creep of fog is drifting down again.

I am dizzy and sick. And it's as though touching her has sealed my fate. I am in this story. She can't be ignored. She's real. I've touched her now. I've been privy to her last moments of heat, her last wisps of smoke. For some reason, I make myself look at her face. I look deep into it. Her expression is strange. Kind of puzzled and surprised and sad and terrified, all at once. And I wonder if this was her expression when the life went out of her. Frozen in time. I wonder if this is what she was feeling. I think about how much she looks like her sister Eliza. And I think about the moment when she'll find out about this, and it twists me in two.

I hear a dim rustle from the other side of the eucalypt. I don't know whether to feel afraid or relieved. I jump to my feet.

"*Jasper!*" I hiss.

And he emerges, carrying a sizeable hunk of granite with both arms. He places it beside Laura's thigh. If I didn't know what that stone was for, if I weren't stunned by what we're about to do, I'd be screaming at him for leaving me alone like that.

I shake my head, slow and low. I am so close to the edge. I really am. Jasper pauses for a moment, and we both regard each other. There's nothing left to be said.

After some time he kneels. Bending, he rolls the rock toward Laura's feet. I watch him take the rope and tightly coil it around the rock; then he threads the end into a knot. He clears his throat and, delicately, lifts Laura's bare feet. They are small and thin and dirty. With the other end of the rope, he carefully binds her ankles together. It hurts him to do this. I think I hear him murmur an apology.

Jasper tugs hard to tighten the knots. Laura's feet rise up as he does so. Like he's tying the shoelaces of a distracted child. His palms must be sweaty, because he keeps running them down his shirt. It is so stuffy and stifling in this place. The air is thick and hot. Hard to breathe.

As her legs rise, her hem spills, and Jasper pauses to adjust it, pulling her nightdress down to where it should rightfully sit. He smooths it over her knees. Even now, though it's just us here, even though we're preparing to discard her, he's trying to afford her some dignity. Trying to treat her the same as he always might have. And it seems to me that maybe they were closer than Jasper let on. He seems sort of familiar in touching her tenderly. Maybe they were in love. Maybe she was his girl.

Jasper gives a couple of neat pulls to the rope, at each of the knotted ends. He runs his hands over the stone and seems grimly satisfied.

Laura Wishart is dead and anchored to a piece of granite. And Jasper Jones is kneeling, watching over her quietly. His eyes slit and he breathes deep and he crouches there for a long time. Just looking. As though he has just lullabied her gently to sleep and he's just sitting at the end of her bed for a time before he leaves her bedroom.

And I don't know what to feel, taking this all in. It's sad and it's warm, but it's so chilling and surreal. I no longer have to remind myself that she is dead. I've seen her eyes. I've touched her. She's no longer here. Really. She might be warm, but she's not in this space anymore. I can tell; I can feel her absence. And whether she's slipped through to someplace else or she's just been switched off like a light, I don't know. But suddenly all that doesn't seem so important anyway.

Jasper Jones shifts, edging closer to her face. He runs the back of his hand down Laura's cheek. I see it for certain this time. And it stings me. He runs his open hand straight down her face, a gentle brush, and her expression changes. Her eyes are closed, but she doesn't look at ease. I want to rearrange it, sculpt it. She looks strained with a distant worry, like she's wincing in the midst of a horrible dream. And I don't want her to bear that forever. I don't want to do this. I don't want to send her sinking to the bottom of this water hole, to damn her to this dam. But I'm part of this. I am the ally of Jasper Jones. I'm committing a crime. This is not an honorable act. Look at her! Look at what she's telling us with her brow, with her tight mouth! She doesn't want this! She doesn't want to go!

Jasper rises, and I step back. He turns.

"Okay, Charlie," he says.

And I don't know what that means until he points at her. He stands behind the rock. I am to grip her between the shoulders, under the arms. This is my task. I am to lift her. Heavy and yielding. I am to carry her toward the water.

And that's what I'm doing. I am bending, grabbing, and struggling with her weight. I shuffle for balance. Oh, she is warm. Her head lolls to the side. I grit my teeth and shaft air through my nostrils. I look at Jasper, who holds the rock to his gut. We're not moving anywhere. She is bowed in the middle. Like she's lying in a hammock. She is slipping. And so is her hem, again. And I know it makes Jasper Jones uneasy, because he frowns at it.

"Are you ready?" he asks.

"She's slipping," I say. "I'm going to drop her."

"Get your elbows under her arms and hold her across her chest. Be easier."

But I don't want to do that. At the moment, I am cupping her armpits and losing my grip. I don't want to hold any more of her. I don't want to hug her chest. The more of her I touch, the more guilty I am for this. She is slipping. I shake my head.

"I'm going to drop her! Put her down! Put her down!" I say, panicked.

"Careful! Careful!" Jasper instructs, as though she's a piece of brittle furniture and we might break her easily. We bend together and lay her down. I'm panting. My mouth is tight and dry. I breathe heavily through my nose. Jasper waits patiently, though I sense that he wants this done.

I've got to get brave.

I wipe my brow. I roll my shoulders and try to stiffen my back. Then I wipe my palms down my shirt. I puff my cheeks. Jasper bends and hoists the rock.

*31*

I have Laura Wishart beneath the arms. Barely. She's slipping again. I shuffle to the side. We are taking her to the water. Just meters away. We are by the edge, which even in summer is sheer and full. It's a broad, still well.

Jasper speaks softly:

"Count of three, Charlie, okay?"

And we swing her. We swing her like we're playing an innocent prank, like we're tossing our friend into the river for a laugh.

One. Two. Three.

I'm not strong enough to throw her. And so the rock that Jasper hurls high and hard simply snatches her body from my thin grasp. And it's a thick, deep splash. A plunk. And I almost hold on. I almost follow her in. It's a rough and sickening jolt, having her torn away, but Jasper steadies me with a hand my shoulder. And we watch. For a moment she floats. Then we watch her sink. It's messy and it's graceless. The bloated bubble of her nightdress. We, the undertakers. We watch her go. We can't save her. We watch the ripples reach for our feet. And she is gone. She really is gone.

We have drowned her.

We are monsters.

I stand motionless. My hands by my sides. And I watch the last pulses of the water, the softening frill of wake. I watch it right till it stills. And I am mesmerized for a time by the plain somber surface, like glass. Strange to think that this afternoon Laura Wishart might have been walking around Corrigan, carefree and unaware. With her friends. With her sister. Now she's anchored to the bottom of this dark pool by the rope she was lynched with. Laura Wishart has been swallowed by the earth. Never to return. And I helped her on her way.

I fear I might stumble forward, follow Laura's descent. I even feel a faint pull toward the water.

Until I hear Jasper Jones. He's no longer at my side. I turn, sharply. His back is to me. One hand is leaning on the trunk of the tree for support. And my mouth falls open when I see his shoulders shaking, when I hear the shuddering of his breath.

There is a sting in my throat. I should stride over there, say something strong and assured and wise. Look him right in the eyes. But I don't. I just spectate. His other hand is to his face. This is real. His knees are bent and his muscles are taut. My lip begins to twist down at the edges.

And I sit down heavily and cry with my head between my thighs. Very quietly and measuredly. I snatch my glasses and wipe my eyes with the back of my wrist. I don't understand what just happened. I need a shit. I need to bathe. I need to sleep. This night has pickpocketed me of precious things I can't ever get back. I feel robbed, but I don't feel cheated by Jasper Jones. It's a curious emptiness. Like when you move to a new house and there's no furniture or familiar walls, the same sort of weird alloy of abandonment and upheaval. It's a lonely sensation.

I squeeze my eyes tight. I don't want to sniff—otherwise Jasper will know I've been crying too—so I pinch my nose and drag.

When I look up and slot my glasses back on, I see Jasper is sitting now, leaning on the curved base of the tree. He looks exhausted. He has a bottle in his lap. It's full. It doesn't have a label. His eyes are glassy. He looks up and slowly rolls his head side to side.

He takes a quick swig. Then glances down and tilts the bottle my way. I am sorely tempted, but I shake my head and show a palm.

Jasper runs his hand roughly down his face and pulls at the skin on his chin. He lights a cigarette. Rests his arms on his knees.

"Give us a smoke?" I ask.

Jasper smiles. He strips one from its pack and straightens it. I purse the cigarette hard between my lips as he offers me a light. And I lean tentatively toward the flame, like I'm moving in to kiss a horse on the arse, waiting to be kicked.

"Waitwaitwait!" Jasper interrupts, still smiling. "Other end, Charlie. That's the filter, see?"

He steals it from my mouth and lights it himself, then hands it back.

I expected to cough, but not as much as this. One breath of it wrings my lungs like a washcloth. I splutter and spit. I try for composure and fail.

"It's the . . . asthma and that. All the . . . humidity. Yeah. Usually I'm . . ." I squint down my nose at the cigarette in my hand, as though it has just said something to confuse me. I needlessly tap ash from its hood, singe the tip of my index finger, and drop the cigarette. Of course, my instinct is to reach and catch it, which, to my surprise, I manage to succeed in doing, and so I burn the inside of my left palm. I hate this cigarette. And now I have to smoke it.

I tear at the soft grass between my legs. It feels like we've weathered a storm and we're sitting among the wreckage. We sit under that blanket of quiet for a long time.

Jasper keeps pulling at his bottle. I don't know what to say. It is so

33

unearthly quiet I can hear the crackle of the paper when he inhales his smoke. The slight puck of his lips. I let my cigarette burn out discreetly between my fingers.

"It feels like I'm dreaming this whole thing," I say.

Jasper raises his eyebrows. "Yair. I know it. This whole night. This whole crazy night. Fuckin hell, I wish it were a dream, Charlie. I can't tell you. It's like somethin's bin ripped right out of me."

He grinds his cigarette and pockets it. I take the opportunity to do the same. He lights another and goes on.

"Laura, she were the only person I ever felt like I *knew*. Like I dint even have to ask questions. I just felt comfortable. She was like my girl and my mum and my family all at the same time, you know. Everything was always easy. I mean, she would sometimes get in these moods where she just sat there quiet and never said nothing, but for some reason I understood that too. And I get like that anyway. But most of the time, she was real funny. And smart, Charlie. Like I said."

Jasper is sucking down that bottle. It's half gone already. I frown. I worry that should he get too drunk, we may not make it back through the bush.

Jasper reads my mind.

"It's orright, Charlie. I can hold my licker. Not like my old man, and he's the whitefella. You want some? Here, garn."

I reach tentatively for the cold, wet bottle, more to slow him down than to quench my own desires. I sniff the lip and recoil.

"What is it?"

"Bushmills. Tastes like piss and oil."

I take a small incendiary pull. Of course, it attacks my mouth and burns down the length of my throat. I gag immediately, wiping my lips, trying to keep my lungs at bay. I slant my head and pretend to read a label that isn't there through my clouding eyes. This shit is poison. And I realize I've been betrayed by the two vices that fiction promised me I'd adore. Sal Paradise held up bottles of booze like a housewife in a detergent commercial. Holden Caulfield reached for his cigarettes like an act of faith. Even Huckleberry Finn tapped on his pipe with relief and satisfaction. I can't trust anything. If sex turns out to be this bad, I'm never reading again. At this rate, it will probably burn my dick and I'll end up with lesions.

I glance at my sandals and try to play down my disgust. "Yair, shit. I usually drink . . . what is that . . . *single* . . . malt?"

"No idea, mate. Dint get much time to read the label. Beggars can't be choosers, Charlie. You take what you can get."

"You mean you *stole* this?" I ask, handing it back to his outstretched fingers.

"Well, I dint *pay* for it. Lifted it from my old man. Right out from under him. He was out of it, huggin an empty one, so I helped meself to the full one on the table."

I nod slowly as Jasper pauses to swallow.

"But you probably already bin told I'm a thief, right? I'm a lifter? I steal stuff."

I pause. Trying to choose the right words.

"It's okay, Charlie. You can't help what you hear. But it *is* what you heard, right?"

"Yeah, I guess."

"Well, what you don't know, Charlie, what nobody will ever be tellin you except me, is that outside of my old man's pocket, I *never* stole a thing I dint need. For certain. I'm talkin about food, matches, clothes sometimes, whatever. Nuthin big, ever. Nuthin people couldn't go without. And, see, it's these people who expect three meals a day, who got pressed clothes and a missus and a car and a job, it's them that look at me like I'm rubbish. Like I've got a choice. Like I'm some runt who just needs to lift his game. And they're the ones tellin their kids that I'm no good. They don't know shit about what it is to be me. They never ask why. Why would he be stealin? They just reckon it's my nature. Like I don't know any better. And you know what else, Charlie? I never once bin caught. Not even close. They all just suspect it. They expect it. *Of course he's a thief*, they say. *Of course he burned down the post office. Of course he hanged that poor girl. That poor girl.*"

Jasper's lips are wet. He is starting to merge his words.

"Your dad doesn't even buy food?" I ask, and regret my incredulity. "You're joking, right?"

"Well, I don't know. What does he spend his money on?"

"Grog and whores and horses, mostly. But even that's slowed down since he was laid off. He hasn't had a job in months. The useless bastard should join the army. Go to bloody Vietnam or whatever and stay there. I'll sort meself out."

"So what do you steal off him?" I press.

"Well, mostly the stuff that I want. Smokes, drink, money when it's there. Whatever's in his pockets. Trick is to do it when he's stone-cold gone; that way he can't be sure if he lost it, drank it, smoked it, or spent it. If he's really bin cooked, he never even notices anyway. It's always different. Sometimes, after he's been layin it on, if he suspects me of clearing him out he might let it slide on account of him feelin guilty, but that's not often."

Jasper scratches his chest, offers back the bottle. I scrunch my face.

"Do *you* ever feel guilty? For taking his things?"

"Not even once, mate. See, from him, I just figure I'm owed. He's not a father's arsehole. I *got* to take it, Charlie, because it's never gonna get offered. And all my life so far, shit's bin taken off me, so I'm evenin the ledger a bit."

I nod. Jasper continues.

"But you can't think that way all the time. It's a poisonous way to think. There's no point sittin down feeling sorry for yourself because other kids are gettin Christmas presents or their old men give a shit, or they've got a mum who's a top cook or whatever."

"Yeah, but you're still entitled to . . ."

"Nah, bugger that, Charlie. I tole you, I don't want to think like that. There's nothing in it. I don't know. I don't want to have one of those bum lives where you just always expect your luck to be fucked because that's the way it's always bin. No. We always reckoned that things would be different once we got out of this town, you know? That's when we reckoned it'd all turn itself around. We'd move to the city, make millions. For certain."

"We?"

"Yeah. We." Jasper looks down and thumbs the bottle neck. The heaviness drifts down again. I want to keep it at bay; it's easier when he's talking.

"What's your plan? When you get out, I mean."

"Well, I haven't thought it all through as yet, but I'll think of something. I got some irons in the fire. Footy, maybe. Who knows? Oysters up north. There's good money in them little buggers. Or I could work on a mine, maybe; put some gold in me pockets. Learn a trade. I don't know. Anything but a shoe-shiner. What about you? Probly the university, right?"

I squirm a bit. Awkward. It suddenly feels disrespectful to be talking about this right now, talking about the future when Laura Wishart has just been robbed of hers. It doesn't seem like it *matters*. But maybe this is the point. Maybe all this talk is for Jasper. Maybe it's doing the same thing as that horrible bottle. Trying to slow our minds down, sandbag some of the panic.

37

"I don't know," I say. "I've always loved reading and stuff. Books, poems. So maybe a writer. I always thought that would be the thing. To write books. Make up stories."

I try to couch it with an ambivalent shrug, like it's a fleeting thought, like it's not the single thing I've had my heart set on since I could first read.

To my surprise, Jasper nods his approval.

"Yeah. I reckon that's you for sure, Charlie."

"You think?"

"No doubt. Reckon you'd be great. Move to some big city with a typewriter. Meetin people, tellin their stories. Maybe you could write my story one day. Then we'll make a film out of it, for certain. Imagine that."

And I do imagine it. Jasper makes it sound so possible and plausible, that I might leave Corrigan to be a writer. To tell tall stories for a living. Real, important literature. When the mood strikes me, I sometimes like to imagine myself as a famous author in an austere candelabra-lit ballroom, where I am bantering with beat poets and novelists like Harper Lee and Truman Capote.

But Jasper Jones interrupts my musing. He's up and lurching, huddled over like he's been shot in the stomach. Before I can panic, he starts evicting that noxious liquid in a thick sheet that seems to almost glow. He grips the empty bottle. It smells sour, his sick. It's bursting out of him. He locks up violently, like he's being held and punched in the stomach by invisible assailants.

Jasper retches and coughs, breathing heavily on his haunches. He spits and groans softly before retching again. Then he finally stands up straight.

"I thought you said you could hold your liquor?" I ask.

Jasper spits again, wipes his mouth, and smiles. "Yeah, I can. Just not for long."

He turns and stumble-steps toward the dam. Kneeling, he fills the bottle with water. He looks precarious. And he collapses back against the tree before he can drink any. The bottle spills. He's out to it. Oblivious and gone. Maybe that's all he wanted.

I notice that it suddenly seems lighter in this space. First I wonder if I've just grown accustomed to the dark, if I've adapted. Then I shoot from my feet like a firecracker and shake him awake.

"Jasper, *shit*! It's almost dawn! We have to go back. Now! If my parents know I've been out, I am right in it!"

Jasper Jones squints and slowly glances up.

"What?" He seems to ponder it. "Yeah, you're right. Okay, Charlie. Juss a second."

His words are slurred. Now I really fear getting lost on our return. But not nearly as much as I fear my parents finding my bed empty. I can't even imagine.

"No, we've got to go now!"

Jasper stands unsteadily and treads heavily. He slaps a hand on my shoulder. Looks at me, intent yet vacant. Full of sorrow. His breath is like acid.

"Orright. Less go."

He pauses. And, swaying slightly, he lingers and looks up at the ghostly eucalypt. In spite of my worried hurry, I don't rush him. He takes it in one last time before we turn to go.

The walk back feels much faster than when we first set out. Perhaps it's because I'm aware of where we're headed, or because I am almost treading on Jasper's Achilles in my haste.

His shoulders have fallen forward slightly. He doesn't walk with that straight-backed poise or intensity he had earlier. He shakes his pack of cigarettes. Empty. So he shoves his hands into his pockets. We walk silently and quickly. Overhead, magpies stir and warble their morning song. The sun is coming, like a harbinger of doom. Strangely, the easier it is to see and navigate, the more afraid and apprehensive I am. But at the least the night is over. There's some relief in that. I don't have to bury anybody else. I can sleep soon. Maybe. For a couple of hours at least.

We track back onto the narrow path. And when we walk along it, I feel a weird sense of kinship, like we're old friends. It's not without its share of comfort. I know where we are. There is nothing but familiarity in front of me. It's the same when we push through the bush and onto the road. It's as though I've been away a long time and I've finally arrived home. With a horrible secret that I've got to cauterize and keep down.

The light is gray and grim, but strengthening quickly. We might make it before the world wakes. We just might.

Now I walk side by side with Jasper Jones. I ponder whether or not we should split up, whether it's dangerous to be seen together. Or, more to the point, I understand that if I'm seen with Jasper Jones, it might arouse suspicion. I breathe in quick, about to broach it, but I check myself. I suddenly don't wish to. And it's not a question of bravery.

39

I don't know. It seems that because we've ridden through something serious and substantial, I feel a real sense of loyalty. I feel as though if we were to separate here, it would sully some kind of tacit pact. We're comrades in some private war. Suddenly it feels important to stay together, side by side.

And so, as we reach the sepia center of Corrigan—the Miners' Hall, the Sovereign Hotel, the newly refurbished post office; then the crouching loom of the police station—I realize I am in this. Right in it. To whatever end. Of course, I'm afraid. But walking in his shadow, I'm also buffeted by a sort of anticipation. Me and Jasper Jones, sleuths and partners. Thick as thieves. In spite of everything, it excites me a little to know I'll certainly be seeing him again. That he needs my help. I don't feel so ridiculous walking next to him anymore. I don't feel like an incongruous sidekick. While the rest of this town looks at Jasper Jones like he's no good, it thrills me that he treats me like I'm equal.

As we turn, finally, into my street and we stride quickly before broad front yards, skirting the side of my house, I'm afforded some slim relief. It seems my parents are yet to stir. I haven't been caught by anybody. Yet. I don't imagine I'll hold this sense of fortune for long. Tonight's events still lurk in me, cold and uneasy. Anchored in and stuck, like that poor girl we tethered to a stone. When I'm less stunned and tired, it's going to hurt. It's going to bubble up and burst in me, I know it.

It is dawn. It is light. But it still feels like the night.

I turn to Jasper. He looks exhausted. And it occurs to me that there is no break in this for him: there's no comfort, nowhere he can go and lie down and be looked after. Not anymore. If he had anywhere in this world, it's the place we've just come from, the place that has just broken his heart and put him at risk. He's right: shit has been taken from him his whole life.

He looks done in and drunk, but he arches his back with a jolt, projecting that toughness again.

I wonder where he's going to go now. If he's going to go sit someplace quiet and wait for the riot or if he's going to go home, if that's what you would call it.

It makes me feel rotten for what I have. For what I've always had. I feel stupid and petty for ever having complained about anything. I feel like a spoiled little bastard, about to crawl into my safe nest while Jasper Jones shoulders his burden alone. It isn't fair. It isn't fair at all. I want to invite Jasper in, give him my bed, and I hate myself because I can't and I won't. I feel sick that I'm going to wake up and have my breakfast made. That my mum is still alive and my dad is a kindly tee-totaller. It isn't right. It just isn't right that I have so many things that he doesn't. I might blub again, but I reckon I'm too tired even to do that. I'm so overdone and overwhelmed.

I wipe my forehead. I was right; my relief was short.

Jasper Jones gives a weak, quick grin and claps my arm. He pockets his hands. We don't say a word. We just look and nod and shift our feet. There's nothing to say.

I shuck off my pansy sandals, move quietly up to the window. I hoist myself up and hold, like I'm on a pommel horse, but I'm stuck. I turn my head and hiss:

"Give us a hand?"

And Jasper strides over and hefts me easily. I'm through. I made it. Back on my bed.

"Thanks," I whisper through the window.

"Yeah, same to you," he says. "I'll see you, Charlie." He lingers, as though he has more to say, but just offers a brief wave.

And he's gone.

I slot the glass plates back in. It feels like I've broken into my own room. It doesn't feel like the same place I left. It doesn't feel like home, but it feels safe. I can feel the heat of the day threatening already, and the light is still blue-hued. I notice how dirty I am, how sweaty and scratched, how urgently my heart bangs at my ribs. Laura Wishart is gone. She really is. She was killed, in a strange clearing only known to Jasper Jones. And I saw her, hanging by a thread. Already dead. I helped carry her to a water hole and I dropped her down and she sank with a stone. That's irrefutable. That's truth. That's what we know. I'm thirsty. I'm in trouble. I feel sick and I can't still this tremor. For some reason, I just know that if I'm in Jasper Jones's corner, it's going to be okay. That there's some kind of protection and rightness at work. I lie down. And it's over, for now.

# 2

am covered in sweat when I wake. It must be late. The sun is beaming directly into my eyes. I squint. I feel like I've just emerged from an operation. It certainly feels like my innards have been pulled and scraped. I wonder what time it is.

Last night comes to me in strange fragments and shards. It doesn't take long to sink in. One bilious moment, a weighted white dress. Then I remember it all.

And I sit up, startled. I expect police with whistles and urgent orders. Sirens. Bells. Spotter planes. Bloodhounds. Yellow tape and busy-looking people. I expect a red sky and ominous clouds. I look through the window. It is utterly serene in our backyard, save for a castanet chorus of cicadas. Even so, I suspect I'm being watched. I peer at length through the window, making sure I'm not being surveyed.

I get up and glance at my bed. There's a dark patch where I slept. I touch it. It's wet. Sweat. But around that is a thin layer of grime. It looks like the chalk outline of a murder. Like I died during the night. Or I shed my skin like a snake.

I need to piss. Urgently. But my dick is cruelly jutting at my underwear, trying to assert itself. It's rock-hard and disobedient. I rearrange myself and grab a towel, then slip quickly across to the bathroom, hoping I don't encounter anyone on the way. Thankfully, the coast is clear. I slam the door and toss the towel. My aim is appalling, but the relief forces a thin smile.

I sit on the edge of our lime-colored bath. Naked and solemn, I run the water, flinching when the first spurts scald my fingers. It pools and burns my feet. I hold them aloft. Goddamn. Has someone lit a fire underneath our water tank? I want to yell at my parents for this. Finally it eases to a lukewarm stream. It's the best I can hope for. I splash water on my face, rub my neck. I wash myself thoroughly with granite soap. It feels good to scratch and scrape at my skin. I don't mind that it hurts me a little.

And I sit. Head bowed and whirring. Dripping. Ashamed of the lack of meat on my body. I'm skin and bones all the way down. It's the gangly body of a kid. No bumps and curves or lines and scars. Nothing like Jasper Jones.

I linger. It's cooler in here. And to be honest, I'm nursing a distant urge to cry. I still feel tired. And angry and sad. Kind of the way I get when I'm on the cusp of a cold or something. Sad and weird. My belly is tender. It's like I've been shaken and pounded and stretched. I want to cradle my head in my hands, but I don't. I won't. I'll blub if I do.

My head whirls.

What if it really *was* Jasper Jones? What if he did this? What if he killed Laura Wishart? What if he killed her and I said nothing? Could I go to jail? Could he really have hanged that girl in that quiet clearing? The notion seemed so implausible in his company, but how well do I know him, really? He could have been feeding me bullshit the whole time. It could have been him all along. I dig at my ear with a knuckle.

But then why on earth would he seek me out? It makes no sense. There's no chance anyone would enact a murder and then go find a witness. That's just stupid. So he can't have. Surely.

But aside from that, I trust him. I really do. And not because I have to. I think he's probably the most honest person in this town. He has no reason to lie. He has no reputation to protect. Last night I never suspected him of pulling the wool. Not once. The way he talks to you, it's like he's incapable of being deceitful. He says things with such conviction that you're sure he believes them to be true. It's just a feeling you get.

See, most people you meet, they'll talk to you through fifty layers of gauze and tinting. Sometimes you know they're lying even before they've started speaking. And it seems the older they get, the more brazen and desperate folks become, and they lie about things that don't even matter. Like my dad with his comb-over, or my mum with her russet hair dye. Or when my dad insists he enjoys the challenge of teaching Corrigan kids to love literature, or when my mum assures her sisters in the city that she loves it down here, and no, it's not too hot at all; it's just lovely, it's a wonderful community. I don't know. Maybe they just get so used to it they don't even notice. Maybe it's like a creeping curse and the more you do it, the easier it gets. What's amazing is that they think they're fooling anybody.

Yes. I think Jasper Jones speaks the whole truth in a town of liars. I can tell. See, it's these lies that precede him, these foggy community fibs that I've been led through: they're the source of these niggling doubts in my head. I mean, if it were Jeffrey Lu who'd woken me last night to lead me silently to that awful scene, I wouldn't doubt his story for a moment. I wouldn't even question him. So why should it be different for Jasper Jones?

I hoist myself out of the bath, restless and heavy. And I don't feel much cleaner than when I sat down.

45

***

When I tentatively enter the kitchen, both my parents pause and eye me suspiciously, brows raised. This is how they demand an explanation without asking for it. For a brief, horrible moment, I think they know something. Perhaps my mother has already inspected her trampled gerbera bed and noticed the fingerprints on the dusty glass louvres of my window, instantly surmising with her uncanny facility to accurately persecute without evidence that I must have been out all night with Jasper Jones, that I've seen and done something terrible, that I'm in all kinds of trouble.

But then my father smirks and reaches out to clap my back.

"Rip Van Winkle! The corpse has risen! So nice of you to join us."

I sit and offer a weak smile.

My mother produces a hot cup of Pablo coffee with a fair dollop of sweetened condensed milk. She leans over, hands on her knees.

"I trust you're enjoying your stay at our hotel, Mr. Bucktin, sir. Might I remind you that our turndown service ends at ten sharp. Will Sir take eggs for his lunch?"

My dad snorts. My mother is the most sarcastic person in the universe. My father calls it "droll wit," but I think it's more or less an opportunity to get up my arse without appearing unreasonable. She's most acerbic when she's faintly pissed about something, which is every waking hour of the day.

"No thanks," I say. "What time is it?"

"Almost noon. So you've only wasted half the day. It's nice for some."

Her back is to me. She's wearing a thin floral dress that clings to her in the heat. She looks good today, I have to admit. Usually she only looks like this if she's just come back from the city, where she's been going more often recently. I want to go hug her, to be held by her, but it would be too awkward and unusual. Still, her hair looks nice today.

"Your hair looks nice today," I say.

This has her whirling around. She glares as though I'd just spat her coffee over the table and called her a courtesan.

"What did you say?"

"I said your hair looks nice today."

"Oh," she says, and frowns, searching for a deeper meaning. She cuts her eyes. "What do you want?"

"What? Nothing. I just said your hair looks nice."

"But why would you say that?"

"I don't know. Because your hair looks nice."

Exasperated, I turn to my father. He is nodding and laughing quietly, with his back to her.

After a brief pause, she says, "Well, thank you," in much the same way she might say, "Well, *don't*."

I shrug.

My dad smiles and folds his paper.

"So, my boy. Couldn't sleep, or couldn't get enough?"

I set my glasses and sniff. It's difficult to play this role. *Charlie Buck-tin at breakfast: Scene One.* I don't feel the same. I'm uneasy in my own skin.

"Yeah, no sleep last night. It's too hot. I was just reading, I guess."

"I see. So what's taken your fancy?"

"*Pudd'nhead Wilson.* It's really good."

"Ah." And my father leans in. "It's been years since I've read that. How are you liking it?"

"Yeah, well, like I say. It's really good."

I crimp my lips and raise my brows. I don't want to play this scene out. This coffee is making me too hot. I'm sweating. I'm stuck to this vinyl seat.

Still, it can't mollify that uneasy feeling that I'm about to be caught. There are insects crawling on my shoulders. At any moment I expect blue-suited troops to burst and bundle into our house and cuff me from behind. Neighbors will line the street, spitting and hollering as I am led, roughly, to a flashing wagon.

I nod toward my father's newspaper.

"What's news? Anything good?"

"Same old, my boy."

"Oh, okay," I say, sipping my coffee and looking away.

"You all right, Charlie?" My dad shifts tone. He reaches across and feels my forehead, and runs his thumb over my cowlick. I want to tell him everything. I want him to wrap me in his arms and reassure me.

"Yeah, I'm fine. Just tired, I guess."

"Well, if you're not eating, young man," my mother says, "I suggest you go visit Jeffrey. He's been over five times already this morning with a bee in his bonnet. I told him to go in and wake you up, but he just trotted back home and said he'd try again later. He's too polite, that boy."

Shit. The Test. I completely forgot. Little wonder he didn't want to come inside. He wasn't being polite, he just didn't want to miss a delivery. Right now, Jeffrey will be huddled beside the radio, intently poised, as though it were spilling state secrets. I've never understood it. It's not like the same thing doesn't happen over and over. Cricket is the most repetitive enterprise in history. But Jeffrey will listen to the words—*Wide outside off stump, Lawry shoulders arms*—with as much glee and intensity for the eightieth time as the first.

I don't want the rest of this coffee, but it's not worth the wrath of my mother to waste it. I quaff it quickly, wincing at the bitter bits at the bottom. It burns my innards, but it's gone. I rinse its silt at the sink and exit stage left, offering a casual farewell.

*** 

Jeffrey lives across the road, four houses up. Any further away and I doubt I would make it. This has to be the hottest day in history. Either the earth is being devoured by the sun or the sun is hurtling toward us like an enormous meteor. Our front lawn crunches beneath my feet. Down our street, I can see strange undulations of heat. I arrive at Jeffrey's door feeling like I've endured a marathon, and I knock quickly, surveying the veranda. I greet Jeffrey's grumpy tabby, Chairman Meow, who ignores me and crouches beneath the white cage of Jeffrey's affable parakeet, Chairman Wow.

Mrs. Lu answers.

"Hello, Chully!" she says, and then her broad smile disappears and she looks suddenly crestfallen. She shakes her head solemnly. "It's no good. The test cricket is raining. Come in, come in."

Jeffrey bursts out of the living room. He is wearing all white.

"Where have you *been*? You're an *idiot*."

"I don't know. Sleeping. Is it raining?"

Mrs. Lu suddenly laughs again. "No, Chully, it's very *hot*!" She squeezes my arm, nods once, and walks away, giggling.

"What does that even *mean*?" says Jeffrey, watching her walk away.

I follow Jeffrey into the living room. He has the radio turned right up.

I take a seat on their couch. Jeffrey perches on a piano stool he has dragged over to the radio. It's much cooler in here. Jeffrey recounts the day's action with unnecessary attention to detail. He's clearly disappointed. Doug Walters is on debut, it's the first Ashes Test, and it seems it's going to be washed out for the rest of the afternoon. The notion of rain seems incredibly inviting to me right now. A huge cold shower, harsh and bracing.

Mrs. Lu swathes in with a plate of sweets and fruit, and two tall glasses of icy lychee juice. I thank her, and Jeffrey dives at the tray. She turns and shrieks something stern at Jeffrey in Vietnamese.

Jeffrey, his mouth still full, says, "It's *not* impolite! It's only Chuck! He doesn't care!"

But her fiery barrage continues as she walks away. Jeffrey grins. He takes up the tray and bows.

"Please, O Holy Ombooodsman, take first from our tray of fine delicacies, aye beseeeeech you."

"That's better," I say.

I take something round and bright orange. It is delicious.

"What is this? It's amazing."

Jeffrey squints. "That is Bang Chow Pow."

"That's a lie."

"Incorrect. That's a *fact*. Don't be ignorant."

"You're an idiot."

"You're a communist."

Jeffrey spills his drink as he gestures. He mops it up with a cushion.

"Here's one: would you rather die of the heat or the cold?" he asks.

I lean back and put my feet up.

"Do you mean immediately burned or frozen, or steady exposure?"

He thumbs his jaw. "Steady exposure."

"Well, I don't know. Neither."

"But you have to choose one."

"Why?"

"Chuck! Are you retarded? It's hypothetical."

"But when am I *ever* going to have to make that choice?"

49

"Well, let's just *say* you have to."

"Why would I have to?"

"Because they've got a hypothetical gun to your head."

"Who is 'they'?"

Jeffrey is smiling. He's perched restlessly on the edge of the piano stool.

"I don't know. The Russians."

"Why do the Russians want me dead?"

"Because they're evil and hypothetical! And you're a spy. You've been selling their secrets."

"To who?"

"Ze Jarmans."

"I see. Well, I'd choose to be hypothetically shot in the head, then. I mean, if I'm going to die anyway, why hypothetically suffer?"

"Okay. One: you're an idiot. Two: you're making this too hard." Jeffrey ponders for a bit. "Okay. They've got your parents too."

"Jeffrey, you're just sweetening the deal."

We both laugh. I take another orange ball. Then Jeffrey clicks his fingers and looks at me slyly, still smiling.

"Okay, okay. What if they've got, say, Eliza Wishart too. Eh, Chuck? What do you do then? You can save her by choosing one or the other."

The mention of her name rattles me. It makes me realize how much I'd pushed Laura aside since I got here. I set down the sweet. I feel like throwing up.

I tell Jeffrey to piss off. Of course, I let this slip just as Mrs. Lu strides back in with more food. I freeze, eyes wide, expecting to be dressed down, but she appears not to hear. Jeffrey is quietly asphyxiating at my expense.

"Here, Chully," she says cheerfully, and refills my drink. She exits as swiftly as she entered. I watch her go, wondering how I have skirted a certain death.

"It's okay, she doesn't know swearwords," Jeffrey says when he's recovered himself. "You should have seen your face!"

"Really?"

"Yeah. Listen to this." Jeffrey yells toward the kitchen: "Ma! Chuck really fucking loves these orange balls! *He really fucking loves balls!*"

There is a loaded pause as we both wait for a response.

"Okay! That's good! Thank you, Chully!" she calls down the hall.

We have to bite our fists to stop from shrieking.

I lounge back. But then I suddenly remember again, and that fist of queasiness rocks me forward. It's a roller coaster in my belly. I wish I could tell Jeffrey everything. I really do. I wonder what it is about holding in a secret that hurts so much. I mean, telling Jeffrey doesn't change anything, it doesn't take anything back. It's just information. It doesn't dredge that poor girl from the depths of the dam, doesn't breathe her back to life. So why do I feel like I need to blurt it all out? Is it just the fact of telling him? Loosening the screws, getting the horrible mess out of my body? Maybe if I spill it over, it's a little less of the burden that I have to carry. By that logic, if I told everyone in Corrigan, or Australia, or The World, if I gave everyone a share, it might become bearable.

But I can't anyway. It's locked in me tight. It's not that I don't trust Jeffrey, it's that Jasper Jones trusts me. It's an unusual contortion of my loyalties. I know I can't say a thing.

Jeffrey suddenly clicks his fingers and points at me.

"Okay. Got one." He spreads his hands, showing me his palms like a mime, the same way he always does when he's telling a joke. "Okay. Why are pirates called pirates?"

I look at him blankly.

"Because they yarrrr!"

He dies laughing. He almost chokes. He has to stop to cough.

"Jeffrey, that is the worst ever. And I mean that. The *worst*."

Oh, come on! Chuck! You're being harrrrsh!"

I laugh. I can't help it.

"Really. Stop. It's bad."

"No way! You can keep that. Tell it to Eliza Wisharrrrt!"

"Jeffrey, I'm going to hold a non-hypothetical gun to your head. If I have to kill you, I will."

"Pffft! You couldn't do it. Not to this handsome face."

***

We stay in Jeffrey's living room until the broadcast ends. Despite the fact that there is no chance of play continuing for the day, Jeffrey doesn't want to run the risk of missing any developments.

Jeffrey soundly defeats me at Ludo, and then I destroy him at Scrabble. He shrugs and says: "My ingrish. Is no goot."

We get restless. Jeffrey suggests we head to the nets in town. I'd much prefer to stay inside and arse about in Jeffrey's living room, but I know there's no chance of that. Jeffrey is ushering me out the door like we're fleeing a fire. He yells behind him: "Ma! We're going into town to play some fucking cricket!"

We pause.

"Jeffrey! Wait! Okay? Wait!" his mother yells sternly. I detect a moment of panic on Jeffrey's face when Mrs. Lu charges down the hall. But she holds out two cold flasks of water and smiles as she shuts the door.

"You should have seen your face!" I say.

He laughs as we run out into the street.

***

Jeffrey tosses a polished red ball in his hands as we make our way into town, snapping it with his wrists and his fingers, fizzing it into the air. The seam is a whirring blur.

I don't especially dislike cricket, but it requires some special kind of pathology to give it the kind of devotion that Jeffrey shows. I don't know. Maybe it's because I'm rubbish at it. I am really bad. Of course, being born without courage has proved to be a significant hindrance, but mostly it's the fact that my limbs have never acted in accordance to what I intend for them. It's like they're being controlled by some vindictive puppet master.

But Jeffrey Lu is uncanny. His skills are so impressive, I'm not even envious. The things he can do with that red rock in his hands are amazing. Really. And his batting is incredible, he's so compact and powerful. Despite being roughly the size of a garden gnome, Jeffrey can manage to be intimidating. He's not so affable with the pads on and the bat in hand. He's like an animal, aggressive and focused. Or some kind of sword-wielding hero. You can't put the ball anywhere when his eye is in.

Granted, I'm not much competition for Jeffrey, but I think if he ever gets the chance to play a real game, he's going to be brilliant.

We walk slowly, favoring the shade. Although it's late afternoon, it is still stupidly sultry. It's a dry and inert heat that seems to press from all sides. Jeffrey is dwarfed by his gear bag.

"See, I was thinking," he says, catching the ball and thrusting a finger into the air. "The thing about Spider-man is that he is completely useless outside of New York City."

"How do you figure?"

"Well, okay, par exemplarrrrr: if he were to fight crime here in Corrigan, he'd be rubbish. There's nothing for him to swing between. He needs a . . ."

"An urban environment?"

"Exactly, sir. I mean, who is Spider-man going to save in the Gobi Desert? Or Antarctica? He's rooted."

"True," I say. "But he still has sweet powers."

"I understand *that*, Chuck, but they are rendered virtually ineffective by the environment. He's immobile. All you need is a camel or a husky sled and you can outrun him. He's nothing. And he's sticking out like a dog's bollocks. Suddenly he's just a weird-looking guy with snot shooting out of his wrists."

I think about it.

"Fair point," I say.

"Of course it is. And that's why Superman is the *best* superhero," Jeffrey says, and tosses the ball high in the air. "He's all-terrain. He can cover the globe in a second. He's the greatest. Simple."

53

"I disagree."

Jeffrey drops his ball.

"What? Excuse me? You *what*? How could you *possibly* disagree with that? You're an idiot."

"Think about it, you little bigot. Superman is boring. He's *too* accomplished. There's nothing interesting about him. There's no story. He's too good. It's not even an effort for him to apprehend criminals or save children from fires. In the end, they had to invent some stupid arbitrary green mineral to give him a weakness. Whatever. It's boring. You know it."

Jeffrey squints at the sun and groans with his mouth open.

"Chuck, you're a fucking *communist*. Firstly, he *does* have other weaknesses."

"What? Bullshit. Name one."

"Love, *okay*, dick*head*. Obviously. His family. Lois Lane. They can be used against him."

"I don't care for Lois," I interject.

"Because you're queer?"

"I'm not queer. Idiot."

"Secondly, the fact that he doesn't *interest* you doesn't mean he isn't the best. You're not the king of opinion. It just means you're foolish and narrow-minded."

"No. It means you have no taste. And no idea what you're talking about."

Jeffrey laughs. "Well, who's better, then?" he asks.

"Batman. Easy. The greatest superhero of them all."

"*Batman?*" Jeffrey stops walking, and looks around as though he's appealing to a jury. "You *are* queer!"

"I'm telling you, Jeffrey. The greatest."

"Chuck, you're an *idiot*! That is the stupidest thing I have *ever* heard. Batman isn't even a superhero!"

It's my turn to stop.

"Shut your mouth!" I slap the ball out of his hands. It skips down the street.

"It's true! He's not a superhero!"

"Jeffrey, you're an idiot!"

"*You're* an idiot! Batman doesn't have any superpowers. He's not superhuman. He's not *super*. So therefore he can't be a *super*hero."

"Jeffrey, *what* are you talking about? He's *Batman*!"

"What does that even *mean*? Batman is just an eccentric billionaire with insomnia! He's a vigilante, not a superhero. Because he doesn't have *superpowers*. He just has a cool car and a handy belt."

"Jeffrey, you are insane. For a start, I disagree fundamentally that you need superpowers to be a superhero. But I would argue that he is super anyway, given that 'super' just means *greater than usual*. So in every aspect he *is* superhuman."

"So Doug Walters is a superhero because he possesses superhuman abilities?"

"No, Doug Walters is an alcoholic. Are you listening? Batman is the *ultimate human*. He is flawless, yet he is capable of being flawed. He's mastered the way of the ninja. He's one of the world's greatest scientists and detectives. His body is in peak condition. He is a man of unfathomable mental toughness. He *is* human perfection. He's a Renaissance man. And it's the fact that he is just a normal guy with a bumload of money and a burning vendetta that makes him the greatest. And because he can fight against and alongside people *with* superpowers. He is a superhero, and you, *sir*, are an idiot."

55

"Charles, you are the very *essence* of stupidity. I'll say this slowly: *Batman does not have superpowers. He can't be a superhero.*"

I know I'm winning when he calls me Charles.

"He doesn't *need* superpowers. That's my *point*. You're an *idiot*. He can hold his own. He has an alter ego. He has a costume. He fights for Truth and Justice. He has arch-enemies. And he does all this without any weird mutations. He's just really *determined*. That's what makes him interesting. The fact that with enough dedication and desire, we could all be Batman. Bat*men*. Bat*people*. And that's what makes him the best."

Jeffrey closes his eyes and puffs his cheeks.

"You know I'm right, Jeffrey. It's just like Lex Luthor doesn't need superpowers to be a supervillain. It's called *context*. Look it up. It's a goddamned comic. I win. You're wrong. Doug Walters is a hero. Muhammad Ali is a hero. Batman is a *super*hero. Simple. And the thing that makes him the *best* superhero is exactly your stupid, ignorant assertion: that he's just a guy. He is fallible. And unlike Superman, he requires courage."

"Charles, what the *fuck* are you flapping on about? Superman is *clearly* the bravest superhero. You've lost your *mind*. Superman invented courage. He steps in front of bullets. He doesn't consider risk. He delves into danger without a moment of thought."

I spread my arms.

"Of course he does! He's Superman, you idiot! Jeffrey, he's invulnerable."

"So what?" Jeffrey scrunches his face.

"So that isn't *courage*. He's a man of *steel*, you retard. He's invincible. He doesn't need to be brave. If a bullet can't possibly hurt you, how is it brave to stand in front of one?"

Jeffrey frowns doubtfully and stays silent.

"See, Batman is different. He's mortal. He's got a real life to risk. Superman just has to avoid Kryptonite. Big deal. Superman fears nothing because outside a few very specific circumstances where he might encounter some stupid rock, nothing can possibly do him in. Batman has the same vulnerabilities as the rest of us, so he has the same fears as us. That's why he is the most courageous: because he can put those aside and fight on regardless. My point is this: the more you have to lose, the braver you are for standing up. That's why Batman is superior to Superman, and that's why I am infinitely smarter than you."

I am a genius. I have won.

"*Pffft!* Whatever. I'll bet Batman won't be too loud about his superiority when Superman is belting seven shades of shit out of him."

Jeffrey executes a number of weird kung fu thrusts, then shrugs and pulls a face. He drags his feet as we reach the eastern end of town. Suddenly he grins, slyly.

56

"I hope *you're* feeling brave." He points.

It is Eliza Wishart.

The brick in my belly sinks a notch.

She's wearing a plain sleeveless cream dress with a lime stripe. Her hair looks thinned out. Maybe it's the heat. Her skin is blushed pink. Usually it's lily-white. And she's outside the bookstore in the shade of a jacaranda, examining the cheaper secondhand paperbacks stacked on trestle tables. She has one open in her palm. I wish I could see what it is.

Nobody knows about Laura. That's what this means. Except me and Jasper. But I wonder how Eliza Wishart can be here when her sister is clearly missing. How can she be browsing books as she is? Looking, as she always does, so distant and sedate?

Eliza's manner has always intrigued me. She seems troubled, yet infinitely untroubled. Sometimes at school her heart beats too fast and she has to sit down. She goes quiet and pale and tells everybody she's fine, even though she's breathless and sweaty. And I just want to hold her hand and slow her pulse and calm her down.

I wonder how it is she's not panicking today. How is she not belting on the glass door of the police station? How is she not yelling her sister's name down side streets, banging pans, corralling locals?

I prod my glasses and tug my ear. We're getting closer to her. The urge to blurt everything out is at me again. To spill this illness. It sounds stupid, but I want to take her hand and lead her to the leaf-littered bank of the Corrigan River. Someplace cooler and quiet. To tell her what I saw, what I did, what I suspect. I want to tell her, assure her, that Jasper Jones didn't do it. I want to ask her not to listen to what people say. With air in my chest, I'll tell her that I know him. That he's a friend and I know what he's like. That he *can't* have done it. That it makes no sense. That I think he loved Laura. And I want to tell her that I feel horrible. I want to apologize. I want to tell her how her sister's face looked last night. That before we moved her, she looked strangely peaceful. I want to ask her if she knows who would do this. If it was just shit luck or something more sinister. I want to look her in the eyes when I tell her. I want to hold her tight when she cries. I'll wait until she's calm. And then make her promises. Say all the right things.

I watch her as we move closer. Wary. As though she might detonate. Jeffrey, because he is a dickhead, does a lot of throat-clearing and foot-scuffing as we approach. I want to clap his head from both sides and squeeze until it bursts.

She looks up from her book. My body knots.

"Afternoon, Miss Eliza," Jeffrey sings, and doffs an invisible cap. I will kill him for this.

Eliza's eyebrows leap slightly. Her nose is specked with barely visible freckles. And her lips just look perfect. Red and varnished. But I can't shake her resemblance to her sister. She has those same eyes, and the same dark moons beneath them. It panics me. My fingers quake, so much more than when I usually encounter her.

"Hello, Jeffrey," she says chirpily; then she looks at me. She tilts her head and leans on one leg. "Hello, Charlie," she says.

My mouth is dry, and so my response is a mute whisper followed by a single nod and a tight smile. I am an idiot. I consider trying again, once more with feeling, but in the time it takes me to decide, we've already walked straight past her. Should I turn around? I should. I should probably turn around. I'm going to turn around.

But I don't. I look down. So much for taking her hand. So much for leading her to the riverbank.

Jeffrey is grinning. When we're out of earshot, he says: "Saving all your words for Scrabble?"

"Piss off."

He tilts his head back and laughs.

"You *love* her, Chuck."

"I'm going to kill you, Jeffrey. One day, honestly, I will end your life with my bare hands. That's my promise to you. You're the most irritating little man in history."

We are nearing the oval. I want to go back and try again with Eliza

Wishart. No awkwardness this time. Strong and forthright. I want to look at her face, see if I can detect anything out of the ordinary. Anything amiss. Anything suspicious. I want to know what she's reading. Maybe her book will have answers. She smelled good, though. Real good. Better than good. She always does. The thought of it makes my blood thinner and my head lighter.

We arrive at the oval. It's a lush, pristine vista, the one part of Corrigan that is maintained with care. An old man in khaki is in the center, watering the turf wicket.

The nets are occupied by the Corrigan Country Week side. I'm intimidated and disappointed. I can hear the cracks and thuds issuing from those two lanes. From afar, the squad looks like some kind of piston-pressed engine. I stop and half motion to turn around and go.

"Shit luck, eh?" I say.

"It's okay, Chuck. We'll still get a bowl in."

"You're joking, right? Jeffrey, they won't let you! They never do. Come on, let's just go back. We'll go play in the street."

"Yeah they will, Chuck. C'mon."

Jeffrey scuds down the grassy embankment toward the nets.

"What planet do you bloody live on?" I call after him and shake my head, but he's smiling lazily and pressing on with infinite optimism, kitbag in tow. I stand my ground, but I'm teetering. He's insane. Or he has no memory.

I decide to follow him, but at a distance.

As I approach, I'm not surprised to notice the team is littered with my nemeses. The arch of these, Warwick Trent, stands at the back, slowly rubbing one side of the ball against his nuts. He has the broadest shoulders and the longest run-up among them. He's one of those kids who's always been two years bigger and broader than anyone else his age. He was probably born with a beard and chest hair; wailing and stinking like the enormous, fetid shit that he is.

Warwick Trent holds the record for the most peaches stolen from the tree of Mad Jack Lionel. He's got four pits in his pocket from four separate excursions. He's had real, actual sex. More than once. He's been in more fights than anyone, and won most of them, including one with a middle-aged miner outside the Sovereign. He is feared and revered, and he knows it. He has a tattoo. He is surly and volatile. I hate him like poison.

And, probably due to the fact that most of his bodily resources are diverted directly to his pituitary gland, he's also an affront to academia. Seldom is this boasted about, but he also holds the record for most grades repeated (two). It's a little fact that renders me smug, but also sore, because his stupidity has placed him in my grade.

See, in class, if I use a word that he believes is too clever, or isn't one of the half-dozen monosyllabic commands that he readily understands, he and his henchmen will seek me out, either at lunch or after school, and will repeat the offending word like a mantra, each time punching me on either shoulder.

"Monosyllabic." *Ow.* "Monosyllabic." *Ah.* "Monosyllabic." *Uh.*

If I run, I'm caught and floored and nailed. If I try to fight back, I risk complete annihilation. If I insult them, the same. If I tell someone about it, it's a suspended death sentence. If I well up and take my beating like a girl, I am killed on the spot.

So I stand there and mutely accept the punishment that is meted out at their discretion. Mostly it's quick and painful. But if I've been particularly clever, or if I've especially pleased our teacher, I'll have my glasses slapped off my face and my thighs corked, with some other public humiliation.

Their message is simple: *Don't be too clever.*

All this has done, really, is firmed my resolve to get smarter. And not without a measure of spite. It's made me thirsty for new words. Every time I encounter one for the first time, I look it up and bank it. Every new word is like getting a punch back. No matter how obscure or archaic, I eat them up and let them settle. And I vow not to forget them. I collect words and lock them away, stored like a hoard of gems.

Every night I use them. Every night I pick the lock. I have black pens and yellow notebooks. And every night I write stories and poems. I polish my jewels. Sometimes I imagine spitting my poems at these boys, though I know it would be like thrashing them with a feather. I know they'd just laugh. And, of course, I know they'd thrash me back with something significantly harder. But there is a grim satisfaction in knowing something they don't know, in having something they don't have. That's what I think about when I'm silently accepting their punches.

I position myself at the top end of the nets. I'm far enough away to remain reasonably inconspicuous. I'll stay here and collect the balls that get straight driven or lofted out of the nets, and I'll roll them back with my head down. I don't expect grateful waves, but I hope it might save Jeffrey some grief.

I'm still nervous, though. I look at Jeffrey, casually laying his gear bag down among theirs. So laconically bounding in and meshing with the pack of bowlers, as though he's part of the side. He looks tiny. It's like watching a puppy crossing a busy street. Jeffrey stamps and scrapes his bowling mark, but he is shoved, hard, out of his chosen net. I hear someone say, "Fuck off, gook," and my gut knots. 61

I don't understand, because Jeffrey has tried this before and it never ends without some kind of humiliation. I watch Jeffrey hover around the crease on the inside net, not taking his mark, waiting for a chance to cut in and bowl.

But the same thing will happen, I know it. Jeffrey bowls slow spinners, and so whoever is batting just invariably tries to hit the ball as far as they can. If they miss, which they often do against Jeffrey's bowling, the batsman will retrieve the ball, loft it, and crack it out of the nets. And Jeffrey will genially jog after it and come straight back, fizzing the ball in his fingers.

Sometimes Jeffrey mistimes his run and is more or less shirtfronted by one of the fast bowlers running in. For this, of course, he's angrily pushed and rebuked: sometimes by all the bowlers, who shove him around like a pinball, trip him up, kick his ball away.

Very rarely, Jeffrey will be allowed to pad up. Right at the end, when it is near dark. It's never a lenient act, though. They take bets on body hits, bowling short and over the crease, as fast as they can. Jeffrey, of course, is resilient and impressive, but occasionally he'll be hit in the chest or the shoulder, and there will be a thrilled roar and an exchange of money or something valuable. Jeffrey stays down there, though, on the back foot, right until they tire and walk off.

I watch Jeffrey bowl his first ball, and it's right on the spot. In fact, it dips and turns sharply, clipping the off stump of Jacob Irving, who planted his foot and took a ridiculous swipe. Jeers and laughter erupt from the bowlers. As I expect, Irving bends and plucks the ball from the back of the net, and belts it hard and square. He spits toward Jeffrey, then claps his gloved hands together and sneers, "Ah, me so *solly*!"

Everyone laughs, watching Jeffrey jog out to fetch his ball in his pressed whites. He is jostled and bumped around the pack. He's so small. Someone kicks his ankle and says, "Fuck *off*, Cong." Jeffrey stumbles, but keeps going, head high. I am so ashamed. It hurts me to see. I want to run over to Jeffrey, tell him we should go. But I don't. Even the coach is cackling. A red, ruddy man with a clipboard and a cigarette. He has an oily film of sweat across his brow. When he laughs, it sounds like he's coughing.

It continues in much the same way. Jeffrey retrieves the ball, bounces back, waits patiently for another turn. I wait and I watch. No batsman can get him away properly, they nick and swipe with no reward. Why can't this stupid coach see that? Jeffrey is the only spinner here, and he's bowled three out already.

See, I always thought that eventually there would be a sort of grudging respect for Jeffrey's talent. Much the same as there is for Jasper. The Corrigan Colts side wouldn't win a game if weren't for Jasper Jones. He raises the eyebrows of even the most ardent bigot on the sideline. He's a phenomenon, a cut above. It's impossible not to be impressed. He never trains, doesn't listen to the coach, doesn't play a position, just does his own thing. He doesn't own his own shoes. Jasper is the toughest tackler I've seen. For someone five years younger than the rest of his competitors, he intimidates his opposition more than any beefy monster on the field with fire in their eyes. Jasper has incredible hands, and amazing instincts for the game. And he has a vertical leap and a burst of speed that can have a whole crowd gasping at once.

It's hard to understand. The folks who watch Jasper play, who barrack for him like he was one of their own, are the same ones who might cut their eyes at him should he walk their way a few hours after the game. But they'll smile and cheer and shake their heads in wonderment if he takes a run through the center or if he nails one from the pocket. His teammates too. They'll surround him and scruff at his hair in celebration, they'll applaud and pat his arse, but once the game is over, the pattern returns. He's back to being shunned by the boys and privately reviled, and privately adored by the girls. Jasper hands his shoes and his jersey back, and leaves them to their changeroom.

It's hard not to believe that something in that uniform is powerful, and that its number is significant. When fat, angry bastards are screaming advice to the best athletes in town and when women are shrieking blue murder, it's hard not to feel as though Jasper Jones has forged himself some kind of momentary peace, because it's patently clear that he's a champion among them. They're forced to accept it. That he's the best going round. He's one of them. Jasper Jones is the player on whom they pin their hopes.

I wonder why it can't carry on. Why Jasper Jones has to strip off his shirt and hand it back at the end. And I wonder why Jeffrey can't even get a slice of that, fleeting as it is. Maybe it's because he can't assert himself like Jasper, who broke three collarbones and two noses this season.

Jeffrey's next delivery produces a leading edge, and it skips past him at the non-strikers' end. Most of the bowlers let it run through them; one of them kicks it along. It bounds toward me. I trap it, roll it back. I hear them talking.

"Got your boyfriend here, Cong?"

"Chorlie loves it in the orse!"

"Eh, you love him long time, Cong?"

Someone pushes Jeffrey in the face. Someone else prods his arse hard with their finger. "Hey, I thought *he* was supposed to be Charlie, anyway?"

They all laugh at this with curled lips. Especially the coach, who looks up from his clipboard. His teeth are the color of bath grit. Warwick Trent picks Jeffrey up by the front collar with one arm. They cheer, and he throws Jeffrey backward, his thin arms flailing. More laughs. Jeffrey picks himself up quickly and resumes his position.

I don't want to watch this anymore.

I wish Jasper Jones were here right now. I wish he were standing next to me. Then I could holler everything I want to holler. I could point and swear. I could single this coach out. Tell him he's a bloody disgrace. That he doesn't know a thing about the game. Then I'd tell Warwick Trent he's a smug, odorous fool who will never leave this town, that he'll be trapped here forever by his own stupidity, like a rat in a wheel. I'd sneer and tell him he's got the cerebral finesse of an amoeba and delight in his squint of confusion. Then I'd punch him, hard, in the shoulder, repeating those words: *Cerebral. Cerebral. Cerebral. Amoeba. Amoeba. Amoeba.* Then I'd tell Jeffrey to put the pads on and I'd make them bowl at him and they'd realize he's the best among them. He'd carve and slice their bowling around so effortlessly, they'd have no choice but to admire him.

But that won't ever happen.

I scratch my chin with my shoulder. It's twilight. And in the copper glow, I see Eliza Wishart making her way across the oval. She is still carrying that book.

Everything feels so pronounced today. All my senses are tender and buzzing. The slightest tremor feels like a quake. I feel harassed by the busy sounds of insects around me, like I'm trapped in an enormous thriving hive. I'm watching Eliza Wishart walk and I'm transfixed, she's so assured and demure at the same time.

I think she sees me. She looks up. I look down. I can't help it. And when I glance back up, she is giving a short wave. I return it with a smile. I should go over there. I should go over there and say something witty about her following me around. And we'd laugh. Then I'd ask her about her book. And then we'd talk. Maybe hold hands. I'd ask her if she wanted to meet me later, by the river. I'd look her in the eyes, like it's important. And she'd be so stunned and impressed by my forthrightness, she'd immediately agree.

So I should. I should walk over there right now, like Jasper Jones: broad-shouldered, with a long lope and a knowing grin. I'm going to go over there. Right now.

I shove my hands in my pockets.

Behind me, someone wolf-whistles. Then all of them do. I whip around. They're laughing. Warwick Trent puts a palm to his mouth.

"Shars yer tits! Oi!"

Eliza looks down, walks a little faster.

I am horrified. I hope she doesn't think I'm with them. Warwick Trent has his cock out and is waving it at her. They all cheer. Thankfully, she has turned away.

65

They laugh. They turn. They lose interest. Eliza Wishart is almost gone. I watch her disappear. I should have said something, I should have stood up. Defended her honor. I'm an idiot. I want to go. I sit down, a little woozy.

Laura Wishart is dead. Her sister doesn't know. But soon everybody in Corrigan is going to know. I'm in the eye of the storm. The world has come apart. I don't know what this town is going to do. It's as though I'm waiting silently for the battle to start, knowing I'm slowly being ambushed. There's a coil round my chest being bound ever tighter. For once, there is no comfort in knowing something nobody else does.

How can Jasper Jones expect us to go back and unravel everything? We tied her to a stone. We *buried* her in water. We *did* that. We can't hope to solve this mystery. It's too much. It's too big and unwieldy. Where would we start?

Laura Wishart is dead. And she is just hours away from being reported missing, unless she already has been. And they're not going to find her. Unless someone confesses. Unless Mad Jack Lionel steps into town with his wrists ready for the cuffing. So what is going to happen? We've bought Jasper Jones some time. But how much? How long until they give up? How far will the search spread? How thorough will it be?

What I really can't begin to understand is how it happened. How somebody could do it. How anybody could kill a girl. How they could take her into the bush and beat her down and hang her from a bare limb in her nightdress. How they could watch her die. How they could leave her there. How they could be capable. I snatch at a mosquito in front of my face. Wipe it on my shorts. I flinch. They're everywhere. I hate insects.

Laura Wishart is dead and I touched her warm body and she's cursed me with dread and sorrow. And I can only hope that they don't find her until we get to the truth.

Jeffrey turns and looks around. No one has started their run in. One of the other bowlers gestures him through. Jeffrey smiles. He turns to stride in and bowl. And just as he pushes off, someone swiftly pulls his white shorts to his ankles. He stacks it, hard. They erupt again. The coach wheezes. The ball skips down the pitch. Jeffrey stands and retrieves his shorts, his little arse like a tan plum.

Meanwhile, the batsman has trapped the ball. He turns and claps the ball high and hard over the back of the nets, into a vacant block of trees and scrub. A huge hit. It's a lost ball. Jeffrey watches it go, and it breaks my heart because that ball was a birthday gift that he'd sweated on for months.

And my eyebrows furrow and my nostrils flare as I watch Jeffrey cut his losses and walk toward his kitbag. I watch them ruffle his hair and shove him lightly.

And I look at this bastard coach. How he stands, how he intermittently pinches at his dick and shifts his weight. How his dark rodent eyes lazily survey this pack of boorish bullies. How his nubby fingers scissor his cigarette. And I think: If he can watch this with a thin grin, what else could he watch? What other cruel things could he view without intervening?

I'm chewing the inside of my mouth and my face is hot. I look away. Part of me is faintly resentful of Jeffrey for joining them in the first place and making me feel like this. I blink hard.

Jeffrey remains unperturbed. As though he were simply undone by fair play. And they're still spitting words at him as he hoists his bag, but I don't want to listen anymore. I just want to go. Jeffrey walks toward me. There are grass clippings in his hair.

His head is bowed as he approaches. But when he gets closer to me, his face lifts and splits into a smile.

"Did you see that first ball? Drifted in, spun out. Bang! Top of off! Thanks very much." He spreads his hands like the ball actually exploded off the pitch.

"It's true. It did, a fair bit," I say, and it feels good and defiant.

"A *bit*? It did everything, Chuck. That second-last guy got a good square drive in, but I've got a deep point, so it's covered."

"I bet you've got a lot of fictional fielders in the right position once they've belted it." I'm anxious to keep talking and diverting.

"Charles, if you knew anything about the game, you'd understand that you've *got* to have a deep point. It's fundamental. You want to get them on the back foot, so you invite that shot. Then, bang! You've been trapped in front. Or you kick one up and you've got him at first slip." Jeffrey executes some frenetic shadowboxing combinations, punctuated by sound effects.

"Easy, Muhammad."

"Float like a butterfly, sting like a bee. Your bat can't hit what your eyes don't see. Bang!" He kisses his fists.

"You're insane."

"What's that, Chuck? I'm the greatest?"

"No, you're a . . ."

"You're probably right. I *am* the greatest." And Jeffrey bursts into

67

round two, bobbing and feinting, his kitbag flapping on his back. Still, I shake my head, angry.

"I hate those bastards."

Jeffrey sighs.

"Chuck, if nobody had stolen his bike, Muhammad Ali wouldn't have hit anybody." Then he stops and points a finger up at me. "Meanwhile, you're an idiot."

"Why?"

"Because you didn't go and talk to Eliza."

"So?" I shrug.

"Chuck, you are the *king* of idiots. It's not like she came this way because she didn't know you were down here. She *loves* you."

I shake my head.

"You're blushing!" Jeffrey says dramatically, pointing like a witness before a police lineup. "You make me *sick*!"

"Jeffrey, firstly, I'm *not* blushing. I'm hot. It's been a hot day. It's the heat. On my face. Second, there is no way Eliza could have known we were going to the oval, so she couldn't have gone that way purely to see me. Which means, *essentially*, you have no idea what you're talking about."

Jeffrey snaps his head back and drones, stumping along like a zombie, "Charles, you know *nothing* about the world of seduction. You need to be advised by an expert, namely me. I know *everything* about girls. They're too stupid to be a mystery."

"Jeffrey, you don't know the first thing about girls."

"Bollocks! What's not to know?"

"Plenty."

"I know why they wear makeup and perfume."

"Why?" I sigh.

"Because they're ugly and they stink!"

We lip-flap for the remainder of the walk home. Jeffrey spies a ripe snottygobble tree that hasn't been raided yet. He picks a fistful and we share them as we ponder the motives of the person who first discovered milk from a cow, who it was that arranged the letters in the alphabet and why they decided on that order. We also question why kamikaze pilots wear helmets. But my heart is never really in the conversation.

When we turn into our street, I find myself slipping in behind Jeffrey, expecting dark and daunting vehicles to be parked at jagged angles on our lawn and people in suits and sunglasses to be waiting, pointing as they see me appear. Loudspeakers. Planes. Shocked on-lookers.

I'm safe, but I feel no relief. If anything, it allows my unease to compound. It adds freight to the weight.

"Stop staring at my arse!" Jeffrey says. I absently move up to his side.

Our street is a little busier than when we left it. In the cooler air, neighbors natter over front fences, watering with hoses or zinc cans. Toddlers stagger about in the nude; other kids squeal and zip around beneath rotor sprinklers in their underwear. Dinner smells seep out of open front doors. You can hear television babble, parental censure, and laughter.

Jeffrey's dad, An, is out front, working his garden with care. He grows various odd fruits and vegetables out in back, but out here is a neat and perfect presentation of color.

An Lu is an engineer at the mine, but of an evening he'll be obsessively tending to either his produce or his flowers, even if he's had to work late. Jeffrey's front yard is like Corrigan's own botanical garden. It's easily the most impressive scene on this street. Jeffrey says An orders in seeds and saplings from all over the world, and he has a logbook for how and when each should be set in soil. An has his land planned with the precision of a symphony. There's a year-round blush of hues, even through the Corrigan winter, but in spring it explodes like a frozen firecracker. And An is always there, coaxing and summoning its blooms like a conductor.

Most folks plan their evening stroll around An's eruption of color. They like to point and pick out the wisterias, the wild poppies, the jasmine, the heirloom roses. They like to wonder aloud what the more exotic plants could be, and they marvel at the selection and the scent.

But of course, all I can ever see is the shifting constellations of insects that hover above the petal bursts, and I stay as far away as I can. I'm deathly afraid of them. Bees. Wasps. Hornets. Anything that flies or crawls or hops or stings. My mother is especially entertained by my phobia, but Jeffrey is the worst. One of his favorite jokes in the world is to warn me there's a bee on my back, or a redback on my shoulder. He pauses, wide-eyed, and says *Don't move*, like I'm about to tread on a land mine. It gets me every time.

One day I may be able to survey An Lu's beautiful garden up close for what it is without my skin crawling at the terrifying hum of a million poison-tipped assassins. But for now, my most comfortable vantage point is where I'm standing: outside my house.

Jeffrey hoists his bag further up his back. I peel off onto my lawn.

"I'd ask you round for dinner, but I really don't like you," I say.

"Pffft! I'd rather lick my own arse than dine with your kind."

"Bollocks." I say. "You'd rather lick your own arse because you like it."

Jeffrey laughs. "It tastes better than your mum's cooking!"

"Touché," I laugh.

Jeffrey turns to go, but spins back, grinning.

"Hey, Chuck?"

"What?"

"What's the hardest thing about liking Batman?"

I close my eyes and sigh. "I don't know. What?"

"Telling your parents you're queer!"

Of course, he dies laughing.

"You're an idiot. That doesn't even make sense."

"*You're* an idiot. That's hilarious."

"I'm not the one licking my own arse."

"If you had *this* arse, you would." And Jeffrey's shadowboxing recommences as he wanders away. "I'm so pretty! So *pretty*!"

"Bye, Muhammad."

"Because they yarrrrr, Charrrrrlie! Because they yarrrrr!"

Jeffrey skips home. As he arrives, An stands abruptly and jabs his secateurs in his direction, yelling something stern and fierce. Jeffrey stands bolt still. It looks like he's in the shit. I watch him duck his head and mooch inside.

I do the same.

***

During dinner, I try to sound my parents out about any news, but they don't offer up anything. Afterward, I take my coffee straight to my sleepout. I'm not in the mood for television or talk. My dad asks if anything is wrong, and I just shrug and say I feel like reading.

I set my brew and open my louvres. I peer through them for some time, hoping to see Jasper Jones waiting in our backyard. He's not there.

I try to read, but I can't concentrate. I lay *Pudd'nhead* down. I use a dirty shirt to swipe the sweat from my face. I think about this time last night, and it seems a world away. It's like I used to inhabit some other dimension, some other body.

Restless, I pull out my old brown suitcase from beneath my bed, unlock it, and take from it my yellow writing pad. I tuck myself into my desk, full of promise. Ready to spin the black silk. And I need it. The urge is urgent. I need to spill some of this over. I need to tell some of my secrets. But my pen won't push. It's still and dry and useless. I stare at the page.

I think I hear something. I leap onto my bed, squint through the louvres. I hiss Jasper's name. Nothing.

So I sit back down. Clean my glasses, tap the lamp with my pen. Still nil. The strange thing is, I'm boiling over with words, they're like a swarm in my head; I just can't order them. They swirl and dip like insidious insects. Haunting and noisy and nonsensical.

I sigh and toss my pen aside, rest my cheek on my palm.

I need to see Jasper Jones. And soon. It's not right having all this

71

to myself. Laura Wishart is dead. And we buried her. In a water hole. We tied her to a stone. We did that.

And until I see Jasper Jones again, I can't even begin to make sense of it. I can't hope to get to the root of things. I need to talk to him about the likelihoods and contingencies and strategies and problems that are bubbling and spitting in my head and my belly. It's like I've started to read a tragic book from the last page and I need to try to fill in the gaps, to write what came before. But I can't. Not without Jasper. Not without the truth. And there's just too much I don't know.

Suddenly I frown and clutch my guts. I burst out of my room and smother our toilet a moment before my arse ejects something foul and molten. And there's a moth. Right there. On the ceiling. A huge moth, big as a bird. Do they bite? I close my eyes and pretend it's not here.

What do we do if somebody actually comes forward with information? It's unlikely, but what if somebody really were aiming to set Jasper up? What if they saw what we did? What if Mad Jack Lionel calls in, tells the police where she is, and she's not there? What happens to us? How much trouble are we in? Would Jasper be true to his word? Would I still be safe?

The moth applauds the light globe above me, casting strange distorted shadows. It's enormous. It's a giant moth. It probably has fangs. It could eat a rat in a single gulp. There are centipedes in the Amazon that eat bats. They hang from the ceilings of caves and snatch them as they flap past. I grit my teeth and turn away as more acid jets out of me.

And why hasn't anything been reported yet? Aren't the Wisharts worried? She's the daughter of top brass, and high-class; where are the search teams and the news people? I palm my forehead. It's this hot tension I can't stand. The sleeping giant. The ticking bomb.

I retreat back to my room. I check my window again.

I quickly down my cup of joe, and it gives me a little buzz. I try *Pudd'nhead* again, forcing myself to follow the words, intermittently glancing out the window.

Something stalls me at the beginning of chapter twelve. From Pudd'nhead Wilson's Calendar: "Courage is resistance to fear, mastery of fear—not absence of fear." My head tilts. Exactly. That's what I'd wanted to say to Jeffrey about Superman. I wish he were here; I'd wave that quote like a red flag.

I run my thumb over those words. Maybe my father was right. Mark Twain has something smart to say about everything.

I shift to my desk and write those words down. Then I write around them and under them, shielding my words with a cupped palm, the same way I do in school. And I keep going, I strike up a rhythm, and it feels good.

See, I think it's harder for me to get brave. It's harder for me to suck it in and square up and bunch my fists. I think the less meat you've got on you, the more you know, the more you're capable of being beaten, the more it sets you back. The lower your weight division, the more often you're swinging up. I think the more you have to defend, the harder it is to press forward without looking back. I'd have Superman's swagger if I couldn't get hurt, but I've got the Charles Bucktin slouch. Because I bruise like a peach. And I'm afraid of insects. And I don't know how to fight.

Does that mean it's easier for Jasper Jones than me? But what about Jeffrey Lu? I don't know. Maybe he's bravest out of all of us.

My scribbling is interrupted.

"Jesus *Christ*, Charles Bucktin! What have you been *eating*?"

My mother has just walked into the toilet. I smile to myself. I have a dozen wisecracks about her cooking tickling the tip of my tongue, but each one would be a death sentence.

I keep writing. It's aimless and desultory, but it feels good. Like I've loosened a valve. Like I've shared some of this mess, pared it off me.

It's late when I ease up, exhausted. The house is hot and quiet. I slip onto my bed and check the window again. I whisper Jasper's name to the space I want him to be standing in and give my eyes more than enough time to adjust. Nothing. I sigh.

73

I clear up my desk. Lay my yellow pad back in its case. Before I snap the combination lock, I thumb through the thin pages of my filled pads, just to touch their grooves and ridges. Right at the bottom, a thick brown paper package makes me smile. I untie the red string and sift through the bundle of pages.

This winter, Jeffrey and I spent rainy days writing a novel together. It was a penny adventure that quickly spiraled out of control, through no fault of my own. I'd sit with the pad on my lap while Jeffrey Lu paced in front of the fireplace, one arm behind his back, gesturing with an empty pipe, garrulous with wild ideas. The plot had more twists than a hurricane. Jeffrey took care of the action and the intrigue, mostly in the form of kung fu bouts and hot pursuits, while it was my responsibility to concoct an actual story (which Jeffrey dubbed "the girly stuff") around these sequences. I was also dubbed Minister of Witty Dialogue.

Our fast-paced adventure involved a jaded ex-cop from Detroit called Truth McJustice who, after his wife mysteriously disappeared, quit the police force with an impeccable crime-fighting record and buried himself in his first love: archaeology.

What followed was a series of barely believable plot developments, with Truth discovering the Holy Grail, Joseph Stalin masquerading as a furious faux-Pope after kidnapping the real one, and Truth's missing wife emerging as a brainwashed assassin called Ivana Knockyourblockov, hired to execute him and recover the precious artifact.

Of course, it ended in a flurry of martial arts in the Pope's chambers. Truth was passionately reunited with his wife, while Stalin was duly hanged in St. Peter's Square for heresy.

I didn't really agree with lynching Stalin, but Jeffrey said we had to in order for his title to work. He wanted to call our masterpiece *Pope on a Rope*. I was more inclined toward *Truth Will Set You Free*. In the end, we agreed to mesh them together and make my suggestion a subtitle.

After we'd decided on a fitting nom de plume (Clifford J. Brawnheart), Jeffrey wrapped our manuscript in brown paper and concluded that therein lay *the* Great Australian Novel.

"But how can it be, really?" I argued. "It doesn't even feature any

74

Australians. And besides, to be honest, the coincidences seem a little outrageous. Our critics will lambast us."

Jeffrey's head snapped back and he groaned.

"Chuck, you are officially a Luddite. There will be no lamb-basting. You know *nothing* about literature. You need to understand that truth is *stranger* than fiction. Listen: people are willing to swallow any old tripe as long as you say it without flinching. They *want* to be told stuff. And they don't want to doubt you either. It's too hard. So if you say it like you really mean it to be true, then you're away. Conviction, Charles. You could do with some. Look at Dickens! He got away with murder! And don't get me started on Cheeses Christ and all that zombie resurrection bollocks. Now, *there's* a twist ending that's hard to sell. He's dead, he's dead—no, wait, who is that crawling out from behind that rock? Noooo, it couldn't be! Oops, wait—yes! He's alive! Hello, Zombie Cheeses! He's back!"

"Sir, with respect, that seems a little cynical."

"It's not cynical if it's factitious."

"Factitious? That makes no sense. It's not even a word."

Jeffrey prodded his pipe in my direction.

"Charles, the problem with you is that you're not worth a damn. Now, if you'll kindly refrain from slowing my progress with your impertinence, I'll remind you that Clifford J. Brawnheart is always right. End of story."

And it was. *Pope on a Rope* has been since been stashed in my suitcase, and though its merits have often been discussed, it hasn't been read again. I doubt it's my gateway to the literati, but I do know that one day I'm going to work on something big and significant. I'm going to stun this know-nothing town, and I'll be Manhattan-bound with a book bearing my name.

I've often wondered if my father has been working toward the same thing in his library. I've long suspected him of secretly writing something in there. He steals away most nights and stays up for hours. Sometimes he falls asleep at his desk.

He's *got* to be working on something. I wonder what it's about. I

75

wonder if he's close to finishing. I wonder how long it is—how many pages, how many words. It's been years since he first began going in there, always locking the door behind him, which I never understood. I mean, I was never going to burst in there unannounced, and my mother hasn't entered that room for eight years. See, my dad's library used to be a second bedroom, painted lilac and decorated for the arrival of my younger sister, who died just before she was born. It almost cost my mother her life and stole her chance to ever try again.

Still, it's strange to think of me and my father both scrawling clandestinely through the night, threading lies and secrets from under the same roof. I wonder, if I told him about my writing, would he talk to me about his? Would he let me read some?

I carefully close my suitcase and lock it. I slide it beneath my bed. Then I cup my temples and look out the window for the last time. Jasper Jones is not coming. I'm on my own tonight.

I turn and lean back on my pillow. I look down at my chest and stomach, frowning at my stick arms and my ladder of ribs. My lip curls. I spill onto the floor and embark on a set of push-ups, full of resolve. I make it to ten before I almost enter a coma.

Back on my bed, sucking in air, I tuck my hands beneath my head and think about Eliza Wishart.

It sounds ridiculous, but I can almost smell her. I close my eyes. I should have talked to her. I should have crossed that oval, my pockets brimming with all the right words. I want to see her in a way that almost hurts.

I wonder what is unfolding at her house right now. Is she asleep, or is she awake and frantic? I imagine her parents. Speculating and supposing. Panicking. They must have involved the police. The Authorities. The people whose job it is to locate the missing. They're probably over there right now. Dozens of them. Specialists. They probably have maps and blackboards and switchboards on trestle tables. They're getting organized. They're drinking black coffee. They're talking fast and loud, punching out their cigarettes dramatically. Collars pulled, ties loosened. Positing and arguing. Embarking on a fresh trail of crumbs and hot leads that will lead them directly to me.

This dread is lousy. When it hits, it's like someone has turned the dial that controls gravity. Everything sinks hard and cold and fast. It winds you. It's that same feeling, that same sad panic you confront when you can't sleep, when your mind wanders and you remind yourself, for no reason at all, that you're going to die one day. That you will end, you will be buried and forgotten. And everything and everyone you know and remember and love will be void. And in that act of knowing, something rushes inward and twists at your heart and you can't breathe right. The knowing, it's a cold kiln for this brick. It's stuck firm. It's not going anywhere. And you come to understand that in a hundred years from now, everyone presently in Corrigan, in Australia, in the world—every parent, every child, every animal, everyone—will have died. It's a weird and unspeakably sad feeling that leaves you hollow but heavy.

That's what I'm beset by. That's what Jasper Jones has led me to.

And so I roll onto my side and I think about Eliza. And I recall her scent and my dread spreads and bursts into butterflies. And I think about how soft her cheeks look, and how it might be to press my lips against them. How it might be to say things in her ear that might make her smile slightly, that would settle her frantic heart and have it beating like the sure tick of the Miners' Hall clock tower. How it might be to encircle her waist with my arms. Tight. How warm she might feel. And I shudder.

must have slept solidly, because I wake in that same position, curled on my side. I feel old and sluggish, like I could sleep the night through again.

I blink. Twice. And my eyes settle on the window.

There's a paper wasp. Right there. Perched on the edge of the glass slats. It looks busy. Its backside bobs, sinister and slow.

My fear spreads like a dollop of molasses. Dazedly, I seem content to observe it, and then I suddenly leap from my bed like I've just had volts shot into my body. I have never moved faster. Nobody, ever, has moved faster. I am a mess of limbs, and my mouth blurts a series of vowels. I grope at my nightstand and throw a book at it. *The Naked and the Dead* misses the wasp entirely, but hits the louvre lever, snapping them shut.

I snatch my towel and leave. I'm not sure if I just locked the wasp in or out of my room. My fear tells me inside. *And*, it whispers ominously behind the back of its hand, *You just pissed it off.* My heart is thrumming like a speed bag.

In the bathroom, I splash my face with warm tap water and try to calm down. Rather than risk an encounter in my room, I take some clothes from our washing basket and throw them on.

Of course, I'm assailed as soon as I walk into the kitchen. My mother doesn't even turn around. It's as though she can sense the grit and the rumples.

"Charlie! Take those off. I haven't washed them yet!"

My mother sets a cup of Pablo in front of me and tugs at my striped cotton tee. I rub my eyes and sigh.

"But it's not even dirty. It's fine," I say, and sip at my coffee.

78

"No, it is not *fine*, Charlie. I won't ask you again."

She fixes me with a glare that could swipe a swath through an iceberg. But this morning, I just don't give a shit.

I keep quiet, which I am sure she translates as grudging assent. I chew the toast she presents and uninterestedly flick through one of the papers my dad isn't reading. He's especially quiet this morning. He's usually a little distant in a distracted sort of way, but this morning he's like a ghost.

My mother pretends to busy herself, wiping down her immaculate kitchen. She talks sternly at me while looking out the window.

"Charlie, if you're going to Jeffrey's today, I'd like you to stay there or on the street, where I can see you, please."

I pause and frown.

"Why?"

"Because I said so. That's why."

I look to my dad, but as ever, he offers no opinion from the other side of the table. I may as well be sitting with a well-fed bloodhound. I hold my hands up, like I'm holding an invisible bowl full of questions.

"How can that *possibly* be a reason?"

"I'm your mother. I don't need a reason."

"That doesn't even make *sense*!" I blurt out, and she whirls around. I am in it now. The glare returns. Those eyes could make a eunuch out of Errol Flynn. You have to squint and look away; it's like trying to look into the sun.

"Are you going to continue to backchat me, or are you going to do what you're *bloody told*?"

I hate this rhetorical standoff. I can't win. There is never any winning. I can't even forge a stalemate. I have three red doors with three labels: SILENCE, AFFIRMATION, and FATAL BEATING. Opening any of them hands her the victory.

At the moment, I hate them both like I hate wasps: my father for being bewildered and useless, my mother for flying the red flag.

I open the red door that says SILENCE. The least painful loss.

79

"Good." My mother turns to wipe her clean bench.

Quietly fuming, I finish my toast and bide my time, with the occasional betrayed glance toward my father. I skim over the newspaper headlines and read about how Americans are saving the Vietnamese and more Australian troops might be sent there soon.

It's confusing, because my dad hates the war. He wanted to drive to the city to join the protests, but my mother wouldn't let him. She said it was a waste of time and money to drive out there just to take a stroll with a crowd. I wanted my dad to be defiant, to drive up there anyway. I might have gone with him. But he stayed.

Eventually my mother leaves the kitchen, speaking loudly about doing a load of washing. I listen to see how busy she is. Then I quietly up and leave, gently shutting the front door behind me. The second time I've snuck out in as many days.

I walk quickly to Jeffrey's, intermittently looking over my shoulder. I imagine that my mother has just swung open my bedroom door to a rapacious swarm of insects so thick that they coat her entire body like chain mail and buzz louder than a sawmill.

Fear of retribution propels me through An Lu's death garden without pause. I knock on Jeffrey's door with some urgency. To my surprise, he answers it. This has never happened. His face is a caricature of disappointment.

"Hello, sir," I say to him. "I've come to talk to you about Cheeeeses. A moment of your time, sir, I beg you. For Cheeses Christ arrrrr Larrrrrd."

Jeffrey's head snaps back like a PEZ dispenser. He sighs upward.

"None shall pass, Chuck."

"But, sir! The Cheeses!"

"No, really," Jeffrey says, his hand still on the door. "You can't come in. And I can't come out."

"You don't have to. Everyone already knows you're queer." I smirk and move to go inside.

"Shut *up*, retard. I mean it. I'm grounded."

"Really?" I stiffen.

"Really."

"How? What did you do? I saw your dad yelling at you last night."

"Well . . ." Jeffrey sniggers slightly and whispers. "Yesterday, Mrs. Sparkman came over to borrow something, and just as my ma answered the door, Chairman Wow whistles and goes: *Ma! We're going into town to play some fucking cricket! We're going into town to play some fucking cricket!* And so of course she blushes and tells my ma what it means and how rude it is. Stupid bird ratted me out."

I die laughing. Jeffrey holds a finger in front of his grinning lips.

"I *know*. It's hilarious. But she went crazy. She was like a tornado, Chuck. A tornado of *fury*. But it's *fucked*. She won't even let me listen to the Test Match. I'm going *mental* in here, Chuck. Do you know the score? Is Doug Walters in yet?"

"I have no idea."

"*Fuck!*" he hisses, and he clicks his fingers in a jerky movement like a thwarted villain. "You're useless to me, Chuck."

"*I'm* useless? What am *I* supposed to do now?"

81

"I don't know." Jeffrey smiles. "Go find Eliza Wishart. Go have a picnic in a meadow and make daisy wreaths and . . . what's the word? Frolic. Go frolic in a meadow."

"I think I'd rather give you a vivisection. With my hands."

"Queer."

"How is that even remotely queer?"

"I don't know. But it is."

Behind him, his mother shrieks something. I don't understand the words, but the tone translates clearly.

"I have to go, Chuck," Jeffrey says sullenly, and I sigh and wave as he shuts the door.

Our quiet, clean street belies its weight of oppression. An's garden, the creeping heat, my wasp-hive bedroom, the brick in my belly, the she-devil awaiting my demise at home. I start walking aimlessly toward town. Maybe I'll go to the library. Or the bookstore. I should have brought some of my savings.

As I walk past the school oval, I watch some kids trying to get a kite started. Looks like they've fashioned it themselves from a dowel and newspaper and fishing line. I don't like their chances. The air is static as an oven, and just as hot. Still, they sprint in straight lines, with their kite scudding and skipping behind. From here, it looks like it is chasing them.

I arrive at the library. Save for Mrs. Harvey, the librarian, it is empty.

Since I've been devouring my father's books, I've spent less and less time here, so it feels a little like I'm visiting an elderly aunt. It has a familiar spicy smell; I feel instantly at home.

I spend some time browsing the general fiction aisle, but my eyes glaze over spines. I amble on. It's only when I reach the crime section that my heart kick-starts and I stop and peer. My finger hooks out titles and I bundle books in my arms. When they get too heavy, I carry them all to a desk in the far corner. I put them down and switch on the lamp. I feel suddenly excited and full of purpose. They're all true-crime books, their covers featuring grainy mug shots or creepy urban scenes. The word *chilling* appears in most of the blurbs. I check to see who has borrowed these books before me, whether there are any names that repeat themselves. They are indistinct and mostly illegible. No Jack Lionel. Nobody I even recognize.

It's compelling reading. I pore over the misdeeds of famous and infamous killers, fascinated by their stories. I learn that Jack the Ripper was never caught. I read about Burke and Hare, who killed for money, selling the corpses to medical colleges. I suck in the words furiously. It all seems so gothic and surreal. Then I read about Albert Fish, the man they called the Brooklyn Vampire, whose written confessions make me so queasy I can't even finish. I slap the book shut. Look left and right. I am galled and enthralled. I open it back up.

His photograph stuns me. The face of a child-eating monster. His hawkish, asymmetrical face and sinister eyes. I have to look away. It's everything I would imagine Mad Jack Lionel to be. That bleak expression, sharp and volatile. As though he could snarl and bite at any moment.

82

I skim through the other titles. They're intriguing and harrowing. I bow close over the pages, but something seems slightly unsatisfying. New York, London, Paris. They all seem so far away and long ago. The cases feel a little too much like fiction, like too much is left to imagination.

It's at this point that I recall the Nedlands Monster, and I know it's him that I really want to read about. What I remember mostly is his hanging last year, which everyone except my dad seemed to welcome. I don't know much about the events.

So I slide the crime books to one side and walk quickly toward the newspaper archives. I spend an hour collecting issues that mention him on the front page, building a hefty stack to my right. Mrs. Harvey sternly reminds me to put them back in the right order, but I suspect she's secretly pleased someone is finally making use of her work.

I haul them back to my desk and try to read about the case chronologically. From the lurking shadow that slaughtered five people on a single weekend almost three years ago to the quiet harelipped man they finally apprehended and hanged. It's macabre and unsettling, more than the other stories, because these are places I recognize and it's a time I can remember. The headline hysteria makes me uneasy even though I know how the story ends.

83

And clearly, it's not just me. I skim over editorials and letters which gather in intensity as the crimes continue. A fever of panic against an unseen evil, as though Perth were Gotham City itself. I imagine worried denizens clutching their coats and walking quickly as a cool wind herds leaves around their ankles. I read on. Reporters tell folks to lock their doors, recommending curfews and urging ladies to wear full-length clothing. There are double-page spreads, rife with wild speculation and concern, on how to secure your home. Nowhere was safe, nobody was exempt. It could be *you* next.

And then they caught him. Eric Edgar Cooke, who came looking for his gun and was ambushed by the law. He must have wondered what took them so long.

I stare at his photograph. The thin, bowed man who tormented a city. The man who had them running for the exits, had them turning against each other. He looks a little like a beaten and battered Jack Dempsey. He looks harried by demons and ill at ease.

There are stories etched into that face, but what I'm really searching for is *why*. Why he stabbed a woman in her own bed. Why he shot a man between the eyes as he answered his door. *Why?* Why did he kill all these people? I need to know why he wanted a whole city to close in on itself.

I shake my head slowly and read on and on, no longer interested in the crimes themselves. I find it strange that even after he was caught and caged, even after he was revealed to be such a small and sallow sight, the panic in the articles doesn't relax. The people still are rattled.

I finally begin to piece together a portrait of his life and his childhood. I read about him being ruthlessly bullied on account of his cleft palate. About his loneliness. His abandonment by everyone except his pitying mother. About his abusive drunkard father who beat him ferociously with his fists, sometimes with a thick belt. Who spent his wages on drink and let his family go hungry, which meant Cooke had to thieve for their livelihood.

It is horrifying and sad. But I still don't understand. Was this really *why*? Are these the ingredients of a murderer? I hold my head in my hands and I think about Jasper Jones. An orphan, or as good as. Whose dad hits the drink as hard as he hits his only son. Who also has to steal to eat. I can't even begin to imagine what has happened under that roof. I think about Jeffrey Lu, bullied every day of his life. I think about Sam Quinn, a boy at our school with a cleft palate. Or Prue Styles, a lonely girl who has a ruby-red birthmark like a bloodstain down her face. And I think of Mad Jack Lionel. I imagine his face as a composite of Albert Fish and assorted movie villains. I think of him alone on his veranda in the still of night. His crooked face, his evil eyes. Surveying his moonlit property. Watching a girl in a nightdress hastily making her way to the river.

I push my glasses to my eyes and peer at Cooke again. And it occurs to me for the first time that people can do this to each other. People really can. And I wonder: How thin is the line? Is it something we all have in us? Is it just a matter of friction and pressure? Is it shit luck and a poor lot? Is it time and chance? I scratch at my scalp and sniff. Maybe Mark Twain knows.

To my surprise, the next volume holds Cooke's own answer.

The paper is dry, and it crackles as I navigate through it. It smells musty. I turn to the right page. There is a small tear in the bottom corner, and my spine sparks cold at the thought of someone else being privy to this. There's a different picture of Cooke. This time he looks more pathetic. Almost resigned. I read hungrily. Finally, at last, a reporter asks him *why*. Why did he do this?

Cooke replied: *I just wanted to hurt somebody*.

I sigh and rest my cheek on my fist. I glance out the window for a time. That can't be it. That can't be all. I reach for the newspaper dated the day after Cooke's hanging, but I find no report. I frown and lean forward, scouring the sheets in front of me. It's only when I'm deep into its innards that I realize my mistake: October 27, 1965. I'm a full year out.

85

But underneath the date, I'm drawn to a headline that stops me cold. I pause to clean my glasses with my shirt. I hold my breath and pore over the box of text beneath it.

I read about a girl from America called Sylvia Likens. The police found her dead on a dirty mattress. She was sixteen. The same age as Laura Wishart. And I feel myself lured down a path I'm not sure I should be treading. The outline of her story seems so black and obscene. I'm ill and cold and empty, but hungry for more. So much so that I'm driven back to the newspaper stand to take every edition since October back to my table. Mrs. Harvey eyes me over the rims of her spectacles. I sit down heavily. And I read on with my brick sinking, patching together the story of Sylvia Likens.

Sylvia's parents were carnival workers and often moved from city to city. A few months ago, in July, they were due to leave for another stint. They couldn't afford to bring all their children with them, so her father called on a recent acquaintance of his, a woman called Gertrude Baniszewski, and offered her twenty dollars a week as board for Sylvia and her younger sister, Jenny. Baniszewski, described as a sickly and severe woman, accepted the offer despite having seven children of her own and an estranged husband.

It seems that as soon as the door was closed on Sylvia Likens, the nightmare began. Gertrude Baniszeswki was at once bitter and suspicious, then jealous and sinister. She took an immediate dislike to the girls, particularly Sylvia, and often falsely accused her of thieving so that she might punish her.

After the first week, the stipend promised by the girls' father did not come. Enraged, Baniszewski thrashed Sylvia with a wooden rod. This became the first of many beatings. The violence became routine and grew in intensity. Sylvia must have been terrified. After a few weeks, she started wetting her bed. But it wasn't just Baniszewski. As the abuse escalated, Gertrude somehow enlisted her own children and others from the surrounding neighborhood, inviting them to enact awful cruelties upon Sylvia. They did unthinkable things. They stubbed cigarettes out on her skin. They cut her and beat her. They pulled her hair and they spat on her. They made her strip her clothes and dance in front of them. They made her put a Coke bottle inside her private parts.

Sylvia's torment got worse. Every day she was kicked and punched and hit and burned. She was just a grisly game for them. They tortured her methodically, all at Baniszewski's bidding. They began lowering Sylvia into baths filled with scalding water, holding her down as a means of cleansing her of sin. Then they rubbed salt into her open wounds.

Eventually, Sylvia tried to escape. She was caught on the landing. She didn't even make it to the front yard. Baniszewski dragged her inside. She shoved her down the basement stairs. From then on she was made to live in the cellar with the dogs. Baniszewski treated her like one of her animals. Worse. They starved her, feeding her nothing but crackers. They wouldn't allow her to wear clothes. They wouldn't let her go to the bathroom. They made her eat her own shit and piss and vomit.

Sylvia had told Jenny that she was going to die soon. She said she knew it. She must have been so afraid. It sounded as though she was giving up. She'd borne too much. She was letting go.

Sylvia's single act of defiance was to spend a night banging a shovel against the walls of the cellar. But nobody came. Nobody saved her.

She died in the bath. Of hunger and shock. She just slipped away. When they made the discovery, Baniszewski and her daughters carried Sylvia's body and dumped it on a filthy mattress across the hall. They folded her arms across her chest. Then they called the police.

What they found was a tiny body scratched and torn and bruised and branded, still wet from the bath. She had open sores from her scalding. She was stippled with puckered cigarette burns. She had teeth missing. Two black eyes. Her nails were broken. She'd bitten right through her bottom lip.

87

Before the police left, Jenny Likens quietly tugged at the shirt of an officer. And she said: "If you get me out of here, I'll tell you everything." Later that day, Baniszewski was arrested.

I stop reading.

One of the hardest things for me to understand is why Jenny waited until then to speak out. She'd watched for all those months; she'd been there for every savage act. She had the chance. Hadn't she been at school while Sylvia was housebound? She could have told somebody there.

But it's not just Jenny. It's the whole choir of mute voices that puts the lump in my throat. Why didn't anybody help her? The neighborhood knew. Oh, they knew. The folks next door, the Vermillions, had been there and seen the extent of Sylvia's injuries. They'd heard the screams and the commotion. The thumping of the shovel. But not a sound came from their side. They let it happen. Did they not care?

Whole blocks of people. Whole towns. A whole city. Whole clusters of families. Not one of them uttered a word.

And how was it that Gertrude Baniszewski could seduce so many children into committing these acts? How could they turn up, day after day, to do the unspeakable? And how could they return home of an evening, no words of shame or remorse tumbling out of their mouths? What did Sylvia Likens do to deserve this? Or was it just shit luck and chance?

Everything bubbles up in me. I have to snatch it and squash before it boils over.

I've read too much. I've seen too much. I'm in a strange daze, angry and bewildered. I don't know what to do with myself. I want to wash my shaking hands of all this. I want to clear my head. I wish I could unknow all I've learned. Exorcise the memory of Eric Cooke and Albert Fish and wring my heart dry of Sylvia Likens. And Laura Wishart? Right now, I'd tear it all out of me in a second. I'd choose to forget. I'd sleep safe in my settled snow dome, and I'd close my window to Jasper Jones.

I hastily stuff the books and newspapers into a shelf in a back corner and leave the library feeling exhausted. I squint in the sunlight and wonder where to go. After a whole morning's reading, I've collected more questions than answers.

I decide to head back home by way of the bookstore. I look at my feet as I walk, my head circling and cycling dizzily through too many avenues of thought. I feel like swimming. I want to dive straight into the Corrigan River and ripple my body and have the heat fizz off my brown skin. I imagine scrubbing at myself with grit from the bottom. Then lying on the surface and floating downstream like a raft. Or a corpse.

As my mind wanders, I trip and stagger on a raised pavement slat. I don't fall, but my recovery is just as spectacular. I stumble like a duckling on ice. When I right myself, I look up and see Eliza Wishart outside the bookstore. She looks both amused and concerned.

"Are you okay, Charlie?"

I forbear a shriek of pain and put my hands on my hips. I force a smile and hold up my hand, which must end up looking like some sort of strange, leery wince, like I've just swallowed a glass of somebody's urine and I'm recommending it.

"Yeah, nah," I say, flexing my back. "Yeah, look, I'm fine. Didn't hurt. At all, really. Just. Yeah. Bloody . . . town council and that. These slabs are . . . dangerous."

Christ. I'm afraid to look down. I must have stubbed the bastard clean off my foot. I hold my breath. I want to either die or cry or take to this footpath with a jackhammer.

But she smiles and everything ebbs. She is beautiful. She looks a little like Audrey Hepburn today.

"Well, you know, I'll let my father know. I'll make sure it's the first thing on the agenda at their next meeting."

"Oh, no!" I say, realizing. "I didn't mean, you know . . ."

"It's okay, Charlie. I'm joking."

"Oh."

"Where is Jeffrey? Playing cricket?"

"No, he got grounded. He's stuck at home."

Her eyes widen conspiratorially.

"Oh, really? What did he do? Is he in a lot of trouble?"

"Just general stupidity. Nothing, really, you know, *bad*."

I am nervous. Where is the sharp ballroom wit that I always imagined would punctuate this moment? My wit has abandoned me. Just when I need wit, I am witless.

"So, what have you been doing in town?" Eliza asks.

"Oh, nothing," I say, and look down. "I was just at the library."

She nods.

"Yeah, just, you know, *reading*."

"At a library?"

I am momentarily confused, and she smiles. Oh. She's outwitting me. Deftly. I need to lift my game. I can feel myself blush. I scuff my heel.

"Yeah. Well, it's less suspicious than pretending to browse outside a bookstore."

"What's that supposed to mean?" She shifts her weight onto one leg and tilts her head.

"Well, you know, it *appears* as though you're casually looking, but I know you're just reading for free. The jig is up."

She smiles and rolls her eyes.

"Yeah, you got me. Red-handed. You'd make a fine detective, Charlie."

That snaps me back. My head whirls and my toe throbs. I smile weakly, trying to stem my nausea. A dragonfly jets past my waist and I recoil like I've been shot.

She raises her eyebrows.

"I have to get home, Charlie. I had to slip out as it is."

"Oh. Okay." I nod excessively, like a pigeon.

Eliza waves the short novel in her hands and smooths her dress. "I just have to get this," she says quickly, and then she pauses as she opens the door. "You want to walk me home?"

My mouth is open. I shrug and keep nodding.

The small bell on the door chimes as it claps shut behind her. There is certainly not enough time for me to compose myself. I inwardly admonish my decision to wear dirty clothes. I hope I don't smell.

I'm just sniffing my armpit as Eliza walks back out, her book in a brown bag. I snap my arm down so hard, I wind myself.

We set off. I am shitting myself. Should I hold her hand? Should I do that? I should. I should do that. But my palms are sweating. Profusely. Surely that would be bad. Off-putting. It would be like giving her a clammy invertebrate to hold. So I shouldn't. I shouldn't do that.

But I walk close as we near the oval. I hope those belligerent dickheads are training at the nets so they can see me with her. But they're not. The oval is empty, save for an old man practicing his golf swing under the shade of a fig tree.

I pretend to watch him with interest. I'm panicking. I should be regaling her with chatter. I should be squaring my shoulders like Jasper Jones. I scour my stupid empty head for witticisms and repartee.

"What book did you buy?" I ask, nodding toward the brown bag.

"Oh." Eliza holds it up with two hands. *"Breakfast at Tiffany's."*

I nod once and open and close my mouth like a large fish. I silently scold myself for not having read it. And I resolve to. Tonight.

"I've seen the film four times," she says. "But I haven't read the book yet. My mum says I'm not allowed, which is so stupid because I already know what happens, but I'm going to anyway. I can't wait to read it. I wish I lived in Manhattan."

"So do I. Or maybe Brooklyn," I say.

"Well, I'll live in Manhattan, and you can live in Brooklyn, and we'll meet at the Plaza Hotel for high tea. And I'll wear a fox-fur coat and penny loafers, and you'll have a tartan scarf and a brown pinstripe suit. And a pipe."

"Sounds swell."

91

Past the oval, we make our way down the pea-gravel road to her house. This is the old part of town, where two-story houses with large trees out the front are common. It is the only part of Corrigan which hints toward any division of class. It's eerily quiet today, though. No cars swish past; there are no kids or pets about.

"Do you like Audrey Hepburn?" I ask.

"Yes. Absolutely." Eliza seems to ignite. "I think she's *brilliant*. And pretty. She's so . . . *dignified*. Do you like her?"

"Are you joking?" I'm pleased she's excited. "I mean, she's beautiful. Really beautiful. Stunning. She's perfect. She's my favorite, you know, *actress*. For certain."

She smiles. I hope I'm not being too obvious. I can't control my hands. They're flapping about like I don't own them. I must look like I'm unraveling my own innards. I go on.

"And talented. Of course. Obviously. I mean, she's not just, you know, *pretty*. She's smart too. I really like her. A lot."

Eliza seems amused. "Have you seen *Breakfast at Tiffany's?*" She looks up and squints as she asks.

"Well, no. Not yet I haven't."

"Really? You should. What films, then?"

Shit. I am in it now. What films, then, Charlie? Idiot.

"Oh, um. Well. Probably my favorite would be . . . it would have to be . . . the last one. With . . . ," I stammer.

"Rex Harrison?"

"Yes!" I almost burst with relief. "I'm no good with names."

"*My Fair Lady,*" she says, and I could kiss her.

"That's the one!" I say. "She was amazing. Really."

"Is that because her name was Eliza?"

"Oh. Oh, of course," I say, and blush.

Eliza smiles and looks down. I'm eager to move away from this conversation. We go quiet for a time.

We round into Sullivan Street, which seems significantly busier. The lawns are lush and thick and well kept, and two rows of trimmed peppermint trees track down its length. Eliza slows her pace.

"So you've probably heard, then?" she says softly.

My stomach wrenches and my body tenses. I'm not sure what to say. My breath stalls and that familiar dizziness returns. I want to run away.

"No. What?"

"My sister. She's gone missing. Since yesterday. We don't know where she is."

I stay quiet. We stop and duck under a tree a few houses from hers. We peer out through the thin strands of peppermint branches. Eliza looks very small in the dappled shade.

"My parents are going crazy. Well, my mother is. She hasn't stopped shaking and crying. My dad is just trying to be normal, which means, you know, stinking of beer and yelling a lot."

I can't speak. My mouth is too dry.

"The police have been at my house all morning. That's why I had to sneak out. I hate them being here."

"Do they . . ." I clear my throat. "Do they have any idea where she might be?" I ask. There's a tingly rash on my neck, as though I've already been caught.

"No," she says. Her tone is strange. Like she's describing someone else's family. There's no sign of panic. Neither of us can look each other in the eye. Eliza looks down; I look over her shoulder. "No, they don't have any idea, really. They're going to start searching soon. Sometime this afternoon. I think they're organizing some people from town as well, and there are special police coming from the city."

"Oh, okay. My god. Eliza, this is terrible. You must be . . . Are you all right? Do you know where she might be?"

I should place my hand on her shoulder. Or rub her back. Or say something comforting. But it would feel trite and stupid. And dishonest. Because I know exactly where her sister is. Because Eliza Wishart is hurting and I'm just trying to cover my arse. I feel like such a phoney.

Before she can reply, a loud shriek cuts the street. It is Eliza's mother, coursing this way, not quite running. Her face is red and her eyes are pink and puffy. She looks haggard and furious. I step back.

93

"What are you *doing*?" she screams at Eliza, and ducks into our umbrella of foliage. Her mouth is turned down sharply at the corners. Eliza remains passive and calm as her mother shakes her roughly by the shoulders, which has her head rocking wildly back and forth. Eliza looks so brittle, as though she might snap, but she stands firm.

"What are you *doing*? You *stupid* little girl! Where have you been? Why on earth would you leave the house without telling anybody? We have been looking *every*where! You stupid, *stupid* little girl! What are you trying to do to me?"

Eliza's mother is trembling with feeling, and clearly attempting to smother her sobs. She keeps her grip on her daughter's shoulders.

Eliza looks engulfed, like she's been caught by a bird of prey. Her voice is soft.

"I just came down the street for a while to see Charlie. I wasn't far away. I've been right here. I told Dad before I left."

"Don't tell me *lies*!"

"I'm not," Eliza says plainly, with a shrug.

Her mother slaps her hard, just once, across the face. I feel ashamed and awkward. Eliza seems unmoved.

"Where did you get this, then, young lady?" Eliza's mother snatches the book from her hands and holds it close to her face.

Eliza's composure impresses me.

"Charlie bought it for me. That's why we met up, because he wanted to give me a gift. That's all."

Her mother glares at me for the first time, seething and suspicious. It's clear she thinks it is bullshit. My face is a mix of fear and earnest corroboration.

"Well, I should think it's time for you to head home now, if you don't mind," she says to me tersely before grabbing Eliza tight by the arm, tugging sharply.

Eliza turns and smiles thinly as she is led away.

"Bye, Charlie. Thanks for the book."

"You're welcome," I call out, then add, "I'll see you at the Plaza," but I don't think she hears, and so my first hint of wit gets caught in this wall of leaves.

I pull back the green ropes and watch Eliza's mother huddle over and shake, sobbing into her hands, as they walk toward their home. I notice the balance has shifted—Eliza is now leading her back. Her arm around her waist. Leaning in.

I think about Eliza's manner. So dry and centered. So matter-of-fact amid the panic. I watch her climbing the garden steps to their front door, holding her weeping mother. Someone is there to meet them with an outstretched hand and a look of concern. I shrink behind the branches. And then, swift as a knife, it occurs to me. A rash of sparks coats my skin. My heart almost leaps from my chest, and my brick slides.

Eliza Wishart knows something.

\*\*\*

Before I can close the front door, my mother has slapped me. Hard and sharp. Much like Mrs. Wishart, but with considerably more venom. It stings for a long time. I touch my face, shocked. My mother calls out to my father:

"It's him, Wesley! It's okay!"

It is rare for my mother to slap me. It is even rarer for her to call my father Wesley. I can only assume this means I am right in the shit. As I'd walked back down our deserted street, I had hoped she might have forgotten my stealthy exit this morning.

Then she slaps me again. Harder. I cry out in protest. The interrogation begins.

"What in *Christ* do you think you're doing? Where have you been?"

"At Jeffrey's!" I yell at her and look away, scowling. I hope my eyes aren't glassy.

"Bullshit, Charlie. Don't *lie* to me!" She slaps me again, and shakes me by the collar.

"Stop it! It's *true*!" It obviously isn't. I am a terrible liar.

"I was over there three hours ago looking for you, young man! You're lying! Where did you go? Where have you been?"

"I just went to the library! Calm *down*. I'm sorry!"                    95

"Calm down? *Calm down!* Jesus *Christ*, do you want people to think you have no parents?"

I want to slap her wrist from my collar. I want to kick her shins and run back outside.

"What does that even *mean*? I just went to the library!"

"Oh! You *just* went to the library, did you? After I *told* you not to leave this street. After I *told* you not to leave this house without changing your clothes. It is *dangerous* out there, Charlie, okay? Do you know that? There's a bloody kidnapper on the streets, and you're walking about like you're lord of the manor! Who do you think you are?"

"What?"

"A girl is *missing*, Charlie," she hisses at me, close to my face. She digs her nails into my arm. "Laura Wishart. She has gone *missing*. Do you understand that?"

"Missing or abducted?" I ask. I want to know what she's heard.

"Don't answer *back*!" she snarls, and moves to slap me again. I shift my weight, and she cops me across the ear. It chimes through my brain.

For a moment it feels like I'm underwater. Without thinking, I push her off me. She looks stunned.

"Go to your room!" she screams.

"I can't! There's a wasp in there!"

"What?"

"There's a *wasp* in there! That's why I couldn't get changed!"

"I don't care!" she yells, pointing toward the back of the house.

"Well, that's been patently obvious for some time!"

"Ex*cuse* me?" She leans in, aggressive, speaking through her gritted teeth.

"God*damn* it!" I yell. "I'll go and get bloody stung!"

And I march off, with her close behind. I don't know what's wrong with me. I just *swore* in front of my mother. That's as close to hara-kiri as you can get without a sword. I slam the door and chock it with a thin Penguin paperback before she can burst in and thrash me to death.

She's hollering from the other side, but my immediate concern is the wasp that may or may not be trapped in here. I quickly scan the walls and the ceiling. I snatch my open copy of *The Naked and the Dead* from my bed and retreat into a corner. I wonder what Norman Mailer would think of me right now. He'd probably smirk and shake his head and call me a fugging pussy. Probably come at me with a penknife. I am hot with anger and shame.

The yelling ends. Book poised, I search every inch of my sleepout. It seems, miraculously, the wasp is gone. For now. But elsewhere, of course, I've shaken up a whole hive of problems.

My mother bursts through the door like she's the Gestapo. The wedged paperback skids across the floor. She glares at me and issues a beckoning finger like a gnarled coathook. She is holding a shovel. I don't know why. I hope it's not a weapon.

"Come with me," she says.

I don't argue.

I follow her outside. It's the middle of the afternoon and unbearably hot. I squint through the glare. I stand motionless as she aims and

96

stabs the spade tip repeatedly into the ground with purpose, like she's chasing something she wants to kill. I cock my head when she stops. She's fashioned the outline of a circle, roughly the diameter of my armspan. I frown.

My mother thrusts the shovel at me. I take it.

"What's this?" I ask.

"A shovel," she says shortly. I can't place her tone. I can't tell if she's hurt or angry or pleased with herself. Perhaps she's all three.

"I know that," I say.

"Well, start digging, then. Right here." She thrusts a finger at her crude markings.

"What? Why?" I ask meekly. I'm genuinely confused.

"You'll find out later. When it is deep enough, you can stop."

I shake my head.

"*What?* No! It's too hot!"

Her nostrils flare as her finger lifts and jabs at my chest.

"Charlie, I'm *not* going to tell you again. You will keep digging until this hole is deep enough. If you do not, you'll spend the rest of this summer in your bedroom, wasps or no wasps. Do you understand? And I will take your books away. Every single one. Those are your choices."

"What? But how is this fair? This is ridiculous!"

"I'm not here to be fair. I'm here to teach you how to do what you're told." She starts to move back toward the house. She knows she's won. She always wins.

I grip the shovel limply and stare at this patch of ground like it has betrayed me. Like it's the portal to hell itself.

I scowl and shick the spade into the earth and imagine I'm slicing clean through her neck. I'm sweating already. Flies are hovering around me like I'm the Holy Grail and I spasm in fright when I feel them land. I stab, lever, and lift, cursing my mother in the dirtiest language I can muster. This is a whole new degree of vindictiveness. Maybe when I'm finished with this hole I can throw her in it. The

97

work is made a little easier by my anger. If anything, it's cathartic for a short while. But this only lasts until the sandy top layer of earth melds into a dense clay and a blister forms on the webbing of my palm. I strip my wet shirt off and throw it to the ground. I kick some clay over it, knowing who will have to wash it. I am thirsty. I am dying. I am so bloody hot, I feel like I'm digging my own grave.

I try to think of what purpose this hole could possibly serve. I am hoping, maybe because I am roasting out here, that it is to accommodate some breed of shady tree. Like a blue gum or a paperbark. Or an enormous mulberry tree, like Mr. Malcolm down the road has. Something to read beneath. That would be nice. Maybe even a peppermint tree, broad and moppish and spicy, like the ones lining Eliza's street.

I think of Eliza and me, standing in the shade. Her clean girl smell, the bloom of heatblush on her cheeks, her sad turndown eyes. The strange, absent way she looked toward her house when she told me about Laura. I wish I could have held her hand, or brushed her cheek. I wish I could have told her everything was going to be okay. That Laura would turn up soon.

98

But Laura Wishart is dead. I know that. I watched Jasper Jones cut her down. Then we threw her in the water. And now they're looking for her, and when they find her, they'll come for me.

I wish I'd asked her more. I have so many questions. Eliza may not know what I know, but I think she has something up her sleeve. Does she suspect anybody? Does she know about Laura and Jasper Jones? Does she know about Jasper's grove? Does she know Laura used to steal away there of an evening? Surely not.

But maybe.

Eliza Wishart holds the pages of the book that leads to that horrible ending. Or at least some of them. But how to pry them out of her fingers? I have to see her again. And soon. So I can give something to Jasper when he comes to my window. So that we might clean up this mess.

My blister bursts. I suck in air through my teeth. And I look down to see a copper-colored centipede just centimeters from my foot. It's huge. It's as big as a python, surely. Does it eat bats? It could take down a cat, easy. Or a small child. I gasp and drop the spade, and run to the fence.

Of course, it's at this point my mother emerges from the house like an angry outlaw exiting a saloon. Our flyscreen door claps against the side of the house, then slaps back into place. She looks sharply from the hole to me.

"Excuse me, I don't remember telling you to stop! Keep digging, Charles Bucktin," she says sternly.

I close my eyes and exhale.

"I have a blister."

"And I have a lazy son. Both of them are painful. I'll give you some iodine when you're done. Come on! *Dig!* Is that your *shirt?* Get it out of the dirt, you filthy boy! Now! Show some *respect* for your things!"

Walking back to the hole, I smirk inwardly at having pissed her off, but it's a fleeting comfort. I take up the shovel and hold it aloft like a spear, but the centipede has disappeared. It's worse when I can't see it and I know it is there. It's probably lurking underground, waiting to strike, like some maniacal alien tentacle from *The War of the Worlds.* My spine is tingling. I suddenly need to piss.

"Dig!" my mother yells, and I do so.

My mother has become so *hard.* It's perplexing. She's always been curt and impatient, but there used to be warmth beneath it all. I don't know. Maybe she's finally fed up. It's crystal-clear to everyone except my father that she hates Corrigan. I suspect she always has. Of course, I can only speculate, but the fact that my parents were married and moved here six months before I was born suggests that maybe they were shamed into eloping and alighting someplace far from the city. Or maybe this was the only place my father could get posted. Maybe it was a sense of adventure: a fresh start in an expanding coal town.

Seems unlikely.

See, my mother comes from old money. And I've gathered from

overhearing various snide comments that she was expected to marry into more of it.

But my father comes from no money at all. My grandfather was a laborer who died early from tuberculosis. From what I've pieced together, my dad's elder brothers were forced to leave school to keep them in food and board. Being the youngest by far, it was easier for my dad, and he was able to stay on at school, where he excelled. They were all convinced he would become a doctor or a lawyer. They wanted him to have the opportunities they never had. And so I think he disappointed everybody when he announced he was going to study literature.

My parents met at university. It's hard to think of them as young people, with healthy hair and shiny skin. It's even harder to imagine them in love on the banks of the Swan, excited to be with each other. I wonder if my dad intended to be a writer back then. I wonder if that's what drew my mother to him. I don't know. But he was a long way removed from what she had grown up with.

When she fell pregnant with me, there was just enough time for them to elope and for my dad to finish his degree before the bump was too pronounced. My mother never completed her studies, and my father never published a novel.

And thirteen years later, a cave full of bats could see that she's bitterly unhappy here. That she's dissatisfied with her lot and her plot. After my baby sister died, I think she gave up for a while. I think it was with a sense of resignation that she played out a role for herself. She joined the Country Women's Association, mixed with Corrigan's leading ladies, helped cater for events, and joined all the amateur pleated-skirt sporting fraternities and committees. She ticked all the community boxes. But now? Now she's just angry. The varnish is tarnished. She can't be bothered retouching the gloss. She's at the end of her tether.

Recently she's taken to visiting her family more and more often, particularly over this summer. Where before she might go to the city once or twice a year for an extended stay, she has started taking more frequent weekend and overnight trips, and she rarely even announces that she's leaving. She just makes sure my father and I have meals and clothes and she leaves without fanfare, as though she's off to the butcher.

And it used to be that she would go away and come back refreshed. She'd be lighter on her feet. She'd bring gifts and gossip. Her mood would have lifted, and she'd be less stern with me and kinder to my father. But now when she arrives home she's bitter and irritable, as though she's been led back to her cell after a foiled escape.

And it's occurred to me that one day she might not come back at all. She might simply refuse. I know her family pressure her. I know they coddle her with self-serving concern, that they constantly remind her of the things she's missing, the things they feel she deserves. And I don't really blame her for being seduced by it. It's what she grew up with, I guess. It's right up near the surface of who she is, the girl who always got what she wanted. But I *do* blame her for feeling ashamed of us. I get that prickly sensation every time she returns these days: that she doesn't think we're good enough. And that, I can't abide. My father is infuriating, but he's a good and honest person. I know how other fathers treat their sons, and I know I've lucked out. And as for me coming along as I did, I had no choice. I was timing and chance. I was shit luck. But I didn't do anything wrong.

I sink my spade into the hard clay and think about what my mother was born into. Her luck and lot. As though there were any difference between us other than that. How does it *mean* anything? I don't know. But what about Eric Edgar Cooke? What about *his* timing and chance? If he were born in Nedlands like my mother, would he have visited it all those years later like he did? Would he have wrought such terror in those streets?

I pause and wipe my brow. It lacquers my hand. I could lick it, I'm so thirsty. What is this bloody hole *for*? A koi pond? A bomb shelter? I am hot and filthy and fed up. The clay is hard and dense and heavy. The clump of dirt to my right has attracted a brazen pair of kookaburras, whom I welcome with relief. They sift through the mound of earth and feast on insects. I pause to watch one glug down an earthworm.

"You're welcome," I say.

It tilts its head, regarding me with what feels like pity. Its friend suddenly flutters away to a neighbor's tree to laugh at my misfortune.

"Your friend's an ungrateful bastard," I growl. It looks at me shrewdly and then seems to shrug.

I shake my head and keep levering up half-spades of caramel clay. One thing that strikes me is the silence of our street. Usually it would be humming, but it's quiet as a church out there.

In a few hours I've dug to the depth of my thighs. My burst blister is beyond pain now. This surely can't go on for much longer. This is like Dickens or something. Surely the Geneva Convention protects me from having to dig anymore.

I keep going.

And I settle back into considering Cooke and his simple, bitter reason. He just wanted to *hurt* somebody. It sounds so vengeful. But was that really it? Was he out there laying into some kind of version of his father? Was he fighting back through other means? But why would Cooke prey on women, then? Why would he make victims of the innocent, like his father had done to him? It makes no sense. So maybe it was that sense of power that he wanted. After a life of being force-fed shit, of beatings and being trodden, he wanted to turn it right round on itself. Maybe he wanted to *become* his father. To swap roles. To finally be on top. He wanted people at *his* mercy. He wanted to *hurt* them. Just like he'd been hurt. Maybe he wanted a whole city to know that fear. Could that really be it? Could that be the same of Mad Jack Lionel?

Laura Wishart is dead. Someone killed her. That's all I know for certain.

I need to see Jasper Jones. I need to see Eliza Wishart. I need to know more about Mad Jack Lionel. I need to know more about Laura. About Corrigan. About the things that make people do what they do. I need to narrow things down, start pruning back. Until then, I'm a whirring zoetrope of half-thoughts and worries. Beset by bright, dizzy flashes and harried by harpies.

I start to dig like it means something. I try to lose myself in the task. I don't want to think anymore. It feels like there's a tourniquet around my head. I never asked for this.

By twilight I am up to my ribs and I feel as though I have acid coursing through the veins of my arms and my back. As soon as I lay down my spade, I feel stiff and exhausted. I lean on the wall of the well and inspect my palm. My glasses are grubby, but I have nothing clean to wipe them with.

As though she has sensed my lack of activity, I hear my mother burst out the back door and stride toward me. I don't turn around. She stands at the edge of the hole in front of me, hands on her hips, nodding slowly. I'd like to think she's grudgingly admiring my craftsmanship.

I'm waiting to hear the reason for which I've been toiling in soil all afternoon. I look at the hill of earth to my right and can't help but feel a little proud of my work. There's a small blush of real achievement. And there's another part of me that craves her approval. I want her to admit that this is a bloody brilliant hole. I want her to recognize my effort. To tell me I've done a fine job. That it is perfect for its purpose. *103*

But I'm not going to ask what that is.

I keep my head bowed, thumbing my palm. It probably looks insolent, but I don't care.

"Okay, Charlie," she says, in a tone that is still stern. "You can stop digging."

I remain silent, but I look up as she points to the mound of dirt.

"Now: fill it in."

It takes me a moment. She starts to walk away. I look in horror at the dirt pile. Then I wheel round.

"*What?*"

"Fill it back in," she says with her back to me.

"What do you *mean*, fill it back in?" I yell, and I feel a fullness in my throat and a heat on my face.

She turns around. I can see that she's pleased with herself. She suddenly looks like her father. Like a haughty marmot.

"I mean, fill *this* hole back up with *that* dirt, Charlie. You're not leaving it like that. I don't want a great big dirty hole in my backyard. It won't take you long. And hose yourself down before you come inside, thank you."

I am furious. Down the street, I hear the kookaburras start up again. I shake my head.

"No," I say firmly.

"Excuse me?" Her eyes widen. "What did you say?"

"I said no. This is ridiculous. I'm exhausted. I'm not filling it in. If you didn't *want* a hole, you shouldn't have *asked* for a hole. Forget it."

"What did you just say to me?" She leans forward.

"What are you, deaf? I said I'm not filling it in! This is stupid. I worked this hard for nothing!"

"Well, you're not the only one, young man. That's life!"

"No it's not!" I shriek at her. I don't care anymore. "That might be *your* life, but it's not mine!"

"You watch your mouth!" She's yelling too. An angry vein embosses her forehead. "Charlie, you either turn around and finish your job or you will spend the rest of the summer in your room. I mean that. And you can forget about Christmas! You want a purpose for this hole, young man? Why don't you drop your bloody attitude in there and bury that? What's it going to be? It's your choice, Charles Bucktin."

That's not a choice. That's holding a turd in either hand and asking me to eat the one on the right or the left. I turn my back on her. I don't want to give her the satisfaction of an answer, or a look at the salt glaze filming my eyes. When I think she's gone, I clamber out slowly and sniff. With a heavy heart and legs, I glower and scrape the earth back in, cursing her under my breath, muttering that I might like to bury her ugly bloody head in this pit of injustice.

Of course, she hasn't left yet. And of course, she's just heard every word of vitriol. I realize this when she clamps a hand on the back of my neck and squeezes like she's trying to dig out my vertebrae. Her nails are like razors. She hisses in my ear.

"You are a *very* rude boy!"

And she shoves me onto the mound of which I'd been so proud. The dirt is soft and cool and yielding. I move to shield myself from her, but she doesn't hit me. She just snatches the spade from the ground and marches back to the house with it.

"*Now* fill it in!"

\*\*\*

It is almost dark when my father lopes out into the yard. I've almost finished. I'm covered in dirt and so exhausted that I can't stifle a groan every time I doze more earth with my palms.

"Okay. That's enough, Charlie. Come on."

I don't look up. I keep working to display my anger.

"Charlie! Did you hear me? Come on, I said stop. We'll clear it up later."

I want to keep going, but I can't. I rest on my knees.

"Mate, what on earth is going on with you?" he asks. I am immediately defensive.

"What? Nothing. I don't know. Why?"

"Well," he says, with endless patience, "because you're a smart and reasonable kid."

"Not really a kid. I'm fourteen soon," I interrupt. I'm not sure why.

"Well. Okay. Exactly. Even so, I've *never* heard you swear, least of all at your mother. You've never disobeyed a strict instruction either. It's unusual, isn't it?"

I want him to keep talking to me like this. Like a contemporary. A colleague. Like I'm smart enough to keep up.

"Listen, Charlie," he goes on. "If you needed to go into town today, you should have asked one of us. Okay? It would have saved a lot of grief. Particularly for you, by the looks." He gestures toward the filled hole.

"It's not that," I blurt, but stop myself. The urge is there to tell him everything. To let him take care of it. But I shake my head quickly. "Forget it."

"Your mother is worried, Charlie. And you can't blame her. To

105

some extent, we both are. Something very unsettling has happened. You've heard about Laura Wishart. Nobody is quite sure what is going on yet. So, in the meantime, we're trying to do the right thing by keeping you as safe as we can. It's most likely nothing, Charlie. I certainly hope so. But you can see why we might want to be careful just now?"

Why does he have to be so sensible? Why does he have to phrase things so well? He should have been a lawyer, like Atticus Finch. But he'd have to stand up for something then.

I look down. That's not at all fair. But I don't care. I'm angry. And sore.

He kneels and sighs.

"The world seems to be shifting, Charlie. It's different to when I grew up. It's really starting to change. Even here."

"You're right about that," I say bitterly.

"A lot of people are scared. Especially right now, with Laura missing. There's a lot going on."

It's rare for him to talk to me like this. The last time was when he offered me the golden ticket to his library. I feel awkward and a little exhilarated. I'm not sure how I should respond. So I nod.

"Anyway," he says, hoisting himself up. His knees crack. "Your mother has just declared that you're to go without dinner this evening, and she will be alerting you to this as soon as you get inside. But what I suggest you do, instead of arguing, is to nod and take it on the chin. Okay? It's her bridge night tonight, so you can have something to eat after she leaves. I think you've been punished enough."

"Are you sure? I mean, I can build you a shed out here and then knock it straight back down if you want."

To my surprise, he laughs.

"You're just like your mother, Charlie."

"Rubbish," I say. "Don't tell me that."

He chuckles again.

"She does a lot for you, you know."

I stand up and spank the dirt from my shorts.

"Yeah, well, so could a maid," I say quietly.

He frowns.

"What does that mean?"

"Nothing."

He breathes out through his nose and keeps his big doe eyes on me in a way that makes me feel childish and uncomfortable.

"Listen, she just wants to feel as though she's respected. I know you're growing up, Charlie, but she's still your mother. She wants the best for you. But if you still have a problem with something, there are smarter ways around it. You just have to be a bit more canny, okay? More diplomatic. Believe me, my boy, you'll do better than to try to lock horns with her. Do you understand?"

"I guess," I admit sullenly.

"Concession doesn't necessarily mean defeat, Charlie."

"Who said that?"

He smiles. "I did."

We linger a moment beside the filled pit in the fading lilac light.

107

"Where have you been this afternoon, anyway?" I ask.

He raises his eyebrows.

"Actually I've been at the Miners' Hall, helping to organize the search. They started just after lunch."

My chest tightens and I feel hackles bristle my neck. This is my first real chance for answers.

"Really? What do they think? Where is she? Do they know? Where are they looking? What will they do?"

"Well, these things start small, Charlie, then the arc widens. The longer she's missing, the harder and wider they search. For now, though, the best thing to do is to keep calm and look in the likely areas."

"What likely areas?" I ask.

"Like along the river, the immediate surrounds. And I'd imagine her family and friends are being interviewed. Then they'll start to piece together an idea of what may have happened. But I have a feeling she'll probably turn up tonight. I bloody hope so."

"But what if she doesn't?" It feels dangerous to be asking these questions. There's a woodpecker tapping at my sternum. But my father fields my concern as thoughtfully as he does any other.

"Then the arc will widen. They have spotter planes on standby for tomorrow. Also, they've requested dive crews from the city, to search the river, but I hope to Christ they won't be necessary. I'm not sure, Charlie, until it happens. Volunteers will probably keep pressing further into the bush, and there will be town meetings and the like, to gather support and information. Every day that she is missing, efforts will get more desperate."

"But what if they still can't find her? What if she's still missing? They can't look forever, can they?"

What if they find Jasper's clearing? And the dam? How clear are the clues? Would they send down a dive crew? Right to the murky bottom? Could they really find her?

"Well, no. Of course they can't. There's only so long that these resources are available."

"How long?"

"I really don't know, mate," he says. My interest does not arouse suspicion. He doesn't narrow his eyes, he doesn't ask me questions.

"Okay," I say. He claps a hand on my shoulder and then thumbs my grubby cowlick. Gives a reassuring smile.

"Listen, as I say, it probably won't come to all that. She'll turn up soon. My guess is that she is staying with a friend, or that she's run away from home. Something of that ilk. Don't get too worked up, Charlie. People disappear and reappear all the time elsewhere, but in Corrigan events such as these get amplified, simply because everybody knows everybody, because it's otherwise so quiet."

I nod.

"Do you know Laura well?" he asks.

"No. Not really. I know her sister, though. Eliza."

"Right. I don't know Eliza. But I've taught Laura for a couple of years now. She's a quiet girl. Very smart. Very independent. But as I told these people today, there's something about her that seems troubled and volatile. It's as though she holds you at a distance, so I don't know her as well as I know some of my other students. But hiking on out of here on her own sounds like something she might try to do."

"Really?"

"It's what I suspect, Charlie. I'm not sure what their household is like, I don't pretend to know what happens under their roof. I mean, it's not fair for me to speculate as to *why* she would want to up and leave, but I do feel there's a streak in her character that could lead her to do something like that. To leave without telling anybody. They'll probably pick her up someplace close, or she'll be in contact when her money runs out."

"You think so?" I ask.

He scratches his chin and flattens his hair. "I really think it's most likely, yes."

"Is it just you who thinks that way?"

"Everyone has the same end in sight, Charlie; everyone wants her home safe. But they have to be open to all possibilities."

109

"Like kidnapping? Or murder?" I blurt. And then I freeze, like I've been caught out. Like I'm holding her under the arms, staring into a spotlight. I am terrified. I hold my breath.

He sighs and tilts his head. He speaks softly.

"I suppose that is a possibility, Charlie, but it's a very, very unlikely one."

"Really? Then why would you have me stay inside? Why isn't anybody playing out on the street?"

His mouth opens and closes again. I've got him.

"I said it is unlikely, but it's not impossible. See . . ." He pauses, choosing his words carefully. "With things like this, when people don't really understand what has happened, they'll assume the worst long before they have to. It's a little like when people are afraid of the dark. Often it's not the darkness they're afraid of, it's the fact that they don't know what's in it. And because they can't see, because they're not sure, they start to imagine there are more sinister things afoot than there ordinarily would be. Does that make sense?"

"I think so."

"All I'm trying to show you is how quickly reason can be put aside once things like panic and fear start to seep in. Especially in a town like this, where people gossip like they're bloody spies. So, for now, don't worry too much about Laura. She'll turn up, mate."

I look down at my filthy feet. It's her turning up that I'm most worried about.

I give a short, involuntary shrug, feeling the heat of Laura's truth and the coldness of my lie. The invisible ants are crawling all over my body again. I need to bathe. To go soak in a cloak of furiously hot water. I want to scrub the skin off my body, to scratch out the grit.

But while I've got him here, like this, I want to keep it going. I want to ask him about Mad Jack Lionel. I want to hear the true story of his horrible crimes and pin them up against the others I've steeped myself in today. But I can't risk it. If he suspects me of knowing too much, of being *involved*, then it could all unravel. It could imperil Jasper Jones. I decide to wait.

I must look impatient, because my dad claps my arm and bids me inside.

"Remember," he says. "No dinner for now, and just take it on the chin, okay? And tell her you're sorry. See how much easier life can be if you just give in a little."

We move inside, his hand resting on my bare back.

*** 

Later, after our front door has closed behind my mother and her friend Beverly, who has come to pick her up for bridge, my father oversees my construction of a corned beef sandwich.

"Make sure you leave everything as you found it," he warns. "And don't cut too much of that loaf. Otherwise she'll find out, and I'll be the one digging a hole, for both our bodies."

"It's a grave matter," I say, and shake my head slowly and theatrically. My mood is considerably less shitty since I've bathed and she's left.

"And I'm dead serious." He smiles. The kettle whistles on the stove top, and he kisses his mug to it. He makes me a coffee with plenty of condensed milk. I press my sandwich so hard that red-onion relish bleeds out the sides. At least the work today has blessed me with hunger.

As we both fork off to our respective rooms, I stop him just before he heads in.

"Are you writing in there? I mean, a book?"

He pauses, startled. He regards me quizzically.

"Why do you ask?"

"I don't know. I just thought that maybe that's what you were doing in there, is all."

He shifts his weight back as he answers, turning his head, surveying his library.

"No, no, mostly I read in here, Charlie. I do all my marking as well. That's how I spend my time. Best leave the novels to the novelists, I think."

"You're probably right," I say quietly, looking away. We both shuffle away and close our doors. I sit heavily and set my plate down on my desk and think about the way he flinched and looked away when I asked. And I wonder why he lied.

*111*

\*\*\*

Jasper Jones has not come to my window.

I've been waiting here for hours now. I've even removed the glass slats from their frame for a quick exit. But all I've done is offered entry to all manner of insects, which busy themselves around my lamp. I try to swat at them, to no avail. So I try to mash them between two books which I clap together like cymbals.

Jasper Jones is not here and I need him to be. I wonder where he is. I wonder how he is doing. If he's lying low, or if he's out investigating. I wonder how close he is to finding an answer. I hope he hasn't been back to his clearing. What if they followed him there? What if they went looking for him?

Though I reckon he's more cautious than that. I figure that it's probably caution that has kept him out of my backyard. Things need to settle down before we meet again, before we really begin to sleuth for the truth.

Even so, I could do with a reassuring dose of his company so I don't feel so alone in this.

I'm tired, but I'm restless. The night is breezeless and balmy. I crawl out through my window, just to see if Jasper might be lying in wait for the rest of our lights to blink off. I stand in our backyard. It's absurdly quiet. I think of the search party. Whether they've retired for the night, or if they're pushing through the bush, wielding torches, calling out Laura's name.

I turn. Down the side of our house, my father's library light casts a hazy yellow rhombus. I feel a little piqued. Hurt, because he confided in me so recently and then drew a curtain across it.

A cruel part of me urges me to sneak up to that window and peek in. To peel back the curtain like a magician unveiling a trick. I want to catch him in the act, reveal the lie.

Maybe I should start another novel. A less ridiculous one. Prove to him I'm smart enough. I could write it about Jasper Jones. And it could stand alone as he does; shoulders squared, spine straight. And I could throw it on my father's desk one day, after it's been published and he still has no idea. Casually, like it's nothing. And I'd tell him that life might be easier if you give in a little, but it's better if you hold on to something so hard you can't give it up.

A car pulls up abruptly outside our house. I press myself against the boards. It's not Beverly's car. Perhaps it's the police. Maybe they're waiting for Jasper. A stakeout. Maybe they've come to get me. For questioning.

The Hillman sits and idles for an eternity. Then, finally, my mother emerges, laughing. It's a strange sight. I think maybe she's quite drunk. She leans back in, looks like she's rummaging for something. Then she slams the door and waves, retreating slowly. The car departs with her smile. When she turns to walk back inside, her face is as blank as when she left.

Back in my room, my eyes are heavy and my body feels beaten. Despite the insects, and the heat, and my desire to wait for Jasper, I begin to slip away with Mark Twain spread on my chest. And I don't protest. I let go easy. Being, as I am, back in the dappled peppermint shade with Eliza Wishart, with all the right words at the tip of my tongue, saying all the things I should have said, doing all the things I should have done.

# 4

tell Jeffrey I had a nightmare about *The Wizard of Oz*.

Though I don't tell him I was dressed as Dorothy in ruby shoes, or that my mother was the witch, in Jasper's glade.

"*The Wizard of Oz?*" he says, screwing up his face. "Really? But there are so many cooler things to have nightmares about. Like sharks. Communist sharks, with razor-sharp fins that can walk on land."

It's the lunch break at the Test Match. We drag a wooden crate into the middle of the street to use as makeshift stumps. Jeffrey is batting.

"Mind you," he says thoughtfully, "it could work. Think about it. Synopsis-wise."

"Think about what?"

"*The Wizard of Oz*, dickhead. Okay. Listen. A young girl arrives in a strange place where she discovers she has killed someone. After she loots the body and recruits three friends, she travels to another city, where she commits her second murder and steals again. Then she flees. It's all about how you tell it, Chuck. Nothing can be trusted."

"It's not all singing midgets, is it?" I say.

"Murder, Chuck. *Murrrderrrr!*"

"Little wonder I can't sleep at night."

"Oh!" says Jeffrey, jolting upright, then leaning forward. "What about Eliza's sister? What's-er-name, *Laura*. She's disappeared. You heard, right? What do you reckon has happened?"

"What? How should I know?" I snap.

He rears back a little.

"Ease up, *retard*. There is such a thing as speculation. *Obviously*, I don't expect you to *know*. Unless it was you who abducted her. Did you abduct her, Chuck?"

I weld my eyes shut and breathe deep.

"Yes. It was me. You're an idiot."

"*You're* an idiot. I don't believe you, anyway. At the very least, you would have abducted Eliza, not Laura. So you could take her back to your dirty lair for some sassytime. Because you *love* her."

"*Sassy*time?"

"Sassytime, Chuck."

"What does that even *mean*?"

"Oh, *you* know." Jeffrey winks at me with his mouth open. It takes all my mental resolve not to beat him within an inch of his life. I decide to change the subject.

"What happened yesterday in the cricket?"

"Nothing, I didn't miss anything. It was rained out for the whole day. So I was lucky."

"You're lucky you're not still grounded. How'd you get out of it?"

115

"Oh, I think my ma just wants me out of her hair." Jeffrey shrugs and wipes his cheek with his shoulder in a strange way.

"I don't blame her. I'd make you live outside in a tent."

"Pffft!" Jeffrey faces up, tapping his bat against his foot. I bowl to him for around half an hour. True to form, he belts me everywhere without even trying.

The street is hot and eerily quiet. It's so empty. It seems this curious curfew is still in place and most kids are being kept inside. It feels like we've been left behind from something.

I send down an offcutter on a fairly good line and length. Jeffrey, brazen now, kneels and sweeps it hard and square. It skips straight into An Lu's Garden of Certain Death. Buried under a bloom of something white.

"Bang!" Jeffrey exclaims. "You know, Chuck, some batsmen will just block a length ball, play it safe, but not Jeffrey Lu. He's all class. It's controlled aggression, Chuck. Measured flair. This kid's going places."

"Yeah, like over there to get the ball."

"Bollocks! It's your turn."

"Bollocks nothing. You're closer. Go get it."

I can see the bees from here. Waiting for me.

"It's your *turn*, dickhead. Go get the *ball*. You can't bowl that rubbish to Jeffrey Lu." The shadowboxing resumes.

"Piss off. If you want me to keep bowling, you go get it."

"This is an outrage! How is it that *I* am being penalized for *your* mediocrity?" Jeffrey throws his hands in the air like he's appealing to the sky for answers.

"Because you're an idiot."

"This is discrimination!"

"I can't help that, Jeffrey. I'm a bigot."

"Okay. *I'll* get the ball. *I'll* brave the insects." Jeffrey stomps over there histrionically, amusing himself. "Will our intrepid hero make it back? Or will he be defeated by hordes of dangerous ladybirds?"

116    "Shut up, retard. It went to your left."

"What's that, Chucktin Bucktin? Chuck Buck-buck-buck-buck-baaaarrktin!"

"You're nowhere near it. And you're crushing those pink flowers. Your dad is going to go mental."

At this moment, I freeze upon hearing the distant drone of two spotter planes. I look up. The cold brick. They're coming for me.

"Sweet! Look at that!" says Jeffrey, bounding toward me with the ball in his hand. "They must be here for the search. I wish we could see them land."

I watch them. Silently. Two black dragonflies in the sky.

"I'm going to go in," I say.

Jeffrey taps his enormous black wristwatch.

"Actually, fair call. The second session should be just starting."

"Nah. Look. I'm just . . . I'm going to go back to my house," I say distantly, still looking up. I'm rattled. I feel a desperate need to get under cover.

"What? But the Test is on!"

"Yeah, look. I'll see you in a bit. I've just got to . . ." I tail off, walking away, head tilted.

"Okay, loser," Jeffrey chirps. I hear him behind me, dragging the crate back from the road. Hurrying in case he misses a single delivery.

I want to ask my dad about the planes. I want to know how useful they are. How far they can see. But he's not home. The library door is ajar. He must be out, helping with the search. I wish I'd asked to go with him. I'm an idiot. Tomorrow I will, though I don't like my chances.

My mother asks if I want lunch. I politely decline.

"You see the planes?" she calls out.

"Yes," I reply, and softly close my bedroom door.

\*\*\*

A few hours later, there is a frenzied rapping on my louvres. I almost burst. Jasper Jones has finally come. I leap onto my bed and pull the lever like it's a carnival machine.

117

My window opens and reveals an animated Jeffrey Lu. I frown. He has never come to my back window before.

"Chuck! Chuck! Chuck! Chuck!" He is grinning madly.

"What?" I can't conceal my disappointment.

"Doug Walters!"

"*What?*"

"Doug fucking Walters! He just made a century! A Test century! One *hundred* runs, on *debut*!"

I don't say anything.

"I told you!" His delight is a little infectious. "I *told* you, Chuck! He's a champion! He's better than Bradman."

"Jeffrey, it's his first innings."

"He's already got a better average!"

"You're an idiot."

"Can I come in? Stay for a bit?" he asks, hopping and skipping.

I open the back door for him.

"Who is that?" my mother snaps loudly from the other end of the house.

"It's just Jeffrey," I call back.

"Well, in this house we come through the *front* door, thank you! Remember that for next time, please."

I shake my head and roll my eyes at Jeffrey.

In my room, he takes up a book from my nightstand.

*"Tropic of Cancer,"* he says. "What's this one? Any good?"

"Lots of sassytime," I say.

"Really?"

"Really."

He looks distracted. Agitated. He does that thing again where he scratches his cheek with his shoulder.

"Why do you have all that dirt in your backyard?" he asks, looking out. "Is that where you buried Laura Wishart?"

I close my eyes. Breathe in. And out.

"Yes. Idiot."

"No, really. What is it for?"

"My mum made me dig an enormous hole, and when it was done, I had to fill it back in. With my hands."

"What? Why?" Jeffrey scrunches his face.

"Well, you're not the only one who got busted for swearing at their mother. Except mine was a little more directed."

*"What?* Really?" Jeffrey bites his fist. "How are you not *dead*?"

"Because that would have been easy. She wanted me to suffer. She wanted me to experience all the pain of death without actually going all the way. Thus, the hole was dugged."

"Chuck, that is hilarious. She is an evil *genius*."

We shoot the breeze a while longer. I sit on my desk, he perches on my bed. I notice Jeffrey looking down a lot. Every so often, something washes over his face like a glaze. I wonder if he is ill.

And then he just says it. Simply. Like any other sentence.

"Some of my family got killed."

Jeffrey kicks his legs on the edge of the bed. There is a long pause. I don't know what to say.

"Jeffrey, that's horrible. When? *Who?* What happened? Jeffrey, that's horrible."

"It happened yesterday. It was my ma's brother and his wife. My aunt and uncle. They won't tell me much more than that. It happened in the village that she grew up in. I don't know. I think it was a bomb."

"A *bomb?*"

"Yeah."

"Jeffrey, I don't . . . This is really horrible. Are you okay?"

Jeffrey doesn't look at all rattled. His legs keep up their rhythm.

"Yeah. I'm okay, Chuck. I didn't know them or anything. I never met them. But it's sad. It's worst for my ma, obviously. Mostly I just feel really bad for her. She's not in a very good way. She hasn't stopped crying and, you know, *wailing.*"

"Yeah."

I nod slowly and look at my feet.

Silence spreads in my room like a thick, discomfiting fog.

"Did they have any children?" I ask after some time.

"Yes. Yep. Two. A boy and a girl. One, the boy, is my age, and the girl is four, I think."

"Are they okay?"

"Did they get bombed, d'you mean?"

"Well, yeah."

"No. They're still alive. And I don't think they were hurt or anything. My parents are trying to get them over here to stay with us, but I think it's hard to do that sort of thing."

"Really? But why? They're *orphans!* They should be able to come here straightaway!"

Jeffrey shrugs.

"So what will happen to them?" I press. My chest is winding ever tighter.

"Well, I guess they'll stay with our other relatives in the village.

119

But it's a big strain, I think. So I think my dad is going to send them a bunch of money." Jeffrey rubs his nose with his palm.

"Are they going to go over there, your parents? For, you know, the funeral and things?"

Jeffrey cocks his head. "Well, I heard my ma talking about it last night when she was really upset. She wanted to go back straightaway. She started packing her bags and everything. But my dad stopped her."

"How come?"

Jeffrey looks momentarily startled. "Well, because there are *bombs*, Chuck. It's a war. It's pretty dangerous. Even for me."

"But they should be able to *do* something," I say.

We slip into silence again. Jeffrey bobs side to side on my bed. I wonder what he's thinking. I wonder if he came especially to talk about it, or to escape it. I really don't know what to say, or whether to say anything at all. I never have the right words. I guess it is customary to offer condolences. That's what they do in books and films.

120

"I'm really sorry, Jeffrey."

"It wasn't your fault."

"You know what I mean. Dickhead," I say with a small smile. I bow my head. "I feel really bad for your ma. She must be really heartbroken."

"Yeah." Jeffrey nods. "She's really angry too. Screaming and things. She even started yelling 'fuck' last night. 'Fuck' this. 'Fuck' that."

"Really?"

"Yeah, really." And Jeffrey grins.

"I can't imagine that."

"I know. It's weird. You should have seen my dad. He was shocked. He looked straight at me, like it was my fault."

We both giggle. Out of relief. And then it gets infectious and we laugh long and hard. Can't help it.

Then we get to talking about Doug Walters again. Jeffrey assures me that he hasn't finished yet, that he is sure to go on with it tomorrow. I don't have the heart to disagree. We discuss the merits of nipples on men, and decide that there is no earthly purpose for them. We ponder how it is they get stripes into toothpaste.

Then I ask Jeffrey if he thinks animals other than humans know they're going to die one day, or if it just comes as a surprise to them.

"Of course they don't," he says. "They're idiots. Except monkeys. And oliphaunts, they might know. It's about communication, probably. Per exemplarrrr, if you were the unwanted baby of a pirate and they left you marooned on an uninhabited island and you had no contact with another human ever, I don't think you'd know about dying and stuff."

"Reasonable assertion." I nod. "Still, it's a curious gift. You can't *not* feel sad, knowing that you and everyone you know will die. So what would you rather? Would you rather not know and have it surprise you at the end, or know it your whole life and dread it coming?"

Jeffrey looks thoughtful.

"I reckon most people wouldn't want to know. I reckon they'd rather not have to think about it. But I think I'd choose to know. Yarrr. Otherwise you'd just be fat and lazy and you'd just put everything off until some other century. If someone told you that you were going to die next week, you'd probably try to fit in as much as possible, go skydiving or whatever."

"Right." I nod.

"But you *can't* not know it. Which is probably why they made up all that rubbish about heaven, to make people feel better about the whole thing. When Cheeses started saying, 'Oh, you know, don't *worry*. It's not *all* over. After this stuff, you get to sit on a cloud and learn the harp and play volleyball in the nude, as long as you're good,' everyone just nodded and smiled and worried about behaving themselves instead."

"I think Cheeses hates your tone."

"Of course he does, Chuck. I am the speaker of the troooth. I should start a cult."

The sky is a bright orange now. I can hear birds calling out in the cool. And the whirring squeal of the kids next door, swinging on their clothesline over a sprinkler. Jeffrey kicks to his feet.

"Righto. I got to get back, Chuck."

"Yeah, okay."

His head snaps back and he slaps his forehead.

"I *forgot*. My dad is cooking dinner tonight because my stupid ma won't come out of their bedroom. Cheeses Christ, it's going to be a *nightmare*. Everything he cooks feels like phlegm and tastes like pus that's been soaked in brine. Salted pus, Chuck. It's like my mouth is trying to turn itself inside out. He thinks he's the greatest chef in the world, but he is *lousy*."

"Sounds like my dad too."

"They should be banned. There should be laws against it." Jeffrey says as he walks out.

"Motion approved, sir."

I see him out the back door. I know I should say something appropriate and comforting, but I can't think of what. Words fail me. Like they always fail me when I need them. I just crimp my lips and look hopeless.

Jeffrey salutes me.

"Chuck, I bid you a Jew."

"And I owe your revoir," I say, and watch him leave. He scuttles off, his shoulders rounded slightly in a way I've not seen before.

*** 

I sit and watch the news bulletin with my dad. Our ceiling fan rocks and spins above our heads, and we both nurse a glass of lime and bitters with ice chips. I'm expectant, hoping to hear something about Jeffrey's relatives. Some kind of outrage. Marching and chanting in the streets, like I've seen before. But there is nothing about Vietnam at all. No report. No mention.

Instead, I'm shocked to see the Miners' Hall on-screen, and people milling around Corrigan's town center. Right there, inside the television. At first I don't recognize it. My father sits forward in his chair, almost spilling his cradled drink. He calls my mother, who bustles in from making dinner, drying her hands with a thin plaid towel. A frown of concern pushes her face down. She stands with her hands on her hips.

And there's Laura's photograph. Black-and-white. It's a forced smile, like someone had to prompt it. There's something missing in her eyes.

The news broadcaster is saying that it's most likely she ran away, and he's urging people in the city to look out for her. To call the police if they know anything, if they've seen her. The brick groans in my belly. And there are Mr. and Mrs. Wishart. Side by side in front of their house. Pete Wishart stands stoic. An awkward, resolute calm. Mrs. Wishart is a little less composed. Her face hangs, haggard. Her eyes are puffy. She doesn't speak. She just nods with her mouth set tight as her husband cordially asks that people assist in any way they can. It is horrible to watch. At least Eliza isn't there.

The news skips to another story. My father turns to me.

"I didn't know about this at all. The report."

123

"So what does this mean?" I ask.

"Well, it certainly means she hasn't turned up yet, mate. Perhaps she made it to the city. It's worrisome. I'll admit that, Charlie. I really had a feeling she would turn up today. Maybe she got further than we thought."

I am breathing fast. Fidgeting with my drink.

"So you still don't think anything, I don't know, more sinister?"

He sighs and shifts his weight toward me.

"I talked to you about that."

"I know, but . . ." I point to the television.

"Listen. There is still nothing to suggest that there is, Charlie. Okay? Laura Wishart was at home and in bed on Thursday night. Her parents have verified it. And she wasn't there in the morning. It's as simple and as difficult as that. There are no signs of interference or struggle or anything of that nature. Everything suggests she might have just slipped out of her window and left."

"By herself?" I ask.

"Probably. Apparently, I discovered today, Laura had a tendency to go out at night for long walks, but she'd always be back by morning."

"Do they know where she went?" I am on the verge of panic. There's a midge in my drink.

"No. Strangely, they let it lie. They didn't talk to her about it. But it's opened a can of worms. Now they're thinking she may have been meeting someone at the river."

I swallow heavily.

"Do they know who?"

My mother interrupts.

"Wes, I don't think we should be discussing this. Not in front of Charlie. I think that's enough."

"What? Why not?" I object loudly.

My father shows a calm hand.

124      "Your mother is right."

"*What?* Why? *Why* is she right? That makes no sense! Of *course* I should know about this!"

"Charlie!" my mother snaps.

"Charlie!" my father warns.

I glower. My mother flaps her tea towel.

"You *see*, Wesley?" She is brimming with emotion. "He's just like you! He won't bloody *listen!*"

She storms out. She slams the door.

I am dumbstruck.

"What was *that* about?" I whisper, gesturing at the door.

My father sighs again, and leans forward.

"Charlie, do you remember what I said? About diplomacy?"

"What? Sure. But . . ."

"Listen, you and I can always talk about this stuff *later*. Okay? Be smarter about it. Don't provoke her. And believe me, I'm telling you more than enough. In other families, you wouldn't hear a thing about this, so be grateful."

He is right. He is always right. But something stubborn and unresolved in me still has to press at it.

"Okay. I understand. But just now, please, while we're talking about it, answer me this: do they know who she was meeting?"

I can't help it. I have to know.

My father's face broadcasts dwindling patience. I am pushing my luck.

"No. They have no idea. And I couldn't help them either. She wasn't sweet with anybody at school, that's for sure. She didn't have a lot of friends. But it's still conjecture that she was meeting anybody at all. It's just as likely she was heading out by herself."

"So does this mean that they will stop looking here? In Corrigan?"

"*Charlie . . .*" My dad glances up at the door. We're still whispering.

"What? She can't hear. I *need* to know."

"I know you're concerned, mate." He pauses and observes me for a moment. "Okay. No. It doesn't mean they'll stop searching. There's lots of bush out there. They have the spotter planes for a little while longer. A few more days, I should think. And the dive crews are coming tomorrow. The search teams will operate as long as there are volunteers. But it's a real needle in a haystack. She really has disappeared without a trace. It's hard to know where to begin. She could have gone anywhere, really. She's a clever girl. And if Laura doesn't wish to be found, then that makes it all the more difficult. People are doing their best with very little. So I don't know. I feel so terrible for her family. They must be going through hell."

We fall silent. I stare at the floor for a time. Then, as casually as I can, I ask: "Can I come with you tomorrow? To help with the search?"

My father just frowns.

"Of course not, Charlie. No. Under no circumstances. No. End of discussion."

He half smiles as he rises and rubs his thumb along my hairline.

"Remember what I said, too." He points toward the door. "You've got a good head. Use it."

I smile back weakly and nod.

\*\*\*

Later, when I think about Jeffrey, I wish I'd tried to talk to my father about Vietnam. About the war there, and Jeffrey's family, and how they got killed. None of it makes any sense. I want him to explain to me just how it could happen.

Strangely, of all the horrible things I've encountered and considered recently, dropping a bomb seems to be the least violent among them, even though it's clearly the worst. But there's no evil mug shot, no bloody glove. It's hard to figure out who to blame. There's something clean about all that distance. Maybe the further away you are, the less you have to care, the less you're responsible. But that seems wrong to me. It should be in the news. It's wrong that they died.

But if they weren't Jeffrey's family, would I care so much? That's hard. Probably not, I guess. I mean, if you took every bad event in the world to heart, you'd be a horrible mess. You'd spend your life crying, wading from one tragedy to the next. You'd be a wreck. Maybe that's why people stay in Corrigan and pull their hats low. The less you know, the further away you are, the easier it is to shrug and tut and move on. And so Corrigan remains a town of barnacles. A cluster of hard shells that suck themselves stuck and clench themselves shut and choose not to know about dying. And the way I feel right now, I don't blame them.

I flop my pen up and down between my fingers so it looks like its made of jelly. I sigh. It feels like somebody is ripping my insides out. Like some kind of mongrel dog has ahold of my intestines, and it's tugging at and wresting them right there in front of me, low and angry. And I feel like letting go, truth be told. I feel like letting the dog have me, letting myself spool out like an old woollen jumper until I'm empty and light.

What kind of lousy world is this? Has it always been this way, or has the bottom fallen out of it in the past couple of days? Has it always been so unfair? What is it that tips the scales so? I don't understand it. What kind of world could let pretty girls get beaten and hanged? What kind of world gives birth to Fish and Cooke, lets them fester and hate, lets them torment the innocent and make good people afraid? What kind of world punches someone for using big words?

Verbosity. Verbosity. Verbosity.

A world that kills parents and makes orphans of children and kicks away cricket balls and lies through its sharp teeth. That makes a decent person feel like rubbish all his life because he's poorer and browner and motherless. That hosts three billion folks, each of them as lonely as the other. A world that's three-quarters water, none of which can quench your thirst.

Bugger it. There is nothing directing this stupid play. There can't be. If there is, He's a crueller bastard than they give Him credit for. It's timing and chance, isn't it? Shit luck and good luck. You dodge bullets or you get hit.

Laura Wishart got hit. She's dead. She really is. I buried her with Jasper Jones. I touched her while she was still warm, I carried her. And they're out there, looking. They're out there now. The police, the news, Corrigan. And I'm afraid they'll find her. Somehow. And then they'll find us.

127

Only one other person knows where she is, and I don't know how Jasper and I can ever find out who they are. It seems the most impossible of tasks.

And what if we don't? What happens then? If the search is abandoned, and if Jasper and I finally admit defeat. When Laura is just a bundle of lonely bones tied to a stone, do we leave the Wisharts to cling to their threadbare hope? Leave them to a life of speculation and prayer? I wonder if preserving the part of them that believes she made it to the city might be a good thing. The part of them that believes she might still be out there someplace. That there's a chance, no matter how slim, that she's making a life out there. That she's doing okay. I wonder whether it would be comforting or torturous, to never fully know, to never put the matter to rest.

I guess, over time, you'd want to protect that fool's-gold glimmer, like you'd clutch a candle in a jar down in a cave. And eventually that hope, that faith, would become a kind of truth. *She'll turn up. She'll turn up.* They would be more than bittersweet words.

But you could never move on from it, could you? You could never set things right in your heart. You'd spend your life wavering between the flickering spark and the dark tunnel you're in, and you'd seek solace in your little bottled lie each time, instead of heading for the real light at the end.

I think the comfort would be thin and hollow. I think the knot of not knowing would be the worst. You'd be at the behest of your howling imagination, beset by it. It would never let up. The possibilities, the frayed ends, the fragments and scenarios. Forever out of your reach. You'd crave the truth most of all, wouldn't you? No matter what it meant. Even coming to know that your daughter, your sister, is anchored at the bottom of a water hole. That she was assailed and beaten and hanged. That she was taken from you. Stolen. And buried without you bearing witness, without you tossing dirt or murmuring goodbye.

128

I put my pen down. I fold my arms and lay my head on them. And I think of Eliza. Her cheeks and her smell. I have to. It's the only way I can distract this hungry dog, the only way I can ward off the insects itching my eyes, the only way I can still the hurricane in my snow dome. *What a world!* said the green witch in my *Wizard of Oz* dream. I bet she was happy to go. I bet a part of her was relieved to melt into nothing. For some people, it must be nice to know about dying. It must be a relief. What a world. And I fall asleep like that, my suitcase yawned open by my feet, a spread of pages under my arms.

And Jasper Jones doesn't come.

# 5

He doesn't come, he doesn't come, and then he does.

Jasper Jones has come to my window.

It is a week since Laura was killed. It's been a week since I've seen Jasper. It feels like my whole life.

*** 

Nothing much had happened since everything happened. The Ashes Test was a draw; not even Doug Walters could swashbuckle a result. Jeffrey failed to make the Country Week cricket team, which came as no surprise. My mother was irritable, my father quietly concerned and serene. I had been getting less and less sleep. I finished *Pudd'nhead Wilson*. I started *Innocents Abroad*. I didn't have to dig any more holes.

The black dragonflies left and the search teams began to disperse. There were only a few locals and some people from neighboring towns still left to scour the bush. The water crews dived and surfaced with empty hands.

The latest round of draft letters was delivered. I heard that three young men from Corrigan had been called up for National Service. My father shook his head when he told me.

It was a whole week since we drowned her body. And Laura Wishart was still where we left her.

Corrigan was slowly lifting the curfew on its children, but the panic remained. Kids were allowed outside again, and there were color and noise back in the street. But doors were being snapped shut and locked come dusk, and parents remained taut and watchful.

Tonight there was a twilight meeting at the Miners' Hall. It was standing room only. The Wisharts weren't there. I was hoping to see

Eliza. Jeffrey was there with his mother, but they arrived late and were toward the back, so I couldn't talk to him. The local chaplain and a few senior members of the local council took the floor. None of them could answer any questions with any certainty. They blustered and touched their collars and said the same things over and again. *It's a complete mystery*, they said. *There is no evidence to suggest anything untoward. It's as though she simply disappeared.* They said the likelihood is that she hitchhiked out of town. Therefore, the search had broadened to other states, and they have issued bulletins nationwide calling for information. I took a long, deep breath. The chaplain, who everybody calls Reverend Gooseberry because he only has one testicle, took to the lectern with theatrical gravity and self-importance. He led the gathering through a prayer, and assured us that God would see her back to us safely. I looked up and saw my father narrow his eyes and thumb his jaw. Before people began to file out, they were reminded to stay vigilant, to keep their eyes peeled. And if anyone had any information that might be of use, they were urged to come forward immediately.

130

I slowly allowed myself to exhale.

I'd never felt so utterly alone as then, hemmed in and trapped by every person in this town. It felt as though I was made of different stuff. As though I was from a different place. Like I spoke a different language.

There, among the local police and the firm-lipped city coppers, among the volunteers and the hysterical mothers and the breast-beating fathers, I'd been right in the hornet's nest. And it struck me afresh, the deed that I'd done, my collusion with Jasper Jones. The heft of it. If any of these people knew what I'd done, I would've been spat on and screamed at.

But they didn't know anything. They had no idea. And nobody in Melbourne or Sydney or Adelaide could possibly come forward to lend assistance. Nobody outside of this town could know what I had seen.

Jasper and I were in the clear for now. Laura had not been discovered, and nobody had seen us in the streets that night. For this

I felt grateful, of course, but I still despaired. If these folks couldn't get anywhere with their search teams and sniffer dogs and planes and dive crews and interviews, if they couldn't unearth any clues, then what hope had we?

After the meeting, in the open vestibule of the hall, there were trestle tables stacked with urns and plates of baked goods. The parents milled about and spilled out of the entrance, slapping the hands of their children. It was a chance for Corrigan to gossip en masse, for rumors to flap and slip from the lips of high-eyebrowed wives, to be refuted and scorned by their husbands.

Out the front, children played chase among the lanes and parked cars. Kids closer to my age mingled and loitered, daring each other to pilfer from the feast inside. Summer couplings stole a chance to spend some time together, looking conspicuously around before sneaking behind the hall or across the road to the back of the hardware store to kiss and grope.

I found Jeffrey pretty quickly. He was chewing a ginger snap that he'd boosted on the way out.

"Quick hands, Chuck," he said. "Like the Artful Dodger. I could have taken a whole tray and they wouldn't have even noticed."

"Then you'd be the Fartful Podger."

Jeffrey smiled with his mouth full.

"They don't really know anything, do they?"

"What d'you mean?" I asked.

"I mean the police. It's stupid. They called a big meeting just so they could tell everybody they know about as much as we do. I reckon they were just hungry." And he stuffed the rest of the ginger snap in his mouth.

"You're probably right," I said.

"I'm always right," he said after a lengthy time chewing. "I'm a genius. And I'm bored too. A sharp mind like mine needs stimulation. Go in there and tell them you did it so we can all go home."

Then there was a commotion. It cut the air and made everything

131

CRAIG SILVEY

still. From inside the lobby of the hall, I heard a single scream, a crockery crash, the gasp of a crowd, then a sustained barrage of sobbing and screeching. It was loud and unintelligible. Heads turned.

This is what had happened:

A woman called Sue Findlay, whom I'd never met, had walked from the hall's belly to see Jeffrey's mother quietly pouring water from one of the urns into her teacup. Sue Findlay was a boxy woman with a thick bob, and from what I was told later by my father, she just detonated. Her eyes had lit up like someone put a penny in her. She screamed until her face was red, then stomped over to Mrs. Lu. She slapped her cup up, right into her chest and her chin, staining her thin summer blouse and scalding her skin. The cup smashed. Mrs. Lu, stunned, had bowed slightly and backed away. But Sue Findlay hadn't finished. Jabbing her finger, she screeched the most horrible words, the nastiest things imaginable, her voice uneven with tears, her eyes crazy. It happened so quickly. The surrounding folks just stared. I don't know where her husband was. It was only when she reached out to snatch at Mrs. Lu's hair that Reverend Gooseberry pushed through to grab her firmly by the shoulders and lead her away.

Mrs. Lu just quietly reached a trembling hand out to unsheathe a napkin. Nobody took her by the shoulders.

Then Jeffrey pushed through the milling cluster. I was right behind him. He walked straight up to his mother and touched her hip as she daubed at her chest.

"Ma, we should go now."

It's all he said. Plainly. As though nothing had happened. Mrs. Lu nodded. She must have been in a lot of pain. Jeffrey led her out with his chin up. Like it was all just an unfortunate accident. Mrs. Lu looked shaken and embarrassed. People slowly made way. I followed them outside silently.

Jeffrey opened the door for his mother and people looked on, watching like they were some kind of exhibit. As their car started, Jeffrey wound down his window and waved.

132

"Bye, Chuck," he said.

Words deserted me. I held my hand up weakly.

Afterward, I orbited my parents. I listened to my father air the same platitudes to every concerned parent who wandered our way. And I watched my mother fawn and cluck in an overbearingly sympathetic way. I felt galled. Nobody talked about what had just happened. Not one word.

Then someone mentioned Jasper Jones. The same way they did when the post office burned to the ground. With tilted eyebrows and suspicion. And my father listened blankly, like he was barely tolerating them, like he knew better, but he said nothing in Jasper's defense. None of the things I wanted to holler. So I sighed and turned and kicked a honky nut as hard as I could. It skittered across the road. I left them and sat in the backseat of our car. And there I scowled and sweated, watching this town through our grubby windows. I was so full of sadness and hate. I wondered how many of them had mentioned Jasper's name over the past week. Probably all of them. I wondered how many of them might be talking about him right now.

*133*

And I understood then that maybe we really did do the wrong thing for the right reasons. If we'd left Laura Wishart where she was, they would find her. Someone, somehow, sometime, would stumble across that glade. And soon enough, they would link Jasper back to that spot. He was right. This town was looking for an excuse. And that coincidence would be more than enough for them.

He would have been cuffed and caged like Eric Cooke. He would have been beaten and lynched like Laura Wishart.

I stared into my lap. Suddenly the thought of being in New York City with Eliza seemed the most wonderful thing in the world. I rested my head against the window and thought on it. I imagined meeting her in Manhattan for high tea, whatever that was; all I cared about was that it was far away from here, from these people. I imagined holding her hand and buying her things. Kissing her cheek goodbye as we parted company. I could live with Jasper Jones. In Brooklyn. We'd be safe there. No one could find us, no one would suspect a thing. Jasper Jones would make New York City his own, and I'd be walking alongside my girl, on the other side of town.

My reverie was interrupted by the Miners' Hall's front floodlights. The sun was bleeding out, and the thick yellow light filled the air abruptly. As though on cue, mothers started rounding up their children and men started wandering to the pub to drink their pay. I saw Sue Findlay treading the wooden steps of the hall, holding a white handkerchief to her face, being led by a tall man I didn't recognize. I wanted to spit poison at her. I watched her with my lip curled.

My father approached and bade me into the front seat by pointing. My mother was staying on to help clean up.

On the short trip home, he explained to me the cause of Sue Findlay's outburst.

Some months ago her husband, Ray, had been killed in the war. They'd had a rocky marriage, but she'd taken it very badly. And only yesterday her eldest son had announced he'd been balloted through to Vietnam. She'd taken that even worse.

"That doesn't make it right," I said indignantly. "That's got nothing to do with Mrs. Lu! It's not fair!"

"Charlie . . ." My dad dipped his head to the side and sighed, showing his dimples.

"Nobody even helped her!" I exclaimed loudly. "Nobody even thought to help her."

My father didn't say anything.

***

Jasper Jones is at my window.

My mouth goes dry and my heart tries to escape as I climb onto my bed to flip the louvres.

*"Charlie!"* he hisses, and taps again.

The first thing I notice is his face. His left eye is like a cricket ball. A shiny bulb with a single seam. There's a dried cut on his lip.

"What happened to your face?" I ask, urgent and quiet.

"Tell you in a bit," he says, scanning my room. "Can you come out?"

It's late. My father is in his library. My mother hasn't yet returned from the hall. I weigh up the risks. It's touch-and-go.

"Where?" I whisper. But he has moved back into the dark. I peer out, but don't see him. I hear a soft thud and a small grunt from Jasper. Next door's dog starts barking. I hold my breath.

I stack the glass plates as quietly as I can. For some reason I hide them under my bedsheet. I meet Jasper in the backyard.

"Who's gone and dug a great big hole in the middle of your backyard?" he says, brushing the dirt from his shirt.

"It was me. Long story."

"Well, shit, Charlie. Fill the bloody thing back in properly at least."

"Where have you been?" I ask. I want to tell him how relieved I am to see him. But I don't.

"I've bin everywhere and nowhere," he says, and scruffs at his hair. "You ready?"

135

That rash of fear and exhilaration is all over me again. I don't have a choice but to follow. I'd sooner take the risk than keep another vigil, worrying and wondering. I'd rather be in jail than be left to my own devices any longer.

We head out, skulking down the side of our house and onto the street. I feel eager and important.

"Are we okay to do this? Aren't they patrolling?"

"Nah," Jasper replies without turning to me. "They stopped that two nights ago. They're all out pissing it away at the Sovereign tonight, anyways."

"Really?"

"Really."

We move quickly, cautious and wary. We keep away from streetlights and push through vacant lots when we can. I have to stop a dozen times to pry prickles out of my pansy sandals. Jasper waits impatiently. On Clement Street, we hear a car approach, then see the soft sheen of its headlights round a bend. Jasper grabs my shirt and tugs me into someone's front yard, and we crouch behind a broad spicy shrub. I recognize the coarse adhesion of a spider's web and feel something crawling on me. I want to whimper. Jasper is still clutching me as we wait for the car to pass. I am sweating. Every muscle is taut. I want to run and squeal and clap at my body.

Of course, the car slows and pulls into the driveway of the very house where we've sought refuge. I could burst. I could self-combust right here. The car shudders to a halt. Just meters away. The door yawns open. This is like a horror film.

A man emerges. He's old. And he's drunk. If he catches us, we're in for it. We watch him stumble across his lawn toward the front of the house. Leaning on a veranda beam, he pauses and tries to unhitch his belt. I hate him. Bloody hell, *something is crawling on me*. I want to strip off my clothes and roll around like I'm on fire.

After some fruitless fumbling, the man lifts his hand like a sock puppet and regards it quizzically, like it's something he's trying to read without his glasses.

Upon trying again, he unbuckles and unzips and unleashes a ridiculous torrent of piss onto his garden bed. It goes forever. He must have a bladder the size of an oak barrel. I've seen smaller streams of fluid from a firehose. I have some breed of noxious spider on my neck, poised to strike with inch-long fangs, and this man is siphoning the Ganges with his dick. I want him dead. I want him struck from above. I've never longed for divine intervention more fervently than now. I watch him, my face creased in agony. He sways his hips and buries his chin deep into his chest as he hums "It's a Long Way to Tipperary."

Finally he staggers inside. As soon as the door slaps shut, we spill out from under our canopy. I run like my limbs belong to somebody else. At the end of the street, I stop and frenetically scrub at my hair and tug at my shirt. I wipe my neck and slap at my chest and stamp my feet. I must look demented.

"Charlie! What are you *doing?*" Jasper hisses.

I pause, having taken my shirt off and flogged it.

"Uh? Oh, I thought I had a spider on me. You know. A deadly one."

Jasper nods once, slowly. Then he shakes his head.

"Christ, I thought you were dying."

"So did I," I say, and carefully slip my T-shirt back on. "Anyway, what was that bloke, a camel?"

To my surprise, Jasper laughs. It's a broad and cheeky grin. I notice he has dimples. I smile too, a little proud I've inspired it. After a bit, he waves me on.

We don't speak when we're on the path to Jasper's glade. It's strange. I feel obliged to stay silent, to walk behind.

When we reach that curtain of foliage, I feel uneasy. Like I'm about to see Laura again, as she was. It's a revolting, queasy sensation. It puts lead in my heels and kneads at my heart. That huge jarrah looms big and dark. I don't want to go in.

"You ready?" asks Jasper Jones.

*137*

I look at him dazedly.

Jasper doesn't wait for my response. He peels back the wattlebush and holds it open. I bow and enter. I have to.

I push through with my eyes closed. When I open them and look around, it feels eerie, but deeply familiar. Though I've only been here once, it feels like a place I've visited all my life, and I've just come back after a long absence.

Jasper is by my side. He's frowning.

"Feels strange," he says.

"Yeah. I feel it too." I tilt my head and look around. As though the strangeness could make its presence known in the surrounding trees, like a sickly green fog.

"No, I mean, it feels . . . different."

"How so?"

"I dunno. It's hard to tell. It's a creepy feelin on the back of my neck. It's like someone else has bin here. That's what it feels like."

"Is that possible?" I ask.

"Course it's *possible*. I don't reckon it's likely but."

Jasper eyes everything carefully. Like he's suspicious of the surrounds. He strides, bent-backed, to the edge of the dam, then under the hollow tent of the tree, then out of my sight. I stay where I am.

When he returns, he stands with a hand on his hips, the other thumbing his chin.

"Nah," he says. "They can't've."

It sounds like he's convincing himself.

"Who? The police, you mean? Why not? They've been out here all week, right?"

But Jasper appears unwilling to regard that as a possibility. Suddenly he shrugs and shakes his head, surfacing.

"Smoke?" he asks me, presenting a battered packet of Luckies. I decline after feigning consideration, and follow Jasper to the water. He sits, leaning his back on the tree, then strikes a match and shields it with his palm. His injured face glows orange and lights the night for a moment. I sit cross-legged nearby, but not quite so close to the water.

"You got any whiskey?" I ask.

Jasper raises his eyebrows. Then he grins with one side of his cut mouth. He reaches down and reels in a thin line hooped around a root just by his leg. At the other end is a bottle. The dam's ripples are unnerving. I look away.

"Here we go, Charlie. Black Bush. This is top-shelf, mate. Not a bad one at all." I turn and Jasper is proffering the bottle, wiping his mouth with the back of his hand.

"Here. Fill yer boots."

And I do. Well, I fill my sandals. I take a thimbleful into my mouth and it's as scaldingly poisonous as the first time. My lips try to squirm away from my face. I have no idea why I felt the need to request this. But now I'm stuck with this bottle, and I need to make some show of reducing its content. I breathe out and choke its neck tight. Then I take an almighty swig. My eyes burst open and I have to wrestle every impulse to keep the fiery stuff in my stomach.

"Yair, Christ. That's . . . better," I wheeze, and hand the bottle back. I can barely see Jasper through my tears. "I bloody needed that."

Surely I'm not fooling anybody. Nonetheless, I kind of like the spread of heat it gives my belly. It crumbles and corrodes my brick. I look at Jasper, feeling a little looser now. A little lighter. That hideous potion works. I point at him.

"Was it your dad who did that?" I ask.

He sits up a little straighter.

"Was what my dad?"

I draw a circle round my face.

"Oh," he says, and touches his bulbous eye with a finger. "Nah. I haven't seen him, actually. He skipped town last Friday. Wasn't there when I got back."

Last Friday. I frown and let it sit there. I don't know. Maybe I'm being hysterical, but I can't help being suspicious. If someone leaves town the morning after a murder, isn't that telling? Jasper quickly snuffs the notion.

139

"And he dint kill Laura either, if that's what you're thinkin about. No chance. He might be a worthless, jobless drunk, and he might come home swingin from the fuckin bootstraps some nights, but he hasn't got *that* in him. He couldn't kill his way out of a morgue, my old man. Probably be too much effort, if anything. That, and Laura would've beat the piss out of him first." Jasper smiles ruefully.

"So who *has* done that to your face, then?"

Jasper drags deeply, then gently coaxes a perfect silver smoke ring from his mouth. He frowns.

"Charlie, come on, mate. Who d'you reckon?"

"I honestly have no idea," I say with a shrug. I don't.

"Sarge. The local constabulary, Charlie."

"What do you mean?"

"Exactly that. They asked me in for a visit, and had me locked in for the weekend."

"What? Why? Are they allowed to do that?"

"They don't need a reason, mate. Besides, who am I going to report it to, anyway?"

"So then they did *that*?" I gesture toward his face.

"Sure did." Jasper spits and stubs out his cigarette. He pockets the end. Lights another. He mumbles with the fresh smoke between his lips, "My ribs hurt the most. Steel caps. Bloody brutal."

"But *why*? Why would they do that?"

"Shit," Jasper says without menace. He holds the whiskey aloft for me to take, and I oblige. "It's obvious, innit? They reckon I got somethink to do with Laura being missing, and they wanted me to say as much."

"They wanted you to confess?"

"Pretty much."

"So what did you tell them?" I suck at the bottle and wince. I feel the heat sink, then lift through me.

"I dint tell them nothing, Charlie. Not a word. Not a single word the whole time. That's why I couldn't breathe right until yesterday."

"That's horrible." It's all I can say.

"That's one way to describe it." Jasper smirks. "But one good thing about it all is that it let me in on what they know, which is fuck-all of nuthin. That's good for us, mate. Means we're in the clear for a bit. But it don't help us in nailin the bloke who really did this to her."

I take another tug at the bottle and hand it back. It still tastes molten and revolting, but it feels nice. I'm beginning to understand why you'd want to pour it down your neck.

"There was a town meeting tonight. Everyone seems to think Laura ran away. They're all saying she hitchhiked out of here. It was on the news too. On the telly. They were asking people to help."

Jasper nods slowly. "They're either lying on purpose, or they're fuckin stupid. Think on it, Charlie. Why would they say that? They *know* that Laura dint pack any clothes, she dint take any money, she dint leave a note or nothing. Know what I reckon? I reckon they're saying that because they haven't found anything. They're tryin to cover their own arses, trying to make it someone else's problem. Takin the attention away."

"Would they do that? I mean, Laura's dad was even on the news, asking people to come forward, asking people in the city to keep their eyes out."

"Mate, Laura's old man is the worst out of the whole lot."

I am taken aback.

"How do you mean?"

"Let's just say he was down at the station as well," Jasper says bitterly.

"What, and he knew they were beating you?"

"Knew? He dint just *know*, he was sticking the boot in most of all. Pissed as a rat and twice as angry. Screamin at me, spittin. *Where is she? What did you do?* Stinkin of turps, worse than my old man."

I can't believe what I'm hearing. It seems so far-fetched. My head is spinning, and I'm not sure if it is the Black Bush.

"But . . . but he's the shire *president*."

"So?"

"It's just . . . it's hard for me to believe, is all."

We slip into silence. The heat is thick. I listen to the rustles and the creaks of the bush. The walls of the glade look formidable. It makes me feel small.

I watch Jasper blow another smoke ring. A large one. And deftly, he slices his cigarette right down the middle of it. For a moment before it dissolves, it takes the shape of a heart.

"That's a neat trick," I say. He nods.

"Laura used to like that too. She tried for ages, but she could never do it."

"You must miss her," I say plainly after a time.

Jasper grinds his cigarette and nods to himself. He upends the whiskey bottle, takes a solid hit of it.

"You know why else she wouldn't have left here, Charlie?" He pauses and shakes his head. "Because we were gonna go together. We were gonna get out. She wouldn't have left without me. We had it planned and everything. I was working the orchards to get us some money up. *That's* where I'd bin the couple of weeks before. And she were gonna fleece a few quid from her old man shortly before we went. We were goin up to the city to live. She was gonna study. Do a course to get into the university."

"What were you going to do?"

"Dunno. Whatever come my way up there, I guess. Anythin. I don't know. I got a few ideas, you know. Boxing. Footy. Get a trade. It weren't ever a worry. I mean, shit, even if I had've come down here of a weekend and taken back a sack full of crayfish, I would have killed the pig up there. It's crazy, Charlie. It's money for nuthin. If you know the right people, if you get friendly enough with the folks that are exportin em, you're makin out like a bandit. It's good money for good sizes. And I know all the spots down here that nobody goes. Where the big ones are, in deep, big as your arm. You spend a night setting traps, take them up fresh. You could make a good living, for certain. So, you know, I got irons in the fire."

Jasper sighs, and his body rises and falls sharply, like a single hiccup.

"I bin thinkin a lot about poker too."

"Poker?"

"Yair. Never lost money. Not once. I got a gift, I reckon. I could scratch out a living during the week, then make it tenfold again over the weekend. That's what I do at the orchards. Work hard during the day, pocket my coin, then go find a game and make some real money."

"Really?"

"For certain. Easy. See, poker isn't about luck, Charlie. Luck's got nuthin to do with it. It's all about acting. It's all about how you comport yerself at the table. You got to give nothing away. Or, if you *do* give yerself away, it's got to be on purpose, you got to be hamstringin them." Jasper pauses to strike a match and feed it to another smoke. "But mostly it's about readin people. And that's what I do best. I reckon

I got a gift for it. True. Like a sixth sense or something. See, when it comes to pounds and pennies, it don't matter who you are, at some point it means something. And when there's enough of it out in the middle, blokes'll tell you things with their eyes. It's almost like I can smell it when they're lyin.'"

"I got that too. It's like I can tell before people even open their mouths. Specially my parents."

"You'd be a good poker player, then."

"Nah, I don't think so. I can't lie so well. I just blush and squirm a lot."

"You don't have to lie, Charlie. You just have to look like you don't give a shit."

"I can't seem to do that either. I wish I could."

I take the bottle again. Then I look down and rub the back of my head. Maybe that's how he does it. Maybe that's how Jasper Jones navigates this world and comes out on top, in spite of the shitty hands he gets dealt over and over. That poker glaze, like a superhero mask. Hiding his suspicion, giving nothing away. But it is still a lie, isn't it? It's just a deflection. That's his trick. That shrug is just a big act. A myth. It's his way of hiding his rubbish cards.

*143*

Like Laura, for instance. Like when he cried that night with his back turned, and then nodded so vacantly when I asked him if he missed her just now. The mask is back on, the alter ego.

Jasper Jones has lost his girl, maybe his best friend too. His only friend. It seems so infinitely sad to me, I can't even imagine. To lose someone so close, someone he had his hopes pinned on. Someone he was going to escape with, start anew. And to see her, right here, as she was. Right where I'm sitting. What a horrible series of events this has been. But Jasper Jones has to keep that poker face. He has to throw that cloak over his heart. I wonder how much of Jasper's life is spent pretending he doesn't give a shit.

It must be a lonely way to be. I wonder if Jasper really needs me here to help solve this or if he just needs company. I wonder if he considers me a friend. I hope so. I imagine him sitting here with Laura, shooting the breeze. I wonder if he has anybody else to talk to. I guess he doesn't.

I think that maybe I'm drunk. Am I drunk? I don't know. I feel a little woozy. I can feel my pulse on the sides of my head. I put the whiskey to one side.

"So are you still going to go? To the city, I mean."

"Yair, probably," Jasper sniffs. "I bin thinkin about it. After this whole mess is sorted, I'll head out. Not sure exactly where, though."

"But doesn't it seem too soon?" I ask. "You're only a year older than me. We're still kids, really. Don't you want to wait?"

"Wait for what? And I haven't ever felt like a kid, Charlie. You don't unnerstand. I bin lookin after myself since I can remember. And that's food, clothes, where I sleep, the whole lot. I tole you, it doesn't *matter* how old you are. Everyone ages. Everyone can learn a trade and pay taxes and have a family. But that's not growin up. It's about how you act when your shit gets shaken up, it's about how much you see around you. That's what makes a man. And if I can do it here, in this town, I can do it anywhere, I reckon. What's for me here, anyway? There's no reason to stay. It's a dead end, this."

"I'm starting to feel the same," I say. I flick a twig into the dam.

"So you *do* unnerstand. And don't worry about me, mate. I can look after meself."

"Oh yair," I say. "Oh shit, yair. I know that."

Jasper lights yet another cigarette.

"It won't be for a while, anyway, I don't reckon. Not until we can get enough on Mad Jack Lionel."

"So you know for sure that it was him?"

"Dead set. I reckon so, Charlie."

"How?" I lean forward, intrigued.

"Well, that's what I bin wanting to tell you. See, I bin walkin past his house every night this week."

"On your way to here?" I ask.

"Yeah."

"But isn't that dangerous? Coming here while they're searching?"

"Nah, not really. I only come here late at night. And it's dead easy to slip the patrols. It's no problems."

"Right."

"Right. Well, I tole you that every time I walked past that house, without fail—and I mean *every* time—Lionel would come out his front door and start yellin out at me. Waving, calling out my name. Or at least I think he was. I could never tell what he was saying, the house is too far away to hear proper."

"Okay." I nod.

"Well, it's been the same as last week when we went there and waited by the gate, remember? Nuthin. Not a word. He hasn't come out once. Maybe he's skipped town, who knows? There's no sign of him at all. And I bin there *every* night, waiting."

"For *what*, though? What will you do?"

"Go in there. Talk to him. It's not trespassing if he's out the front, hollerin my name all over the place." Jasper motions for me to pass him the whiskey.

"Surely you wouldn't go in there!"

"Course I would. Why not?" Jasper frowns.

"Are you insane? It's Jack *Lionel*! You don't know what could happen!"

"Well, there's only one way I'm gonna find out, Charlie. What's the worst that can happen?" Jasper sucks at the bottle.

"What do you *mean*? I don't know: a *bullet*?"

"Maybe. But I got to get to him somehow, right? I got to talk to him."

"But it could all just be a coincidence, him suddenly being absent. There's a big chance he's got nothing to do with this at all."

Jasper nods.

"Could be. You're right. But I don't reckon. I got a feeling, Charlie. It's hard to explain. There's *somethin* that links him into this. I just

145

know it. And I got to talk to him. Think about it: for *years* he's bin coming out that door, callin out *my* name. And I got to find out *why*. He's seen Laura too. Seen me with her. And now, starting from that night, I haven't seen him once. That in itself is worth investigatin, let alone what we already know about Mad Jack Lionel. That he's killed before."

Jasper sniffs and blows smoke out the side of his mouth. I fiddle with the buckle on my sandals.

"What do we even know about that, though?" I ask.

"We know the fact of it."

"*Do* we, though? Who did he kill? And how? I mean, I don't know, was he even convicted?"

"As good as."

"What does *that* mean?"

"It means that from what I've heard from my old man, he was lucky to escape the gallows. He only ever talked about him just the once. But I never seen him so worked up about somethin without being half drunk. He went wild. Says he should have bin locked up for what he done. Says he's a waste of a living soul, that hell's too good for him."

"Christ," I say. "I wonder what really happened."

"So do I, Charlie. And that's what I intend on findin out, among other things. I don't know. See, what I bin thinking is, there's every chance Laura might've bin walkin past Lionel's property on her *own* that night. She might have bin tryin to find her way here by herself. And he took his chance. That's what I reckon."

"Why would she try to do that?"

Jasper shifts uncomfortably. Takes a long drag at his fag.

"Well, see, thing is, usually she'd just wait for me to come and get her. I'd come to her window of a night, then we'd come here. Or she'd creep out and meet me under one of them peppermint trees in their street. But some nights she got tired of waitin. And she'd come to my house, come lookin for me. And lately, over the last few months, she bin wanting to see me *all* the time. She wanted to come here every other day. Like she really dint ever want to be at home, you know." Jasper crushes and pockets another expired cigarette. He scratches his neck and pulls at his nose. Fidgeting in a nervous way. I edge forward.

"But the truth is, Charlie, I hadn't seen Laura for a bit. As I say, I'd bin out on the orchards picking the early stone fruit, trying to get some dough up for when we left. Thing is, I never told her, I just went. I knew she wouldn't want me to leave her for so long, so I just went. It was stupid, but I just had to. Not only because I dint want to leave town with nuthin in my pockets, but I wanted to have some time for meself again. I was missing just bein here on my own. The way it always used to be. And with us sposed to be leavin soon and all, I dunno, I just wanted to be alone for a bit." He shrugs.

"That's okay," I say. "I understand. I get like that."

Jasper shakes his head and looks up. He breathes in deep.

"But the strange thing is, last Thursday night I came home, dog-tired, money in my pockets, and the first thing, I went out looking for Laura. I was worried about her, to tell you the truth. And I *wanted* to see her, I admit. I missed her. Thought about her the whole time I was away. So I went up to her window, like always, but she weren't there. But I saw her window was open, so I shut it and went back to my house to see if she might be waitin for me. But I couldn't find her. So I went lookin through town, down to the river, the same route we always took. Nuthin. And then, finally, I made it back here." 147

"And then you found her," I say. Jasper nods slowly.

"See, what I think might've happened is, she must've bin tryin to get here at the same time I was out looking for her. She probably got fed up waiting, and snuck out to try to make it out here on her own. That's where she would have walked past Lionel's place, see? That's what I reckon, Charlie. That's where it all went wrong, mate. I dunno. Maybe you're right. Maybe she really *did* know the way here, or she was bullheaded enough to try. Maybe Lionel follered her. Or maybe Lionel had follered us both here one night, maybe *he* knew the way."

I try to reason it through as Atticus Finch might. But it's hard when

Jasper seems so resigned to this scenario, as though he's accepted it as truth. I shake my head. It's too much for me. Jasper coughs and spits.

"And that's where I fucked it up, Charlie. I left it too long, I should never have gone away without tellin her first. I should've seen her sooner; I should've written, at least. See, it don't matter who done this"—and Jasper points up at the branch overhead. "Because it's *my* fault. It's my fault this happened."

"But, Jasper," I appeal, spreading my hands, "we don't *know* what happened. That's the thing."

"We know what happened, Charlie. We just don't know *how*. Or *why*."

"Either way." I shake my head. "There's no reason for you to feel guilty. That's absurd. It had nothing to do with you. It doesn't matter what we find out. It's not your fault. You didn't do this. Jasper, we don't know *anything*. We don't know if it was really Mad Jack Lionel. We don't even know if Laura left her bedroom by herself. It's just a story we're telling ourselves."

Jasper sighs.

"You're not listening, Charlie. If I'd have bin with her, like I *should*'ve bin, this would never have happened."

"Well, okay. But we don't know that either. And that's no way to look at things. That doesn't make it your fault. The fact is, you weren't to know. How could you? By that logic, every horrible world event would be your fault because you didn't stop it. I don't know. You should have warned Kennedy not to ride in a convertible."

Jasper shakes his head. "It's *different*. That's not my fault, because them people never relied on me, like a family would. So I dint let them down. And I let Laura down. I should have come back sooner, or left her a letter. I should have known she would come here lookin for me. And that's my fault, just like everythin that come after. I had a . . . a *duty*. To protect her. To help her."

"Protect her? From what?"

"Nuthin. Forget it." Jasper sniffs and sighs in a way that suggests he's unwilling to talk anymore. He slides out another cigarette and, with a knitted brow, lights it.

It's irksome. I get the sense he's withholding something from me. I'm always a step removed. Eliza, Jasper, my father. I can wade through the dark, but I can only see as far as the guttering candle allows me.

All I know is the end, the part where I walked in. But the rest of the story, all the parts before it, is still just a litter of torn leaflets. It seems so helpless and hopeless. I'm so small and weak in the wake of all this, in its sinister ripples. I wonder if we will ever find out for certain. I wonder how much I should really stake in Jasper and his assertions. Of course, it's an attractive notion: pinning it all on the town recluse with the shady history. But it seems so filled with coincidence and chance. It seems too convenient. Then again, maybe the simplest answer really *is* the most accurate. I wonder too if Jasper actually needs my help. Whether he came to my window looking for Atticus Finch or Tom Sawyer. A brain or an ally. Maybe both.

I don't know.

149

We stay silent for a time. I don't ask any more. I take on some more whiskey, though.

After a while, Jasper shuffles and looks up.

"You reckon they'll get a man on the moon?"

"They say they can do it."

"Seems impossible, don't it?"

"Sure does," I say. "We can't even get to the bottom of the ocean, let alone all the way up to the moon."

"I reckon they might, you know," says Jasper, with a small smile and a shake of his head. "I reckon they'll get there. Imagine it."

"It'd be something," I agree.

"You know, Charlie," says Jasper, scratching at his calf, "I don't get how people can look up at the moon and still reckon they're the *center* of everythin. When I sit here sometimes and take it in, it makes me feel like I'm just the smallest piece of dust in the universe. Like I'm nuthin. It's a lonely feeling, but it sort of makes me happy too."

CRAIG SILVEY

"How do you mean, the center of everything?"

"Laura once told me that they reckon that over a hundred billion people have lived and died on the earth, in the whole history of it. A hundred *billion* have come and gone and had lives before we even got here. You can't even imagine it. But when you think about it, you realize you're stupid to think that you're the one who found this space here, that it's your bit of the earth. Unless you're the lucky bloke settin foot on the moon, I reckon people are fools to be claiming this or that for themselves, drawin lines and territory. Just like they're fools to be thinkin that some big bearded bastard gives two shits how much money they throw in a tin tray or if they eat fish of a Friday. It's all rubbish."

"You're talking about Catholics?"

"No, not just them, Charlie. But it's some of it, yeah."

I think about it. "Well, see, I think it's that most people don't like that lonely feeling. People don't like looking up and feeling small or lost. That's what I think prayer is all about. It doesn't matter which stories they believe in, they're all doing that same thing, kind of casting a line out to outer space, like there's something out there to connect to. It's like people make themselves part of something bigger that way, and maybe it makes them less afraid."

"Do you do it, then?" Jasper looks at me quizzically.

"Me? No. Course not. I'm a speck of dust like you."

"Does it make *you* sad?"

"Sometimes, I guess. I mean, it's bleak to think about."

"Like an empty feelin."

"Right. I guess it must be comforting to actually believe in God and Jesus and all that. It must fill in all that space so you don't have to worry about it anymore. But it's a bit like closing a door when there's a cold draft, isn't it? It's still cold out there, it's just that you don't notice anymore because you're warm."

"Exactly," Jasper agrees.

"But all that stuff has never worked for me anyway. I've listened to Gooseberry and read bits of the Bible and all. But there are too many holes and gaps and slippery bits that I can't get past, and I just keep thinking about them. I have too many questions along the way for any of it to stick to me. It just hasn't ever made any sense. Sometimes I wish it would, though, just so I don't have to feel so tiny."

"But that's not so bad, Charlie. Take it from me. I bin made to feel small all my life. I'm used to it. And all it's ever done is made me want to fill it up meself, you know? To do big things. That's the good thing about havin nuthin to lose. There's no use havin a cry about it. And if this is all you believe in, this time and place here, then you're not likely to waste it, are you?"

"Makes sense," I say.

Jasper nods slowly. He coughs and flicks ash into the dam and presses on.

"Somethink else I could never understand," he says, "is how people, ages ago, could look up at the moon and still reckon the world was flat. *Flat*, Charlie. See, that's what I mean by people thinkin they're the center of things. Everythin comes back to what they could *see*. Nobody ever thought they might be a small cog in a bigger engine, just one of those billion little balls spinning through space. Everyone was convinced it was orbiting round *them*, not the other way round. It's crazy. Like they were living in the middle of one of them snow domes. You know, the ones you're supposed to shake up."

I nod. "I know the ones, yeah."

"You see what I'm saying?" Jasper asks.

"Yeah. Yeah, I do. You know, in India they believed the world was a big flat board that was carried on the back of a turtle."

Jasper smiles. "Bullshit," he says.

"I'm serious. A turtle."

"Bollocks, Charlie, I don't believe you. That's the grog talkin. A giant space turtle? That's what you're tellin me."

We're both laughing.

"That's right. The earth is a big biscuit, and we're on the back of a turtle. Shooting for the moon."

"That's crazy." Jasper shakes his head.

"You're right, though. People just kind of used what they saw around them, and made it up from there. And you can't really blame them for trying to make sense of it. It's when you know better and still believe it, that's when there's a problem, I think. Have you ever heard of Easter Island?"

Jasper quaffs and coughs. Wet-lipped.

"Is that the one with the big stone heads?"

"Yeah, that's it."

"And they used all their trees to build them, and so they couldn't make canoes anymore. So then they died because they couldn't catch any fish."

"Yeah, that's pretty close. Anyway, they were the most isolated civilization in history. Completely marooned. Thousands of miles from anywhere else, water as far as the eye could see. So you can sorta see how *they* might have thought they were the center of the universe. All they knew about were fish and potatoes, and birds, who they worshipped most of all. And off the main headland of the island, there were a couple of smaller rocky outcrops where these birds would nest. And when this started, they saw it as their god's announcement of the birth of the new year. The eggs were gifts."

"Right."

"So what happened was, there was this race. All the chiefs from all the different clans on the island would choose their fittest bloke, and they all had to swim out to these rocky outcrops through shark-infested waters to try and steal the first egg of the laying season. Once he had an egg, he had to swim back, climb up a *thousand*-foot cliff with the egg strapped to his head, and present it to his chief, who was waiting in a stone hut. The chief who received the egg first then became the Bird Man."

"*Bird Man?*"

"Well, he was like their spiritual leader. Kind of like their god's ambassador or representative. Like the Pope of Easter Island. And for that year, his particular clan had total dominion over the island. Also, he had to seclude himself from everybody else. He painted his face red and black. He wasn't allowed to cut his hair or his fingernails. And he had to strap a dead bird to his back."

"A dead bird to his back?" Jasper raises his eyebrows.

"A dead bird to his back."

"Probably a good thing he was secluded, then."

"Good point."

"And best of luck wiping your arse with foot-long fingernails." Jasper smiles.

"I never thought of that. But I'm sure he had someone to do that for him."

"Now, there's an occupation, Charlie."

"Come on. That's an honor, not a job."

"You can wipe my arse with honor anytime you like, mate."

"Only if you tie a dead pelican round your neck for twelve months."

Jasper laughs out loud. It looks like his face hurts when it spreads. He touches the side of his mouth with his tongue.

153

"Deal," he says. "We have an accord, Charlie, my boy. I'd shake your hand, but I just found out where its bin!"

We laugh some more. We have some more whiskey, too, which is much closer to the bottom of the bottle than the top.

"Still, it's kind of fascinating, though, isn't it? When you think about those people trying to answer all those questions just using what's in front of them on a tiny bit of the world."

"Well, that's the thing, isn't it, Charlie? It's all just a big Easter Island. A giant snow dome. Whether it's Bird Men or sun gods or giant bloody space turtles or Jesus himself. But what I want to know is, why can't we think like that now about the earth? Now we've learned about other planets and stars and galaxies, now we know it's round and spinning and tied to the sun, now that the earth isn't all we know. Why are we stuck? And why does everything have to be for *us*? Why are *we* so special? There's no such thing as God, Charlie, at least not how they say. Just like there's no such thing as Zeus or Apollo or bloody unicorns. You're on your own. And that can make you feel either lonely or powerful. When you're born, you either luck out or you don't. It's a lottery. Tough shit, or good on yer. But from there, it's all up to you. There's nuthin up there that gives a shit if I took a pack of smokes or lifted a tin of beef. I'm left with meself, and I know what's right and what isn't. Nobody would ever give me a job in this town, so I had to make things work when I could. Soon as you can walk and talk, you start makin your own luck. And I don't need some spirit in the sky to help me do that. I can do it on me own. But, see, that's what I reckon God really is, Charlie. It's that part inside me that's stronger and harder than anything else. And I reckon prayer is just trustin in it, havin faith in it, just askin meself to be tough. And that's all you can do. I don't need a bunch of bullshit stories about towers and boats and floods or rules about sin. It's all just a complicated way to get to that place in you, and it's not *honest* either. I don't need to trick meself into thinkin anyone else is listenin, or even cares. Because it doesn't matter. *I* matter. And I know I'll be all right. Because I got a good heart, and fuck this town for makin me try to believe otherwise. It's what you come with and what you leave with. And that's all I got."

We pause for a while. I pick at the dry grass by my feet. We share some more whiskey. The bottle makes a wet plinking sound as we pass it back and forth. It doesn't taste quite so lousy now. And that heat seems to have cloaked my whole body, mostly the front of my brain. It almost feels as though the world *is* orbiting around me. There's a slow spin to the trees. A green mesh, a gray mash.

And I don't think, I just ask.

"You're half Aboriginal, aren't you? D'you know much about what they believe in?"

"Nah, not really, Charlie. I never really knew me mum, so I never learned about that stuff. And she weren't from this town, so I've never met any of her family."

"Do you remember anything about her at all?"

"Nah, mate. She died when I was still pretty young." Jasper clears his throat. He flares up another cigarette.

"What happened?" I ask, then say, "I'm sorry. I shouldn't be asking about all this."

"No, that's okay. You're all right, mate. Truth is, I don't know that much. It was a car accident. Real bad one, from what I can gather. Tryin to get my old man to talk about it is like tryin to get him to find a fuckin job."

"Maybe it makes him sad."

"No doubt, Charlie. But it's no excuse anymore. He's just wasting his life and his money. He's a joke. I'm ashamed of him, tell you the truth. You know, down at the footy club, they talk about him like he's royalty. Reckon he was a champion in his day. The best player goin around. They reckon he could've gone on with it, could've gone anywhere. And I look at them like they're pullin the piss. I can't even imagine it. He fucked it all up, Charlie. No heart. He just quit. Just like that. It got too hard. Then my mum got up the duff with yours truly, and that was the end of him. He never went back. He hasn't stepped foot in there for years now."

"That's a real shame," I say, but I'm slightly distracted. I give my head a brief shake. The world is blurring and stirring further still, and there's a tribal thrum in my head which is pounding ever louder. I'm in some trouble, I think. I absently look down and try to gather myself. But my vision keeps shifting in a weird fashion, and my belly is roiling. My mouth is pasty. I can't feel my arms.

Messily, I up and stumble, like I'm being led by invisible reins. And then it's like an exorcism. That horrible spirit leaps from my body in a wet, acrid shower. I stop staggering and rest my hands on my knees as that vile shit keeps wrenching my guts. It dribbles off my lips as I groan. And I learn that whiskey doesn't taste any better on its way out.

And then I'm just buckling and flexing with my mouth open. There's no Black Bush left to purge. I feel Jasper's hand on my back, warm and comforting.

"You right, Charlie?"

"No. I think I'm dying," I sputter.

"Close," says Jasper, "but not quite. Here, get this in you."

He holds out a jar of water. I shake my head.

"I can't. I can't drink any more," I say.

"You got to, mate. You'll feel better. C'mon, just a bit."

Against all my instincts, I grab at the jar and suck at it sloppily. I try to straighten up, to square my shoulders and man up, but I've been robbed of balance. I'm back on my haunches again. Trying to breathe deeply.

Then I realize that the water I've been given has likely been scooped from the dam, at the bottom of which Laura Wishart sits still, pale and soft. I can't help but think of her, swaying like an angel in the water, her hair slowly twisting. Silky and serpentine. Just as quickly, I imagine I've drunk odd flecks and flakes of her skin, bits of her body. I retch it up instantly, grunting like an animal.

156

My knees are weak, but Jasper steadies me. He leads me back to where we were sitting, helps me down, sits the jar beside me. I'm wheezing, my stomach is sore, but I'm not vomiting anymore. The spinning has eased. I'm not so dizzy. But I still feel like I've been beaten up from the inside. I feel weak and embarrassed.

I hug my knees to my chest. We knock around a little while longer, talking back and forth, though I do considerably more of the listening and grunting of assent. Jasper breaks sticks in his hands, and I concentrate on stopping the world turning like a money wheel. I slowly improve, but my tongue still feels like a dead mollusk and my belly feels like it's been wrung out like a sponge.

It's only when Jasper rises from where he's been sitting all night that I frown and tilt my head and I see it. There. Low. On the trunk of the tree. He's had his back to it all this time, completely concealing it. I hold my breath and question myself. Doubting my eyes. Making certain it's not some whiskey apparition. Or that I hadn't seen it there before tonight.

No. No, I would have noticed.

Which means, of course, someone has put it there. Recently. My chest tightens.

"Jasper?" I say, tentatively. And he emerges from inside the tree's hollow base on the other side.

"What?"

And I point and he looks and it is clear he has not seen it, it is clear it is not his doing; it's not born of *his* sense of guilt. He steps up to the tree trunk urgently. He kneels. Touches it. Runs his fingers over it lightly. I meet him over there, and we examine it carefully.

We don't speak, we just take it in. Right there, scratched into the tree. A single word.

*Sorry.*

\*\*\*

We barely speak as we trudge back. I imagine Jasper's mind is turning and churning like mine. I wonder what he's feeling.

I stumble along behind, my legs heavy and disobedient. My guts are still sickly and tender. I'm tired and queasy, but I'm still buzzing around that word.

*Sorry.*

Jasper was right. Someone *had* been there. Tonight, maybe. Someone had pushed through, someone had invaded that glade. Somebody else knows about his space.

Not only that, but someone has more or less confessed. *Sorry.* An admission of guilt, carved into that tree. Cut into its body, like a tattoo. A word with so much weight. A word that now can't be taken back.

I think about *how* it was written. What was its nature and purpose? To brave the searches, to risk being caught, means that it must have been etched with strong feeling. So was it remorseful? Regretful? Angry? And who was this apology for? Laura Wishart? Her family? Jasper Jones? God?

One thing is certain, they're here. Whoever has done this is still in Corrigan.

It also means they've been back there and found her missing.

157

Gone. Taken from where they left her, all traces removed. I wonder if they suspect the police of having found her. Or, if they know about Jasper Jones, whether they assume it was his doing. I wonder then if this means trouble for Jasper. And if this means trouble for Jasper, then it might mean trouble for me.

We approach Mad Jack Lionel's place. The lights are out and it is eerily quiet. Could it *really* be him that did all this? Has he just been out, carving his misgivings? Jasper pauses at the gate again, staring at the house, which slumps dim and deep into the property. I urge him to move on. It's still dark, but there can't be long left. We need to hurry.

When we reach the center of town, I'm surprised and worried by the amount of activity. Jasper must be too, because he turns to me as we duck and slip behind a building to dodge the lights of two oncoming vehicles:

"This is strange, Charlie. The patrol cars are back. And they haven't been out this late since the first night. Maybe they got a tip. Maybe they're out to make an arrest."

My chest is drumming as we press our backs flat against the wall.

"Are you sure? It might be a bunch of blokes driving home from the Sovereign. Maybe they just closed up," I whisper.

"I'm positive, mate. Lickered-up miners don't drive slow like that. And I've seen them cars before. It's a patrol, Charlie. For certain. We got to be careful, orright?"

I nod. We move out. Walking as quietly and alertly as we can, close to shrubs and buildings. We cut across properties and empty allotments, slipping behind covered areas. My legs are still leaden, but my mind is a little sharper, my vision a little clearer. There's a sour taste in my mouth. My sweat feels oily. I long to get home. I wish I'd never left.

The closest call comes at the intersection of Simpson and Bourke Streets, where the patrol car appears without us hearing it first. Seeing the lights, Jasper tackles me down hard and we roll into a drainage ditch at the roadside. I hold my breath as the sheet of white passes. We stay down. Jasper shifts and turns to me.

"I don't get it, Charlie. This is real strange. There's never bin cars out like this. Specially this late. And they don't usually come through here. I don't know what's goin on. But we should probly get back in a hurry, that's fersure."

"It's not far now. I'm only a few streets away," I say quickly, distressed.

I pause, on the cusp of saying more. I want to suggest we split up. I want to tell Jasper he should leave me here and get home as quickly as he can. I know it would be the best idea. But I can't bring myself to do it. Even though I know what it would mean if Jasper were caught out. But I can't do it. I can't. The thought of being out here on my own scares me rigid. And I hate myself for it. I feel like a grubby piece of shit. Selfish and spineless.

Jasper has no intention of separating. He smiles and winks at me.

"We'll be right."

Just as we move to rise, Jasper deftly shoves a palm onto my back and shoves me back down hard as another car whispers past. This time it heads up the lazy hill that stretches toward my street.

159

"Shit. That one was close," I say.

"C'mon, quick. We'll stick to this side," Jasper hisses. We run, crouching, soft as we can. Gravel and sticks crackle underfoot and sound loud as fireworks in the tense, hot air. Thankfully, no more cars threaten as we make our way to my street. We round the corner. It almost feels triumphant.

And then we see it. We both stop abruptly.

Jasper swears and slinks away immediately, and I press back toward him. He grabs my arm. Holds me firm. Keeps me where I am. They haven't seen us. Yet.

"Charlie, don't say nuthin. *Nuthin.* Unnerstand?"

I nod fast. Swallow heavily.

"But what do I do? What do I do?" I hiss, panicking. My eyes sting.

"You keep walking. You make somethin up. Just don't say *nuthin* about me. You'll be orright, Charlie. It's fine, mate. They won't suspect anythin. You haven't done nuthin wrong."

I breathe out. Look down the street. Then I turn back. Now there's no choice. He can't come with me any farther.

"You've got to go, Jasper. Quick! You've got to get out of here."

He's already shrinking away.

"Listen, I'll come round soon. Remember: don't say nuthin. G'luck, mate."

And he slips away.

I am shit scared. Poison dribbles into my chest and seizes it.

I am in real trouble.

I stare down the street at the scene that confronts me. The scene I've been dreading. There, illuminated by the glow of our dim peach veranda lights, are two police cars angled across our lawn. Another two cars sit across the road, their lights on too. And a cluster of people stand out the front. I recognize our neighbors. And An Lu, standing cautiously to the side, his hands behind his back. I don't know why, but seeing his quietly dignified figure suddenly embarrasses me. Then there's my mother. Someone has her by the shoulders, dipping their body in a comforting manner. My father stands with a group of men on our lawn. He is nodding and thumbing his chin.

I am a dead man walking. I pause. I can't escape this. My heart is fluttering. My brick is back and made of heavier stuff than ever. It's a jagged lump of pig iron. Cold. I want to run away. Sneak in from the back maybe, then come out the front and ask what all the fuss is about. But I can't. It's too late. I've got to get brave. I've got to stride up to them, I've got to take it like a man.

But I'm about to be skinned alive. I'm about to be beaten with blunt clubs. I am about to be disemboweled. I have never known trouble like this.

And just as I move forward, I am spotlit from behind. I jolt and freeze. I am caught, guilty, covered in white. Red-handed. Red-faced. This is it. This is the moment. And it's dreamlike, surreal, but nothing like I'd imagined. My ears pin back like a frightened animal. It's a patrol car. And before I can think to react, their horn peals, piercing the night. I see the heads of the folks on my lawn turn toward me at once. I hear the car door slam behind me. My first thought is to distantly hope that Jasper has made it out without being seen. Then I see my mother break her loose embrace and begin running messily my way. She's screaming my name in a way that cuts through me and makes my spine spark. She's sobbing. Her hair is ruffled and her clothes are tousled. Her breasts jounce about and her face crumples as she runs right up to where I stand. I don't even notice the man gripping my arms. But I notice her kneeling down and beating at my chest. Then clutching hard at my face.

"Charlie! We were so afraid! We were so *afraid*! Where have you *been*?" Her face is wet and glossy. Her makeup runs dark columns down her cheeks, a shadow of her tears. She holds my head in her hands and shakes it.

It's only now that I understand the real gravity of being missing. Of being gone. It's only now that I get a taste of what absence can invite. The angry, taut knot of not knowing.

*161*

For some reason, my mind pulls away and I think of the other side of town. I think of Eliza Wishart not knowing where her sister is, living with that button of panic in her chest. And to think that I have the means to take that away hurts me like nothing else ever has.

And I think of Laura. The heavy ghost. So horribly vivid in my mind. And I think of that single word of apology, of admission and regret, tattooed into that eucalypt where she no longer hangs. *Sorry*. I look at my mother's face and all I can think about is Laura and Jasper and their plans to leave this town, to start again in the city, to fill it up and live big together. And I just think it is such a *shame*. No one deserves to have their dreams end like that. Then I think of Mrs. Lu, and I think of Jeffrey leading her out of the hall just hours ago. And it's too much. Far too much. This whole horrible alloy of sadness. And everything spills out of me. Like a stutter at first, and then I'm at it like my mother. It all catches up. I crumble and I weep. At the worst of moments, when I'm headlit and center stage, when all of Corrigan is staring at me, I'm blubbing like a girl. And I can't stop. My mother cradles my head roughly. She smells like wine and perfume and something sour and sweaty I can't pinpoint. My shoulders are quaking. I'm glad Jasper's gone. If he were here to see this, I'd die.

The thought of him finally allows me to straighten my back a little. I sniff and get some control. I look over to our veranda, that soft light. I've got to be strong enough to hold out against their questions.

My mother grabs my hair and shakes me again, speaking forcefully through her teeth.

"You stupid, *stupid* boy! Everyone was so afraid. Everyone was so *afraid*, Charlie. Where did you go? Where have you been? What *happened?*"

By this time, my father and a fair portion of the neighborhood have surrounded us. I'm so embarrassed. By all of this. All of them talking around me and about me like I'm not even here. Like I'm a child who doesn't know any better. Their mild admonishments and bullshit concern suddenly just make me angry. It's like I'm surrounded by clucking parents. I want to kick at their shins and tell them to piss off and run back to my room. They don't know what I know. The lights behind me have attracted insects. I slap something away from my cheek. Some idiot kneels down and grabs me under the jaw and places his palm on the top of my head. It's Keith Tostling. He inspects my face, particularly my eyes. Like he's a bloody physician, which he's not. I don't know who he's fooling, or impressing—everybody knows he shears sheep for a living. I shake him off and take a step back, bumping into the man who had my shoulders. I accidentally stamp on his foot.

"Whoa, easy, sport."

Finally, my father presses through and puts a hand across my shoulder. He does that thing where he thumbs my cowlick. I've never loved him more than now.

The sarge leans toward my father and says they'd like to talk to me now. My father nods.

"Of course."

We walk into the house. He looks at me strangely. I can't quite place his expression. Confused and thoughtful, maybe. He doesn't say a word.

I look over at An Lu, who is returning to his home, his hands behind his back, his chin on his chest. I wonder what he's thinking. There's something about his posture that convinces me he's judging me poorly. I feel so ashamed. I feel like everyone in this town is disappointed in me.

And that's when I resolve it, with my father's hand on my back. When Jasper Jones goes, when he leaves town after this mess is over, I'll be going with him. I'll be leaving too. Leaving Corrigan behind. For good.

# 6

wasn't killed.

But I was tortured. I was thrown in the hole. They imprisoned me in my room up until this morning. It was supposed to be until after the New Year, but after a brief hearing I've been granted parole for good behavior.

It's the day after Boxing Day and the start of the Country Week Cricket Carnival. Jeffrey has been made twelfth man for the main team, but it's no sudden admission of his ability: they just need someone to run errands without complaint. In the same way, the seniors team always give a jersey to Neville Schank, a cricket tragic who has Down syndrome and performs menial tasks with pride and enthusiasm. Not unlike Neville, Jeffrey is the embodiment of excitement. He's been round twice this morning, his whites starched stiff, begging me to try to make it down to the oval. Both times I had to remind him I was grounded. But to my surprise, my parents have relented and they've let me out early. My purgatory has ended. I can stand in the sun. It's been a long couple of weeks.

That night, after we came inside, I was expecting to be thrashed to death. Instead, our living room was full of tense, cautious concern. The house smelled of lamb fat and cold gravy. I still felt sickly and drunk, but sober enough to act straight. The police stayed: two locals and one from the city who wore a gray suit and a hustler's hat. My mother perched on the edge of our couch. Turned out she'd arrived home and noticed my lamp was still on. After knocking on my door to no response, she'd burst in to find my room empty, my louvre plates stacked beneath my bedsheet. Then she panicked.

My father stood in the kitchen doorway and looked on as they asked me questions. They asked me if I'd been with Jasper Jones.

I was terrified, but something kicked in me. I discovered a gift for lies. I looked straight at them and offered up the best story I could muster. It was like I'd clicked opened my suitcase and started spinning a thread at my desk. Weaving between the factual and the fictional. It was factitious. And Jeffrey was right, it was all in the delivery. I had them. I'd reeled them in. They all nodded like it was truth, writing it down on a yellow pad.

I started talking about Eliza Wishart.

Blushing, I told them I was very fond of her. I told them that I hadn't been able to sleep that night. I was beset by thoughts of her, worried and alone. I told them I kept thinking of her lying awake too, wondering where her sister was, whether she was all right. I couldn't bear it any longer. I told them that all I wanted was to comfort her, because I knew she was upset. So I snuck out with the intent of going to her house, just to talk to her, just to see if she was okay. To my surprise, they nodded, taking it in. Growing confident, I furthered my lie by saying that I'd been to see her before, on the day I'd said I was at the library, but I'd been too embarrassed to admit it at the time. I figured my saying so might give credence to this lie should they investigate it, given that Eliza's mother had seen me with her that day.

I also told them that I had failed to make it out there tonight. As soon as I'd noticed the patrol vehicles, I stopped and hid from them in a nearby front yard. I didn't want to get into any trouble, so I slowly made my way back home the long way, hoping to slip back in without being caught. At no point had I thought the patrol cars had been for me. Which was true.

I was relieved to look up and see that everyone had swallowed the whole thing. Jasper Jones was in the clear. Laura Wishart was still lost. The city cop clapped his yellow pad shut. They nodded to themselves.

Then Sarge leaned in and spoke to me the same way he would talk to Neville Schank. Slow and officious and patronizing, which

I was more than happy to absorb, considering. He told me I was a very lucky boy. That Corrigan wasn't as safe as it used to be. I couldn't just wander about at night on my own. The streets were dangerous. He said that although my intent may have been admirable, it was still wrong and foolhardy to set out on my own. That I should have used the telephone, or visited during the day with my parents' permission. He winked and reminded me that *Romeo and Juliet* didn't have a happy ending. But if either one of them had exercised some common sense and clear thinking, they might have come out all right.

The sarge might be a philistine, and his advice might have been hackneyed and pointless, but there was something comforting in his expansive frame and his certain tone. And glancing across at my mother, who looked like a snake poised to strike, I almost wished he wouldn't leave.

Hoisting himself up, he smiled and ruffled my hair.

"He's a good kid," he told my parents, winking at me again, as though he were only ever here to give an appraisal of my character. Then he nodded once and collected his hat.

I remember thinking that if I hadn't seen the cuts and bruises on Jasper's face for myself, I wouldn't have thought for a second that this burly paternal copper was capable of locking up an innocent boy without charge and beating him. If Jasper Jones hadn't shown me the cigarette burns on his shoulders just hours before, if I hadn't touched their ugly pink pucker with my fingertips, I wouldn't have suspected this man to be the monster he was. My top lip wouldn't have curled up at the edge as he turned his back and showed himself out.

And he'd never imagine I was partly responsible for quietly dropping Laura Wishart's body to the bottom of a still pond. He would never narrow his eyes and suspect me of being a loyal friend and ally to Jasper Jones, the poor bastard who had been victim to such assumptions his whole life.

After they left, the room felt empty and hot. I sat with my head bowed. I tented my fingers and waited.

Then it began.

First, my mother rose and pointed and told me I was grounded until well into the New Year. I wasn't to be out of her sight for a second. This time, I didn't answer back. I didn't complain. Her voice was quietly charged.

It started civil, and then suddenly erupted. The strange thing was, I was virtually absent from the fight. My mother was furious, but not at me. She began screaming at my father, worse than ever. She gestured wildly, crying, throwing things. I sat stunned. She called him a poor parent, a useless husband. She accused him of not caring for either me or her, not for anyone other than himself. Said he locked himself in the baby's room night after night, and couldn't give a shit about how she or I felt. She said he was so distant and self-involved that his own son could walk out in the middle of the night and he didn't even know. She asked him what sort of *man* he thought he was. She asked him what he thought it was like for me to grow up with a father who had no love for his family. She held her arms toward me like I was an art exhibit and said it was little wonder I was so insolent and disobedient, that I was probably just vying for his attention.

I sat there, frowning. Part of her may well have apportioned my father some blame for not hearing me sneak out, but it really looked like it was just an opportunity for her to be vindictive, to get some shots away. I was shocked by the injustice, bewildered by the scene. I felt horribly guilty and so sorry for my dad, knowing that I had brought all this upon him. It was really all my fault. I wanted to intervene, to yell and tell her she was wrong, but a sly part of me was relieved that it wasn't *my* arse being gored.

My father looked nonplussed anyway. He just stood stolidly in the doorway, leaning on the doorframe. He volleyed nothing back and took it all in. He looked at her in that same faintly curious and disappointed way, the same expression he'd greeted me with outside.

Still, I wanted him to hook in. I wanted him to step up with a fierce piercing gaze. I wanted him to state his case. Firmly and fairly.

167

Tell her that she didn't know what she was talking about. I wanted him to take umbrage with her questioning of his heart and his loyalty. But he didn't. He absorbed it all. And she got away with saying all those awful things. And again I was left to wonder whether he would ever stand up for what he believed to be right.

Toward the end, she was hysterical, my mother. Out of control. She began blaming Corrigan for everything. It was harming her family. It wasn't safe anymore. She said we needed to get out, start somewhere else. Then it clicked for me. I knew what she was doing.

And maybe my father did too. Finally, he pushed off the doorway and stood straight. He was so calm.

"Ruth, there are things in this world that you don't think I know, but I do. For now, I think it's time you went to bed. You too, Charlie."

"Don't start telling him what to do now! Me either!"

My father just sighed and closed his eyes. He looked down at me.

"You shouldn't have heard all this, Charlie. However, you and I will talk later. I'm very angry at you."

"Oh, you'll talk later!" My mother swayed unsteadily on her feet. I wondered if she'd as much to drink as I had. "You'll talk behind my back and you'll blame all this on me! I *know* the things you tell him!"

Then she screamed in frustration. The final word. And she stormed into their bedroom and slammed the door shut.

"Go to bed," my father said simply.

I nodded and left. He just looked sad and tired. I sighed. Everything had gone to shit.

\*\*\*

It was a strange couple of weeks in purgatory. I scoured the papers looking for news about Laura, but the columns just got slimmer and shorter and then disappeared. Still, there were horrible things to catch my eye. I followed the Baniszewski case closely. I read about a hideous couple in England who were caught and charged with slaughtering children and burying them in the Yorkshire moors. They even took photographs of their crimes. I read about *how* this and *how* that, but still I could never find *why*. Why any of it had to happen, why these people did what they did. But the newspapers seemed to shrug back at me, content to assert that some people are just born depraved.

Just as every kid was being let outside again, I barely left the house, only to do chores in the backyard. I read a bunch of books, though. They couldn't bar me from visiting those worlds. My favorite was *One Flew over the Cuckoo's Nest*. I thought it was beautiful. I read it twice. I really liked McMurphy. He reminded me of Jasper Jones. It made me miss his company.

Of course, I missed Eliza the most. I often daydreamed of waiting for her outside the bookstore. A chance meeting, so I might see her and smell her, ask how she was doing, talk to her about books and art.

My father got a bunch of new novels when we went to the city over Christmas. I sifted through them, took a few back to my room. He didn't stop me. He didn't ask me about them afterward either. There was a new Truman Capote book in the pile. I tried to read it, but I couldn't. I just couldn't do it. Every time I opened it, I felt as though insects were crawling over my scalp and down my neck.

169

Mostly, I spent the time writing. Almost obsessively. Every day and every night. It's the thing that gave me company. Along with reading, it's what got me out of the house without them being able to stop me at the door.

Though it only seemed to work when I was doing it. A little like squeezing a sponge in a bucket of water. As soon as you released your grip, it filled right back up again.

Sometimes, once I'd sat my pen down, exhausted, I'd close my eyes and be in my softly lit Manhattan ballroom, Eliza's arm linked to mine, an outrageously large engagement ring adorning her gloved finger. We'd navigate our way across the floor, nodding at random well-wishers and the venerable handwaves of the press, with their importunate requests for exclusive photographs politely declined. We'd pause behind a group of suited men, overhearing their conversation. Eliza would smile bashfully because they'd be talking about my latest novel.

A broad-shouldered man with his back to me, lauding my work. I'd blush and attempt to move away, but the bearded man would wheel round with his eyebrows high. And it'd be Ernest Hemingway. We'd be the same height, we'd have the same-colored eyes, and he'd incline his head respectfully.

"Papa," I'd say, and smile. He'd clap his hands on my shoulders, run his thumb over my cowlick, and tell me how proud he was.

***

My new flip-flops are cutting into my toes, but I don't care. I'm too happy to have somewhere to wear them. And it feels good to have finally abandoned my pansy sandals. I've got my face out the window of our car like a dog, sucking in hot air and liberty. I've got my new plaid shirt on. I feel clean and fresh and new. Filled with the thrill of being outside.

I look to my right. My father drives with an arm out the window, humming. He and I never really discussed the night I was caught out, but his manner toward me has changed. I don't know. He's a little harder, maybe; a little distant, a little less forgiving. Something has shifted away. I wonder if he's still angry at me. But then I wonder if he's thinking I might have shifted away and he's letting me go without pulling me back. I wonder, then, if this is what it is to be treated as an adult.

He drops me off. A part of me wishes he'd wink and thumb my cowlick, but he doesn't. I peel away and give a short wave. The game has already started. Cars cluster round the oval like a necklace of unpolished gems. There must be over a hundred people watching.

I walk down the slow slope to the oval and suddenly stop. I can scarcely believe it. Is it? I squint. It is. It's Jeffrey. He's on the field. He's right on the boundary, but he's actually in play. He really is.

I move quickly. My knees jolt as I jog. I see the players break for the end of the over, and Jeffrey starts a straight line to the far end of the oval. They've got him running the whole length of the field. As he sets off, he sees me and flashes a grin. He waves me to the other side. He runs with his chin up and his back straight, clapping encouragement as he skips through the middle. He's bouncing up and down when I catch up to him. My heart is high.

"Chuck, you're *not* going to believe it!" He points at me with both hands, two dueling pistols.

Then he turns suddenly and walks in, stern and focused, as the ball is bowled. It slides through to the keeper. He turns back, animated once more.

"Here's one: who's got two thumbs and is *officially* playing in this game?"

"*What?*"

Jeffrey grins and thrusts his thumbs back towards his little chest and says:

"This guy!"

"No!"

"Yes! It's unbelievable, Chuck! I'm in!"

"In? How?"

"Jim Quincy! He's out!"

"What do you mean, *out*? Out how?"

"Out! Out-of-the-match out! We started warming up before, and then all of a sudden he went down like a bucket of shit! Turns out it's his appendix! They rushed him off to hospital, he has to have it out!"

"Out?"

"Out, Chuck!"

"So you're in the side? *Officially* officially?"

"Well, yair. They already handed in the team list, so they couldn't pick anybody else. So now I'm playing! People were *pissed*, Chuck. You should have seen it. All these parents crowding round the umpires and coaches, trying to get someone else in. But the umpires wouldn't have a bar of it. Huzzah for protocol! Bang! Jeffrey Lu on debut!"

He shadowboxes between deliveries. His excitement is infectious.

"I can't believe it. D'you reckon they'll let you bowl?"

"I don't know!" Jeffrey smiles. "They'd be practically retarded *not* to. They should have made me captain, Chuck. This field is the *essence* of stupidity. Look at it! It's an outrage. Look at this bloke. He's rubbish. He's all over it. He couldn't hit a cow's arse with a banjo."

"A who with a what?"

But it's the end of the over again, and Jeffrey skips off. I sit down on the boundary and watch him go. I'm anxious for him.

I survey the other side of the field, taking in the activity. It seems like an awful lot of people for a junior Country Week game. It's strange. Clusters and lines of people are in and around the pavilion. I can see members of the shire council milling around in suits, backs straight with self-importance and station. They look staunch and proud. There are trestle tables with food and drinks, and ladies behind them fussing and nattering. Beside them, a canvas sheet held straight between star pickets that boasts the town emblem and creed. The Australian flag hangs limply over the clubhouse.

I wonder what has brought all this on. I know that we're playing Blackburn, a neighboring shire, which makes it something of a grudge match. But even so, it seems a lot of bells and whistles for a relatively small event. I ask Jeffrey when he swaggers back.

"Yair, I don't know," he shrugs. "It's certainly queer, Charles. Like you."

"You're an idiot."

"*You're* an idiot."

Jeffrey walks in crouching, walks back relaxed.

"But it was really weird before the match," he begins. "One of the town councilors addressed all the players like he was bloody Winston Churchill or something, saying how great Corrigan is and how rich our history is, how proud our traditions are, all this bollocks. I didn't know what was going on. But people clapped at the end of it. Some women were getting a weep on, dabbing at their faces with hankies. It was mental."

"That *is* strange," I say.

"Humans, Chuck. There's no telling what they'll do next. Unless it's this batsman. Watch. Next ball, he's going over the top, I bet you. He's impatient, he's rubbish, and he's all bottom hand."

Sure enough, the next ball is whipped high over mid-wicket. One bounce and it is over the line.

"Told you," Jeffrey says with his hands behind his back. "Lucky shot. We'll get him soon, but. He's going to sky one. You wait. I'm the finest mind in the game, Chuck. I'm practically a clairvoyant."

"Really? Do you know what I'm thinking right now?"

"Hmm. Let me see. Yes. Yes, I think I do. You're marveling at my sensational cricketing brain, and not only am I completely *gorgeous* to look at, I have unparalleled talents in all facets of the game."

"Yeah. Wow. Actually, that's pretty close to the exact *opposite* to what I am thinking."

"So you're thinking about yourself, then?"

I have no riposte. The little bastard has got me. He laughs.

Another few overs pass. It's largely uneventful. Jeffrey has dubbed the increasingly frustrated batsman the Spider Monkey, because he can't stop swinging. He's starting to flay wildly, looking to blast the ball over the infield, but he's getting bogged down.

"He's not long now, Chuck," Jeffrey says.

And he's right. The very next ball, the crowd gasps. Just as Jeffrey predicted, another wild swipe across the line produces a top edge. It skies high. Jeffrey makes a break for a ball just as I realize it's his chance. He could get there. Jeffrey has pace. He barrels toward it, his little legs like pistons. Everyone is watching. The world has stopped for this moment. This would be the greatest catch of all time. My heart is in my mouth. I don't know if he can make it. The ball arcs and descends. My head snaps up, then down. It's going to be inside the boundary. Jeffrey Lu leaps and lunges. Full length, he snatches at the ball. Has he got it? I jump up. I think, Yes! *No!* It skittles out of his hands as he lands. The ball trickles over the line. It's four runs. He had it. He *had* it! I can hear the disappointment of the crowd from here. Jeffrey doesn't sprawl for long. He scampers after it, throws it back with a glorious arc.

Warwick Trent is furious. He rips off his cap, pelts it at the ground, and kicks at it like the enormous petulant arsehole that he is.

"Fuck *me*, Cong!" he screams at Jeffrey, who trots back to where I stand, a grass stain under his knee. "You're fuckin *useless*. I tole you to get *fine*! Now *stay* there! Fuck*sake*!"

He barks and waves. As though Jeffrey is a disobedient sheepdog. Then he turns with his arms folded, shaking his head.

"Tough chance," I say carefully.

"Yair. Damn!" Jeffrey trots back, grimacing. He punches his palm. "I *had* it, Chuck. It just spilled out."

"It would have been some catch." I try to smile, but I'm so disappointed for him.

"I know. I was so close. I *had* it." Jeffrey holds his hand aloft, like it has betrayed him. "And this guy, Trent, he has to be clinically *retarded* if he thinks he told me to get fine. He told me the *opposite*, the big bloated fucking *ape*. It was *me* that moved fine, because I knew what would happen. If I had have been where *he* put me, I wouldn't have even got a hand on it." Jeffrey hangs his hands on his hips.

"I wouldn't just say clinically retarded," I muse. "I'm pretty sure he's officially brain-dead. Or fully lobotomized. You know how cockroaches can still live for a while without a head? I think he's got a similar sort of thing."

"Chickens too."

"Right. Chickens."

"Apparently there was a chicken in my ma's village that lived for a full year after they lopped its head off with an axe. Did I ever tell you that?"

"Bullshit," I say.

"Are you calling my ma a liar?"

"No. I'm calling *you* a liar. You can't be trusted. How is she, anyway?" I ask after a pause.

"Yeah, you know, she's doing okay. You should have seen the blister on her neck when it burst. Disgusting, Chuck. It was all pink and wet. But she's all right now. My dad is having a bit of a rough time at the moment, though. He's all quiet and weird. More than usual."

"Really? Because of the war and everything?"

"No, it's not that. I think there are some people got laid off at the mine before Christmas, and even though that's got absolutely nothing to do with him, people are harassing my dad about it all the time, because he's only allowed here through some sponsorship with the mine, blah blah blah. Like he's a Bond villain and it's all somehow part of his plan for world domination."

I'm on the cusp of replying when a full-length ball sneaks under the bat of the Spider Monkey, skittling his wicket. The crowd cheers, and Jeffrey pounces in to celebrate. I sit down as drinks are brought onto the ground. I observe Jeffrey standing apart from the group, sucking at a plastic cup as the rest of the team forms a circle that excludes him.

We don't get to talk about An Lu again. For the rest of the innings we babble and ramble and ruminate like always. Jeffrey asks me if I would rather wear a hat made of spiders or have penises for fingers. After a lengthy preamble which identifies the spiders as both poisonous and alive, I choose the penis-fingers. Then I wonder aloud how the earwig got its name. Jeffrey proposes that maybe it burrows into your brain through your ear canal and takes over your conscious being.

"Is that what happened to you?" I ask him.

Jeffrey declines comment on account of it being the end of the over. When he comes back, he clicks his fingers and points.

"Got one for you, Chuck. Now. Think about this carefully. Did the dung beetle invent the wheel?"

"Interesting proposition," I admit. "Although technically a ball of dung is a sphere, and a sphere is not a wheel."

"So the question really is whether a sphere is a wheel," Jeffrey says with his finger on his cheek.

"No, the question is, who came first: the beetle or the Cheeses?"

Jeffrey laughs.

"You're saying Cheeses Christ invented the wheel?"

"Only the big wheel you're standing on right now. A wheel we call earth. He also gave birth to the cheese wheel. Not literally, of course, but it's a symbol of respect. Take a cheese wheel to the Vatican and see if they don't bow and drool in reverence. But it has to be Swiss cheese."

"Why?"

"Because it's holey."

"Oh, fuck *off!*" Jeffrey groans, then scoots away for the end of another over.

The heat drills down as the innings plays itself out. Blackburn begin to score well with the old ball, turning over the strike effortlessly, punctuating their control with occasional lofted boundaries. It's obvious that Corrigan should bowl-spin to try to choke them up, but no matter how often Jeffrey warms up his arms to suggest he's ready and willing, Warwick Trent doesn't relent. In fact, with six overs to go, the repellent turd brings himself on to bowl, and almost every delivery is hit to the ropes. I shake my head, angry and disappointed. This was Jeffrey's chance. He could have made his mark. He slipped into the team through a fluke and they're not even going to use him. He may as well have been carrying the drinks.

And so, at the close of the first innings, Corrigan are chasing a hefty target. I can feel my skin baking brown. The players start shuffling toward the pavilion, knowing they've got work to do.

"Let me know where you're batting," I say, even though I know exactly where he'll be listed.

"Will do," says Jeffrey, about to jog away. Then he looks over my shoulder and grins. "Let me know where *you're* batting."

"What does that even *mean?*" I say, and then I follow his gaze.

Eliza Wishart is sitting at the top of the hill behind me, under the shade of a Moreton Bay fig tree. She offers a small smile and a wave, which I return. Shit. I hope she hasn't heard any of our rubbish. I suddenly feel as though I weigh twice as much as Warwick Trent. I whip back around to face Jeffrey. He grins.

"Sassytime, Chuck!" He laughs and runs off, his legs like stilts.

"G'luck," I mumble after him, then turn slowly.

I try to compose myself. I look down. I'm not sure if my legs will get me up the hill. I'm unprepared. I'm panicking. I need to think of a witty gambit.

In the end, I'm propelled forward after I see a bee behind me. I take the steep steps toward Eliza, wiping the sweat from my brow. It feels like my entire body has sunk down to fill my feet, leaving my head completely vacant.

"Hello, Charlie!" she says. I've thought so often of her voice these past couple of weeks that I'm a little stunned to hear it. It makes my spine chime like a tuning fork.

"Hello," I say. I'm standing awkwardly. Should I sit? I should probably sit. But where? Am I permitted? I'm not sure if my legs will bend, anyway.

"Come sit down," she says, and pats the grass right beside her and shuffles slightly.

"Sure."

The first thing I notice is how thin she is. She looks almost brittle now. Delicate. Her skin like a china doll's. Her hair is uncannily close to Audrey Hepburn's. And she appears to be speaking differently. A little cleaner and crisper with her consonants. Proper. It's almost a British inflection, but not quite.

I sit down. She smells incredible. Amazing. I don't know how anybody could smell like this. Every morning, she must soak in a bath of lavender and rose petals and other assorted girlspices, then spray herself liberally with a silver atomizer filled with the finest perfume ever prepared. Probably by somebody French. I don't know. Either way, it makes me queasy and nervous, and the sudden image of her soaking in a bath has me blushing and looking away.

Damn. I think of a witty opening line, a full minute after I needed it. I should have said, *May I have your autograph, Miss Hepburn?* And then sat down casually as she laughed. No, actually, that would have

177

been stupid. Don't say anything. That's Mark Twain's advice. It's better to shut up and appear stupid than open your mouth and remove all doubt.

So we sit in silence. Parts of the alphabet whirl and slat across my brain like sleet, refusing to form any kind of meaningful sentences. Eliza leans back on her hands. Relaxed and perfect. A paperback in her lap, fanning out from the shallow gully between her legs.

"What are you reading?"

She holds up her book.

I read the title out loud: *"Franny and Zooey."*

"I quite like it," she says, "though I'm not too far in. Have you read it?"

I wish I could say I have. I shake my head.

"New *York*, Charlie. Imagine it. Wouldn't it be a dream? Doesn't it just sound like the whole world has been packed into one city?"

"Well, we're going to be living there soon enough, aren't we? High tea at the Plaza Hotel and so on?"

She looks at me like I've just mumbled something in Ukrainian. I panic. Did I imagine that whole conversation? But then she remembers and laughs, and my heart resumes beating.

"Of course! How could I forget?"

"You almost stood me up," I say.

"That would have been tragic," she says, still smiling. "I would have remembered too late, and then I would have turned up breathless at the Plaza to find our table empty. The waiter would have told me that you had arrived and left already. So I would have followed you back to Brooklyn, searching everywhere, only to finally see you linking arms with some other young belle in a fur coat and a pillbox hat."

"Oh, no. That wouldn't happen," I mumble, then blush and look down. Where is my wit? I am witless. Has my head been infected by an earwig? It's never like this when I daydream this scene. I would have quickly quipped something about the importance of being punctual, about my eligible bachelorship and the slew of society girls waiting to make my acquaintance.

"Oh really? And why is that, Mr. Bucktin?"

"Because I would have waited. All day. Until they closed."

And now she blushes a little, because I've delivered the verbal equivalent of an awkward kiss.

We both look away, out across the oval, just as the game recommences. The Blackburn side run out as a single white cluster, looking confident and intimidating. Their opening bowler is enormous. He looks old enough to have fought in Gallipoli. And he looks angry about it too. He has to be the world's only prematurely balding teenager. Either that or he's swapped birth certificates with one of his children.

The innings starts badly for Corrigan, but brilliantly for me. Warwick Trent is bowled early without troubling the scorers. I almost celebrate his wicket loudly from the sidelines. I'm filled with a spiteful glee as he trudges off the field, slapping at his pads with his bat.

The scoring is slow. I look over to Jeffrey, who sits cross-legged a few meters away from the rest of the team, his kitbag closed behind him. It doesn't look like he'll be in anytime soon.

Eliza tells me she likes my shirt. She touches my rolled-up sleeve, which transmits a shiver up my spine.

"Thank you," I say. "I like your, you know, dress."

She laughs and thanks me back.

I ask softly:

"So how is your family? And how are *you* doing with everything?"

Eliza picks at the cover of her book. She shrugs and speaks with that accent.

"It's all about the same, I guess. But it's all a little less . . . I don't know, *urgent*. It's very strange. And sad. Nobody knows what to *do*. My mother is a mess. You know, Charlie, we still can't sit down and eat at the table without her noticing Laura's empty chair and just bursting into tears."

"That's awful," I say.

"Yeah. And yet my dad is completely different. First he just refused to admit she'd gone missing. Now it's as though he never had another daughter. He's blocked it all out. He's blocked everything out, really. Which must be easy when you're drunk all the time."

She says this last part very quietly. Maybe she doesn't wish to talk about it anymore. But she goes on.

"Christmas was the hardest, of course. All my cousins and aunties and uncles were being so careful and polite. But you could see that everybody was avoiding it. My mother had already bought presents for Laura before she went missing, and so she just wrapped them all up and gave them to me. Then she said that I will have to share them with Laura when she comes back."

And then Eliza starts to cry. I freeze. Her face slowly creases, there's a moment where she is struggling to control it, but then it's unstoppable. Another wicket falls. There is consternation everywhere. Chaos. My mouth is open. I have no idea what to do. Why did I have to ask about all this? Why did I have to invite all this sadness to the surface? I feel utterly responsible. It's hard for me to watch. Her face reddens. Her cheeks are enameled with tears. And I know I can't help noticing her dimples make her even more beautiful.

I want to go back in time, back to that night. I want to make this all right. I want someone to tell me what to do right now. Should I place my hand on her shoulder? Or should I pull her to me like I want to, hold her close?

I remember. I have a handkerchief, I think. I pat my pockets. Yes. I hope it's clean. Please be clean. It is. I am useful. I hand it to her.

"Thanks, Charlie," Eliza says, and gives a short smile. She wipes her eyes and blows her nose. Her mouth is still turned down. Her hands fall heavily to her lap.

"See, everyone is just waiting for Laura to ring or to write and say that everything is okay. Or they're expecting her to suddenly return home, but . . ." Eliza just shakes her head and shuts her eyes tight. Her lips turn down even further and she begins to sob quietly again.

I admit, I'm close myself. I feel the sting in my eyes.

It hurts me that I can't say the things that seem right, because to do so would be an unforgivable lie. I can't give her assurances or comfort, because I know that Laura Wishart is dead. I know exactly where she is. Because after she died I drowned her to save Jasper Jones. I did that. We bound a stone to her feet and watched her sink to the bottom of a still pond.

I suppose that if Eliza ever finds out what I've done, she will hate me for the rest of her days. And I don't blame her. But would she understand about Jasper Jones? If I told her that Laura loved him, that he loved her back, that they were planning to flee to the city together? That if we'd left Laura where we found her, she would have been discovered and Jasper wouldn't have stood a chance? That I'd tried to do the right thing?

"I'm sorry, Charlie," Eliza says, sniffing. She dabs at her face again.

"Please don't be," I respond, swallowing heavily.

She sighs and closes her eyes. I steal an opportunity to look at her closely. I want to tuck her hair behind her ears, wipe her cheek with the back of my hand. She looks so slight, so small.

"I know things, Charlie," she says after a time, and opens her eyes. "I know I'm not a good person. I don't even know why you talk to me."

I frown at her. Ready to defend her virtue. But she waves me away before I get the chance.

"Forget it," she says. "We're all doing okay, Charlie. Really. Don't worry. Let's talk about something else. Anything. Say something funny. Make me laugh."

Laughter? Now I have to induce laughter, after I've just brought her to tears? Of course, I panic.

My brain is a vast, barren, jokeless plain where wolves howl at the moon over rocky overhangs and the wind kicks up twists of sand and tumbleweed. And funny words huddle in clusters at the bottom of shallow burrows. Without thinking, I kneel and reach into the closest one and quickly pull something out. Without thinking, I am quoting Jeffrey Lu.

"Okay. Here's one. Would you rather wear a hat made of spiders, or have penises for fingers?"

As soon as I realize what I've said, I want to crawl out of my own body and thump myself to death. Mark Twain was right: I've just re-moved all doubt. I want to quickly stuff those words back down into their black little hole and rummage about for something, anything else. Idiot.

But to my surprise, she does laugh. She really does. She giggles and rocks back. Her nostrils flare and fall. When she settles, I'm curiously pleased to find her addressing the quandary.

"That's a good question. Hmm. Believe it or not, this is quite a hard one for me, Charlie. I'm absolutely terrified of insects."

"Really?" I ask, almost leaping at her.

"Oh, *terribly*. I am useless when confronted by them. In fact, most of the time there doesn't even need to be a confrontation. Sometimes I look for excuses to stay inside if I know there is a bee nearby. And I *hate* wasps. Even thinking about them makes me all queasy." She shudders.

"Really? You know, I'm exactly the . . . ," I start, then instantly nip it in the bud. A fear of insects is admissible for girls. Not so for me. I urge her for an answer.

"Am I allowed to ask questions?"

"Of course," I say.

"Okay. Well. Are the spiders still alive?"

"I'm afraid so. Yes."

"And are they . . ."

"Poisonous? Absolutely. They are practically oozing with poison. Neon-green poison. Like acid."

"Oh God. Charlie, that sounds like a *nightmare*!" Eliza strokes her chin comically, then holds up her hands. "Okay. I know you're going to think less of me, but I'm afraid my fingers are going to have to become penises."

"I'm sorry to hear that," I say with a grin.

"I *know*. I'm so ashamed. I'm going to miss my fingers. I *love* my fingers." She fans them out in front of her.

"It's okay. To be honest, it's what I ended up choosing."

"Really?" she laughs. "Well, I guess it's a little better for you. At least you're a boy."

"I'm still a boy with penises for fingers."

"It's true. You're a freak, Charlie. We're both freaks. We're outcasts. But at least we have each other for company. We'll have to move to the mountains together, live in seclusion for the rest of our lives."

"We could join the circus," I say.

She clicks her fingers and lights up.

"Charlie, that's perfect! Yes! We will join the circus. Right away. The next circus that comes to Corrigan, we're stowing away inside their carriages. We'll travel the world as carnival people. Carnies! Maybe I can grow a beard too. And you'll wear a cream shirt with navy-blue suspenders, and I'll wear a peach-colored pinafore and have a yellow ribbon in my hair. Oh, and sensible black boots."

"And maybe we can live in New York during the winter, and we'll just wear gloves or mittens to hide our hideous penis-fingers," I say with my eyebrows high.

183

"Perfect!" Eliza says, and laughs out loud. She has a sweet laugh. A high warble. I feel chuffed; I've been able to make her happier on request. She leans the top of her head against my shoulder. Volts of electricity pulse up my body. My stomach wrenches. I've never felt more pleasantly nauseous in all my life.

All the while, the score ticks along. The ball is a little older, and the field spreads out to accommodate the bigger shots. There is a tightening of the atmosphere, a palpable feeling that we're headed for a close finish. An even bigger crowd has developed in the late afternoon. A row of men spectate from the boundary with their arms folded, cans in hand, reaching out to point at field placements or to offer their expert comment on technique.

I can smell the woodfire starting for the post-match barbecue. Children roll their bodies down the steep hill by the clubhouse; others show off their Christmas presents. Jeffrey stays sitting where he's been all innings.

I pepper Eliza with more hypotheticals. I ask her if she'd rather wear the same underwear every day for the rest of her life or have to bite the head off a frog once a week. Astonishingly, she selects the frog. She says I wouldn't understand, because I'm a filthy boy. I ask if she'd prefer to have no arms or no legs. Cleverly, she chooses to have no arms so as to nullify her obligation to have penises for fingers. She seems happy with this, until I remind her that she no longer has hands with which to pick up the little frog she's agreed to decapitate with her teeth. I tell her it will be just like bobbing for apples, except there's only one apple, and it can jump. She asks if I would hold it for her so she could chomp it properly. I reply by saying that ordinarily I would, but in this case the rules forbid it. Eliza laughs and says she hates me.

Then disaster strikes the Corrigan team. We lose four wickets in two overs to a crafty spin bowler. I can barely believe it. The crowd is in shock. And I become intolerably nervous as Jeffrey Lu hurriedly buckles up his pads and briskly canters onto the field for his debut knock. This is his chance. He looks so tiny out there, marching to the crease. Jeffrey Lu, the last man in. Fortune or failure resting on his shoulders. I can barely watch.

The Corrigan side are carrying on as though the game is already lost. Most are sitting with their heads between their knees; some have walked away to the changerooms. The coach is on his haunches, packing up the team gear bag. He's not even watching.

I lean forward as Jeffrey squares his shoulders, asks for middle stump, marks his guard, and stands ready. My heart is pounding.

Blackburn's captain, thinking little of the diminutive player at the crease, has brought his fielders into attacking positions. There are four slips, a close gully, and two catchers close to the bat.

The Veteran runs in. Jeffrey looks poised.

He is bowled. First ball. His off stump cartwheels out of the ground and my heart breaks. Eliza brings her hand to her mouth and lets out a disappointed groan. Blackburn erupt. The Corrigan team begins shuffling onto the field to shake hands with their opposition. But then they stop. Everyone stares in the direction of the umpire, whose right arm is fully extended to the side, like he's reaching for a peach. It's a no ball! The Veteran has overstepped! Jeffrey stays in! In fact, he waddles over to where his off stump has rested, picks it up and resets it in the ground himself. The Corrigan side creeps back. The Blackburn team is furious. They resume their positions, riled and robbed. The game is still alive, by a thread.

Jeffrey's first ball in cricket has ratcheted up the tension. Players from both teams are now standing at attention. The Veteran steams in again. His next ball is short and sharp and it hits Jeffrey flush on the shoulder. I spring to my feet instinctively, full of indignation, but Jeffrey doesn't flinch or go down. He barely even looks hurt. I can hear the Corrigan team laughing from the boundary.

The Veteran wanders down the pitch, his finger a dagger, upbraiding Jeffrey loudly. He spits, just missing his bat, and turns. Jeffrey looks unconcerned.

The next ball is short and fast again, and this time Jeffrey rocks back and swats it smartly behind square with a loud crack. It's four runs. The crowd is stunned. There is no applause, just silence. I can barely believe it. But the next ball too is short of a length and wide enough for Jeffrey to glide through the slight gap in gully for another four runs. The Veteran is livid. Jeffrey is serene. He's out there to win this game. He really thinks he can do it.

Eliza clutches my arm.

"Jeffrey is amazing! I didn't know he was so good!"

"Oh, he can play," I say, feeling simultaneously proud and jealous.

Jeffrey plays the spinner with some caution. He's surrounded by close fielders; they form a tight ring around him. The first two balls he defends ably. The third ball drops short, or short enough for a certified midget like Jeffrey to get underneath it and pull it onto the on side. And the ball sails. He's hit it well. One bounce and it's over the line.

The Blackburn captain has his hands on his head, looking baffled and irritated. The next ball Jeffrey belts hard. The crack of it echoes around this little amphitheater, and all eyes watch as the ball fizzes through the infield. The sideline experts begin to nod and tilt their heads. The Corrigan side cluster around the coach. And Jeffrey Lu, for the first time in his life, might be garnering grudging respect.

At the end of the over, a runner skips out with a drink and a message. The game must be close. I see Jeffrey accept the cup and nod his head. I can scarcely believe it. Not only have they furnished Jeffrey Lu with a refreshing drink, but they're conveying information like he's a real teammate.

Jeffrey jogs back to the crease. He looks like he's been playing the game for twenty years.

The field is slightly less generous. Another small sign of respect. Even so, Jeffrey slots in a boundary with a cheeky glide past backward point, and manages to keep the strike.

I am not sure of the score, or how many balls there are left to play, which keeps my nerves at boiling point. But Jeffrey elicits no signs of panic or pressure. He's playing it smart and sure. He bats patiently, waiting for a half-chance to strike. And when it presents, he executes expertly. Toward the end of the next over, he neatly lofts a full ball straight, which scutters over the line. He plays the same stroke for the last ball, but doesn't hit it cleanly. Fortunately, they run three and Jeffrey holds strike again.

The bowler replacing the Veteran seems just as angry, but a little less consistent. Frustrated, he sprays the ball wide, trying to bowl too fast, and Jeffrey capitalizes.

The next over is the spinner's last, and Jeffrey lays in. He swash-buckles him, picking the gaps with amazing precision. It's risky batting, but it is paying off. I really can't believe this is happening. Eliza and I are smiling at each other, shaking our heads. My spine is tingling. It stuns me to think he is even out there. Jeffrey Lu has taken this game by the nuts. In this frightened town, Jeffrey Lu, its shortest, slightest occupant, is fearless.

It must be getting close. Even tired and bored children are drawn to the sidelines. Even wives who care little for the game sense that something significant is happening. It's the last ball of the over. The spinner stands at his mark, tossing the ball to himself while the Blackburn captain screams and marshals his fielders. Jeffrey, resting the bat on his shoulders, takes in the field, nodding at each one as he counts them.

Jeffrey drives well, but an acrobatic piece of fielding denies him a chance to take the strike for the next over. The crowd gasp and mill about. And I realize the next over must be the very last. I have no idea how many runs we need. I watch the coach, the ruddy self-important bastard, as he skirts the boundary with a cigarette between his fat fingers. I look back to Jeffrey, who is chatting mid-pitch with his teammate, pointing and gesturing. I can't sit still. Eliza grips my arm again, but this time I barely notice. All attention is fixed on the game.

There are six balls left.

The Blackburn captain makes his final arrangements. The bowler takes his mark. He pushes off. Eliza Wishart has taken my hand in hers. This isn't real. It is too much.

Jeffrey's plan is to run on the first ball of the over, regardless of where it is hit. He starts sprinting just before the ball is bowled; it goes on to hit the other tailender high on the leg. The Blackburn bowler, sensing Jeffrey's movement, steps to his right to stand in his path, almost skittling him over and slowing him down significantly. Jeffrey scampers and dives at the crease, but the underarm throw is miraculously wide of the stumps. Jeffrey is safe. Just.

The Corrigan crowd is livid with injustice. They holler and remonstrate from the boundary after the unfair bump. I smile. Not the for the first time this summer, the world has turned on its head. They're screaming on Jeffrey's behalf. They've got his back, they're on his side.

As it happens, the umpire issues a stern warning to the bowler, who shrugs him off and petulantly strides back to his mark. The crowd jeers at him.

The next ball Jeffrey punches through cover, zipping through for two runs. And it is with complete disbelief that I hear real encouragement from the sidelines. His teammates. In unison. Those belligerent bastards, yelling "*Shot*, Cong!" across the field, at once turning an insult into a nickname. Jeffrey's chest is heaving. For the first time, he turns his head toward the pavilion.

The next ball is flipped easily down wide of fine leg. Jeffrey has placed this well, and he flies through for another two. There are more applause, more visible tension and frustration from the Blackburn team. Jeffrey smears away his sweat with his wrist. The crowd are urging him on. It must be close now. They're pressing in from the sidelines. I am squeezing Eliza's hand unbearably tight.

The next ball is short and fast. Jeffrey gets inside it and swings hard, but he fails to connect under the steep bounce. The wicketkeeper takes the ball above his head. The crowd gasps. No score. The Blackburn side applaud and yell their support, walking in like a slow ambush of wolves. The captain runs to his bowler, gives him what appears to be a very clear instruction, then pats his arse and runs back to his place.

188    The next ball is an even higher bouncer, almost impossible for Jeffrey to lay any timber on. I wince and protest, as do the rest of the crowd. It doesn't seem fair. It should be called wide. Some folks begin booing. The Blackburn team clap and yell louder, sensing victory. It's another ball without score.

There is one ball remaining in the innings. I'm not sure how many runs we need, but the way the crowd are huddling and yelling and clapping suggests there is still a conceivable chance we can win. Jeffrey stands at the crease, surveying the field. The boundary is completely protected now, which suggests that a four will be enough to take the game. Warwick Trent stands motionless beside the coach, his arms folded. The rest of the side hollers advice and support. There's no malice or scorn. They're really barracking.

And for some reason, this makes it harder for me to spectate. There's so much more than the game riding on this next ball. I don't want to think of him failing. I don't want to think of these people being let down.

"I can't watch!" Eliza says, and claps her hand over her eyes.

"Come on, Jeffrey," I say through my teeth, willing him on, over and over.

It's happening.

Everything hushes as the bowler streaks in. All eyes are on his path, his heavy tread, his smooth tangle; then on the ball; then on Jeffrey Lu, for the most important split second of his life.

The ball, like the last two, is short and sharp and straight. Jeffrey must have known this. Must have anticipated the tactic. Because before the ball was delivered, I noticed him shuffle slightly, stepping back. Holding his bat high and ready. Giving himself room. And as the ball sharply rose, just above the level of his head, he was ready to play the shot he'd premeditated.

Not even a shot, really. Jeffrey doesn't swing at it. He simply lifts the bat, angles the blade so that the ball is deflected higher without losing much speed. He taps and glides the ball directly over the wicket-keeper's head, just inches away from his outstretched glove, and the ball holds its line, skipping across the only part of the oval left unprotected, piercing the two fielders behind the bat, who chase the ball with a sense of futility.

189

He's done it.

Corrigan erupts. Jeffrey Lu is a hero. Eliza and I jump up and down on the hill, screaming and holding each other. It's amazing. My spine sparks and arcs electric, my lips quiver. And Jeffrey Lu, after calmly watching the ball, turns and thrusts both arms into the air, hoisting his bat high. He grins like a madman. He has done the unthinkable. Blackburn slump in disbelief. The Corrigan side ruffle each other's hair and laugh and mess about. The other tailender walks up to Jeffrey, slaps his back, and wraps his arm roughly around him. Jeffrey is barely as tall as his waist, adding to the awkwardness of this display of congratulation.

What I'm feeling, I think, is joy. And it's been some time since I've felt that blinkered rush of happiness. This might be one of those rare events that lasts, one that'll be remembered and recalled as months and years wind and ravel. One of those sweet, significant moments that leaves a footprint in your mind. A photograph couldn't ever tell its story. It's something you have to live to understand. One of those freak collisions of fizzing meteors and looming celestial bodies and floating debris and one single beautiful red ball that bursts into your life and through your body like an enormous firework. Where things shift into focus for a moment, and everything makes sense. And it becomes one of those things inside you, a pearl among the sludge, one of those big exaggerated memories you can invoke at any moment to peel away a little layer of how you felt, like a lick of an ice cream. The flavor of grace. An inadvertent gift of myth from Jeffrey Lu. And as if to seal it in a chest of treasure, I see him seek me out as he walks off the oval as a match-winner, and he tilts and points his bat at me in triumph. My arm shoots up in a celebratory salute. I'm grinning like an idiot.

Jeffrey has his hand shaken and his hair ruffled by players and spectators. Even Warwick Trent gives a nod and a slap. I realize I'm still holding Eliza's hand. I shiver.

190

"That was amazing!" Eliza says. "I'm shaking!"

"I can't believe it," I say, still watching Jeffrey. "I just can't believe it."

The group disperses; the team heads toward the pavilion and into the changerooms. Somebody is carrying Jeffrey's kitbag for him. The Blackburn team sulk and shuffle, hands on hips. The oval slowly clears. The day is slowly winding toward twilight.

Eliza and I sit down. We're no longer holding hands, but I'm acutely aware of our shoulders touching. We sit silently for a time. I begin to feel awkward again.

But then Eliza leans forward slightly as the sun melts away.

"Can I tell you a secret?" she asks.

I try to read her face. Is it something about Laura? It has to be. Surely. What does she know? What pages of this story has she been pressing to her chest? What does she know about that night? I'm not sure I'm ready to hear it. Not today. Not right now.

"Okay," I say carefully, nodding once.

"Well." Eliza blushes and tugs at her hair. "It's stupid. But . . . I've been waiting outside the bookstore for the past two weeks, pretending to browse at paperbacks, but really I was just hoping I might see you pass by."

My stomach is a hive. My head whirs like a pinwheel. There's dust in my throat. Again, I don't know what to say. I never have the right words in me. I swallow heavily. Blink hard.

"Oh well. I got . . . I was grounded. I couldn't go anywhere. That's probably why . . ."

"I know," she says, "which is why it was so *stupid*, because I knew you'd been grounded and that you weren't going to suddenly appear, but I still kept going there."

"Wait, you *knew*? How did you know I'd been grounded?"

"Sarge told my mum all about it the day after, and then she told me. You know, about how you snuck out to come see me."

"Oh," I say, stunned.

We sit in a bubble of quiet. It's Eliza who bursts it.

"I think you're very sweet, Charlie. And I wish you'd made it to my house that night."

She smiles and shifts her body, turning toward me. I am afraid. And exhilarated.

"You have very nice dimples," I offer. "You know, on your cheeks there." And I point, sharply, at her jaw, as though she requires me to chart exactly where her dimples reside. I am an idiot. My wit, which flowed briefly, has ebbed. The tide has dried. My mouth is parched and unwieldy and useless.

But.

Then.

Mark Twain might well have had an opinion on everything. He might have been bestowed with the wit I don't have and blessed with phrases I can't summon. He might write with the air of knowledge earned; he might invoke laughter or sadness or anger with his herds of words. He might beguile and illuminate, frustrate and affect. He might gift you whole worlds to walk in, wide eyes to see through. But not even Mark Twain could describe just how soft a girl's lips are when they're pressed against your own.

Eliza Wishart has kissed me. Is kissing me. Right here, beneath this tree. And it is lovely and thrilling and terrifying. There is nothing else like it. Not even close. My skin is tight and itching, my neck hot and ticklish.

We pull away, and I feel both relieved and regretful to be doing so. She smiles, bashful. I guess I do the same.

"That was nice," she says.

"It was," I say.

We look at each other. Tremulous and uncertain. Her lips are red and wet. They look a little swollen. She smells incredible, I can't tell you. Neither could Mark Twain.

"Should we do it again?" she asks, biting her lip.

I hold a shrug, because I'm an idiot.

192

"I guess. I mean, well, yes. But only if you want. Which isn't to say I don't, of course, which I do."

She shuts me up. Thankfully. She tilts first, and I follow. And it's so much easier the second time, when you know it's coming. Our bodies don't move. Everything is concentrated on that soft part where we touch.

I feel a little embarrassed, of course. We're out in the open, and this feels very private.

We kiss like we're glued together. Like statues. And I worry that Eliza thinks I'm rubbish, that I'm not doing it properly. And so, when I'm slightly less stunned and more comfortable, I try to execute some maneuvers that I've taken note of previously on television and in books. I open my mouth slightly, and she does too, which leads me to believe it was a risk worth taking. It's weird and nice. A little more confident, I decide to place my hand on her cheek. Unfortunately, all manner of grass and sand has adhered itself to the sweat on my palm, which I duly plaster over her face.

"*Sassy*time!"

Abruptly, we pull apart. Jeffrey Lu is making his way up the slope, beaming.

"Enough of that! Save your love for me! I earned it!"

"Hello, Jeffrey!" says Eliza, unruffled. "Congratulations! You were amazing!"

"You're right," he says, nodding, with his hands on his hips. "I *was* amazing. Eh, Chuck? You, er, saw me out there? Uh? You may have noticed my match-winning performance? Probably saw me score forty-three runs on debut with consummate ease, like a young Douglas Walters? Just smashing a four to win on the last ball of the game? You watched all that, did you?"

"No, I missed it actually. I turned away after your off stump flew out of the ground on your first ball."

Jeffrey laughs.

"He's lying!" Eliza says. "He watched every ball like a hawk."

"I'm not surprised," Jeffrey replies, and sniffs. "He's got taste. He appreciates fine stroke play. When you see perfection right in front of you, you can't help but take notice."

I screw my face up in mock pain.

"Jeffrey, it actually physically hurts me to say this, but that really was incredible. You were really good. I can't believe it. I didn't even think you would get a bat. And that last shot was just *crazy*."

"You mean the shot I played over the keeper's head to win the game on the last ball?"

I puff my cheeks out. "Yes, dickhead."

"I humbly accept your devotion, Charles. You know, I envy you, in a way."

"Why?"

"Well, because, as the hero in question, I didn't actually get to *see* the shot being played. It's my one regret. It must have looked sensational from up here."

"You're an idiot."

"Jeffrey Lu, on debut!" He smiles and starts shadowboxing, short little uppercut jabs that go nowhere. Eliza laughs. He looks ready to go back out there and do it all again.

"It's a fairy tale, Chuck! I'm practically a legend of the game. It'll probably be on the telly. Definitely in the paper."

"You should retire now," I say. "Go out with a legacy."

"Couldn't do it, Chuck. I mean, what about my fans?" He points at Eliza.

"I'm sure the both of you will be okay."

"Both? Chuck, you're an idiot. The whole *world* is in love with me at the moment. It's fact. I'm more famous than Bradman."

Eliza laughs and leans her head on my shoulder. I tense up. I wonder how she can be so carefree about it. I don't know. Perhaps she's really not as shy as I've always thought. Maybe she's changed this summer. Her clothes, her hair, her voice. Or maybe I never really knew her that well. She seems different, though. She's been bubblier and livelier and more vivacious than I can ever remember. And that accent, that curious aristocratic flourish. I've never noticed that.

Jeffrey, no doubt sensing my discomfort, makes a show of pointing, straight-armed, from Eliza to me, then back to Eliza.

"Ease up. That's a sin, that. What about Cheeses?"

"Doesn't apply to us," says Eliza, holding up her hand. "We don't count. We're banished anyway. Because we have penises for fingers."

Jeffrey rears back in shock.

"*No!* You chose the penises too?"

"Fraid so," Eliza says, smirking.

"But you're a *girl*! And you have *penises* now! Ten of them!"

"It's okay. Charlie doesn't mind."

"Of course he doesn't! He *loves* penises!"

"Jeffrey, I'm going to kill you," I announce, meaning it.

"Bloody hell. Pansies! Both of you! It's just a hat!"

"It's not just a hat!" Eliza protests. "It's a *spider* hat!"

"The prosecution rests, Wisharrrrrt. Anyway. Chuck. Come on.

You can fiddle with each other later. Howsabout giving a hero a lift home?"

"Well, okay. But my dad isn't here yet."

"You're an idiot," says Jeffrey, turning and pointing. "He's just over there in your car. Look. He's been there for ages."

I follow Jeffrey's arm. There he is. On the other side of the oval. I had no idea. A cold fish slinks and bucks in my gut. I shift my weight away from Eliza. What has he seen? Am I in trouble? Is this an offense? I don't even know.

"How long has he been there?"

Jeffrey shrugs. "How would *I* know? I'm not God. Though it's an easy mistake to make. But I've been a little busy staging incredible comebacks and rewriting history books."

"He's waiting. We better go."

Eliza squeezes my arm, clutching it secretly from behind. I wonder if this means she doesn't want me to leave. I turn to her.

"Do you want a ride home?"

195

"No, no. It's okay," she says. I want to kiss her again.

The awkwardness resumes. It's hard to know what to do. I feel as though I should say something profound, or enact some rite, or trade something to make it official. I want to transfer some trinket which would allow me to say that she's my girl, some kind of currency that proves to people that she likes me back. Something that would permit me to think about her all the time without feeling guilty or helpless or hopelessly far away. I guess I'm just so excited, I want to cage this thing like a tiny red bird so it can't fly away, so it stays the same, so it's still there the next time. For keeps, like a coin in your pocket. Like a peach pit from Mad Jack Lionel's tree. Like scribbled words in a locked suitcase. A bright balloon to tie to your bedpost. And you want to hug it close, hold it, but not so tight it bursts.

I wish Jeffrey would piss off. But he's lingering, grinning, waiting to leave. I shift around slightly.

"Okay. Well."

"I'll see you, Charlie."

"Soon. I mean, I hope. Yes."

Eliza moves in to kiss me on the cheek. Of course, I misread this entirely and aim for her lips, and I manage to peck her in the eye with my nose. I murmur something, then get to my feet.

"Bye, Jeffrey! Well done!" she says and waves. She opens her book with her thumb. I feel sad to be leaving.

Jeffrey bids her a Jew and we shift off. I catch Eliza's eye and hold it just for a moment as we leave, and it seems as good as any traded trinket, as firm as any gem in my hand.

I turn. As soon as we're out of earshot and walking across the oval, Jeffrey executes some kind of strange cakewalk dance, his kitbag banging against his back.

"*Sassy*time! Sassytime!"

"Jeffrey, I *will* kill you. With my hands. I'm not lying. You're perilously close to a tragic end to your perfect day."

He laughs.

"You *love* her! Chucktin Bucktin! You loooove her! Wait. Who am I? Who am I?" Jeffrey raises one eyebrow and pushes his lips out like a crooner. "Do you, er, want a ride home?"

"You're an idiot."

"*You're* an idiot! I *saw* you! *Kissing!* With your *mouth!* Disgusting!" I have to smile.

"You're just jealous."

"*Jealous?* Chuck, you're approximately *twelve* times stupider than you look. I'm the town hero! I've just created history! Jealous? *Pffft!* No, say I. Why would I be? Superman doesn't lay around smooching Lois, he's got shit to do! Just like me: I've got games to save!"

"I'm sure if Superman had the choice, he'd take some sassytime with Lois over a child trapped in a burning building." I grin to myself.

"Chuck!" Jeffrey groans with outrage. "Cheeses *Christ!* You're not functioning as a human. I don't even know where to start. I'm offended. You've *actually* offended me. You could hand me a turd in a jar and it would be less offensive than what you just said. It's technically blasphemous. Cheeses hates you, Charles. I want you to know that."

"It's true, though."

"Sorry? Come again? You really *are* a communist? Comrade, you've had your brain sucked out through your lips. You're not thinking straight. The Man of *Tomorrow* doesn't care about *girls*. It's fact. Unless they're in mortal danger. And even then they're just a pointless decoy while Luthor prepares to take over the Free World. And that's barely even a distraction for Superman. He *always* chooses to save the world before Lois. And that's the way it should be. Personally, I wouldn't even bother going back for her."

"But you're a maniac."

"True. But I'm a pragmatic maniac. Listen, Charles, and you might just learn something. Lois Lane is more trouble than she's worth. How many times has she imperiled the world just by needing to be saved? Take one for the team, I say. Let her go. Call Luthor's bluff. Actually, Superman should kill her himself. Give her a solid burst of heat vision. Bang. No more stupid moral dilemmas."

197

"You're insane. This is why you're not a superhero."

"Perhaps, Chuck," Jeffrey agrees. "But I'm still the People's Champion."

We laugh and bumble along. I take an opportunity to turn and steal a glance at Eliza. She's still there. The girl with a book under a tree. I feel the strangest, queasiest sensation. I'm full of energy. I want to run toward her and away from her at the same time.

Every instance in my life, I've felt like the exact opposite of Superman. Except this time, this moment right now. I don't care. I don't feel like a weak, insipid sissy. Because right now I know I would save the girl. I know that I would rather risk the planet than let harm befall Eliza Wishart. I would save her in a second. Because I can imagine her and me huddled safe together while the earth falls under evil designs, but I can't imagine the world without her in it.

I smirk to myself. I don't give a shit if I'm not Superman. I kissed Eliza Wishart.

\*\*\*

Jeffrey flings himself into the backseat, scooting into the middle. I sit in the front.

"Congratulations, Jeffrey," my dad says, watching him in the rearview.

"Did you see the game?" Jeffrey demands.

"No, sorry, mate." My dad dips his head with mock regret.

"Foolish!" Jeffrey announces. "You missed the event of your life! It was like David and Goliath, but this time, David was Asian and unbelievably good-looking. And there was no cheating. Turn on the radio, they're probably talking about me!"

We crackle out of the car park, kicking up blue-gray dust from behind. I take a last look at Eliza, still under the tree. I think I see her wave, so I turn and show my hand as discreetly as I can. I hear Jeffrey whisper "*Sassytime!*" from the backseat. I want to hurl him from the car. But then I spin my head toward my father.

198

"Wait. How did you know Jeffrey won the game if you didn't see it?"

"Chuck, it's practically impossible *not* to hear about it," says Jeffrey, leaning in.

"I am starting to get that feeling, yes," I say to him.

My dad laughs to himself.

"Actually, I caught up with Pete Wishart on his way home. He was very impressed with you, Jeffrey. He watched the second innings from the pavilion, though I don't know how much he saw. I don't think he moved too far from the bar. He had a few under his belt. But he was full of superlatives."

I am horrified.

"Wait, Eliza's *dad* was here? I mean, he watched? Jeffrey?"

"That's right," he says. "And it's okay, Charlie, he wasn't watching anything else."

Jeffrey starts giggling from behind me.

"The People's Champion can still be pushed out of a moving

vehicle, you know," I announce over my shoulder. But it just makes him laugh harder. I turn to my dad, and he winks and smiles at me in a way he hasn't for some time. And as the wind spills in cool through the windows of our battered Holden, buffeting my dad's comb-over ridiculously and tweaking my lips into a smile, I tell myself to relax a little. Calm down. Shrug. Because it's summer. Because my dad still loves me. Because Jeffrey Lu finally got one back on this town. And because Eliza Wishart leaned in and gave me what I always dreamed of.

*** 

I can't eat. I'm buzzing and roiling. I push my food around my plate listlessly and recount Jeffrey's heroic tale without the drama and tension it deserves. Either way, my mother's not listening.

"Less talking and more eating, please." She wags her finger at my cold sculpted mashed potato. I sigh. I really can't eat it. I look down at the bland, pasty goo. It's not food. It's that pallid gunk you repair walls with, or use to seal rusted pipes. And regrettably, I've run out of passably tasty items to blend with it.

*199*

I look to my dad, who returns my gaze levelly. He raises his eyebrows. I understand. I blast the stucco mound with an alloy of condiments and get it down as rapidly as I can without complaint. Once it's gone I know that he's right. It really *is* easier this way. I even compliment my mother on the meal. In a way, it feels like a victory.

Later, with my mug of sweetened Pablo in my room, I think about my dad. It's as though we're on equal footing again, like something has shifted back into place.

It seems to me that perhaps he knew I was lying that night. He's not an idiot. He must have smelled the liquor, he must have known I was drunk. He must have seen my dirty clothes, my red eyes. And he's seen me lie before. I remember the way he frowned down at me. I don't think he believed me for a second.

So when he saw me sitting with Eliza today, I think it might have confirmed some crucial part of my story, or enough of it to have him trust me again. Just enough to know my lie wasn't as flagrant as he might have thought. That I might not have told the whole truth, but enough of it was in there.

I wish Jasper Jones would come round tonight. I don't know why, but I want to tell him about Eliza. That I kissed her. That she kissed me.

*** 

He came to my window twice when I was detained. The first was a few days after it happened. He turned up late and full of apology. Whispering, I told him I'd been grounded and I couldn't come out. Jasper kept saying he was sorry, that it was all his fault. He said he should have brought us back sooner. I did my best to allay his misgivings, but I feel he left that night heavier than he'd arrived, harried by guilt.

I'd wanted to follow him out, to assure him I was embroiled in this by my own choice. I could have pulled out if I wanted, but I believed him. I wanted to help. Not that I was much good to him anyway.

I also wanted to tell him then that I'd resolved to leave with him, escape to the city once this was all over.

I'd thought a lot about it. Especially when I was most bitter about being kept inside. My determination ebbed and flowed, but I always held on to the idea. Of course, the notion of running away scared the shit out of me, but the thought of walking out on Corrigan side by side with Jasper Jones was galvanizing enough for me to believe I could actually do it.

The second time Jasper showed up, it was Christmas Eve. This time he was urgent, impatient. Almost the same as that very first night he tapped on my louvres. Breathing heavily, sweating as though he'd just run here. I flipped my window open and found him stepping from one foot to another.

"Charlie, I *know* it were him. I can prove it." His eyes bulged with feeling. He smelled of earth and cigarettes.

"Quiet!" I said to him, holding my finger to my lips. "The walls are real thin. My parents might hear. What's happened?"

"I got him, Charlie. I reckon I fuckin got him," Jasper hissed.

"Who? Jack Lionel?"

"That's right."

"How? What do you mean?"

Jasper told me how he'd snuck onto Lionel's property that dawn, knowing he'd be asleep. He'd come in from the back, ducking through Lionel's wire fence, and started snooping around. He went right past the peach tree and under the veranda, opening dusty cupboards and running his eyes over cluttered shelves, but there was nothing except empty paint tins and tools. I was astonished by his bravery. If it weren't Jasper Jones, I would never have believed it.

He had even peered through the windows of the house, but that didn't give much away either. The kitchen was as good as barren: a small kettle on the stove, a tin mug in the drying rack by the sink. A small table with vinyl chairs. Around the side, under the peach tree, another window revealed a neat brown living room. A single reclining chair. A small radio and television sat on a low table. I pressed Jasper for more details. There were photographs on the upright piano by the far wall, but he couldn't make them out. A landscape painting. A stack of newspapers. A fireplace. Every other window was hidden behind thin beige shades. It didn't sound like the home of a psychopath.

It was only when Jasper gave up and walked back the way he came, past the outhouse and the chicken coop and the overgrown vegetable garden, that he stumbled across it. A way past Lionel's rickety corrugated-iron woodshed, lying in the open among spikes of tall dry grass, was the burned, rusted husk of a car. Jasper had approached it without much interest. The front end of its shell was completely crunched in. Jasper walked around it, peered inside. Gossamer cobwebs hung from crevices, budded with dew. It smelled of dust and rat shit. What little was left of the interior foam had rotted through.

Jasper told me he was about to leave when he looked down and saw it. He said it made him freeze, made him sick to his guts. He thought he was dreaming. There. Right there. On the passenger-side door, etched deep into the rust.

A single word.

*Sorry.*

He had to touch it to make sure. He found it difficult to bend his knees in order to squat down to inspect it further. That word. That same word, this time spelled out in capitals. A good deal older than the one on the eucalypt. It was barely noticeable, but it was there.

"I had to sit down," Jasper told me. "And then I just got *angry*. It was all I could do not to run inside and grab him then and there. I knew it. I *knew* he done it. I just sat there and kept starin at that word. Readin it over and over."

Jasper paused to light a cigarette while my brain slowly churned around this information.

"Are you sure it looked the same as the tree? Was the writing the same?" I asked him.

"The word was the same," he stated, and exhaled.

"Blow away from the window," I hissed, feeling like a pansy. "Or else they'll have me for smoking too and I'll be stuck in here until my bollocks rot."

"Shit. Sorry, mate." Jasper flapped at his silver breath and smirked.

In the short silence that followed, I tried to get my head around the story. It was certainly intriguing. Could it really be truth? Did it really implicate Lionel? Maybe Jasper was right all along. But to whom was *this* apology dedicated? If the etchings were old, as Jasper stated, it *had* to have been for somebody other than Laura. So who? I couldn't make sense of it. The whole thing seemed so cryptic and tenuous.

"I don't know, Jasper. It could all be a complete coincidence," I tried to reason.

"What? Charlie, listen, there's no such *thing* as coincidence. Think about it. Think about everythin we *know*. About Jack Lionel coming out shouting at me without fail, wavin and screamin. Because he's a crazy old *bastard*. About the fact that we know he's murdered before. And now, all this about him scratchin his guilt everywhere. Come *on*, Charlie. It was him. He killed her. It makes sense. It stands to reason. This is it. This is the thing that links him to it, to my spot, to Laura. We knew it from the start, and now we can prove it."

I frowned over these two apologies. One whispered, one shouted. One etched in wood, one scratched in tin. It was compelling, I had to admit. It *felt* like a true clue. And Jasper's certainty was so alluring. I was sorely tempted to agree with him, to grab my pitchfork and run, just to have this solved and settled.

But in order to be useful to Jasper, I had to be evenhanded and logical, like Atticus, like my dad. Critical. I had to fight it with questions. If it stood to reason, it could stand to me.

"But if Mad Jack Lionel is such a dangerous criminal," I whispered, "why haven't the police been round there? Why hasn't he been questioned or apprehended already? Seems to me if his reputation were true, he'd be the first person I'd go talk to if a young girl went missing. I mean, is there a chance he really isn't who we think?"

"First, Charlie, we orready know how smart the police are in this town. Other thing is, we don't know that they *haven't* bin to see Lionel. I don't have his house under constant surveillance. Who knows? Maybe they took him in. Maybe that's where he'd bin, why he hadn't bin out yelling at me while I waited all those nights."

"So you think they *have* talked to him?"

"I'm sayin they *might* have. But the real problem with the police is that they don't even know what they're investigatin. You see? All they know is that Laura is missing. That's all they got to go on. They still think she's just disappeared on her own. They still think she's run off to the city or whatever. You don't start lookin for a murderer until you're know someone's bin killed."

"True," I conceded. I sensed some impatience from Jasper, as though he'd argued this before.

"Anyway," he went on, "he caught me."

"*What?*"

Jasper nodded slowly and crushed his cigarette into the window-sill. "Yeah. See, after I sat there for a bit, I decided to go back for a closer look before I left. Now that I was sure it was him. But I got back within view of the house, and there he was, on the back steps, starin straight at me."

"*Christ*. What did he do?"

"Nuthin, really. I dint stick round long enough. I was angry but. I pointed at him and yelled out, 'I knew it! I knew it were you!' Then I just bolted back the way I come in."

I shook my head and swore.

"I know," Jasper said softly. "It's the closest I ever bin to him. He's not as old as I thought. I should've stayed, but I was so angry, I might've had a run at him."

"Did he yell out to you?"

"Nah, that's the thing. He dint say one word. He just stood there on his back steps."

I paused and looked down.

"So what does all this mean?"

204

"It means we *know* he did it, Charlie. We know for sure."

"But *do* we?" I scratched at my hair. "I mean, I don't know, Jasper. It's unusual, I admit. But we don't know *for sure*, do we? We need witnesses and all that sort of stuff in order to convince anyone else. Something that ties him there irrefutably."

"Well, that's what we get next," Jasper said simply.

"Yeah, but *how*?"

"We get him to confess."

And before I could blurt my next inquiry, there were three loud knocks at my door and my mother called my name sharply. I swatted the air with the back of my hand to urge Jasper away. He vanished. She burst in like she was conducting a raid.

"Go easy," I told her. "I was just trying to get this window open. The lever was stuck."

She surveyed my room like a bird of prey.

"Have you been smoking? I smell smoke. Is that why you're open-ing your window?" She leaned in, stern, looking for any justifiable cause to smite me to a bloody pulp. She'd been doing this for the past two weeks: coming in tense and terse and suspicious, as though I might be digging an escape tunnel or harboring communist spies. She was more aggressive with me than ever. She'd been everything I'd imagined a prison guard to be, but without the uniform or baton or occasional displays of humanity.

"What? Of course not," I answered, crumpling my face into a portrait of confusion and offense.

She humphed, narrowed her eyes, and exited.

I'd embarrassed her the night I was caught, that much I knew. I'd shattered the facade; I'd sullied the family name and her repute. Tongues were wagging. Aspersions were being cast like dandelion spores on hot, gossipy winds. The CWA brigade and the badminton babblers were tutting like vultures. I was no longer a model child and she was no longer a model mother. And a snide, petty part of me was thrilled about it, almost proud.

After she shut the door, I stared out the window. I waited all night for Jasper Jones, but he didn't come back.

It's been three nights since I saw Jasper Jones, and I'm brimming with questions and news.

So tonight, I try to write to make sense of it. I'm anxious and excited after spending the day with Eliza and seeing Jeffrey triumph. But all that is still tempered by the brick in my gut, the wasp nesting in my chest, the girl in the water.

For some reason, I begin by scrawling that word at the top of the page. I look at it. Sorry. *Sorry*. It's a word that haunts and hurts to read. It seems to pardon itself for being on the page. It's a word as clear as it is elusive.

I write around it. Weaving and scratching. I give it story and dialogue. I give it names and places. I give it breath and voice. My writing is fast and messy. I chew the insides of my mouth and barely notice when I taste blood.

And it becomes clear to me that it's a good word used by good people. Nobody is truly virtuous, nobody avoids the creeping curse. Every character in every story is buffeted between good and bad, between right and wrong. But it's good people who can tell the difference, who know when they've crossed the line. And it's a hard and humbling gesture, to take blame and admit fault. You've got to get brave to say it and mean it. *Sorry.*

*Sorry.*

*Sorry* means you feel the pulse of other people's pain as well as your own, and saying it means you take a share of it. And so it binds us together, makes us as trodden and sodden as one another. *Sorry* is a lot of things. It's a hole refilled. A debt repaid. *Sorry* is the wake of misdeed. It's the crippling ripple of consequence. *Sorry* is sadness, just as knowing is sadness. *Sorry* is sometimes self-pity. But *Sorry*, really, is not about you. It's theirs to take or leave.

*Sorry* means you leave yourself open, to embrace or to ridicule or to revenge. *Sorry* is a question that begs forgiveness, because the metronome of a good heart won't settle until things are set right and true. *Sorry* doesn't take things back, but it pushes things forward. It bridges the gap. *Sorry* is a sacrament. It's an offering. A gift.

Yes. *Sorry* is when good people feel bad. And the folks who trouble me are the ones who, through some break in their circuitry, through some hole in their heart, can't feel it, or say it, or scratch it into trees, or transmit it to the sky with their palms kissing. Eric Edgar Cooke never whispered it. Albert Fish never admitted it. The Boston Strangler never offered it up. Gertrude Baniszewski never burned it into the skin of Sylvia Likens. And that's why a part of me is reluctant to believe it was Laura's killer who was responsible for scarring that word into wood. *Sorry.* It *had* to be somebody else. I've read about murderers revisiting the scenes of their crimes, but never out of contrition. Never to make good with a ghost. If you're capable of that kind of evil, can you be capable of an equal share of remorse?

But who else could it have been? Who else knew? Who else could have cause to apologize? Maybe I'm being wilfully obtuse. I'm probably wrong. About everything. And maybe Jasper's right. Maybe *Sorry* isn't as simple as I think it is. Or as honorable or romantic or grand. Maybe it's just the refuge of the weak. Maybe it's just the calming balm of the bad and the ruthless. Maybe it's little or no reward for those in receipt. Maybe it's just an empty promise, the gift of a hollow box. Maybe it's self-serving and loveless. Maybe it takes what it needs and gives nothing back. Maybe it's as stupid and lousy and meaningless as all these yellow slices of hackneyed scrawl, cased up and locked away.

I think about Eliza, and my belly grips and fists and rolls over itself. I tear to a new page and huddle over it, desperate to trap her with words.

> *A tree*
> *doesn't know it's a tree.*
> *It doesn't know how pretty its flowers are,*
> *or how beautiful they smell,*
> *or how soft and sweet its fruit is.*
> *It can't feel how warm I am with my arms*
>     *around it.*
> *It can't hear me when I tell it these things.*
> *It doesn't know anything.*
> *I'm glad you're not a tree.*

207

I read it through and sigh and strip the page from the pad. I scrunch it into a ball the size of a walnut. But I don't throw it away. I place it in my top drawer, even though it's the worst poem ever contrived.

Stuff it. The world is beating me tonight. My brain is a big, sluggish pink mollusk. I toss my pen aside, frustrated. I rest my head on my crossed forearms and close my eyes. And I go to my Manhattan ballroom for solace.

I grip the lectern onstage, my gold trophy resting in front of me. The applause has stopped abruptly, and what remains is a slightly awkward, confused silence. Somebody coughs. I glance down and notice the engraving on the gilt edge of my prize. It's not mine. It never was. Two blue-suited men with shades sweep in from the wings and grab my arms. As they lead me away, I look out into the crowd and see Papa Hemingway shaking his head at a bemused Harper Lee, as if to suggest he too has no idea who I am and what I'm doing onstage. Norman Mailer is grinning smugly. People are tittering. Kerouac and Kesey are under a chandelier, giggling to themselves. Roaring now, these cruel fictioneers, all so smart and assured. I'm horribly embarrassed. I glance to my left and see Truman Capote holding a copy of my poem, cringing and rolling his eyes. And the blue suits lead me blessedly away from their cruel laughter, to someplace dark and quiet.

***

And then the noises pull me back to Corrigan.

I lift my head and frown. At first I notice banging, faint from here. And then shouting. I hear car doors slamming. Then a dog barking. I wonder what the ruckus is, who it belongs to.

208 When it persists, I am compelled to go find out. I slip quietly out of my room and into the living room. I peel back the curtain and survey the street. Something is happening outside Jeffrey's house. My brick sinks and I gasp. I see four men destroying An Lu's garden, headlit by their own truck. It doesn't seem real through this glass. They pull at his flowers, his small shrubs, uprooting everything, throwing the heavier stuff at the house. I'm afraid: more so when the veranda light comes on and An Lu steps outside. I can't hear him, but I know he's speaking to them. He has his palms out, like he's calmly asking for an explanation. Then he points at his garden. But they don't stop tearing it up until it's almost razed. He's walking down his steps slowly. He looks confused. I am shaking.

An Lu doesn't fall down when they hit him in the face. He buckles, but he still stands. He holds his arms out, but they grab him and pull him and keep hitting him. In the body and the face.

It's only when I see Jeffrey and Mrs. Lu at the open doorway that I surface and scream for my dad. My father bursts out of his study. He says nothing, he just follows my gaze. My mother comes out from the bedroom in a thin nightdress, frowning and asking what the matter is. My dad peers out our window.

Then he's out our front door, running at them. I am so scared, but I follow him out. I'm running too. The road is still warm under my bare feet. The night is hot and still. Mrs. Lu is screaming. She's holding Jeffrey back; he is slapping at her grip, but she's got him firm. An Lu is on the ground now. Huddled on their front lawn. And they keep going. They hit and spit on him. Swinging and kicking. I can hear them shouting: *Red rat! Fucking red rat!* My father is shouting too as he runs. Demanding that they stop. But they don't. I find myself shouting too, shrill. Other veranda lights come on. My father catches up. He's so tall. He's so goddamned tall. And I watch as he rips one of the men away and pushes hard at another. There's grunting and the smacking sounds of flesh. Someone takes a swing at my dad, but he's too swift for it. He rocks back like a boxer, lets it slide in front of him. And he's stepping between them and An Lu, who is crawling back toward the steps on his haunches. I can hear him wheezing. My dad has one of them by the collar, a stocky younger man a head shorter than him. He's got him at arm's length, pressing his shirt into his throat. My dad is gritting his teeth, telling him to leave off. Amid it all, I'm shocked to note that he is the stronger of the two. The men have a dog chained to back of their truck, white with a black patch around its eye. It's testing its tether, gnashing and barking.

209

One of the other men steps in to take my dad and I yell out, but behind me, Harry Rawlings from next door has leapt the asbestos fence that divides the two yards and wraps his arms around the assailant. Harry is a broad, copper-haired truck driver and four times regional log-chop champion, and when he wrestles the wiry body to the ground, it stays down.

"Stay there, you bastard!" Harry orders.

The two other men have pushed back toward the truck, but another neighbor from across the road, Roy Sparkman, who is dressed in khaki workshorts and nothing else, has slipped the keys from the ignition and now walks toward the scene. There's a strange silence that follows the cutting of the engine. The dog hushes and whimpers. I notice that almost the whole street has come alight, couples looking on from front steps, keeping their inquisitive kids indoors.

After a brief pause, the youngest of the four men breaks away and bolts down the street. I hear Maggie Sparkman screeching and upbraiding him from across the road as he runs: "It's not like we don't know who y'are, James Trent! You're a bloody *disgrace*! I know your *mother*! You should *all* be ashamed of yerselves!"

The stocky man in my father's clasp suddenly pulls away, ready to scrap, but he backs down when Harry Rawlings steps up and Roy Sparkman falls in behind. My father smooths his shirt and goes to An Lu, who is sitting on the step. Mrs. Lu, sensing it's safe to approach, releases Jeffrey and crouches over An.

Jeffrey, pent up and furious like I've never seen, takes a running dash at the wiry man on the ground, lining up a kick to his face. Mrs. Lu screams at him, holding out her arm. But Harry Rawlings moves fast and collects Jeffrey before he can fully swing his leg, lifting him up easily in a strong tackle. Jeffrey claws and flails to get free, like an angry cat, but Harry has him firm. He plants Jeffrey back on the veranda, holding his shoulders until he's calmed down.

"Charlie, get him inside, will you, please?" my father asks, looking up from his inspection of An Lu's face. I tentatively approach Jeffrey, but I know I'll never get him to move. I stand beside him, ready to hold him if he goes again. But Jeffrey Lu, who was the toast of this town just hours before, stands quietly. He breathes quickly and deeply and holds a level gaze over these men.

The oldest of them walks back from the truck, a little unsteady on his feet. He kicks a clump of jasmine that has adhered itself to his boot. I suspect he might be drunk.

"Give me my fuckin keys, Roy. This is none of your business."

"When you're in my street, it's my business."

"Strike me, you need a red star, you lot," he sneers.

"Fuck off," says Harry Rawlings. "It's not his fault you pissed away your job, you worthless bastard. It's got nuthin to do with him."

"Don't it, now? You big sack of shit. Listen to yerself. Jesus *Christ*, you're all sittin on your hands. He's *involved*. He's red. He's a *red! fucking! rat!*" He leans forward and spits those words at An Lu. "He's got a fuckin card. I know it. He probably killed that young girl. Go back to Hanoi, *rats*."

Harry takes two steps and delivers a swift backhander to his jaw. The dog pulls and barks in a frenzy. I freeze. The man, Mick, keeps his head turned. He spits blood.

"You want some more?" Harry steps up again.

"Leave it," warns Roy Sparkman, who tosses the keys back, hitting Mick in the chest. "Here. Piss off home. We can deal with this shit in the morning."

Mick snatches his keys from the grass. I'm not afraid anymore. The two other men have slunk back to the truck. Mick looks up at Harry Rawlings.

"You just watch yourself, son. You don't know a fuckin thing. None of youse do. You're everythin what's wrong with this country. Use your eyes! The rats are here and they're breedin, mark my words. They're fuckin breedin."

"Go *home!*" my father explodes. He stands up, tall and intimidating. He glares with real anger. And I can't help but feel a blush of pride, seeing it. I've been wrong about him.

The truck shudders to a start. The engine roars. And they tear up strips of lawn with their tires before they scream down the street. They leave a very strange silence behind them. Folks move back into their homes, ushering their kids to bed. My dad helps An Lu to his feet.

"I'm so sorry, An," he says.

An Lu shakes his head and waves him away, offering a thin smile. He climbs the stairs stiffly, his wife under his arm. She's crying. An looks shaken and hurt, but still quiet and dignified. Seeing him struggle cuts straight through me. My eyes sting and I have to look away. My dad follows as far as the door. He leans on the doorframe and says words to them that I can't hear, but they seem comforting. I feel like I should be doing the same for Jeffrey, but I don't know what to say. I open my mouth, but there's nothing. I don't have the right words in me.

Roy Sparkman is standing with Harry Rawlings on the lawn. He calls out to Jeffrey.

"Well batted today, kid. I didn't see it, but I heard all about it. They tell me you're the last ball hero, am I right? What'd you make, forty odd?" ·

Jeffrey nods absently.

"Forty-three," I say. I don't know why I feel the need to clarify it. Maybe I want to distract Jeffrey with his own success.

"Forty-three!" Roy exclaims and whistles, and he seeks and holds Jeffrey's eyes. "Well, you should be bloody proud of yourself. You keep your head up, orright? Y'hear me? You did a great thing today. And no one can take that off you. You understand?"

Jeffrey nods. He shuffles his feet. He stays quiet, his face giving nothing away. He reminds me of An. He's flipped a switch on himself.

I feel my father's hand on my shoulder. He doesn't speak, but I know it is time for us to go. He moves past me, onto the lawn.

Before we leave, I put my own hand on Jeffrey's shoulder, my thumb pressing on his collarbone, trying to transmit the reassuring things I want to say. He nods and tightens his lips. He moves inside.

The street has shut its doors. I tread heavily down the steps and meet my father, who is talking to Harry and Roy. He bids them good-night and absently lays his arm around my shoulder. It feels comfortable and protective and I don't mind at all. I really don't. And we walk all the way back to the house like that. Stunned. To be honest, I'm close to tears, and there's something about my proximity to my father that seems to urge them further. But I blink them away and suck in air.

At our front door, my father pauses and holds me to him. He moves away first and looks me in the eye.

"I'm sorry you had to see that, Charlie. You okay?"

"I don't know. No. Not really." I shrug and look away.

"Well, I'm not either, if that makes you feel any better. I feel lousy," he says.

We stand there for a time.

"Why did that just *happen*? Why would anyone do that to An?"

My father breathes in deeply, carefully crafting a response, but he's interrupted by my mother, who opens the door and calls us in.

We sit at our kitchen table. It's strange. None of us are tired. Neither do we know what to say.

After a time, my father gets up and fusses around our drawers and cupboards. He sits back down with a pack of cards, a bottle of port, and three small glasses. My mother frowns at the third glass, but she lets it pass.

I shuffle as he pours out three plum-colored measures. My mother gets a yellow pad and a pen. I hand the cards across and my dad deals. He hasn't answered my question, so I ask him again.

He sighs. "Mick Thompson is a coward and a fool. He's a man who's trapped in his own gutter. See, it's those sharks in the dark again, Charlie. For some folks, it's easier to condemn another man than have the strength to right your own wrongs. But he'll get his one day, because for every one of him, there are a dozen Harry Rawlingses ready to stand in his way."

I nod, my head bowed, though I still don't understand a thing. It doesn't seem to be enough to fit what I've just seen at all. But I don't want to press him further on it. My mother leans forward and touches my arm.

"Don't worry about An, Charlie. He'll be all right. He's strong as a bull, and so is Jeffrey." She takes a pull of her port. "God Almighty, it's been a *torrid* few weeks. I don't know what is happening to this town."

I look through my hand and wait for her to sound off about Everything That's Wrong with Corrigan, but she doesn't. She sifts through her cards and tuts.

213

"Once again, Wes, you've dealt me the worst hand imaginable."

"It matters not, dear. You'll still somehow engineer an impossible victory," he says.

"I think not, *dear*. You're not sitting where I am. These cards are about as useful as a chocolate teapot. I can't do a thing. You're not dealing anymore. You're banned."

And so we sit and play canasta until it's late. It's hot, and there's plenty of banter, and things are remarkably civil. Our kitchen fan whirrs and stirs above us. I take tentative sips at my port, feeling like I'm getting away with something.

Just as my father predicted, my mother still beats the pants off us. She's crafty and relentless at cards, especially canasta. My dad always lays his melds too early, and I never seem to get the right cards when I need them. But my mother is uncanny. She always hoards her hand, cursing her luck, giving nothing away until she suddenly presents her columns in one satisfied flurry, grinning.

214     My dad and I groan as she neatly lays down her last card. She reaches for the pen and the tally.

"Add em up, boys," she gloats.

"How does she keep doing this to us, Charlie?"

"Because I'm brilliant. And I have fine instincts."

"I think she cheats," my dad says to me, shielding his mouth with his hands and winking.

"If you sorry lot ever became a threat, maybe then I'd consider being underhanded. But I've got no need to bend the rules. It's like shooting fish in a barrel."

"You know," I say quietly, lifting my glass of port, "I never understood why you would ever feel the need to *shoot* the fish in the barrel. I mean, they're in a *barrel*, you've already caught them. The hard work's done, they can't escape. So if you want them dead, just drain the water out. Why bring guns into it?"

My dad laughs.

"See, Ruth, this is why the boy is going places. It's a fair point. And one worth remembering, should you ever encounter a man pointing a rifle over an open barrel of trout."

"Drain the water, save your bullets," I say, shrugging.

"It's an *expression*," says my mother. "You two aren't right in the head. Anyway, give me your scores."

We read out our numbers. I know that my dad just made his up, and I smile in collusion. When my mother writes, her tongue presses out the side of her mouth. It makes her look girlish. She whistles at the scores on the pad.

"You're on a train with no brakes, gentlemen."

"Come on, Charlie," says my dad. "We need to put a halt on this loose caboose. It's not over yet. The Good Luck Express over here has got to run out soon."

"Luck?" my mother exclaims. "It's skill. Don't be so obstreperous."

"Obstreperous?"

"Obstreperous."

We all smile. It's nice, I guess. It's obvious that we're all trying to make each other feel better. I wonder if they're playing canasta at Jeffrey's house. Probably not. I hope he's okay. I feel like knocking on his window like Jasper Jones.

My mother cocks her head, biting her lip.

"Gentlemen, I've got some *devastating* news." She starts laying down her cards in columns with a smirk. We both groan and lean back.

"Already? You're ruthless as a sack of snakes."

"Add em up," she says, reaching for the pad.

"I don't think there'll be any need." My dad tosses his cards onto the table. "This spells the end for us, Charlie. Time to surrender. We've been plundered. To bed with ye."

I get up. And as I do, there are sudden Gatling gun pops on our roof. We all flinch and look up. It's raining. Slow, then a heavy barrage. Fat silver sheets of it. I can see it through the kitchen window. It silences us for a time.

"Hell's bells," says my father. "It's really coming down."

My mother unlatches our windows to let the cool air in. The roar of the rain gets louder, and a sheet of white flashes.

Thunder erupts soon after, and it startles my mother. She clutches at the back of my father's chair.

"Christ *Almighty*," she says. "That's it! That's enough. I'm going to bed. Night, Charlie."

My father clears the table, and I stand and set my chair.

"You all right?" he asks, pausing.

I nod, but I'm not really. Not at all.

I don't know how my parents can distance themselves from what just happened out there so easily. How they can put a lid on their outrage and bang it shut. I keep thinking of An Lu being held steady by his wife, trying to stay level and dignified. And Jeffrey. For the first time in his life he looked defeated, and it was on the first day in his life he'd bloody *won*. I don't know. Maybe there's something wrong with me. There has to be. Because it feels as though there's something squeezing my heart and I can't breathe properly and I just want to lie down and think of how soft and warm Eliza Wishart felt today, but even that's displaced by her face when she cried, her wet dimples, the creases at her eyes. She told me she wasn't a good person, and I countered it with nothing. Because I'm an idiot. I didn't say any of those things I'd always meant to tell her, the hundreds of words I'd scribbled in preparation. I stayed quiet. I didn't stand up for her. Whereas my father tonight, he proved me wrong. *He* stood up for something. He really did. And I was so impressed, so awed to see him lean in with that kind of aggression. But not even that stays in me unchecked; there's a low dog with its teeth in my shirt, hassling and tugging and pulling me down with the insistent thought that it wasn't *enough*, that it would never ever be enough.

Because Jeffrey Lu was a hero today and when he got to the top they dragged him back to the bottom. They showered him with shit. They made him feel like rubbish when he should be kite-high.

Because those men struck his father, over and over, and they destroyed something beautiful. And nothing will ever happen to them.

Because a girl goes missing in this town and it's Jasper Jones who is held and threatened and belted for days, but somehow those monsters will arouse no suspicion.

Because now Jasper Jones has to leave Corrigan before it breaks him. And I have to go with him, knowing what I know, having done what I've done, feeling as I do.

Because Laura Wishart is dead. She was beaten and hanged. Maybe by Jack Lionel. Maybe by those men. And we took the rope from her neck and wrapped it around her ankles. We tied her to a stone and we threw her in the water and we sunk her.

And because Eliza Wishart will hate me if she ever finds out what I did to her sister after she died. She'll never clutch my arm or lean on my shoulder. I will have kissed her for the last time. But I still feel the need to tell her. To unburden us both. To assure her I tried to do the right thing. To etch that word.

Oh, I've got myself into trouble. I know they're coming for me. The blue suits, the dragonflies in the sky. It's the waiting that's the worst. I can feel something slowly closing in, a slow choke. An ambush. And I don't want to be alone with this.

It's pissing down now, blanketing our house. And heavy as I am, the snow dome won't settle. Perhaps it never will.

"Good night," I say.

217

# 7

ate in the morning on New Year's Eve, Jeffrey Lu is declaring his intention to master the One-Inch Punch.

"You have a one-inch what?"

"You're an idiot. The One-Inch Punch. It's *karate*. It's Bruce *Lee*. He introduced it to the greater martial arts community. Jeffrey Lu is going to make it famous."

We drag our wooden crate out onto the road. Jeffrey rests his bat over his shoulder and squints in the sun.

"See, Chuck, while you're mincing about saying clever things to girls, some of us are training themselves to a point of *immaculate* perfection for your protection. It must be nice for you to have a horse like me in your stable. You're a citizen. You can afford to rest on your laurels. Because you know that Jeffrey Lu is standing in the path of tyranny."

"Sir, your sacrifice means everything to me."

"It's hardly a sacrifice. I'd rather hone my superior skills to infallible sharpness than swan about smooching girls."

"Because you're queer?"

"*You're* queer," Jeffrey sighs. Sensing his impatience, I ask him to reveal the secrets of the One-Inch Punch. Jeffrey sighs again and lays his bat down.

"For the ignorant and uninitiated, the One-Inch Punch, *essentially*, is the fierce concentration of energy to a single place in the body that can be released in a moment of explosive power. Like this." Jeffrey steadies. He crouches, his fist out in front; then he spasms suddenly and pads me deftly on the shoulder.

"Jeffrey, that's the stupidest thing I've ever encountered."

"*You're* the stupidest thing I've ever encountered!"

"But how is that at all useful? Unless you're fighting someone in a phone booth, there's no benefit to doing that. Just wind up and swing like a normal person."

Jeffrey groans.

"*Charles*, you know *nothing* of the world. There's no use in me trying to illuminate the ways of the elite martial artist. Your inner pansy just scrambles a perfectly sensible message. It's like I'm talking a different language. *Obviously*, I didn't want to hit you that hard. My hand would have gone straight through you if I'd unleashed all my reserves. And I don't need a murder on my hands."

"Murder? Jeffrey, all due respect, but a strike like that wouldn't even cause noticeable discomfort to a newborn rabbit with some kind of brittle-bone disease."

Jeffrey shakes his head.

"See? This is what I'm talking about. You're incapable of understanding the fundamental principles of physical combat. Your giant blouse drowns out the information. You're an idiot. Stick to skipping stones and making daisy wreaths and chasing rainbows and writing stupid sonnets or whatever." Jeffrey picks up his bat and shakes his head.

"Sure," I laugh. "And you stick to tapping your enemies politely with your fist."

"It's explosive *power*, you *dick*head!"

"You want explosive power? Face up, little man."

I walk to my mark. Jeffrey surveys his imaginary field. I push off.

Of course, he belts me everywhere. His eye is too good. He invents shots, doing what he wants with the ball. And it's frustrating, given that my line and length aren't too bad today. I get the feeling he's exacting some revenge for my disrespect.

For the first time, I'm not afraid of retrieving the ball from their front yard. An Lu's garden is dun and dusty now. Just a lumpy, barren bed of soil. The insects are in exile.

There is a cluster of color under the veranda, though. After they heard what happened, a few folks from town delivered cuttings and grafts and flowers from their own gardens for An Lu to use. Of course, they're nowhere near as pretty or exotic as An's own collection, but it's nice they did that. It seems like it's their way of saying they're sorry for what happened. But I wonder if they would have brought anything if his garden hadn't been razed. Nobody brought anything for Mrs. Lu after she was scalded and scolded by Sue Findlay. Maybe because his garden was a beautiful thing everyone could share in, they felt like they lost something too.

My stomach churns and gurgles. I skipped breakfast today. I haven't really been eating much at all. My gut is a cavern of nesting butterflies. Jeffrey says I'm afflicted with Lovetummy, a known side effect stemming from excessive sassytime. I'm living off occasional buttered bread slices and sweetened Pablo. Even my mother has given up trying to force-feed me. Now she just shrugs and reminds me not to blame her when I expire.

For that I'd have to hold Eliza Wishart responsible. Every time I think of her, which is often, my body tenses and my stomach squeezes and my blood is filled with a strange alloy of exhilaration and fear. At night, I think of seeing her. I think of what it might be to creep across her back garden and tap on her window like Jasper Jones. To look past the sunflowers sitting on her sill, to see her reading on her bed. To whisper a sweet greeting when she approaches, taking care we don't get caught. To ask if she's okay. To put my finger on her jaw, to kiss her again. And this time I might lean in of my own volition. I might hold her hand. Her inside, me outside.

But I can't. Of course. I know it. And it makes me horribly lonesome. It makes me ache.

I haven't seen Jasper either, since he was at my window last. And I'm worried; he was so full of intensity and intent. I'm afraid he might have done something. That he might have been caught. By the police. By his father. By Mad Jack Lionel.

I need to see him soon. Strangely enough, spending time with Jasper always seems to quell the swell. He somehow sets things right, despite him pulling the storm clouds over my head in the first place. He has a sort of infectious strength, and I need a dose of it. I really do.

Jeffrey crouches in readiness. I roll in again. This time, the ball kicks up on a shard of loose gravel, forcing a leading edge. I stumble forward and take the catch like a bear snatching at a salmon. However unconvincing, the wicket remains. I toss the ball into the air. It's the first time I've legitimately dismissed him this summer.

"Your reign is over! Pure talent has prevailed."

"Pffft! That's barely your wicket. That one goes down to the Law of Averages. Or the Infinite Monkey Theory. Or both. If enough chimps hurl balls at a master for long enough, eventually he's going to tire of belting them all over the place and make an uncharacteristic mistake."

"It must be exhausting."

"The belting?"

"No, the constant kissing of your own arse."

Jeffrey laughs as we swap weapons and change ends. He tosses the ball hand to hand as I face up.

"You ready?"

I give a single nod.

He bowls me. First ball. Around my legs, the ball spinning sharply in. I swipe at it, but to no avail. The crate clatters. Of course, Jeffrey dies laughing. I throw the bat down in a mock tantrum and walk away, which has Jeffery cackling louder. He drags the crate off the road. It's game over. I've had enough.

We sit on Jeffrey's back steps eating angles of watermelon. Being hot and thirsty, I can manage to get this down.

We compete, seeing who can spit the seeds the furthest. I'm currently leading by an intimidating margin of around two feet.

"Your ninja skills are no match for my superior spitting."

"Bollocks. I just haven't had the right pips. My pips are rubbish."

"A poor pip-spitter always blames his melon."

Jeffrey isolates a black seed on the tip of his tongue. He stands and rears back like a javelin thrower. He breathes in sharply, which serves only to dislodge the seed and suck it to the back of his throat. He sputters and coughs and pulls forward onto his haunches. Then he spits, dribbling the seed in a pink pupa of mucus over the rail of the steps. I laugh as he sits back down.

"This contest is stupid," he rasps.

"It appears you've been pipped."

"*Charles*, what have I *told* you about puns?" Jeffrey clears his throat and throws his melon rind under the house. I swivel and do the same, just as Mrs. Lu appears with an empty basket to collect the linen from the clothesline. She frowns at me. Jeffrey, knowing I've infringed, makes it worse.

"Chuck, *Cheeses*! I've told you before not to throw things under the house. It's disrespectful. And in front of my *mother*. What are you, a *communist*? Go pick it up!"

222    I mutter and shake my head at him. He raises his eyebrows and opens his mouth, daring me to say something. I crawl beneath the veranda to collect the dirt-crusted pieces of melon. When I emerge, Jeffrey is smiling a little, but not enough to give himself away. We sit in silence as Mrs. Lu folds sheets and hums to herself. I try to make a point of holding both rinds for her to see in an attempt to incriminate Jeffrey, but I fear she just assumes I'm a gluttonous dual offender.

Finally she leaves, giving me a single satisfied nod, like I've learned an important lesson. When she's out of earshot, Jeffrey dies laughing.

"One day I will end your life with my hands," I say.

Jeffrey shrugs. We stretch and lean back on the steps, sitting silent in the shade.

"Know what I don't understand?" I ask eventually.

"I don't know: pretty much fundamentally everything in the history of the world?"

"Mermaids."

"Mermaids? How d'you mean?"

"I mean, why are they considered so seductive?"

"Easy. Because they yarrrrr!"

"That's not a reason."

"What are you talking about? You're so *ignorant*. It's their boobies. Obviously."

"Obviously. But they're half a fish! They're freaks! They have a scaly fish tail, with fins and things. Surely that alone is going to negate the thrill of boobies."

"What? Of course not. Chuck, it's harrrrd being a pirate. It's lonely. You take what you can get on the open seas."

"Noted. Sure. But I feel we're missing my central point here, and that is: they're half a *fish*. You could potentially deep-fry the lower part of their body with chips and it would be delicious. If you *actually* saw one, boobies aside, you would be disturbed, if not repulsed. You would harpoon them for science or something."

Jeffrey shakes his head.

"Incorrect, Chuck. It's not the fish part that's the attraction. Pirates see fish every day. Their trick is just to focus on the boobies and squint away the fishy bits, which is easy with enough rum. As a pirate, you take your boobies, you enjoy them, and you don't complain. Pirates aren't fussy. It's really one of those 'glass half full'–type things."

223

I hold my hands out. "Again, all due respect to your insight into the mind of a pirate, but I firmly believe that no matter how optimistic you are, or how desperate or carefree, the issue remains, sir, that should you choose to become romantically entangled with a mermaid there's going to come a point where the *fact* of their weird fish body is going to present a problem. Do you understand?"

"But, Chuck, the *boobies*."

"Forget it."

"You can't arrrgue with a pirate."

"Or an idiot."

"Yarrrr!"

I shake my head. Jeffrey leans back and yawns. He scratches his chest.

"I feel like an icy cold beer," he says.

"What? Why?"

"I don't know. It always looks so refreshing. I wishhhh to be refreshhhhed by an icy cold beer."

"But you've never *had* beer."

"So?"

"So how can you feel like something you've never tasted?"

"You never kissed Eliza Wishart before, but you still wanted to do that."

I roll my eyes at him.

"That's a lot different to a beer."

"Telling *me*. A beer is farrrr superior. You don't have to sit around holding its hand and saying nice things about its hair."

"Jeffrey, you're a volcanic eruption of stupidity."

224

"I'm a volcanic eruption of the *truth*; you know it."

I grin and get up, wiping my sticky hands on my shorts.

"Are you going to the Miners' Hall tonight for the fireworks?"

Jeffrey shrugs heavily and looks down.

"I don't know. I don't think so. I think we're just going to stay here. I heard that they moved it forward a couple of hours anyway, so it's not even for the New Year."

"I heard that too. I think parents don't want their kids out so late. But I'm not going either. Mum's going in to help with the kitchen, but I'm probably going to stay home with my dad."

"Really? But won't Ee-*laye*-za be there?"

"I don't know. Maybe." I shrug.

"Don't you want to go see her so you can link arms and finish each other's sentences and share pieces of food and smooch under the fireworks and serenade her with panpipes?"

"Panpipes?"

"Panpipes, Chuck. It's been verified by scienticians. In Paris.

Which is a city full of blouses like you. Girls can't resist being seduced when you blow bamboo flutes. It's fact. It's in their fizzyology."

"You're a very strange little man."

"Incorrect. I'm practically a visionary. I've got so many feathers in my cap, I'm practically an Indian chief. Why don't you go home and rub a photograph of Eliza all over your body like a bar of soap?"

"Honestly, you're starting to genuinely unsettle me. Have you thought about electrotherapy?"

"Charles, I'm shocked."

"Did you just break your own pun rule?"

"No. The rule is that *you're* banned from pun-making. My puns are witty and superb."

"You're an idiot."

"If you're not going tonight, you should come over and have a delicious refreshing beer with me."

"But you don't *have* beer," I insist.

"Don't I?" Jeffrey says, arching an eyebrow.

225

"No. No you don't."

"You're right. I don't. Which is just as well. I have to keep my body in peak condition. I have to resist vice and temptation. You don't see Bruce Lee with a refreshing beer in his hand. Probably why he's so alert. My body is a temple, Chuck. A temple of explosive power. A cathedral of virtue. My fists are like . . . gavels. Gavels of stone. Stone-cold justice. I bleed integrity. It's practically my destiny." Jeffrey hops up and shadowboxes, huffing "I'm so pretty, I'm so pretty" under his breath. I bid him a Jew and leave him to defeat his gray ghost.

As I walk home, I wonder if I could just up and leave Jeffrey here when I turn my back on Corrigan. It's always been so easy with Jeffrey. I've never felt the need to act stronger or smarter than I am. I've never had to try to be somebody else. I wonder if I can really do it. For some reason, I dread leaving him behind more than my parents.

One of the hardest things about this whole mess has been not sharing it with Jeffrey Lu. Not to discuss or dissect, just to have him know, to put a piece of it in his pocket. It feels so strange and alien to keep this all to myself.

It should be getting easier; the tide of anxiety should be creeping back. But even as the fever around Laura's disappearance dissolves, that red stripe of mercury climbs higher inside me. My breath gets shorter; that knot in my chest gets tighter. Eliza Wishart has taken my appetite; Laura has stolen my slumber. I've traded my pansy sandals for heavy boots. Because I know they'll come for me one day. The buzzards will always be circling.

What if Laura rose to the surface? What if the rope frayed; what if they found her floating? What if someone came forward, or discovered her by chance? Would they cuff me and beat me like they beat Jasper Jones?

And if they caught me, would I tell them everything?

If I see Eliza, I might. Though I long to see her, to make sure she's okay, I'm afraid of what might spill out of me. It's bubbling closer and closer to the surface. And I'm worried I'll burst. The temptation to end the misery and mystery, to make amends, to try and explain it, to carve that word. But doing so will put Jasper Jones in jail. And maybe me too.

She'll be there tonight, at the fireworks, and so I have to stay home. I can't let myself see her, though I want to so badly. I can't risk my promise to Jasper Jones.

And I know that if I tell her, she'll hate me. She won't understand. No matter how much I try to explain that I tried to do the right thing.

And that's why I have to leave with Jasper. Before they discover us, or I give us away. I've got to leave everything behind, with our secret in a bindle bag, tied tight. I know we won't ever solve this. I guess I always knew. So I've got to crack open the snow dome. I've got to get out, get brave. And I know it will be okay if I'm with Jasper. With him, I feel as though we could really do it. We could move to the city, maybe. I could still go to school somewhere. Or work with Jasper. We could go up north. Travel to places where it's always summer. We could be entrepreneurs, partners. Shoulder to shoulder. We'd outsmart them all. Dodger and Charlie. We could sneak back to Corrigan and make a killing with crayfish. We could work orchards when the seasons are right, pick peaches at dawn and hustle poker games at night. Oysters. Pearls. Gold. I could sneak into universities, learn for free. We'd grift and get by. I could write in my yellow pads. Everything and anything. Letters to Eliza. And I'd finally have the right words in me, all the things I'd meant to tell her. I'd be wittier than Wilde. I'd make her heart melt from a thousand miles away.

We'd be like Kerouac and Cassady. We could steal away in boxcars, ride all the way across the country. Melbourne, Sydney. Every town in between. I could document our adventures. Maybe one day I could get our story published under a nom de plume. I'd have to move to New York City. The famous writer who fled from his hometown and shunned the limelight. And every morning I'd wait awhile at the Plaza Hotel to see if Eliza Wishart might happen by. And one day she'd appear. She'd stop in her tracks, making sure it was me. She'd be wrapped in a thick coat, her hair tied up. She'd say my name and she'd drop her bags and run toward me. We'd kiss again, and hold each other in the cold. She'd wipe her lipstick off my lips with her thumb. And then we'd go inside and take high tea, and I'd tell her everything about Jasper and Laura—I'd unpick the lock and she'd understand because she'd be older and wiser and the hole in her heart would have healed some. Maybe.

I don't know. This whole mess.

*** 

In the early evening, my father knocks on my door after my mother has left.

"Are you going into town to see the fireworks?"

I shrug.

"Why not?" he asks.

"I don't know. I just feel like staying here. I might go see Jeffrey later."

My father nods slowly with his bottom lip out and his eyebrows high. He seems distracted. It's strange for him to linger like this.

"Listen, Charlie. I have to tell you. You were right, you know."

"Right about what?"

"About me," he says softly. "I *have* been writing. In my study."

I frown and sit up. He goes on.

"I've been working on a novel. For a long time. And I've finally finished. Today. I wanted to show you first. Actually, I wanted you to be the first to read it."

He opens the door wider and reveals a manuscript in his left hand. I wonder how I never heard him typing it. I don't really know what to say. I should feel honored and proud, I should be full of congratulations and awe and support. But as he lays his bundle on my desk, I just feel tired and pissed off. I look down at it the same way I might observe a cold bowl of boiled cabbage.

228 "It's a bit of a surprise, I suppose," he says, hovering over me. I peel away the first sheet of paper and read the title. It's called *Patterson's Curse*.

"Well," he says, rocking back on his feet and thrusting his hands in his pockets. He looks shyly excited. "I guess I'll leave you to it. Take your time and have a good think. Who knows, Charlie. I might try to get it published. A book on the shelves, imagine that!"

I smile with pressed lips and nod as he backs out of my room. He closes the door behind him. I look at the pile of sheets in front of me, as thick as a Bible. My thumb strums through the pages, fanning hot, musty air back into my face. My father's name is beneath the title. *Patterson's Curse*. My lip lifts into a surly curl. *Bucktin's Envy*. I can't help it. I want to tear it all up, scatter it around the room. I want to throw it back in his kind, genial face. I always thought this would be something amazing we could share, but the truth is, I just feel betrayed. I feel like something precious has been ripped out of my chest, which makes me a sour-lipped, small-hearted bastard, but I can't shake it. Not just because I know it's going to be brilliant. But I always imagined it would be *me* walking softly into his office with a secret and a bundle of hard-earned pages. I always thought they'd be *my* words, *my* little stamps of ink. My moment of accomplishment. My name under my title.

I lean on my elbows and scratch my scalp, staring at the title page. My curiosity and resentment work against each other like a knife on a whetstone. I don't know what to expect. My heart is racing.

I pinch a page. Flip it. The first line.

Jasper Jones has come to my window.

*"Charlie!"*

I start and wheel around. For some reason, I feel the need to conceal the manuscript with my arms.

*"Charlie!"* he hisses again.

"What are you doing? It's still light outside!" I climb onto my bed and flip the slats. He looks restless. It's strange to see him with the sun still out, albeit fading fast.

"Tonight, Charlie. We're gonna do it. Are you ready?"

"Tonight we're going to do *what*? What do you mean, *ready*? Ready for what?"

"Mad Jack. We're gonna go there tonight. Me and you. Right now. Are you ready?"

"*What?* Wait. Go up to his house? Why right *now*? And why do you need *me*? I can't go there. It's Mad Jack *Lionel*. He'll shoot us before we get inside the bloody gate. It makes no sense."

"I tole you, Charlie. We're gonna go there to get it out of him. We're gonna get him to own up to what he done."

"But *how*? How are we going to even talk to him?"

"The man's been calling out my name for as long as I bin walking, Charlie. Tonight I'm gonna call *his* out."

I sigh, with my eyes closed tight.

"Okay. Look. Even if we get in there without being shot, he's not just going to throw his hands in the air and admit he did it. That's for books and films. It doesn't happen. We can't send him to jail on our own."

Jasper shakes his head quickly.

"You don't have to say nuthin, Charlie. Just be there. I'll do the talking. I'll work him round. I'm gonna tell him that we know it were him. That we know how and where. That we were there when he did it, hidin; that we saw the whole thing. I'll even tell him we saw him scratch that word in the tree, same as the rusted car in his yard. Then I'll tell him that if he don't come forward and turn himself in, we'll go to the police. We'll back him into a corner, Charlie. He'll *have* to talk."

"He'll never believe you," I argue.

"Only one way to find out."

"Why do you need me there, then? If you're doing all the talking?"

"Because I reckon it's more likely he'll believe me if I say it was both of us who seen him do it. And also, I need you there as a witness, Charlie. You got to corroborate my story. If he talks, and if I go to the sarge by meself, it's my word against Lionel's. I got no chance. But if you're there too, they *got* to believe me. But we've got to go now."

"Why? Why right *now?*" I'm getting flustered; my voice shifts higher in pitch. I can't think straight.

Jasper slaps at a mosquito on his forearm and wipes it on his shorts.

"Because the whole town is on its way to the Miners' Hall for New Year's. There's no curfew tonight, which means nobody's going to ask any questions if we're walking to somewhere. Even so, we'll separate while it's still light. So you go in there, tell your folks that you're going in to watch the fireworks; then you walk into town the main way, and I'll meet you at the railway station. No one will suspect anythin. And we'll go to Lionel's from there. Orright?"

I pinch my nose.

"Jasper, it won't work! This is *ridiculous*. I mean, we don't even *know* it was him."

Jasper shakes his head, setting his upper teeth behind his lower.

"Jesus *Christ*, Charlie. Listen. You can either help me or not. It's your choice. I don't give a shit. You don't owe me anythin, it's true. But you tole me you were in for the pound, Charlie, and I took your word. But I reckon you're just fuckin scared. That's all. All this bullshit right now, that's just you bein afraid. And what did I tell you, right at the start? I *promised* that nuthin would happen to you. I tole you that I'd make sure you were safe, that you never had anythin to worry about. And that's still the same for tonight. It's up to you if you trust me or not. Now I'm gonna wait for you at the station until it gets dark. If you're not there, you're not there. No hard feelins. It's orright. But I hope y'are, because I need your help, Charlie. I got to set this straight, and not just for me, remember. I got to do what's right. I got to put this bastard away."

Before I can respond, Jasper slips away.

I'm rattled. I pace my room for a time. I stare out the window at a peach-colored sunset that stains everything with its glow. And then I kneel and put on my shoes. I walk to my father's study and tap on his door. He looks a little surprised to see me. I explain that I've changed my mind, I'm going in to see the fireworks with Jeffrey. When he responds with more enthusiasm than I'd usually expect, I know I've disappointed him by not sitting down to read his novel. A nasty shard of me is pleased he's upset.

I have to slip out of our street quickly, lest Jeffrey sees me and decides to come. I stroll down the hill, kicking at bits of gravel. Most families are making their way in now, dressed to the nines and mucking about. I wish I could walk in their shoes.

The world is aflame. The sun is a giant red ball. And by the time I pass the bowls club and approach the council gardens, the sky is a thin violet, stunning and clear. I'm not far from the middle of town. The main street has been blocked off, and folks are milling and trilling. I keep to the roadside, ducking behind ambling families, worried that Eliza might be among those ahead. Light is fading fast, and I don't know if I'll have enough time to take the long route round the oval. I'm not sure how long Jasper will wait. A strong part of me, the part that's making my legs heavy and sluggish, hopes that I'll find the station steps empty.

I can hear the warble and shriek of the street crowd now, and the thin pacy melodies made by the bush band up by the pub. I decide to stick close to the family in front of me, who are certainly broad enough to use as a screen, and hope that Eliza doesn't pick me out.

I can hear laughing and chatting. Kids have organized a game of British bulldog on either side of the main street, and they duck and slip around people like slick fish in a stream, bending and arching their backs so they don't get tagged. There are stalls and attractions. A raucous ring of two-up outside the hardware store. There's an enormous bonfire in the pebbled car park of the Miners' Hall, a pyramid of old railway sleepers feeding the flames. Against the wall of the hall, there are crates of fireworks, a few of which, no doubt, will sting the fingers of the pissed idiots who'll swagger in to light them later.

Behind the hall, they've shoveled coals into a long hole, above which a half-dozen skewered lambs twirl and roast. The aroma is thick and moreish.

232

People spill out of the hall like wasps from a hive, nursing small refreshments. I duck my head as the crowd gets thicker. A line dance has formed before the band, and partners stomp and skip out a heel-toe polka. A happy arc of observers clap the rhythm, laughing and cheering. The beer garden has sprawled out onto the street; they've even wheeled out kegs to keep up with demand.

Then there's a tap on my shoulder. I freeze and wheel around. Of course, it's Eliza Wishart, and she's beaming, her dimples like pretty buttons, her skin like milk. I must look horrified, because her expression immediately falls.

"Charlie, what's the matter?"

"Oh, no, nothing. At all," I sputter, and shake my head. I try to smile, but my weight is on my heels. I'm lost for words. She smells amazing.

"I've been looking everywhere for you! I'm glad you came. I haven't seen you for a while."

I open and close my mouth. Take a small step backward. She glances over my shoulder with a frown.

"Are you here by yourself? Where's Jeffrey?"

"He didn't come. Actually," I begin, my voice strangled, "I can't stay. Here, I mean. I've got to go. I'm on my way to . . . somewhere. I can't say. I mean, it's nowhere, really. It's just . . . I can't . . ."

My hands are flapping. I'm buggering this up.

"Well, are you coming back? I thought I might be able to see you tonight. I need to talk to you, Charlie. It's important." Eliza sounds distressed; her eyes even glaze a little, which makes me ill to see. So I do it. I put a hand on her shoulder and I squeeze. And I give in to the creeping curse. I promise her I'll be coming back. That I won't be long. She looks down and nods. I think she can tell I'm lying. Either way, it's clear I've disappointed her. I wish I could tell her everything. But I can't. I have to go. I have to disobey every impulse and leave her here for Jasper Jones, for Jack Lionel, for this horrible mess.

Everything is so loud and boisterous around me. Thumping through my brain. The light is leaking. But I gather myself long enough to commit an astonishing act of bravery. In the middle of town, in front of everyone, I lean in, then and there, and I kiss her, quickly, on the lips. And they're as soft as I remember. I hope I haven't impaled her eye with the frame of my glasses. But when she looks up, she seems a little lighter, a little less sad. I try to reassure her.

233

"I'm very . . . fond. Of you. I'm sorry," I say. She smiles. I tell her I'll see her soon.

"How soon?" she asks anxiously. She seems edgy. She wells up again and it melts me. I wonder if anything has happened.

"Soon," I say, and I pull away. I feel like dirt. Eliza squeezes my fingers as I turn, gives them a weak tug. I didn't even realize we were holding hands. I leave her and walk toward the junction, concentrating hard on not looking behind me, because doing so might have me abandoning Jasper Jones altogether.

I arrive in time. Jasper is leaning on a pillar beside the timetable corkboard, casting a long shadow across the gritty slats of the station floor. He smiles, his teeth bright white in the dimness.

"I knew you'd come, Charlie. I knew you'd do the right thing."

I say nothing and climb the stairs. I can't shake Eliza from my mind.

"Are you ready?" he asks, tapping a cigarette from its crumpled pack. He offers one. I decline. I don't even feign interest.

Jasper pats his pockets.

"Shit. You have a light?"

I look at him blankly, then shake my head.

"Fuckit," he mutters. "We have to go, Charlie."

We set off, and it gets suddenly very real. We walk side by side and don't speak. The stars emerge. Gravel crunches underfoot as we leave the sound of the town behind. It feels so different to the first night Jasper Jones came to my window. There's no thrill to jostle with the apprehension, just a dark thread of dread. I know we're making a mistake. Even in the heat, a chill shudders my shoulders.

We're going to Mad Jack Lionel's. We're really doing it. We're about to trespass on the property of a killer. The town recluse. The unhinged eccentric. And we're not just sneaking in for peach pits. We're not just taking badges of bravery. We're rapping at his door and we're accusing him of unspeakable acts.

And what if he did it? What if it really was him? What if all the rumors are true? What if he's really violent and unstable? These people exist. Albert Fish. Gertrude Baniszewski. Eric Edgar Cooke. They're real people. It's not myth. I've read about them. We trudge closer. I can't do this. There's no way I can do this. I can't walk to his door and accuse him. I have to get out of this. It's a death warrant. Not even Jasper Jones can stop bullets. I want to flee this scene, back to Eliza Wishart.

I speak to Jasper, because I'm nervous.

"What do you think he'll do?"

Jasper scratches at the back of his head.

"Honestly? I dunno. I really do not know."

"Then why? Why do it like this?"

"Just because you don't know how somethin's gonna turn out is no reason *not* to do it. If the world went by that rule, nuthin would ever get done. But the simple truth is, we got to. We've just *got* to."

I wave and clap at a cluster of midges at eye level. Jasper feeds his cigarette back into his mouth. He pats his pockets, looking confused.

"Jasper, you don't have a light, remember?"

"What? Oh, shit. That's right. D'you?"

"No. I don't. I told you."

He shoves his smoke back into his pocket. And it occurs to me that maybe Jasper Jones is afraid, and it ratchets up my anxiety. And that strange admission that he doesn't know what to expect, that he doesn't know what this night will bring. Of course he doesn't. How could he? I know that. But Jasper is normally so reliably forthright, it's unnerving to see him wavering. Maybe I could convince him to turn back. Maybe we could rethink this. Devise something less hopeless and dangerous.

But it's too late. We're here.

We pause. It's incredibly still. Mad Jack Lionel's gate is closed.     *235*

The yard beyond is scruffy and dilapidated. Along the border closest to the river, where the bush meets the property, a thick thatch of blackberries presses through the rusted wire fence. On the other side, toward the cottage, I notice a goat tethered to a star picket and lying on its side. If it weren't for the circle of shorter grass inside its boundary, I'd believe it to be dead. Crows moan from gray leafless branches. They look like silhouettes. Crow-shaped holes.

Jasper unlatches the gate; it swings open loudly. I'm shitting myself.

"Wait! We're coming up from the front?"

"That's right," Jasper says loudly, as though he intends for Mad Jack to hear. His boldness is back. Jasper strides up the drive. I follow as he speaks over his shoulder. "Straight up, Charlie. We want to be direct. I reckon that's the way."

I watch him walk. Straight-backed, chest full of air. And I see it now, just how counterfeit his confidence is. It's a noise, a distraction, hot air. It's Batman's cape; it's my father's comb-over. And a bubble bursts in me. Still, I march behind him, like a tired infantryman, frightened and resigned.

The goat lifts its head languidly, bleats, then rests it again. I interpret it as a bad omen. Beyond, a mob of kangaroos bounces lazily across a paddock. I see a still windmill I've never noticed before. It's dreamlike and intense, this short walk. My heart is a bomb. It's so still, I can hear the fireworks pop and crackle in the distance. I even think I can see their small flashes of color. I wish I was there.

There are lights on inside. He's home. We're close. Jasper walks fast and aggressively. I can see the peach tree hanging laden by the side of the cottage. I can even smell its fruit, sweet and fat and overripe.

The veranda creaks unbearably loud as Jasper treads the boards. I hang back, gripping a support beam as he breathes deep and beats at the door three times with the side of his fist.

"Lionel!"

My legs are useless to me. I hold the beam like I'm caught in a gale. I hear movement. I see a shadow. I hold my breath.

And there he is.

Mad Jack Lionel.

He's not nearly as tall as I expected. Or as broad. The first thing that strikes me, really, is how *old* he looks. Hunkering and haggard and bent. Nothing at all like Albert Fish. He wears a pair of grubby gray workpants and a faded blue tank top with small holes in the side where moths have feasted. His feet are bare. His hair is white and combed; his shoulders are thick with it too. He opens the flywire slowly, confused, a man who doesn't get many visitors. But what surprises me most is Lionel's expression upon seeing Jasper Jones. His blank face lifts in delight. And he smiles a row of yellow teeth. His green eyes get glassy. And he looks him up and down for a moment.

"Jasper! Good God, it's you! How about that! Strike a light, what a surprise! Come on in, come on."

Jasper wasn't lying: he knows his name. Lionel reaches out to usher Jasper in by the shoulder. Jasper responds by rearing and ripping his arm back. I flinch.

"Don't be touching me, mate. That's not happening. Understand?"

Lionel regards him. Then nods once.

"I understand. That's fine. But come in anyway. Please. Come on in."

Lionel turns awkwardly and waves him on, walking down the hall in front of us. He has a pronounced limp, favoring his right side. Jasper glances at me with a furrowed brow. He is sweating. There are beads on his brow. Half-moons under his arms. I hold a shrug. Jasper breathes in deep. His chest swells. And we follow Mad Jack Lionel into his home.

The inside of the cottage is dim. It's a strange light, the color of an egg yolk. The wallpaper is split and faded. Everything smells of dust and turpentine. On my left is a wall hanging of butterflies with pins through their bodies. They don't look very colorful. The hall mantel is full of photographs and trinkets and doilies, but I don't get time to look at them carefully. We shuffle into Mad Jack Lionel's living room. There's a rifle mounted on the wall. I step back. He hasn't seen me yet. Maybe if I remain unseen, I'll get out of here alive.

Lionel extends an arm.

"Have a seat, Jasper. Have a sit. Go on."

"I'm not sittin," Jasper says, firm.

Lionel nods again slowly, arms behind his back. Before he replies, he sees me for the first time.

"Oh, who's this? I didn't see you out there. Is this your mate? Hello, son."

Jasper stands back with his arms folded.

"This is Charlie. That's all you need to know. But it dunt matter anyway, because we come here to talk about what *we* know. About you."

Mad Jack Lionel shuffles on his feet. His face falls. He looks uneasy.

"Right."

"We know it was you. We know you did it."

237

Jack Lionel fixes Jasper with a thoughtful look. His eyes look red and rheumy and sad. He sighs.

"Why don't you boys have a seat? Go on, have a sit and I'll make a brew. I don't have much here, but I got plenty of tea."

He gestures toward two ratty couches by the window. Jasper shakes his head.

"We don't want anythin from you. And I tole you, we don't want to sit. We're not stayin. I want to talk about what you done. That's what I want."

Lionel nods slowly.

"Orright, Jasper. Well, let me sit, then."

He crosses to his couch and gingerly lowers himself.

Jasper narrows his eyes and leans forward. His breathing has gathered pace.

"So you admit it? You admit that it was you? That you killed her?"

The silence is thick and tense. I glance from Jack Lionel to Jasper Jones, who glares aggressively across the room, hands by his sides now, bunching his fists and then releasing them. Then back to Jack, who sits with his elbows nursed on his knees, kneading his dry palms. I think he is searching for words. He rubs at his nose, then reaches to the sideboard for his tobacco pouch and papers. He frowns and concentrates on the task. The thin gully in the groove of his fingers, the peppering of copper flakes.

"Jasper, listen to me, I know you're upset. I know it. You know, though, I always thought you'd've found out before now. I thought that's why you never come to see me. Who finally told you? Your dad? Or have you known all this time?"

I shrink back and swallow hard, bumping the edge of the piano. Is this really happening? Was Jasper right this whole time? I look at Lionel, shocked and shaken. None of this makes any sense. He looks so slight and frail and slow. His manner, his frame, none of it seems right. There's no way he could have restrained Laura Wishart, let alone scaled that tree to loosen the rope. But why would he be owning up to this? He's not right in the head. He's insane. It's the only answer.

238

Jasper tries to settle himself, sticking with his plan.

"Nobody told me nuthin."

Lionel looks doubtful. He licks the adhesive lip of his cigarette carefully, taking his time.

"Nobody told you? But you must have found out somehow."

"We *saw* you," says Jasper forcefully. It sounds like the lie it is. "We saw you do it. Me and Charlie. We both did."

This stops Lionel. He bucks back; his fingers pause. He looks genuinely baffled.

"Jasper, what do you mean, *saw*? Eh? You saw what?"

"We saw everythin. We even saw you scratchin that word onto the tree, days after. So you can't deny what you done. We saw it. Because it's my spot. It's my bit of the bush, it's where I go. You know it. You seen me goin there for years. And I were there that night. Both of us. We saw you do it."

"Jasper, what on *earth* are you talking about?" Lionel shakes his head shortly, but he speaks patiently. "That's not possible. You were barely two years old when it happened. D'you understand? You couldn't have seen anything. Nobody saw anything."

The walls are pressing in. Jasper looks affronted.

"What are *you* on about? It only just happened. Three weeks ago. Don't lie to me. You can't get out of it. I saw you. I know the *truth*. Do you have any idea what you've fuckin done? Any idea?" Jasper takes a threatening step forward.

I wonder if I should intervene. I feel like a spectator in a play. My heart is drumming at my ribs. If Mad Jack Lionel is in any way intimidated, he's masking it well. I wish I had his composure. I want to back out of this house, but my legs won't move. This is a bad dream.

Lionel finishes rolling his smoke, pats his pockets and searches for a light. After he finds one, he flares up, then seeks out Jasper's eyes.

"Listen, Jasper. Look, I understand. I understand why you're . . . *hostile* to me. I really do. I've wanted to speak to you about this for a very long time."

"Well, here's your chance," Jasper says.

"This business about you two *seeing* it? Three weeks ago? Mate, I'm sorry, but I *do not* follow you. That's impossible. You *know* that can't be right. What are you tryin to tell me? What'd you see?"

"We saw you kill Laura."

"Laura? Who is Laura? That wasn't her name."

"Whose name?"

"Your mother's."

"My *mother*? You mention my mother again, I will have you. No lie."

Now Jack Lionel looks completely lost. So am I. He sits upright, his head tilted. I notice a slight tremor in his hands.

"Jasper, I still don't follow you. Who is Laura? Charlie, can you help me?"

He glances at me in appeal, and I blush and shy away, looking down at the dusty piano keys. I shouldn't be here. This is a mistake.

"Who?" he asks again. "Who is Laura?"

"The girl you killed, you sick old prick! You don't even know her *name*? The girl you beat and hanged and whatever else you did to her! I know it were you. I know it."

"Beat and *hanged*? Jasper, good *God*! What in *Christ* are you talking about? *Who* are you talking about?"

They've both raised their voices. I am deathly afraid. I need to piss urgently.

"Who? Laura Wishart. And don't get all confused, like you don't know, because I *know* you seen her. You know exactly who she is! You seen her walkin past with me, out the front there, when you're calling out my name every other night like a fuckin madman. I'm not stupid, mate. Don't try to pull the wool. I *know* what you done! It's over. Just admit it."

Jasper is leaning and pointing now. Looming. But Lionel still shows no sign of being threatened, no fear of having been caught. He mutters to himself, shaking his head, squinting while he tokes on his smoke. He just looks like a confused old man. I fear that Jasper has played his last card.

"*Wishart?* Wishart, Wishart, Wishart . . ." And he looks up suddenly. "You mean that young one who's gone missing? That's her name, isn't it? Laura Wishart."

"Yes," says Jasper impatiently. "You're not all there, are you?"

Lionel leans forward, his brow knitted. He coughs. One of his knees cracks.

"You mean they've found her?"

"*We* found her. Charlie and me. On that night. That's what I'm tryin to tell you. You're good as caught."

"Caught? Jasper, I . . ."

"Listen. We're not gonna do you in straight up. We'll give you the chance to come forward, to tell them what you done. That's why we come here. I reckon you got that in you. It's over anyway. We *seen* you, understand?"

"Hold up, son. Now, wait. What's happened? You're telling me you found her, and she's *dead?*" He speaks stronger now, more assertive. I sense a shift of power in the room.

241

"Don't play the fool. You know exactly what happened. We *seen* you do it. How many times do I have to say it?"

"Oh, Jasper. Oh, strike me." Lionel plants a hand on his heart. "You think it was me? You think I killed that poor girl?"

"I'm saying we *know* it were you."

Jasper is less steady now. Less certain. The venom has left his voice. He looks like the one who's backed into the corner. I'm worried.

"Jasper, that's a bloody lie. That's a *bloody* lie! You're talking nonsense! Jesus *Christ* Almighty. She's dead? Are you *sure?* Or are you playing games here? What happened? And you start talking the *truth!*" Lionel says with feeling.

"Well, you fuckin did it!" And Jasper Jones sounds like a child. Like a bleating, scared, hurt kid. And I feel betrayed for the second time tonight. We shouldn't be here. I don't know who this man is, but he didn't kill anybody. I've done everything wrong. Mad Jack Lionel isn't a criminal. He's probably not even mad. He's just old and sad and poor and lonely.

"Why? Jasper, why do you *say* that?" Lionel's voice is thick and raised, and his red rheumy eyes are glazed over. I think he might be beginning to cry. "Is it because of what happened? With your mum? Is that why?"

This room is filled with a fat fog and I'm utterly lost in it. I want to crawl into a ball.

Jasper squints and shakes his head quickly. He jabs a finger.

"I tole you, if you mention her again, I'm steppin in. I don't give a shit how old y'are. Why are you even bringing her up? She's *dead*, you stupid bastard. You know that? And you got no right at all to be discussin my family."

At this, Jack Lionel bucks back again in his chair. He pauses, then slowly shakes his head. I watch the ash of his fag grow perilously close to toppling onto his foot.

"Oh, good God. Good *God*," he says, still shaking his head, holding Jasper's eye. He looks incredulous. "You don't know. Anything. You don't know who I am, do you? You've got no idea. You don't know a *bloody* thing."

"What? Course I know who you are. You're Jack Lionel."

"More than that, though. About us? You and me."

"What are you *on* about? What do you mean?"

Lionel coughs again, swivels, and stubs his cigarette in an ashtray on the sideboard. He swallows heavily. He looks weary and ragged.

"Jasper, how do you think it is I know your name? Why do you think I'm talking to you like this?"

"I bin wonderin that meself. And why it is you yell out at me every time I walk by, every single night."

"You really don't know? Tell the truth, now."

Jasper shakes his head.

Lionel mutters something under his breath, and then he creaks slowly to his feet. I eye him closely as he hobbles across the room, prepared for anything. But he just waves his hand, almost like he's warding Jasper Jones away.

"Turn around," he says.

"What? No." Jasper steps back. "What for?"

"Just turn around." Lionel is standing next to him now, pointing at something atop the dusty upright. Jasper cautiously does as he is directed. I slink around to see. Lionel is motioning toward three framed photographs. Jasper looks blankly and shrugs. Lionel asks him if he recognizes anyone in them. Looking at the two of them standing side by side now, then at the figures in the frames, I think I understand before Jasper does. It clicks into place, and I really don't know what Jasper will do. But he's not even really looking at them. He shrugs again, showing no interest. He doesn't see. But then Lionel points a gnarled finger, and he says, "That there. That there's your father. And that's your mother." And then he points at the baby between them, and he says, "That's you." Jasper scoffs, but I can tell he's wavering, because he screws his face up and tells Lionel to fuck off. That he's lying. But Jack Lionel, still patient, tells Jasper to look hard and close at that picture, to tell him if it isn't really his old man. Jasper cuts his eyes. He's silent for a while. Then he shakes his head quickly, like a dog trying to loosen something from its collar. He backs away a step. Says it's bullshit. Asks where he got them from. But Lionel quietly points to another photograph, the smallest one. This time, an older man holds the same baby, and it's then that Lionel reveals to Jasper what I know already to be true. The man is him. Jack Lionel is his father's father. Jasper's grandfather. And as Jasper's eyebrows knit together and his jaw clenches, Lionel asks him again to sit down with him, as he's wanted to all these years. Because he has to talk to him about his mother. Jasper is rattled. It hurts me to see. I feel sorry for him. Quiet now, unsteady, Jasper says there's nothing to say. She's dead. She was in a car crash.

And then Lionel says, softly: "I know. I was driving."

*** 

When I'm back in my room, it feels like the first time I've ever walked into it. Nothing feels like home anymore. Even my skin, my clothes, my smell. Everything feels different.

The return journey from Jack Lionel's house was very strange. We walked fast and purposefully. Across the oval, away from the center of town. We could still hear pulses of music and chatter in the air. Thankfully, I didn't encounter Eliza Wishart. I might have melted into her arms, I might have told her everything. Jasper and I didn't say a word to each other. My head was an empty box. Jasper seemed deep in thought. Full of sullen and angry questions. And why wouldn't he be? His whole world had been lifted and upended like a bag of rubbish.

When he left me by my sleepout, all he said was that he was going home to see his father, who'd arrived back this morning from the gold-fields, but not before pissing away the money he'd earned out there. It's an encounter I'll be glad to miss.

I look across at the bundle of pages my own father has left me, like a giant steaming shit on my desk. It's all too much. Like that first night when this whole mess took me over. And it's tightened its grip ever since. It's buckled me. I need to sleep it away. I need to wake up somebody new. I need to leave with Jasper Jones.

244

We'd gone to confront Mad Jack Lionel about murdering Laura Wishart, only to find that he was driving the car that killed Jasper's mother. This world isn't right. It's small and it's nasty and it's lousy with sadness. Under every rock, hidden in every closet, shaken from every tree, it seems there's something horrible I don't want to see. I don't know. Maybe that's why this town is so content to face in on itself, to keep everything so settled and smooth and serene. And at the moment, I can't say as I blame them.

\*\*\*

Jasper didn't sit down. But he didn't look Lionel in the eye either, not after the old man presented him with ragged albums full of other photographs and birth certificates, nor after he showed Jasper his father's old bedroom, which hadn't been touched or troubled in years. There were still clothes hanging out of the drawers, a guitar and a cricket bat leaning into each other in the corner of the room. Football trophies in a cupboard. I peered at the engravings. DAVID LIONEL.

Jack Lionel told Jasper that he'd never wanted him to be born.

Rosie Jones was from a neighboring shire. She and David had met at a dance outside town. They kept seeing each other, secretly, usually down at the Corrigan River, where they could be alone. When she fell pregnant, Jack Lionel railed hard against it. He demanded that they have it dealt with. He said it wasn't right, that David was dirtying the family name. But David pushed back harder. He told him they were in love, they would keep the child. Furious, Jack Lionel banished his son from the house. David snatched up some belongings and left willingly. His drawers stayed open all those years. He and Rosie rented a place in town, and he secured an apprenticeship at the mine. But they were cast apart. Even David's mates turned their backs after saying their piece. Eventually, they all left him alone. The only place he was still tolerated was the footy club.

They were married three months before Jasper was born. Just the two of them, attended in a small church in the city. And it was there that David took the opportunity to change his surname to Jones. Jack said that hurt him the most of all.

245

After Jasper was born, Rosie reached out to Jack. She began inviting him to Sunday dinner every week, which he would routinely turn down. After a full year of cheery requests, he finally relented. He showed up, quiet and tentative, hat in his hand. David pushed past him and went to the pub. But Lionel stayed, and he and Rosie sat and ate.

Jack Lionel learned that he'd been so very wrong about her. She was kind and forthright and beautiful, and she cooked as well as his own wife had ever done. He began turning up every Sunday, spending longer in their house with Jasper and Rosie. David slapped the bar at the Sovereign and stayed out until the bell rang.

Lionel began looking forward to seeing Rosie so much, it became the peak of his week. He dressed sharp and took care and combed his hair. And Rosie, too, began cooking more elaborately and took to wearing her Sunday best. Lionel told Jasper that he came to adore his mother like a daughter, that the two of them became very fine friends. And it wasn't just on Sundays. She often dropped in to Jack's house for afternoon tea with something she'd baked, and he'd unpack the good china cups and saucers. David, of course, stayed away. Rosie held them equally responsible for persisting with their feud: David for being too stubborn to extend his hand, and Jack for being too proud to apologize.

It was on an unseasonably cold April Sunday that Rosie Jones clutched her side and gasped. She insisted she was all right, but when she could no longer stand and could barely breathe, Lionel bundled her into the Hillman and started driving toward the coast. When she started shrieking in the car, Lionel feared the worst. Rosie's eyes were wild, and she sucked and seethed air like she was leaking it through her lungs. Lionel hurtled down the hill, squinting into the harsh twilight sun. Rosie's back was bolt straight, and she pitched and pulled in her seat as though she were in a rocking chair. She squeezed at his hand with such urgency that he hadn't the heart to retract it.

246 If he'd done so, if he'd possessed that shard of cold common sense that would have seen both his hands gripping the steering wheel, he might have better dealt with the jolt caused by a deep pothole that the sun obscured. But as it was, Jack Lionel braked hard and overcorrected on the gravel roadside. They slid toward a wall of trees. And that's all it took. Just a hole in the ground, aligned with a tire. An instant in time. A moment of shit luck in bright light and everything turned to black.

When Lionel came to, he was covered in blood and glass and he was trapped inside the car. The passenger seat was empty. There was a thick, sick quiet punctuated only by insects. The windscreen was gone. Before he blacked out again, he caught sight of Rosie's dress a few meters ahead, and he understood what he'd done with such a heavy dread that he welcomed the creeping dark behind his eyes.

It was her appendix. It was a bubble ready to burst. And so Lionel's instincts had been right in rushing her toward a doctor. But even so, Lionel never forgave himself. He wished it were him that had died, not Rosie Jones. And so too did David, who blamed him violently and entirely, who suspected something far more sinister than an urgent race to the hospital. The last words David ever spoke to his father were delivered that night over his bed in the emergency room. He told him that if he showed up at Rosie's funeral, he'd kill him then and there, God as his witness. And Jack Lionel believed him.

The crash had shattered Jack's leg, left it aching and useless and bent inward. But Rosie's death cloaked his whole body. Weighed him down like chain mail. Because he'd come to love her in that short time, and hand in hand with that chill of responsibility was that he simply missed his friend. He missed her cooking and her laugh and her smell and the way she always sat so straight and dignified in her chair, the way she was always so interested in what he had to say. Jack Lionel packed away the china and hung up his suit and never wore it again. Neither his leg nor the rest of him ever healed properly.

He held his own service for Rosie Jones. When the council returned the crushed husk of the Hillman to his property, it was there that he said his piece, by the passenger side of the car. He cried and he prayed, and then, kneeling in the rain, he used the edge of a penny to etch the word he wanted to last longer than he'd be on this earth to keep saying it.

Of course, Corrigan was ruthless. Rumors spread regarding the circumstances that saw Jack Lionel speeding away from town with Rosie Jones. Some said that he'd abducted her. That he'd become infatuated with his son's wife and had stolen her away, and when she'd fought him in the car, the scuffle had caused them to crash. Others asserted that they'd planned their escape together, and it was their lusty fumblings that had them coming unstuck on the road. There were those that maintained he'd lured her into the car, strapped himself in, and deliberately veered off the road, making her death seem an accident. There were so many competing plots and twists. So many unconfirmed sources and personal accounts and neighborhood testimonies. And they wound around each other so tightly, they seemed destined to strangle and obscure the real truth. Nobody ever mentioned Rosie's ruptured side. It seemed consigned to some other history. And the lies and suppositions were just heaped upon the stack. The story became truth. It became stone. And Jack Lionel's portrait was smudged with ink and smeared in shit, and he made no effort to wipe it clean. And so he became the monster and the killer that they all said he was. A low man, a madman. A pariah. The town turned its back. The church no longer held an interest in his soul. And Jack Lionel, who had always enjoyed the solitude of his property, simply pulled further away. He severed himself from Corrigan. He went to other towns for food and supplies. He lived very simply off his war pension; he grew vegetables and raised sheep and cattle until his leg wouldn't allow it. In recent years, he's lived off tinned food and eggs and tea from tin mugs. And the only people he sees from Corrigan are the few children who dare to steal his peaches, and his grandson, who skirted his property for years, taunting his heart.

248    Jack Lionel always thought Jasper ignored him on purpose as a means of shunning him. Some angry, willful act of ignorance. Not for a moment did he consider that Jasper Jones may not have known the truth.

Lionel expected Jasper Jones to have been poisoned with the lie. Planted by his father and fertilized by the town. And so he desperately wanted to invite him inside, to give him the truth, to scratch that word into the air. But Jasper never stopped, he never once paused to listen. And Lionel, too immobile to rush down to meet him and plead his case, was consigned to yelling from his veranda every time Jasper happened by.

All the while, Jasper Jones had no idea why Lionel kept calling his name. But he'd been singled out his whole life, so he paid no attention. Jack Lionel was just some mad old bastard with nothing to say. But I do wonder how it was that Jasper never found out. It made some sense to me that his father never mentioned the old man, but was Jasper so far removed that nobody, not even the most insensitive of children, ever blurted out what they knew?

Perhaps they didn't have a clue either. I certainly didn't. Maybe they were all like me. They just feared the myth of Mad Jack Lionel without properly knowing the nature of the lie that fed into it. But in his living room, watching him smoke and recount his horrible story, it seemed strange that I was ever afraid of him. He looked so small and tired and wretched sitting there, slowly rolling his cigarettes. He just seemed a decent man who'd been beaten.

I couldn't place Jasper's face. I watched him warily while he stood and listened. He rubbed at his hair and kicked his feet and sniffed. He looked at the ground, fists opening and closing, but I didn't get the sense he was moving to strike. I noticed him stealing glances at the photographs on top of the piano. I shrunk back and listened intently.

And I'm not sure why, but when Jasper Jones quietly accepted a cigarette offered by Jack Lionel, at the moment he pressed his lips and sucked at it gratefully, I thought then that he'd abandoned hope of ever discovering who killed Laura Wishart. I thought the game was over. He'd given up.

249

But then Jack Lionel told us what he'd seen that night.

He recalled the evening easily because it was the night before he'd fallen ill with a virus that kept him weak and bedridden for a fortnight. He'd taken notice of the figure outside because it was unusual to see. He knew who passed his property regularly, he knew the familiar patterns. And so when he recognized that young girl, the one he'd so often seen accompanying Jasper, the one he now knew was Laura Wishart, he took notice, because she was walking past alone. And so he'd waited, assuming that Jasper wouldn't be far behind her. Perhaps they'd had a row and she was walking defiantly ahead. Or she was meeting him somewhere. But Jasper didn't show.

Jasper asked if he was sure she was on her own.

Lionel was. But then his brow had creased. And his head tilted. And he told us that although he hadn't seen Jasper with her, he saw that somebody was following behind.

\*\*\*

I'm sitting on my bed with elbows on my knees when there's a soft rapping at my window. I close my eyes and sigh. I don't even turn. It must have been a quick confrontation. Or maybe his father was out drinking. But I'm not even sure if I want to see Jasper again tonight, I'm so sad and tired.

"Charlie!"

I wheel around, hearing the voice. I flip the slats.

Eliza Wishart has come to my window.

She's here. At night. It's really her. I don't say anything. I just open my mouth and then close it.

"What were you doing with Jasper Jones?" she demands. I pause. I don't have an answer. She must have followed me to the station. I should have turned around. I wonder how far she trailed us.

"Oh. Nothing, really. He's just my friend, I guess. I don't know."

Eliza tilts her head in a way that suggests that she knows I'm lying.

"Charlie, why didn't you come back? You said you would. You promised. And I waited for you. You said you would come back!"

I have nothing to say. I can't tell her the truth, and I don't want to lie anymore.

"I'm sorry," I offer. "I really am."

"Charlie, I really need to talk to you."

"I know."

"I mean *now*. Can you come out? It's important."

I can. I'm reasonably certain my dad didn't hear me return. But I hesitate because I'm worried about what I might say. What she might ask.

And then Eliza says something that shakes me down more than anything I've heard since that first night. She feeds her fingers through the louvres and touches my hand. And she says:

"Charlie, I know where Laura is."

\*\*\*

I slip out of the house in a daze and I trudge beside her, racing through a maze of thoughts. I'm heading into the abyss. I haven't mentioned a word of what I know, in case she leads me to someplace different. Is she taking me to Jasper's glade? She must be. But how big a piece of this puzzle does she hold?

If she knows anything about the clearing, about the tree and the rope, then she must have been there on that night. She must know *something* of what happened, or at least how it ended. And has she been there since? What will she do when she finds Laura's no longer there? Should I tell her everything now?

Was Eliza Wishart the figure that Jack Lionel couldn't make out? Was she the one who followed Laura that night?

The town is emptying out. The Sovereign's sprawl has been reined back inside. The band is still playing. The bonfire behind the Miners' Hall is a mound of red embers. Stray dogs circle the carcasses of the roasting sheep, waiting for the coals to cool so they can pick at the bones. Most families have retired, but a few have stayed on to see in the new year. We walk quickly up the center of the main street. I hope I don't see my mother anywhere. The hall is still open, but activity there has slowed. Sure enough, on the front steps someone is getting their burned hand seen to by a nurse.

A few couples are necking down the alley by the hardware store. They must be drunk enough to assume nobody can see them. A large man is throwing up on the edge of the general store's veranda, leaning on a vertical beam and hacking his guts into a drain. It's the sarge.

Eliza takes me past the station. We don't speak, but I know she's upset. I hope she doesn't cry again. The longer we walk, the surer I am of our destination.

We're into the outskirts of town, where it's still and quiet. We move quickly, stepping in rhythm. I don't know how, but our hands have linked up again. We reach the broad banks of the Corrigan River, onto the open lawns past the traffic bridge. I'm still trying to think of things to say, but Eliza seems so resolute I feel I shouldn't interrupt her.

We slip beneath the paperbark trees, which leer and lean, their scabby skins hanging from their limbs. The grass by the river is soft, and little saplings have emerged with the aid of the recent rain. Eliza bends to uproot a cluster of tiny wildflowers. She fiddles with them in her hands.

And then I see our car.

It's parked by the water's edge, under a tree. It's concealed by shadows, but I still recognize it easily. I stop and squint. Eliza tugs at my hand, willing me on, but then she follows my gaze. I frown. And I say it, absently.

"That's our car."

"Really?" Eliza whispers.

I nod and I hold my breath. I'm not sure what to do. After a time, we slowly make our way toward it.

It's a horrible sense of foreboding. It takes me a moment to join the pieces, and then everything makes sense. I swallow hard. The brick drops further than it's ever been. I feel like that man from France I read about who had a syndrome that compelled him to swallow coins. When he died, they discovered that his stomach was packed like a purse, and it was so heavy it had slid to his pelvis.

I know precisely what I'm about to see, but I edge closer anyway. Twigs crackle crisply under my feet. And I'm close enough to see two of them in there. On the backseat. The sheen of pale skin, slipping and dipping between the shadows. Close enough now to touch the back window. Close enough to see my mother grappling and gripping a man I don't recognize. To see them flinch, then freeze at my interruption. To see my mother glaring out the window, her face spreading from pinched anger to wide horror. The scrabble and untangle. I'm numb. I'm watching this unfold right in front of me, but I feel removed from it.

I step back. My mother has awkwardly pulled her dress back on. The man slinks back in the seat. The door yawns open, and I squeeze Eliza's hand.

"Charlie! What are you doing here? You shouldn't *be* here! What are you playing at? Did you *follow* me? You shouldn't be out here! Why aren't you at home?"

She's hysterical and aggressive. Yelling a mile a minute and waving her hands. I wonder how she has the gall to be furious. I can smell sour sweat and liquor from the car, and it disgusts me. My mother's chest is heaving. She's panicking and she's upset and she's drunk. She keeps shrieking her spitfire questions, just filling up this space with her stupid outrage.

The walls might be falling, but I feel calm. I really do. Even when she slams the door and grabs my arms and shakes me free of Eliza Wishart. And I notice that her cotton dress is on backward, and how ugly and old she looks when her makeup is smudged.

She starts to pull me toward the car. Still yelling.

"You're coming home! You shouldn't be out here! Come on! Get in the car!"

I rip my hands from her grasp with an ease that surprises me. My shoulders are squared. I take a step back, and I feel the balance between us shift. I look away from her. I am so ashamed. Not only because she's drunk and barefoot, and not just because I've caught her fooling around with some fat old bastard while my dad is sitting at home, but because all of this has unfolded in front of Eliza Wishart. She's seen it all. I want to cover this scene in a blanket, draw a curtain. I want to push our car into the water.

"No," I say firmly.

"What did you say?"

"I said no."

"How dare you! Don't you talk to me like that, Charles Bucktin. Get in the car! I'm taking you home. You shouldn't be out here."

"And neither should *you*. This"—I point at the backseat of the car—"*this* means I don't have to do what you say anymore."

I step forward. I'm not afraid of her.

"Excuse me? Yes you *do*, young man! Now get in the car. I won't ask you again!"

"No! *You* dug this hole, *you* fill it in. I'm not going with you."

She's lost. She can't win this. She can't win anything anymore.

253

She looks vile and unlovely. Ghostly white against the mottled gray of the paperbarks. I hate her. I hate her like poison right now, but I also feel sorry for her. She looks like a child. Scared and lost and unhappy. Even more so when her mouth turns down at the edges and her face folds and she begins to cry. As suddenly as she'd risen, she's fallen.

"You don't understand," she sobs. "Your father doesn't love me. He never has. You don't know *anything*. You don't know a thing at all."

She's right about that. I don't understand a thing about this world: about people, and why they do the things they do. The more I find out, the more I uncover, the more I know, the less I understand. My mother shakes her head and sniffs. Her hands go limp at her sides. The man in the car doesn't move. He just sits there. All of this is so messy and awful.

I have to leave.

"Go home," I tell her, and I feel powerful saying it. I sound like Jasper Jones. I get a shot of electricity down my spine. "Just go home."

I turn and I take Eliza's hand. I weave our fingers tight and I squeeze hard. I've been betrayed by both my parents in a single night. And I look her up and down, and then leave my mother standing there, her shoulders slumped and shaking. She calls me back, but there's no venom. There's nothing in it anymore. We leave her behind.

I stay quiet as we walk. Distantly, we hear the car cough to a start behind us, fleeing the scene. My mother and her lover. I wonder if she's going back home to confess to my dad. Probably not.

I must be pressing Eliza's hand especially hard, because she wriggles it a little.

"You okay, Charlie?"

I sigh and scratch my scalp with my free hand.

"I don't know, to tell you the truth. I think so. Maybe. I think it's all too crazy for me to feel anything either way."

She nods.

"I think I know how you mean. That was really . . . *strange*. Your *mother*. It's just . . . I never thought she'd be the . . . I'm sorry, Charlie," Eliza says quietly.

And it soothes me. It's as though she can make everything golden with an apology, even though she's a world away from fault.

I kick at the gravel.

We reach Lionel's property. It looks so different. It's such a desolate plot of land to look at now, whereas it used to throb with threat and portent. I wonder if he is watching us go by.

Jasper and I had left his house as abruptly as we'd entered it. After Jasper milked Lionel of all he had seen that night, he pushed off the wall he'd been leaning on. He'd had enough. He slid his bottom jaw from side to side, took one last look at the top of the piano, then strode out of the house. I followed. Neither of us said goodbye, neither of us looked back. I even felt bad for Jack Lionel, leaving him alone like that in his sad little museum.

I know now we're headed for the clearing, but that's where my certainty ends. I don't know what to expect. I don't know what she has to say, what light she has to shine on this dark mess.

The bush doesn't slow her down. We follow the same narrow kangaroo tracks. I take note of the same landmarks. My legs are scratched by shrubs and low scrub. I hope that Eliza knows the way better than I do. I file behind her, our hands still loosely linked. I can still smell her from here. I can breathe her in and it takes me over. I could follow that scent forever.

Still, the creaks and whirrs and clicks around me make my skin tighten. I don't want to be out here. It feels as though I'm inhabited by a teeming metropolis of insects, trailing up and down my limbs and my neck. Burrowing under my skin. And they won't be shuddered off or shucked away.

Eliza Wishart is taking me to the place her sister was killed. My brick is at its lowest. I'm not sure how much more I can absorb tonight.

Here.

Here it is. The broad spine of that enormous jarrah, standing monumental and alone. I'm being pulled into its orbit. We pause here. Eliza's back is to the wattlebush that opens into Jasper's glade. My head is bowed a little, and I watch her carefully. She opens her thin arms and brushes the musky foliage. I am dead on my feet. Heavier than ever.

"You've been here before," she says plainly. It's not an accusation. It's a simple statement.

I nod, but I can't look her in the eye.

Then Eliza Wishart pushes through the bush and disappears like a ghost. I follow slowly.

It's always strange to walk into this space. The air is different. Everything is utterly still and timeless.

But it's strangest tonight, being here with Eliza. Being here without Jasper. It feels like I'm trespassing. It's so hot and quiet and eerie. It's emptier without him in it. I get the sensation we're being watched.

I follow Eliza across the thick lawn to the water. We sit beneath the tree. I'm shaking a little. Directly above me is the space where Laura died. The hole in the world that she fell through. I wonder if Eliza knows that.

We sit in silence for a long time. I'm not sure where to look. The water, Eliza, the glade. There are lies everywhere.

Eventually, Eliza pulls her legs to her chest and rests her chin on her knees. She looks at me.

"We need to tell each other things," she says.

I nod.

"Do you want to go first?" she asks me.

"No. Not really. If that's okay with you."

Eliza seems to nod without moving. Then she removes something from the pocket of her skirt. It's a folded piece of paper. She turns it over in her fingers.

"What's that?" I ask quietly.

"A letter."

"To who?"

"Jasper Jones."

I frown.

"Is it from you?"

"No."

The silence settles again. Eliza slowly unfolds the paper, then folds it again.

"It's from Laura," she says.

"Did she ask you to give it to him?"

Eliza shakes her head and looks away.

"Did you find it?"

She shrugs, still looking over the dam. We fall silent again. Then I ask tentatively, "What does it say?"

She doesn't answer. Doesn't even appear to hear. Instead her face seems to glaze over. She tilts her head, and she turns and speaks with that strange accent again.

"You know those days when you get the Mean Reds?"

"The what?"

Eliza looks at me with mild chagrin, like I'm getting something wrong.

"Like the blues," she says softly.

"Oh," I say. "So you mean, do I get the blues?"

She lifts a little.

"No, the blues are because you're getting fat or it's been raining too much; you're just sad, is all. The Mean Reds are horrible. Suddenly you're afraid and you don't know what you're afraid of. Do you ever get that feeling?"

"Actually, that sounds exactly like what I've had the last few weeks. The Mean Reds."

"Really?" she asks.

"Really. What about you?"

Eliza stares across the dam again. We sit and we listen to the insects.

Then she turns and looks me straight in the eye. She looks older in the starlight, her face drawn and furrowed. She stares at me for an uncomfortably long time. I wonder if I should say something. But then she breaks the silence.

"I did it, Charlie."

"You did what?" I have to hold my arms to stop my hands quivering.

"I killed her. It's all my fault. I killed Laura."

***

This is what Eliza tells me.

This is what happened.

And I've got to get it out quick, I've got to loosen the valve on it and let it go, fizzing and spraying, because it's too hard, it's too heavy, it's too much. I can't hold on to it for too long because it'll burn. Do you understand? It's the knowing. It's always the knowing that's the worst. I wish I didn't have to. I want the stillness back. But I can't. I can't ever get it back. So. Thisiswhathappened. See, Eliza, she knew all about Jasper Jones. She knew he was with her sister. She knew they were in love. And she knew they went someplace together at night. From her own window, right next to Laura's, Eliza could observe Jasper approaching. When he first started coming round, he was cautious. He'd hide in the shadows and wait and move slowly. Toward the end, he got more brazen. He just sidled right up. Tapped on the window. And Eliza could see Laura striding back out with him across their lawn after climbing through her window. It had been happening all year, even on the coldest of Corrigan nights. They'd skip across the frosted grass and leave Eliza behind to wonder and speculate. As the weather warmed, it happened more and more frequently. Recently it got to be almost every night. Eliza always wondered where they went to. She imagined they were going to the river, maybe under the old traffic bridge. She was curious and envious. She longed to follow them, but she knew she shouldn't. It was all so perfectly romantic to her. Like it was from a book or something. A fairy tale. They always stole away in the dead of night, and Laura always returned just before dawn. The

258

shire president's daughter and the town outcast, the dangerous boy all the girls secretly wanted to be with. Sometimes Laura and Jasper embraced tightly before they parted. And he'd wink at her and leave. They seemed to fit so tight and right. But then, near the end of November, as the summer heat crept in, Jasper stopped coming. Eliza wondered if they weren't going steady anymore. It seemed sad that they weren't, though a part of her felt guiltily satisfied that Laura no longer possessed something that she couldn't have. Listen. Thisiswhathappened. Like a geyser. Like a burst dam, I can't hold it. Because Eliza didn't know, never knew, that her father, the shire president, she never knew that he visited Laura's room as well. But he didn't tap politely. He crept in, drunk. Always drunk. Always discreet. There were no locks. It was all in the letter, see? Long before Jasper Jones came to her window. Since she was a girl. Eliza's age. Thisiswhathappened. Like a cork from a bottle. A train with no brakes. On that night, when I'd been reading, something was happening. Building and garnering and gathering. Something was *up*. It had been strange in the Wishart house for days. It had been tense and sullen. A sickness had sunk. Trouble was brewing. Eliza tried to stay out of the way, as she always did when the mood was foul. Her mother seemed the same as ever, serenely unaware. Her father was louder and angrier; his threshold was thinner. He reeked of spirits and tobacco all the time now. And Laura, who had retreated from them so much this year, who never ate anymore, who never talked or laughed with her little sister like she used to, she was more sallow and sapped and silent than ever. It was as though she wasn't even there. A ghost in a haunted house. She only left her bedroom when her chores needed doing. Eliza thought she must have been upset about Jasper Jones, but she couldn't ask about it like she wanted. Thisiswhathappened. On that night, there'd been a big argument. There had been words in the kitchen which Eliza wasn't allowed to hear. She'd been sent to her room. She didn't want to listen anyway. She read on her bed with the cat on her lap. She listened to Ella Fitzgerald and hummed softly. She tried to carve out a little space for

259

herself, a little vacuum away from the world. And there she stayed. But it wasn't thick enough. It was too brittle. Because later that evening there was a scuffle in Laura's room, right next to her, and that's when Eliza became afraid. Head to the wall, she heard voices, but she couldn't make out words. She knew it was Laura and her father in there. The argument had flared again. She could sense movement. She could hear odd squeaks and shifts. Sounds that Eliza translated in her mind as two people grappling. But then Laura began shouting, screaming, which was soon muffled into sounds that made Eliza feel ill. Thishadneverhappened. She heard a crack and a yelp. She felt something through the floorboards. Something smashed against their shared wall and rattled onto the ground. And then the door slammed. Hard, loud as a gunshot. Eliza started. The house shook, do you understand? Flakes of plaster fell from the molding around the light fitting on the ceiling and were cast broadly by the sweeping blades of her fan. Like confetti. Like snow. Footsteps, marching. Then the silence was swift, sweeping in like backwash. She wondered if she was allowed out of her room. She figured she didn't want to go anyway. She was afraid. And where was her mother? Where was she in all this? She heard their car roar to a start, and she opened her curtain to see her father weaving dangerously out of the drive and down the street. Then she could hear Laura crying through the wall that separated them. But still she didn't leave her little bubble. She stayed. Safe. And she didn't stir, though she was restless and confused. She thought Laura would wave her away angrily. And the house was quiet for some time. After the neighborhood lights went out, when folks had retired for the night, Eliza heard the familiar scrape of Laura's window. Up, up, stop. She spilled off her bed and pressed her face to the glass. Laura was leaving, heaving, but she couldn't see Jasper anywhere. Laura was in her nightdress. She was in a hurry. She was alone. But she was barefoot, so she couldn't have been going far. Maybe just to the end of the street. Still, something was wrong. Maybe she was sleepwalking. Beckoned by something behind her eyes. Eliza worried. And it was worry that propelled her out into the hot night, that had her trailing her sister at a safe distance. It was illicit and exciting. She'd never been out this late on her own. Her body was buzzing, her heart was stammering. Things smelled different, felt different. Trees took a ragged shape. Things felt sinister, threatening. Laura was meeting Jasper somewhere, that's what she figured. But what had just happened in her room? What was the ruckus? Why had she been screaming? What was the argument about? Had her father struck Laura? Is that what she'd heard through the wall? Why had he left so quickly, so angrily? Things had been so horrible recently. She'd tried to ignore it all, but it just welled up and took her over. It loomed until it toppled. Now she had to know. If this excursion revealed nothing, she would interrogate her sister tomorrow. She was going to finally find out. Thisiswhathappened. Eliza skipped lightly to keep up, still with the thrill of being out at night for the first time. Laura was moving fast, bent forward, arms folded. And they walked for what seemed an eternity. Laura didn't look back once. All the way through town. Past the station, past the thick end of the Corrigan River by the bridge and the picnic grounds. Right out past the old pastoral properties that kick-started Corrigan waybackwhen. Past Mad Jack Lionel's run-down cottage, which still had its lights on. Eliza shuddered when she realized where she was. She thought seriously about turning back. But she was committed now. More so when they reached the fringe of bush, and when they pressed into the thick of it. She was terrified of losing Laura. She had strayed out of view a number of times, and Eliza had to pause and listen carefully and follow the path with her head bowed. She became annoyed and confused. She was being scratched and rasped by branches and prickles. She regretted her impulse now. Where was she going? Was this where Laura had been going all year? Where was Jasper Jones? Was he at the end of this journey? She didn't know anything. She felt small and out of her depth, like a child. When Laura paused at the foot of that enormous jarrah and smoothly vanished, Eliza felt a sudden chill. She desperately wanted to go back. But Eliza crept around under the wattle bush and hid in the scrub beneath a bottlebrush. She peeled back the foliage to reveal that strange little clearing. And she crouched and watched Laura very carefully, stunned by this place. This must be where they had been coming all this time. It seemed so perfect. It was so beautiful and serene. It felt ethereal. A timeless little bubble in the world. A secret garden. Her sister walked toward the smooth gray eucalypt that presided over the small dam on the far side, and she peered into what appeared to be a broad, hollow space at its base. When she emerged, she surveyed the glade, squinting intently. Eliza shrunk into the shadows and held her breath. But Laura turned and slumped and sat by the water with her head on her knees. Eliza longed to go to her, but she knew she'd be in for it if she did. It looked as though Laura was waiting for someone anyway. For Jasper, she assumed. So she'd probably just disappoint her if she crept out from the trees and revealed herself. Thisiswhathappened. Laura got to her feet and started pacing under the tree. She looked distressed. She tugged at her hair. She examined the hollow another couple of times. She came out with something in her hands. Then she sat. And she cried. She hugged her belly and she rocked herself by the water. It was hard for Eliza to watch. She wanted to run out there and put her arm around her. And she wept herself, very quietly, watching all this unfold. She had to bite her fist. She had to look away. She desperately wanted to know what was wrong, but she was trapped by her own indiscretion. It was so hard being outside of this, watching it like a grainy film. Thisiswhathappened. Laura bowed and concentrated over something in her lap. It looked as though she might be writing. Then she stood with her arms folded and her head bowed. Eliza could see her shoulders shaking. And then she watched her move toward the eucalypt. And with a strength and ease that surprised Eliza, her sister made her way up the trunk, shinnying in parts, using footholds and hoists in others. Flakes of bark were peeled off by her bare feet. Her nightdress hung loose. She paused in places, but she seemed to make her way up easily. It never looked precarious. Eliza was quietly impressed. Even so, it seemed perilously high. Eliza wanted her to come down. In any other circumstance she would have shouted out as much, would have demanded she descend. But Laura sat on a thick bough that reached across the front bank of the water. Eliza thought she might jump in. It looked dangerous. She was uneasy. But Laura looked relaxed up there. Swinging her legs, her hands holding the branch. She sat on the bough for a long time. Eliza's mind wandered. She adjusted her position, got comfortable. She sat cross-legged, rested her chin on her palm. And she waited. Maybe Jasper was on his way. Maybe Laura just wanted someplace quiet to sit. It made sense. She'd had a horrible time. Maybe she just needed to be somewhere peaceful and nice. Her fortress. Her castle keep. Thisiswhathappened. And it was fast. Too fast. Eliza had no time to think, no time to act. Her mind had drifted elsewhere, was too far removed. She was even a little dozy. She hadn't noticed the rope wrapped around the branch. She just saw it as a natural irregularity in the wood, some strange bind of bark. And so she was slightly bemused when it was picked and unwound. Not worried. Not horrified. Quickly, quickly. She was still a little detached when the halo fell, do you understand? Thisiswhathappened. Laura, with her back to her sister, her back to the town, her hands to her throat like her father tightening his necktie. And then she rocked back and fell. Eliza remembered being startled when she didn't hit the ground. It made it so much more sudden, when she locked and jolted and listed and twisted, with a gap between her and the earth. Then silence. White noise. Eliza didn't scream, she didn't run. She froze. Everything stopped. Everything ceased to be. Do you understand? It was a mistake. Surely. It hadn't happened. She'd dreamed it. She'd fallen asleep. She was flinching out of a nightmare. But no. There she was. There she was. No struggle. A heavy bag. Floating. Slowly turning. Until she was still, and then everything rushed inward: Laura was facing Eliza Wishart, who then ran from her hiding space and pulled at her sister until she realized it would do no good. She'd gone. Snuffed like a candle. Laura had just fallen from grace. She'd disappeared. Gulped and swallowed by something enormous and unseen. Eliza panicked. There was something by her

263

feet. A folded piece of paper. She picked it up. Pocketed it. She didn't know what to do. She was shaking, like her limbs were not her own. She was about to sob, about to scream, but she heard someone approaching. She gasped. She ran back to where she'd been hiding. Just in time. She had to bite down hard to stop her teeth chattering. She'd never been so afraid. This was all a horrible mistake. She hugged at herself, dug her nails into her ribs, and she waited. She breathed in quivering beats. She was close to breaking down. And then Jasper Jones appeared. He slipped in through the wattlebush. A couple of yellow baubles nestled in his hair. And he stopped. Eliza watched him, she saw the precise moment he understood. And he issued a ragged animal sound, like a groan. Then he ran straight to Laura, trying to hold her up, trying to take her weight, to give her air. But she was gone. No matter how high he tried to hoist her, no matter how much he yelled and appealed in a desperate voice that raised hackles on Eliza's neck. She watched the messy struggle, breathing a million miles a

264   minute. It was a macabre acrobatic dance. Some horrid gothic circus act. She shuddered. And she would have cried and shrieked and wailed right then and there had Jasper not suddenly recoiled and bolted from the glade. She was alone again. She crept out. She had no choice. She had to follow. She had no other way of getting back. She didn't know where she was. But she didn't want to leave her sister. Eliza Wishart took her last look at Laura and quickly burrowed through the wattlebush. But of course Jasper was moving too fast, too fast. He knew the way too well. He burst along the kangaroo tracks and disappeared. Eliza was lost almost immediately. She stumbled and staggered on, tired and alone. She followed the tracks that looked the most worn, hopelessly lost. But it didn't matter, because of what she'd just seen. Whathadjusthappened. She seemed to be moving deeper into the bush. When Eliza reached the river, a broad vein of something familiar, she was overcome. She dropped to her knees and she wept until she vomited into the stream, and it carried her insides south in ribbons. She cried because she was afraid. It was too early for grief. Too close.

Something had burst in her, leaving a black hole that sucked and swallowed everything into nothingness. She wanted to dive into the water. To sink, swim, be stolen away by the weak current, she didn't care. But she stayed where she was, curled and furled, until the first light bled through the canopy. Then she scrapped on. She followed the river, hoping that it might lead her to town. It did. By the time she reached the old traffic bridge, her nightdress was torn by blackberry bushes and bracken, her legs were etched with red lines. Her feet were sodden. But she made it home before Corrigan awoke, without her sister. Eliza crossed the lawn. Their car was still gone. The lights were out. Birds were trilling a chorus for the sun. And she crawled wearily through her bedroom window, which she'd left open. And she read on her bed with the cat on her lap. She read a letter which was never meant for her. It was for Jasper Jones. It was a messy scrawl, spidery and fast. Small and scratchy. Which broke her heart because Laura had such beautiful, careful handwriting. And it destroyed her, this letter. It finished her off. It was the saddest, angriest constellation of words she'd ever traced with her eyes. Thisiswhathappened. They were planning to leave together, Laura and Jasper. They were going to run away to the city. To start a new life. And they weren't going to tell anybody. And they would never come back. Despite everything, Eliza couldn't help but feel a cold spike of betrayal. This whole other life that she wasn't privy to. This whole other world, this bubble she wasn't allowed inside. But then Jasper Jones vanished. Laura was confused and upset; she thought Jasper had left her behind. While I knew that Jasper had been working the orchards for those two weeks, Laura suspected the worst. That he had abandoned her and fled to the city on his own. That he didn't love her at all. That he'd broken his promise. And all this had been confirmed for her when there were no fresh signs of him in his glade. The fireplace had healed over. The ground in the tree hollow where they slept was undisturbed. Laura had been waiting to see him that night. Had Jasper shown up, she was going to tell him things. Everything. And she was going to beg him to leave with her before dawn. Because she was in Trouble. She had to go. Now. Urgently. She needed him. Because he was the strongest thing in this town. Because she couldn't go alone. Because they were supposed to go together. Because there was something insidious growing inside her. Do you understand? Something was very wrong. A measure of milky poison had caught hold and infected her, and now she was in trouble. She was rotten inside. Something worse than disease. And she had to leave. She didn't know what else to do. She was afraid. And disgraced. Because she'd come out and said it, she finally pointed her finger, all too late, all too late. This was the night she stood up. It was in the letter. She swallowed her shame and she told her mother what had been happening, all this time, under her roof, what it had left her with, the trouble she was in. She told her why she had to steal out as often as she did to see Jasper Jones, even after she was caught and cautioned. Told her why it was she couldn't stand to stay in that house anymore. What evil befell her during the night. What grim and sinister things her room had accommodated. Why it was she had to steal away to where it was safe, more and more, whenever she could. And her mother didn't believe her, can you imagine? Not a word of it. She defended him. She stood there and called Laura a liar. Her own daughter. And him? He sat at the table, quiet and calm. The shire president. And when he burst into her room later, he hissed and he leered and he threatened her. He wasn't even sorry. He had no love in him. And she spat and yelled and flailed her thin arms with all the courage she had left, and he raised his hand and hit her, hard, in the face, which he'd never done. He knocked her down to shut her up. And he swung again, twice, right at the core of her, right where the trouble was. And as she struggled to suck in air, he squeezed her jaw and he warned her, his ugly red face, his rancid medicine breath, he warned her not to say another word. To anybody. He turned to go. As her single last act of defiance, Laura threw her glass paperweight at his back. She missed. It hit the wall and smashed. He slammed the door. That'swhathappened. And she complied. She never did say another word. Her courage was spent. It gave way to dismay. She wrote, though. She wrote plenty. She poured it out for Jasper Jones. She felt abandoned and heartbroken and bitter and ruined. It was as though she wanted him to hurt like she was hurting. There was nothing left in this world for her. And then she fell back from the bough, like a diver on the edge of a boat, paper in her fist. She killed two birds with one stone. When she left her room, she knew it was for the last time, one way or another. That'swhathappened. It's out. It's out.

***

Eliza reads me the letter in that curious accent, without flinching. As though the story isn't hers and the words have no meaning. As though it concerns people she doesn't care about, fictional people she's never met. Like it's a dream she's just woken from. The missing pages are in place. Eliza Wishart has cleaned this mess with one swipe, but there's no joy in what's left. Just the sadness of knowing.

It's awful. It's mystifying and it's tragic, but it makes more sense to me than condemning Jack Lionel or some other shifty figure. It feels like truth. Laura really could make her own way here, she really could climb that tree. Her father put those marks on her face; he put the fear and the poison in her belly. Despair had her clad in nightclothes and no footwear. And everything else conspired to make her fall.

Her father started it, Laura ended it, and now Eliza is fielding the blame because she saw it happen. I feel so bad for her. I can't imagine what it has been like, holding it in all this time.

Laura Wishart wasn't kidnapped by Mad Jack Lionel. But it seems she was snatched away by something infinitely more sinister and terrifying. By the same thing that had us pursuing Lionel in the first place. The same thing that's thieved my appetite and kept me awake and has me shying away from dragonflies. The thing that makes this town so quick to close in on itself and point its finger, that had it closing its doors and calling its children inside. She just couldn't hold on anymore. She had no one to shield her from it.

I sit and look up at the bough where Laura sat. And a cold part of me is suddenly furious at Eliza for taking that letter. I think about how different everything would have been if it had found Jasper's hands that night. I would have been free of all this. I would have stayed safe in my room. I might have read for a little longer. Then I would have slept like I used to. I would have woken as I normally would have. None the wiser. Much the lighter. I'd never have known Jasper Jones, I'd never have shared his story, I'd never have known this awful brick in my stomach. Misery and melancholy and terror would just be words I knew, like all those gemstones I collected in my suitcase that I never knew a thing about. I'd never have been haunted by Laura Wishart. I'd never have helped shackle her body to a stone, and I'd never have swallowed that rock's weight in sadness. I'd never have had such a secret to guard. I'd never have been burdened with all this stupid guilt. *Sorry sorry sorry.* We wouldn't have accused a lonely old man of murder. I'd never have read those horrible things that people do to each other. I'd never have caught my mother out, I'd never have *known.* And I'd be free to hold the hand of Eliza Wishart without fearing that it might be the last time.

Still, perhaps it was best the letter didn't reach Jasper Jones. I don't know what he would have done, but I doubt it would have been *my* window he visited. My guess is that he'd have marched straight to her old man. And there's no telling what he might have done once he got there. Maybe that's what Laura wanted. To her mind, they'd both betrayed her terribly.

It's futile anyway, that kind of thinking. I can't blame Eliza for picking up that packet of answers any more than I can rebuke Jasper Jones for arriving a few minutes too late. If Jasper had been there that night, Laura would still be here today. She'd still be alive.

But I am afraid of what Jasper's response will be when he learns this. That he really *could* have stopped her. He'll never forgive himself now. It makes me want to conceal the truth from him. To bury it, drown it; to let him believe some other history.

Eliza leans forward.

"Now it's your turn. You have to tell me things, Charlie."

"Like what?"

"Like how you know Jasper Jones. How come you were here with him."

"How did you know I've been here?"

"Because I was leaving here one night and I heard someone coming just as I made it to the road. And it was the both of you. You were on your way here with Jasper."

"You came back here?"

"Yeah."

"How did you find it again, this place?"

"I just remembered somehow. I couldn't forget it. And it's straightforward enough, if you follow the path and don't panic."

I'm silent for a moment, then I look past her to the tree.

"It was you who carved that word," I say.

She looks behind her, and nods.

"I used a church key from inside the hollow of the tree. I came back here to see Laura. After all the patrols and the searches had died down a bit, and after my mother stopped checking my room every half hour, I snuck out. I *had* to come see her again. I had to say some things to her. I don't know what I was expecting, Charlie, but I didn't think she'd be missing."

269

I feel her looking at me. I can't meet her eye.

"What did Jasper do with her?" she asks. "Do you know? Where is she?"

I look at my feet and bite my lip. The creeping curse. It's tempting to absolve myself entirely. I could drop Jasper right in it and run away, make him the scapegoat again. I could erase myself from the whole story, free myself from involvement and wrongdoing. Wash my hands of the whole thing. She would never have to know; she'd have no reason to hate me.

But I can't. I can't do it. I can't keep it in. And I know I'm breaking a promise by talking about it, but it's swelled and welled in me for so long. It's out. It's out. I point at the dam.

"She's in there. She's at the bottom."

"In *there?*"

"Yeah."

"He threw her in the *water?*"

I almost bite my lip clean through.

"We both did. We both did it. I was here too. He brought me back here that same night. The night that Laura . . . I'm so sorry. I'm sorry."

"You came here that *night?* Charlie, you *knew?* And you did that?" She points at the dam.

I nod. "Jasper came to my window after he left here. I'd never even spoken to him before. He said he needed my help. I didn't know a thing, honest. I just followed him here. And then I saw her. I saw Laura. The same way you saw her."

"You *knew?* You knew this whole time?"

I nod again. I feel like shit, but the sickness is shifting.

"I saw her up there, and it was horrible. It was the most horrible thing I've ever seen in my life. And Jasper didn't know what to do. He wouldn't believe for a moment that she might have done it herself. He was convinced it was someone else, because of Laura's face and how her dress was torn and how she had scratches and no shoes. And he didn't think that she could climb that high to get the rope, or even make her own way here. I don't know. It seems so *stupid* now. But we really believed, you know, that someone had brought her here and done this to her. And Jasper was scared because this is *his* place, and if they found her here as she was, they'd say it was him. They'd lock him up for it without asking questions. And so he said we had to hide her. To give us enough time to work out what happened. And so he climbed up there and cut her down. And we tied her to a stone. And . . ."

I shake my head. Eliza doesn't speak.

"Please don't hate me," I say quietly. I'm contorting my hands, like I'm trying to twist them off my wrists.

"Why didn't you say anything to me? That *really* hurts, Charlie."

I hold out my hands.

"I couldn't. I wanted to, I really did. But I made a promise to Jasper.

270

And I didn't know what you knew. I didn't know what you would do if I told you. If you'd have told me all this weeks ago . . ." I trail off.

The silence settles again. I pick at the grass, keep my head down. Eliza remains level and calm. I feel so tired.

"Why did Jasper stop seeing my sister? Did he not love her anymore?"

"No. No, it wasn't that. He still loved her. Very much. Jasper was down south. Picking peaches. He was getting some money together for when they left, enough to get them started. That's what he told me. He got back that night with all his savings. He went straight to your house, but Laura wasn't in her room," I tell her.

"And then he came here. Too late."

I nod.

Shit luck and chance. It doesn't seem fair. Laura Wishart did nothing wrong. She didn't do a thing to deserve this. And the two people who loved her the most are hurting the worst and harboring the most blame, for something they could never have known. And the monster who put the flint and force to this tinder just reels in the pity of this whole town. It's not right.

271

"Why did you scratch that word into the tree?" I ask Eliza.

"Because it's my fault, Charlie."

"It's not your fault."

"It is. I could have stopped her. I should have said something, I should have jumped out and told her to get down. But I didn't *do* anything. I sat and just watched it happen because I was scared. I killed her, Charlie. It's like if you just watch someone drown from the shore without swimming out to help them. That's what I did. It's my fault."

"It wasn't your fault."

"It *was*. You weren't here. I had all this time to say something, and I didn't. I just sat here. And then it happened. And she was gone. Just like that. And I didn't do anything."

"But you didn't *know* what would happen. You didn't know anybody was drowning. You couldn't have known."

"Maybe. But I'm sorry. I just am. I feel terribly and I miss her and I want to talk to her and I feel miserable. I feel awful and rotten inside. I can't even *breathe* properly anymore. And I'm just . . . *sorry*." Eliza shakes her head, holds a hand to her chest.

"I'm sorry too," I say. "For everything. For what we did. I don't know. I know it was the wrong thing to do, but Jasper has this way of pulling you in. I didn't want him to get into trouble. And he would have, too. He really would."

"It's all right, Charlie. I understand, I think. It doesn't matter anyway. Laura's gone. She died. And I don't hate you. I'm upset you didn't say anything, but I don't hate you. In a funny way, though, it almost makes me feel a bit better knowing that you saw it. That you might know how I feel better than anyone."

"I think I might," I say.

"Do you care about me, Charlie?"

"I do," I say eagerly. "Very much."

She smiles flatly and her dimples bud briefly. I blush a little. She pats the grass next to her, an invitation for me to sit closer. I do. Our legs are touching. She leans forward. I lean back and look up.

"Why didn't *you* say anything?" I blurt out suddenly. "Why didn't you come forward? Through all the searches and the curfews and the newspaper reports, everything. You had Laura's letter. You knew where she was, you knew what had happened. You could have stopped everything. You could have ended the whole thing in a day."

"I was frightened," she says quietly.

"Of what?" I say.

Eliza shrugs and leans further forward. Smooths her palms down her shins.

"Of your dad?" I ask.

She stays quiet. This seems to confirm it.

I wrestle with my next question. I sigh and tug at my ear.

"Has he? I mean, did he ever . . . ?"

"No. No, he hasn't," she interrupts, firm. "And he won't. Ever. What a bloody *creep*. What a . . ."

She suddenly shudders and shakes her head quickly, as if to shatter her thoughts back into brittle pieces.

Eliza stands up and shakes the grass from her dress. She turns and offers me her hand. I take it, and she hoists me up. We stand very close to each other. She seems to glaze over, like she's turned into somebody else.

"Do you know how to waltz, Charlie?"

That curious accent has returned. She holds my shoulder and my hand, placing my palm on her hip.

"No," I say, looking down at my feet. "I have no idea how to waltz. I dance like a penguin. I just sort of waddle from side to side."

To my surprise, she rears her head back and laughs theatrically. I have to clutch the small of her back in case she falls. She keeps her smile, and I forget everything for a moment. Eliza takes her hand from my shoulder and playfully pinches my nose.

"You know what's going to happen to you? I'm going to march you to the zoo and feed you to the yak!"

"The yak?"

"The yak."

"I didn't think yaks were that fierce," I say as we sway on our feet.

"Oh, how wrong you are."

I smirk to myself and rest my chin on the top of her head. I'm glad we're dancing, strangely as it's come about. It's so nice being able to hold her, to smell her. To move to some absent rhythm.

I feel as though there is some kind of warm spotlight on us, and within this bright circle everything can be all right. I close my eyes and the spotlight stays with me, and it lances into my Manhattan ballroom scene. It settles on me and stays loyal. The presentations are over. The prize was for my father. Their praise was never for me. But here's the rub: I've got the girl. I've got her like a skipping ball in a roulette wheel finds its fated number, held there still and safe while the world spins. And we move within this bright sphere like a single thing. People have stopped and they're watching. They form a ring around us, admiring

273

how perfectly we move, how graceful our steps are. And I don't care for prizes or praise, because I've got the girl and that's all that matters.

The bubble breaks when I notice Eliza humming. I open my eyes, back to the gray glade. We're barely moving now, just shifting our weight in time, lightly stamping the grass beneath our feet.

"Do you ever think of leaving here? Leaving Corrigan?" I murmur.

She nods her head slowly and sighs.

"All the time. I don't want to be here anymore. I hate this town."

"Well, maybe we could leave together. With Jasper, when he goes. Which might be soon. I mean, maybe we could go as well. The three of us."

Eliza stops moving. She stands very still, but she doesn't pull away.

"Do you mean that? You would do it? You would leave Corrigan?"

"Maybe," I say. "If you wanted to. I would leave with you."

She pulls back and holds my shoulders. Her eyes are searching mine.

274

"Do you *really* mean that?" she demands of me.

"I do. I mean it. I really do."

"If I wanted to leave, you would promise to come with me?"

I nod, and give a short smile.

She holds my eye a little longer and then lays her face back into my chest and clutches me tightly to her, tugging the front of my shirt. She holds me like that for a long time. I'm unsure where to put my hands. So I run them through her hair. I kiss the barrette in her hair. And I think she begins to cry. She's shaking softly. Not for the first time, I'm lost for words. But maybe they're not necessary. I seem destined never to have the right words in me. But maybe I don't need to. Maybe that's it. Maybe it's better I stay quiet. Maybe just gently rubbing her shoulder blades is infinitely more useful than saying something right and trite, or reciting some stupid poem. Maybe I'm finally doing the right thing.

We stand like this for a long time. Eliza begins to breathe evenly again. I listen to the clicks and shifts of the bush, like small detonations in the stillness, and I don't fret. Everything is dislodged, everything is free of its mooring. But I don't want to think of anything other than how pleasant Eliza Wishart's hair smells, how warm her body is. I don't want to let anything else in. Which seems easy enough to accomplish in this little patch of earth. It's so private and sovereign here, so timeless and hushed and sheltered, it's easy to forget the cold inclemency you've stumbled in from.

It's leaving that seems the hard part. Heading back into it. Which Laura couldn't do. She couldn't ever go back, so she made sure she stayed.

Eliza breaks away. She takes my hand and she leads me toward the tree. She ducks and kneels at the hollow. Curiously, I've never seen inside it until now. Jasper has made it his own. He's carved shelves into its walls, where he keeps all manner of items. Tins, tinder, cooking utensils, enamel mugs and plates, cards, pencils, tobacco, tea and sugar. There's even a little Spanish guitar hanging from a railway nail high above me.

275

She crawls inside, still holding my hand. I follow, feeling as though I'm encroaching. Like I'm stealing a space that isn't mine.

Eliza lies down. I do the same. We huddle together. I'm anxious and stiff, but Eliza wriggles her way into a comfortable position. She puts a hand on my chest and leans her head on my shoulder, and she whispers:

"Let's don't say another word. Go to sleep."

I frown. Sleeping is the last thing I'm capable of. And, in a way, I don't want to slow the whirring in my mind, lest I have to really consider all that's come and all that's coming. I don't want to think about what we do now. Laura's letter, Eliza's account. Surely that clears Jasper Jones. But if we come forward with all this, what will happen to me? What will happen to Eliza? Will Jasper keep his word and keep me safe? Will Eliza even talk? And what might it visit upon her father if she did?

And what if we stayed silent? What if this place kept its horrible secret at the bottom of its deep well? And if we walked away with it, kept it locked up? If we never breathed a word, would anything change? The mystery would evolve into a pile of lies that are bound to become truth anyway. And nobody would ever be burdened by the knowing.

What would my father have done? Or Mark Twain? Or Atticus Finch? It's likely they wouldn't be in this mess. But I'm not them. I'm an idiot. And a child. And I've done this all so very, very wrong.

I must have slipped away for a time, because I jolt awake upon hearing footsteps. Eliza is heavy on my arm. She doesn't stir. But I freeze as a shadow is cast over us.

"Jasper?" I whisper.

"*Charlie?* What is *she* doing here? What have you done? What have you said?"

Eliza starts. She grips my arm and shunts back, kicking her feet. Something drops from the shelf and clatters. A fishing lantern. Jasper shows a palm and tells her to calm down. I feel like I've been caught out. Jasper looks hostile.

I emerge from the hollow.

"You broke your promise," Jasper says plainly, standing over me.

I'm about to respond when Eliza steps out and interjects.

"No he didn't. *I* brought him here."

"*You?* Bullshit. How?"

"Jasper, she knows some things," I say.

"Things? What *things*? What have you tole her, Charlie?" His lower jaw juts out.

"Not from me," I say, my hand on my heart. "She knows, Jasper. What happened. She *knows*."

"What, and you dint tell her nuthin?" He regards Eliza edgily.

"Well, no. I didn't have to."

Jasper takes a step back, still looking at Eliza, more uncertain now. "What d'you mean? What does this mean? Why is she here, Charlie? You shouldn't've brought her here."

"You're not listening," Eliza says. "He didn't bring me here. I know the way. I've been here before. I followed you."

"*Follered* me? When?" Jasper looks suspicious; he glances from her to me. My heart has kick-started and it's revving hard. It's all about to come out again. I'm afraid of what Jasper might do. Eliza reaches into her shallow pocket. She extends her hand. Blankly, she tells Jasper that she's sorry. She took something that wasn't hers. It was meant for his eyes.

Jasper shifts his weight from side to side, like a boxer. He looks at the square of paper, but he does not take it.

"What is it?"

"It's a letter. From Laura."

He kicks his chin up and folds his arms.

"What does it say? I can't read it. It's too dark."

I stay quiet. I glance at Eliza. She looks the strongest here by far. She holds his eye. She takes a breath. She keeps the paper closed. And she tells Jasper Jones all that she told me. It's worse knowing what's coming, knowing how it ends.

And Eliza doesn't curb her bitterness. She doesn't conceal a thing. It's clear she's still angry at Jasper Jones, despite what I said to exonerate him. But she spills it all, down to Laura's feelings of hurt and betrayal. Jasper stands and receives it, still and quiet.

He doesn't react, not a flicker or a twitch, until Eliza recounts that horrible moment when Laura swayed back and fell. Then he moves. He shuffles, he slopes back. And his shoulders, broad for so long, they dip and round, and he cups his mouth and his nose, like he's caught a sneeze, and he just slowly backs away, clearing his throat and groaning, staring at Eliza Wishart. I watch him the way you would a cornered animal. I can't help but crouch slightly. And then he bursts. Snaps like a trap. He breaks out and I flinch as he runs past us both and dives straight into the waterhole with a sharp crash and he disappears, leaving nothing but ripples.

Eliza and I are motionless. We watch the surface grow smooth. He

277

hasn't come back up. What is he doing? How deep is he digging? He's not coming up, he's not coming up. For a moment, I think of him tying his own leg to that rope and I panic. What has he done? I look at Eliza. Then back to the water. Frantic, I tear out of my shirt and I shuck off my shoes and I drop my glasses. The ground is cool as I cross it, and I dive into the darkness, I follow Jasper Jones. I kick and I flail, carving my arms into the murky water, but I'm getting nowhere. I can't see. My air is spent. Just as I wriggle to ascend, I am clubbed in the jaw by something unseen. I thrash at it, afraid. But it grips me by the arms and drags me up with it. And when we get to the surface, Jasper Jones gags and gasps for air and he holds me to him, hard. We clutch each other, kicking under the surface, churning at the water. I cough hard, hoarse and ratchety. Jasper tugs hard at the hair at the back of my head, grabs it in his fist and pulls my head toward him so forcefully I think he's trying to drown me. And he bites down on my shoulder and I dig my nails into his slick back. And I know him. I *know* him, and it's the saddest thing of all. As the lost boy who has lost everything. And as much as I was always aware that he was Randall McMurphy and I was every bleating, frightened barnacle that clung to him for their share of counterfeit boldness, I know now that he needed me in this too. Not because I'm smart or reliable or loyal or good, but because he needed someone, anyone, so he didn't have to be alone with it. He sought me out, he came to my window that night, because he was shit-scared and he didn't have a clue what to do. That's all. I think he saw my lamplight and he was drawn to it like an insect to a bulb. He had to share it, to spill some of it over with someone he felt he could trust. He couldn't hold it alone, he couldn't go through it alone. He couldn't drown Laura alone, couldn't face Jack Lionel alone.

And if Jasper Jones is just as scared as the rest of us, I wonder if I'll ever be without fear. But then I think of Jeffrey Lu, and our discussion about Batman, and the light that Mark Twain had shone upon it. Maybe it's not about being without it. Maybe it's about how well you walk with the weight. It makes sense to me now. That's what courage is. Bruce Wayne is still afraid, but he gets it done, because he's bloody Batman. But for the rest of us, it's working out an honest way, that's the trick.

But how? How to balance it all out, between the blues and the Mean Reds? See, it seems to me there's a familiar fork: you can either learn about things and be sad and restless, or you can put your head in the sand and be afraid. But maybe that's where Eliza Wishart comes in, to level it all out with love. And look. She's here, now, standing on the edge of the dam.

My legs are tired as we kick toward the tree. I feel like I've swallowed my own weight in water. Wordlessly, Jasper hoists himself out, then reaches for me. I take his hand, and we stand dripping and heaving. My body made of sticks and stilts, his carved out of wood. I bow and squint for my glasses. And when I rise, we all line the edge of the dam and look down at it.

"She's down there forever," says Eliza.

***

Later, we lie on our backs and stare at the stars. Jasper props his head up on a raised root and sucks a cigarette. He found some matches in the hollow. His chest rises and falls like clockwork. Eliza rests her head on my stomach.

It's strange, the three of us being together like this. There's a lot to say, but it somehow seems the wrong time to say it. I want to ask Jasper how he went talking with his father, if Lionel's story was true, what really happened with his mother. But it seems wrong to do so in front of Eliza Wishart. Likewise, I want to strum my thumb gently down Eliza's cheek, and maybe swipe the hair that has escaped from her clip away from her eyes, but it seems too private a gesture.

Still, if we're to leave this town behind, it'll be the three of us bound tightly together. We'd have to make it work somehow. I turn to Jasper.

"Listen, Jasper. When you leave Corrigan, I think we're going to come with you. I think we're going to leave too."

Jasper at first appears not to hear, but he sits up just as I'm about to repeat it. He speaks levelly. He sounds tired.

"You're gonna what?"

"We're going to leave here as well. Me and Eliza. With you. I don't know. To the city, maybe. Or wherever. We'll work something out. We could do it. I know we could."

"You two? Shit, Charlie, you're both out of your minds. There's no way that could happen. I don't even know where to start. You're not thinkin."

"Why not? Why couldn't we leave too?" Piqued, I prop myself on my elbow, disturbing Eliza. Jasper grinds his cigarette into the dirt and pockets it. He lights another, taking his time.

"Mate, consider it. If the two of you left suddenly, without tellin anybody, what d'you reckon would happen? You saw what happened with Laura: the police, the patrols, the news, all that. You don't reckon the circus will be back in town? And it'll be even worse if it's the *both* of you. They'll drag your arses back here before you're even out of the shire. And if you're with *me*? Shit. They'll probably do me with kidnappin."

"Okay, but . . ."

Jasper holds up a finger.

"And that's assuming you doan tell anyone you're leavin, of course. Because if you do, I'll wager neither of you have a chance in hell of being let out by your folks. Specially you." He nods at Eliza.

"Well, what about you, then?" I ask him.

"Me? What about me?" Jasper scoffs.

"If you just up and left? What do *you* think would happen?"

Jasper smiles and takes a long draft of his smoke.

"Charlie, you'll see what happens when I go. Just wait and see. Trust me."

"What? What will happen?"

"Just trust me. You'll know what I mean. Charlie, you need to unnerstand, this is something that *I* got to do. Not you. And it's nuthin personal. It's just not the right idea, mate. You should stay. Both of you should stay here. I'm sorry."

And like that, I've been dismissed. I feel faintly foolish and humiliated, maybe even a little betrayed. I thought we were friends. Partners.

Eliza touches my arm.

"Charlie, he's right."

I glance at her and frown.

"We can't leave here, you and I."

"But I thought you wanted to," I say.

She sighs. "I just wanted to know that you *would* go with me. That's all. That's enough. But we can't do it. Not yet, anyway."

I nod, slowly, and look away. Silence falls again. I hadn't realized how much I had riding on getting out of Corrigan. It seemed to screw a lid on so many problems, and the thought of staying makes me suddenly very anxious. I feel as though this is all in my lap, and it shouldn't be. Jasper shouldn't be allowed to leave this bag of bricks with me.

"So what do we do now? Now that we know everything? What happens?"

Jasper tugs at his ear.

"I dunno, Charlie. I really don't. Leave it with me. I'm thinkin on it. I'll come up with somethin."

Eliza sits up and picks at the grass.

"I'm going to tell them," she says.

Jasper sits up.

"Tell who?"

"Everyone," she says. "The police. The town. Everyone. It's the right thing. People are still out looking for her, and they're getting colder and colder. Because she's here, she's at the bottom of this water hole. We know the truth."

"And what are you going to say?" Jasper's voice is unsteady.

"The truth! I'm going to tell them all the truth!"

Jasper closes his eyes. He looks resigned.

"You can't do that," I say.

281

"I have to! Why not?"

"Because it'll all have been for nothing. Because you can't *do* what he's done. What *we* have done. You can't throw bodies in the water. They'll lock him up. They'll put him away, that's why."

"So?" Eliza says, defiant. I stare at her.

"What are you saying?" I ask.

"I'm saying I have to do the right thing, Charlie."

"But how is that right? This isn't his fault, and you want him to get punished for it. And me too. You understand that, don't you? If you tell them everything, it means I'm in serious trouble. I was *here*. I did the same thing as Jasper. And you. You'll be right in it as well."

"I won't tell them about you," Eliza says quietly. I sigh.

"Then that's not the truth, is it? And if you can do that for me, if you can leave me out, then you can do the same for Jasper."

Of course, I'm asking her to lie. I'm asking her to pull a blanket over parts of this story. To comb it over, to change its color and complexion. Just so I can stay clean. So Jasper Jones can be given a reprieve. I'm asking her to keep her sister hidden. And I feel terrible. But what's right and just and true here, anyway?

I don't know.

But I also have a suspicion that Eliza might be less concerned with what's right, less concerned about uncovering the truth, than she is about ensuring that she and Jasper Jones, and maybe her father too, are meted out the penance that she feels they each deserve. I think she wants to do something with all this blame and hurt. I think she just wants to tie rocks to all their feet.

Eliza doesn't respond. She continues to uproot blades of grass and tear at them.

"You blame Jasper, don't you?" I say quietly.

She shrugs. I shake my head.

"It's *not* his fault. Or yours. How could it be? Listen, you don't know him like I do. Like Laura did. And I've told you where he was for that fortnight he went missing. You *know* what happened that night.

You saw it. And all he ever tried to do was the right thing. I think you want to get him into trouble, you want to burden him and make him hurt like Laura wanted. And I think you want the same thing for yourself. But the difference is, you know better."

Eliza cuts her eyes and looks away.

Jasper stands. He looks spent. He turns to Eliza, but doesn't look her in the eye.

"Listen, you do you what you reckon is right. That's all."

He offers a slim shrug my way, then shuffles into his hollow and lies down. He doesn't make another sound.

Drowsily, I notice faint slivers of blue light bleeding into the trees. We should head back. But I'm so tired and heavy, and there's nothing but trouble to return to anyway. Almost involuntarily, I rest my head on the ground. Eliza crawls over and weaves herself into my arms. I'm still damp from the dam, but she doesn't mind. She smells so good. I hold her tightly to me. And she nods. Slowly. But it's there. Her nose brushes up and down my neck. And then sleep comes. And it's dead and dreamless, like it hasn't been for weeks.

283

*** 

Jasper Jones shakes us awake.

"C'mon. We should go," he says.

It takes me a long time to understand where I am and why I'm here. I have insect bites on my legs, and my arm is heavy and prickly from where Eliza rested her head. Last night's events drip into my mind like syrup, a series of flickering scenes that shackle me with a dreadful disbelief.

I stand unsteadily. It's hot already. It must be late morning. The glade feels so different in the light of day. It feels barren and ominously calm. Gone is the sense of embrace, the warmth from the walls.

I shuffle to the dam and cup some water into my mouth. It fills my belly but does little for my thirst. Eliza and Jasper stand silently apart. I can hear birds trilling from miles away. Nobody speaks.

We trudge along the trail in single file. Jasper, then Eliza, then me.

I wonder what they're thinking. I try to crawl into their heads, work through their worries. It makes it easier for me to postpone my own. All that's waiting for me at home.

The least of my concerns is being caught sneaking out again, given that my mother resigned all her punitive powers in the back of our car last night. And I have a feeling my father will have weightier problems on his mind. Oh, there's a shitstorm brewing. That's for certain. And I've got to walk back into it. I scratch the underside of my arm. My rash looks red and angry. The bush is a secret switchboard of clicks and busy buzzing, and I'm heading back into the hornet's nest. I know the sad truth. About everything. Jasper, Laura, my mother. It's all come to light, it's all been bared, and it's bowed my shoulders so much I'm too tired to be afraid anymore.

I want to lie back down with Eliza. I want to take small hits of whiskey with Jasper Jones, even just to tip the bottle to my shut lips to pretend I'm sucking it down with him. I want to accept his cigarettes and talk about how broad the world is and how small we are and how easy it is to flip that around just by being bold and living big. I want it to be that easy. I want him to fill my chest with bluster, like he's giving me the kiss of life, and I want to use that air to say wise and comforting things to Eliza Wishart for as long as she'll let me.

284

We stay in the same formation even when we reach the road. I guess everyone's alone with their thoughts. We walk like we're soldiers carrying packs on our backs.

Curiously, we stop outside Jack Lionel's gate. Eliza frowns and flaps away a fly. Jasper rests his thumb on the latch and scratches the back of his head. He looks over at the cottage.

"This is me right here. I reckon I'm gonna go in. I need to talk to the old man again. See what's true and what isn't. I got to see it all with my own eyes again."

I nod.

"You two keep on. But go the long way, less you wanna get picked up. They're probably lookin for you orready."

JASPER JONES

Eliza tilts her head.

"Wait, you're going in *there*? Why? Do you know whose house that is?"

"I do now."

Eliza shakes her head, bemused.

"Listen," I say. "Did you get to talk to your . . ."

"Nah," Jasper says. "He weren't even there. Skipped town again, looks like. He dint even unpack his bag. I got no idea where he's gone to. No clue."

"So why did he come back?"

"Buggered if I know."

Jasper shrugs. We linger there. He pushes at the gate and it squeals like a siren. We watch it swing and settle. Then he marches toward me. Jasper Jones puts his hand on my shoulder and looks me straight in the eye. He holds my gaze so that I can't glance away. He smells of tobacco and sweat.

"Thank you, Charlie."

285

"That's all right." I blush.

He shoves his hand into his pocket for a cigarette. He lights up and regards Eliza with narrow eyes. And he apologizes to her again, under his breath, but it's full of meaning, you can tell. Then Jasper Jones shakes my hand. Firmly. And he winks at me.

"Take care," he mutters with his cigarette between his lips.

It's all he says. Then he turns. I clean the chalky pollen off my lenses, and over Jasper's shoulder I see that Lionel is waiting on his veranda. He's wearing navy shorts and a white tank top. His back is straight.

"Is that Mad Jack Lionel?" Eliza asks.

"The very same," I say. And I watch Jasper crunch down the gravel drive, his open hand trailing the heads of thigh-high weeds, sending seeds into the air. And I can't help feeling it's the last time I'll ever see him.

\*\*\*

From the low moist grasslands, where the shoulder of the river curls in toward town, under the paperbarks where my mother turned her back on my father and me, we can see cars swooshing by through the trees. We only see the white sparks where the sun catches their windows, but it still strikes me as more traffic than I'd expect for New Year's Day.

As we pause at the junction that leads to the bridge, a rusted blue truck sidles up to us slowly and then idles beside us. Its driver reaches past his dog to wind his passenger window down. He nods once at Eliza.

"You Pete Wishart's girl?"

Eliza shakes her head and says no. The man and his dog eye her suspiciously.

"Righto," the man says, and pulls his car into gear. "Keep lookin, though, you two. She'll turn up."

He winks and sputters away, leaving a noxious cloud of diesel. I place a hand on Eliza's shoulder.

286

"We need to keep our heads down. We'll keep to the shade and go round the oval," I say, but she doesn't appear to hear, or care. She seems unperturbed.

In fact, she barely reacts when a horn blasts behind us minutes later and a hoarse voice splits the morning.

"Oi! You two! Git ere! *Now!*"

I wheel around. My heart sinks. It's the sarge. And he doesn't look impressed. He leaves the truck running and steps out. He looks haggard and hungover and pissed.

He points at me, then stabs his finger toward the ground.

"Get in. *Now.*"

I touch Eliza's arm. It's over. We comply.

I sit in the backseat while the sarge dresses us down, his mustache twitching and his red eyes wild. Eliza looks blankly out the window.

"Jesus bloody *Christ*. Do you have any idea what kind of mess you kids have brewed up for me this morning? I got city patrols on their way, I got volunteers giving up their holiday time, coppers from other shires coming in. I'm calling in favors, and for what, missy? Your bloody mother is beside herself. D'you understand?"

His voice rises steadily. The back of his cab smells of grease and alcohol and dirt. I stay quiet, posting my hands between my knees.

"It's not bloody good enough, is it? What were you *thinking*, leaving the house without telling your mum and dad? Now, I don't give a rat's arse what you two have been up to, but that's not on. Not after what you've all bin through. Eh? Can you imagine your mother this morning, finding your room empty? *I* can, because I was over there within the hour, tryin to calm her down, which isn't easy when her eldest daughter is still out there missing. I would think you'd know better. *Both* of youse! Are you listening to me?" He spits out the window and glowers and shakes his head to himself.

We arrive at the station. The gravel car park is full. We lurch out of the car. The sarge leads Eliza to the entrance with his hand on her back. She still hasn't murmured a word. I walk behind. When we reach the mesh door, the sarge leads Eliza in. She disappears. I hear a chorus of voices. I don't want them to take her. I move to go inside, but I'm barred by a bearlike forearm. The sarge turns to address me.

He looms over me. "Piss off home. This is your last warning. You fuck me about one more time, you'll wish you hadn't. Do I make myself clear? You're lucky you've got a head on your shoulders as it is. One more episode like this and you'll be too scared to wipe your arse after I'm finished with you. Understand?"

I nod readily. I do understand. I feel the weight of his threat, I get a real feel for what he's capable of.

I don't leave, though. Besides not wishing to go home just yet, I feel the need to stay for Eliza. I sit in the sun, chasing away my thoughts. I absorb myself in picking up cigarette ends, cleaning up the front garden. I don't even notice the bees scouting the bottlebrush. I wish Jeffrey was here.

By the middle of the afternoon, I am oily and dirty and thirsty. My tongue has cultivated a fur coat. My worry compounds. I wonder what she's saying in there, how much she's telling them, how heavy the interrogation is. Perhaps it's dangerous for me to be here. What if they're drawing up my arrest warrant? What if they're already out, looking for Jasper Jones? I hid a body. I did that. Perhaps I should turn myself in before they have a chance to take me. I'll tell them everything and beg for clemency.

I don't know.

But there she is. Eliza Wishart. Free to go. Being led out of the station by her parents. One on either side. Her mother is red-faced with distress; her father looks pale. Eliza walks solemnly. I try to catch her eye, but she doesn't give it to me until she's lowering her head into their car. And I think she offers me a whisper of a smile, but I can't be sure. Either way, it does very little to assuage my worry.

They drive away, kicking up a plume of dust. I watch them pass. I'm about to topple over. I spend a long time considering the entrance of the police station, then I decide to head home. I want to swim in the river and not come out. I want a lychee drink and a stupid hypothetical.

I shuffle past the school oval, and I notice those kids I'd seen a couple of weeks ago have finally got their ragged kite going. I stop to stare at it.

It's easy to imagine it as a circling bird up there. As though they've tied a long string to the foot of a hovering hawk, keeping it on a thin leash to feel what it is to fly. And you want to let it higher, you want to spool out your line and hold it, just for the thrill, to see how far it goes. But once it's out of view, you want it back again, don't you? Because you're still stuck down here and you can't follow it. But it's nice to know that you had enough weight to hold it down, to keep it grounded so you could admire it for a time. Like something precious that you can pull out and look at. A piece of jewelry. A poem, a song. And you want to tie it to something permanent, put it in a cage at night. Have it for keeps, despite its nature. Like people who put rings on their fingers just so neither of them can leave. But of course you can't do that.

Holding something doesn't make it yours. You realize at some point you're just keeping it back for yourself, because it's pulling away with equal force. You've got to cut the string from your finger and leave that wispy thread, like a baby spider on the breeze.

I look away, and I lock my eyes shut for a long time, concentrating, the way you do when there's a sneeze gathering in you. But my throat caves in on itself and my mouth turns down. And I hurry home before anybody sees me cry.

289

# 8

I don't leave Corrigan. I don't steal away in the night with Eliza Wishart or Jasper Jones. There's no leaping into boxcars, no thumbs out on barren roads. No bindles or sleeping rough under a blanket of galaxy. I stay right where I am.

But my mother leaves.

She left that night. She packed her things and she drove out, our car fishtailing wildly down the street, our curious neighbors forming a loose guard of honor on their lawns. They heard it all unfold. And within hours, the whole town would know everything. In an instant she'd stripped her name of whatever careful varnish she'd glossed it with for so many years. In a single scene she revealed herself, ugly and loud and mean. And they heard it all.

She left that night, but not before she'd ranted and raged. Not before she'd picked a fight and, like always, didn't get one back. My father just let her go. It was like yelling at a statue. He let her scream and holler, let her beat at him and weep. He didn't give her comfort, nor did he give in to any anger.

She left, but not before she tore into my room, hoping I'd be there. She tipped things, stripped things, tore things. Threw and broke things. She found my father's manuscript on my desk and ripped it apart. Cast it across the room. She left, but not before finding my suitcase and unlatching it. The only time I've left it unlocked. She emptied its contents on my bed, sifted through those treasured sheets, searching in vain for her name. And she dragged that empty suitcase to her vanity table. She stole it from me, but she had nothing precious of her own to pack in it. She just shoved in her clothes, her jewelry, her perfumes. She snatched the keys from where they'd skittered after she'd thrown them at my father. And she announced her intentions with our front door open. She finally told my father what she thought. No more threadbare hints or poor metaphors. She finally said what she'd been meaning to say.

Of course, it came as no surprise to my father. He knew she was miserable here, he even knew the company she'd been keeping. He knew all her little secrets, the holes she'd dug for herself. I'm not sure when it was he realized. Perhaps he knew all along. Though I often wonder why he kept it to himself, why he let it go on. Perhaps he thought it made her happy. Or maybe it was easier for him to shrug and sweep it under the rug and pretend otherwise. Or maybe it was to save me the grief. Maybe he wanted to shelter me from the disruption and hurt. I don't know. Maybe he hoped she'd stop of her own volition. That she'd see sense and admit her wrongdoing and they'd mend back to new. Or maybe he still believed in the commitment, the sanctity, of loyalty, so he stood firm even while she strayed away and made a cuckold of him.

I don't know.

But he didn't intervene as she dragged my suitcase out to the car. He didn't implore her to stay. He stood on our veranda and coolly observed. He let her go. He cut the string on his finger. And he watched her weave away and leave for good. She was free of every bind; she had severed ties with the town she hated from the moment she arrived.

And she hasn't once returned. Not in two weeks. She's moved to the city to be cosseted by her family. She's back to being the spoiled girl. They've given her a house all to herself, full of furniture and trinkets and paintings and a cleaner that visits on Fridays. Maybe she thought we might follow her, that we'd call her bluff.

She's spoken to my father only once since that night, on the telephone. She said she wasn't coming back. He said he didn't ask her to. He did urge her to talk to me, try to put things right. But she declined. She didn't say why. Maybe she's too ashamed. Or maybe it's all a part of her being liberated. She's cut me loose too. A whole fistful of kites left on their own to spread in the sky.

So it's strange at home now. I waver between wishing her back because something familiar seems missing, and getting to like this new arrangement with my dad. We're both learning to fend for ourselves. Of course, my dad can't cook worth shit, so I've picked up the slack. Cooking is conducting, knowing when each piece comes in and how strong. It's all about timing. And I enjoy it. I really do.

And it turns out my dad quite enjoys keeping things neat and clean, so he takes care of the dishes and dust and clothes. He likes the simple satisfaction in wiping things away, restoring them to freshness.

I was never aware that his comb-over hadn't been his idea. Within days of my mother leaving, he'd trimmed his hair short and let his scalp shine free. He's even growing a stately beard. He looks like a dignitary, a man of influence and sway. Jeffrey says he looks like a communist.

He's yet to hear from any publishers, though he assures me that these things take time. Of course, he had another copy in his desk drawer, so all my mother destroyed was my chance to read his novel straightaway. I finished *Patterson's Curse* a couple of days ago. I took my time. Pored over it, taking little portions and chewing over them, savoring the taste.

It is so smart and sad and beautiful that I'm not even jealous. And I have a warm feeling in my belly that says someone important is going to believe in it. That one day soon I'll see my father's name on a straight spine on a bookstore shelf, standing proud and strong and bright.

***

Eliza Wishart didn't say a word to the police. Not a single one. But it was clear to them, as it had been to me, that she held an important piece of the puzzle. She knew *something*. So they pressed her for hours. But she just sat in that station and fiddled with her hair clasp and she shrugged, with her lips tight. She stayed firm when they plied her with sweets and lemonade and spoke soothingly; even firmer when they threatened her, when they hissed in her ear and told her she was betraying the people she loved.

When they arrived home, there was no punishment. They didn't even ask where she'd been.

It was after her father left for the Sovereign that she finally spoke. Eliza made a pot of tea and sat her brittle mother down. In her room she'd made a copy of Laura's letter, and she slid it across the table. And she told her that Laura's Trouble was never a lie, it was hideously true. She told her she followed Laura out that night, but she didn't say where. And she told her she crouched and hid in this secret place and watched her sister. She told her that she knew where Laura was now. And she was never coming back because she took her own life in this place. Two lives. Another one that sat inside her like a barnacle. And her mother leaned forward and held the back of her head and silently wept while the sun bled away and their tea went cold. And Eliza offered her neither comfort nor love, because this woman had betrayed her eldest daughter. She turned her back to the truth and now Laura was gone.

But Eliza promised this: if her mother wished to come forward, to declare what was true and see that things were put right, then she'd take her to the place where Laura lay. Until that day, she vowed to stay quiet.

293

So far, neither of them has spoken. The secret has stayed with the Wisharts, sealed shut in a jar, locked in a dusty cupboard. And Eliza thinks that's where it will always stay. Once, I asked Eliza if she wanted to see her father punished. She narrowed her eyes and softly assured me: he'd get his. And that's all she said on it.

I've been seeing a lot of Eliza Wishart. She retreated a little these past couple of weeks, but she's coming back. She's getting some meat back on her bones. As am I, slowly.

She and I, we go to the glade in the dead of night, like Jasper and Laura before us. I've devised a route to her window that means I'm unlikely to get caught. It's the next best thing to digging a tunnel under Corrigan all the way to her street. I tap the glass with my knuckle like I always dreamed of doing, and she swipes the curtain back, pleased to see me. She even has sunflowers on the windowsill.

And we walk together, hand in hand, to that island in the bush, and it no longer feels like we're trespassing. Sometimes Eliza takes flowers and sits by the water's edge with her legs crossed, and I stand apart while she whispers things. Sometimes she brings her sister gifts and she drops them to the bottom like a wishing well. Sometimes she gets quiet and hard and it's best for me to leave her be. Sometimes we muck about, we giggle and dance and have fun. We don't ever swim in the dam. We lie down and drink in the stars and talk about books and cities and things that are important to us. The things we wish for. Who we want to be. I confide in her. I tell her about my father's novel. I even sneak her a copy of the manuscript, which she reads in a single day, and we get giddy over the parts we liked. We talk about how famous he'll be, how one day I might have a book that sits next to his on the shelf.

We sleep in the tree hollow, snug and safe. Eliza and I hold on to each other the same way you'd cling to a lamppost during a blizzard. I put my hand on her hummingbird heart and see that it settles.

294 And we kiss as we lie under the thick tent of that eucalypt. I'm not even nervous anymore. It's the nicest thing in the world. I press my mouth to her neck and I breathe her in and our hands go places. I touch her belly, her ribs, and the warm thrill of her breasts. I was wrong to ever declare there is nothing softer than a girl's lips.

It's our secret. And this one is worth keeping. And I don't feel the need to share or shuck it. This one keeps me light. In a way, this secret has helped untie the knot of the other ones. The hushed stuff in our chests seems to hum and dissolve when we press our hearts together. I look forward to seeing her so much.

Visiting the glade has softened our talk about leaving; it's leached the urgency right out of it. We're mostly wistful and wishful now. We may not have high tea at the Plaza, but billy tea in Jasper's glade is just as nice.

Every so often, when she's particularly low or sad, or thinking on horrible things, that curious accent of hers returns. But I think I understand it now. I've seen the film. I know the flippant and frivolous manner, the snips of scenes. The Golightly voice, it's a wily vice. Eliza WishArt. So I don't ever say anything. I let it pass.

But mostly, Jasper's glade fills our lungs and settles us down. And it feels like love. It really does. It seems to mirror everything I've read about it. And if it's not, then it must be awfully close. I want to ask her to marry me. I don't want anybody else. She's the finest thing in this town. And I don't want to be without her. She's the single sliver of something good that I've got to hold in my hand. And I want to wrap it around my finger and make a ring out of it. One day, when I've got enough courage in me, I'll tell her. I'll say all the right words. And she might even say them back.

# 9

oday is the first day back at school. As expected, the summer's events are foremost on everyone's minds and mouths. The disappearance of Laura Wishart is gossiped about for hours, with the abduction of the Beaumont kids in Adelaide just a few days ago giving the mystery fresh ingredients. Nobody is safe anymore. The air drones with the murmurs of rumors.

The girls cluster and hush when Eliza appears. The boys jostle and grin and elbow each other.

Jasper Jones doesn't turn up late to tick off his name for the football team.

Jeffrey Lu has become something of a minor celebrity, which he doesn't mind at all. Upon receiving his first snippets of praise, he spends most of the morning reliving his heroic stand to anyone who will listen, mapping out his feats with ball-by-ball emphasis and more than a little liberty with the truth.

The day is strange. I feel as though everything has changed, and yet nothing really has. Warwick Trent is even back in uniform. After a lazy summer of booze and depravity, he failed to secure an apprenticeship but managed to knock up Sharon Noonan. So, bereft of options, he's returned to haunt the halls.

And it's this, the reemergence of Warwick Trent, that is the reason I find myself walking to Jack Lionel's property right now, with a coterie of classmates in tow. The final bell has gone. It's hot and dry. And I've made a wager with Warwick Trent.

If I walk to the peach tree of Mad Jack Lionel this very afternoon, in broad daylight, and steal more than four of his peaches, I will be granted immunity for a full school year. This permits me freedom from beatings and assorted tortures, even casual derision. No matter how deep I delve into my vocabulary, no matter how far I goad, no matter how tempting it is to mention my mother, because everybody knew by now. I will have immunity. Also, Jeffrey Lu gets to play the remainder of the cricket season, and not as twelfth man either. He is also permitted to open the batting and to bowl in at least one fixture.

Trent is convinced I'll never do it. He thinks I'll be crippled by fear as soon as I'm there. He doesn't believe I'll even make it over the grid past the front gate, where so many have tried and failed.

I've agreed to an inhumanly cruel punishment should I fail, because I know I can deliver what I've promised. Should I somehow return with anything less than five peaches, my fate is clear and devastating. Not only do I consign myself to being this year's targeted pariah, but Warwick and his coterie promise to strip me naked and chain me to the door of the Miners' Hall overnight, not without first pelting me with eggs, flour, sugar, and water. In short, I'm promised a few hours of pain and shame followed by a lifetime of humiliating reminders.

It's a done deal. Hands have been shaken. Witnesses have nodded sagely.

There must be two dozen kids who have mustered and clustered after the bell for the journey to Mad Jack Lionel's. I'm fairly certain they've all lined up to delight in my failure, but there's a ripple of underdog hope among them: I might be the one to stick it to Warwick Trent.

I walk calmly across the oval, with Jeffrey Lu beside me. Right now I feel like Clark Kent in a gunfight. I've got nothing to lose. I feel invincible, because I'm concealing something powerful. I'm finally holding the aces.

Eliza Wishart intersects the crowd. I long to lean in to kiss her, but I can't in front of everyone. She pulls me aside.

"So it's true?"

"Yeah. I guess." I smile and shrug.

She doesn't smile back. She looks pale and distant. I touch her hand. She stops walking.

"Are you going to come?" I ask.

"No. I can't. I've got to be somewhere."

"Where?"

"Just somewhere." She looks over my shoulder.

"Will I see you tonight?"

She shifts her eyes to mine.

"I don't know. Maybe. You might see me before then."

"What? Where?"

"You'll see."

I frown and take her arm.

"I'll see what?"

She wriggles away.

"I've got to go, Charlie. I'll see you soon."

And she strides off alone, leaving her two friends behind. Too fast and sure for me to pull or call her back. Something is wrong. I want to follow her, but I'm trapped in this procession.

Jeffrey sidles over to my side. He sighs.

"Dames," he says, shaking his head. "Hell hath no fury like a woman's corn. They'll never understand, Chuck."

"I think it's me that'll never understand."

"I'm happy to concede that, because you're an idiot. But the finest minds in the world still have no idea what women are about, so you're in good company."

"I don't know, my company seems fairly poor."

"So what's your plan?" Jeffrey asks anxiously as we turn and catch up to the pack.

"What do you mean?"

"Exactly that. What's your plan? You must have a plan. How are you going to infiltrate the premises? Are you going round the back? Have you set some kind of trap that I don't know about? A pit? Have you dug a pit? Or created a diversion? Have you rigged up explosives? Are you concealing a weapon?"

"I wish I was, Jeffrey, but not to use on Jack Lionel. You're out of your mind. Explosives? Of course not. There is no plan, other than a brisk stroll up his driveway to take five pieces of fruit and then to walk calmly back."

"Simple as that."

"That's right."

"*Charles*, you are batshit in*sane*. You'll die. You'll be *mauled*, you fucking lunatic. He probably has, I don't know, *tigers*. Or he's developed some new savage species of hybrid animal like Doctor Moreau. Like a shark with crocodile legs. He'll probably come at you with a cutlass."

"Jeffrey, he's not a pirate."

"And neither are you."

"What?"

"Exactly. Listen, you don't steal the peaches of a communist psychopath. It's Golden Rule Number One. Understand? And if you do, if you're foolhardy enough to attempt such a thing, then you devise a fucking plan that ensures you're not disemboweled by his bear-wolves or whatever. You're in trouble, Charlie. This is worse than I thought. You're not equipped. You don't even have a basic understanding of martial arts."

"I won't need martial arts."

"You *always* need martial arts, dickhead. That's the point. If you want to be brave, you've got to be smart and you've got to be prepared and you've got to *know* shit. Okay. Look. We don't have much time. I'm going to mentor you as best I can. Here's an infallible move, should you encounter an adversary. Are you listening?"

"No."

"Good. Now. This will save your life one day. It's the easiest move in the book. It's called the Monkey Steals the Peach. Honest. It's appropriate, right?"

"Jeffrey, you're making this up."

"I'm not! Okay. What you do, if you're attacked, is, you drop down on one knee and you slap your assailant fair in the jaffas with

299

an open palm, like an uppercut, or an angry lawn bowler, and then you grab hold and rip the shit out of those peaches. Bang. Fight over. I'm serious, Chuck. People outside the martial arts community say it's a cowardly act to go at the crackers. I say it's smart." Jeffrey taps his head.

"Well, *I* say it won't be necessary. I'm picking peaches from his tree, not between his legs. It will be fine. Trust me."

"Cheeses *Christ*, Chuck! What is the *matter* with you? The man is a *mentalist*. Your head's in the sand. You're like a fucking . . . *ostridge*. You're *king* of the fucking ostridges. This is *dangerous*, don't you understand? Don't do it, retard. It's not worth it."

"It *is* worth it."

"How?"

"It just is."

"Don't *do* it."

"I'm *doing* it!"

300   Jeffrey tugs at his ear and shakes his head.

"Fuck it. Then let me come with you. If we go down, we go down together."

"Jeffrey, no."

"I will, Chuck. I'll do it. I'll go in with you," he says resolutely.

He really would, too. Even though Jeffrey Lu doesn't know what I know. I have no reason to be afraid, but he does. He's as transfixed by the myth of Jack Lionel as anyone in this town, yet he's willing to put that aside to see me through safely. He's the bravest person I'll ever know.

"You don't need to, Jeffrey. Really. Besides, I'll lose the bet if you come with me."

"You'll lose more than that if I *don't*. Charles, you're not *equipped*."

"I'm equipped. Trust me, I'm equipped."

"No, you're *ignorant*, remember? You don't know the first thing about combat. You couldn't hit the ground if you fell over. And yet here you are, staging a peach mission with no preparation or reconnaissance, with no fundamental understanding of martial arts and no fucking *plan*. You need me with you. You'll never make it otherwise."

"You can't come with me, Jeffrey."

"Well, *shit*. Then lie back and think of England, Chuck Bucktin, because you're about to get *fucked*, one way or another. It's been nice knowing you, at times. I may have mentioned this before, but this time I *really* mean it: you're an idiot."

I put my hand on his shoulder and squeeze it.

"Jeffrey, you're the best friend I'll ever have. You're like a brother to me. You should know that."

"What? Why are you suddenly queer?"

"Because I love you, little man. And this is something I have to do. Understand? And trust me, it's going to be the most straightforward thing in the world. Everyone in this town is going to see that there's nothing to be afraid of. And then we'll get the spoils."

He shakes his head in resignation and mild disgust. After a little while, he asks:

301

"Can I have a peach pit, if you get one?"

"Jeffrey, you can have them all. You deserve them."

We trudge the rest of the way in silence.

At Lionel's, they gather in an arc around the front gate. Some kids even hang back across the road, keeping their distance. It's tense. Warwick Trent sneers at me and smiles as though his point is already proven.

"Well? Go on, dipshit," he says, motioning his head toward the cottage. "We dint come here for nuthin."

They expect me to prevaricate. To shiver and shake as I survey the scruffy landscape and haunted architecture. They think I'll back away and say I can't do it. There's a sense of fascination and foreboding among this group. All eyes are on me, on what I'll do. But I've been inside. I know the truth. And so I look Warwick Trent square in the eyes, and I unhook the latch on the gate and give it a single shove. I step over the grate. I think about turning and saying something pithy or profound, but I don't. I pause and straighten my back and stare straight ahead.

"He's shitting himself," I hear someone say. They're probably surprised I've made it this far.

I stride down the driveway. Completely in the open. I take no shelter in the weeds. I don't crouch or step lightly. I walk up like no peach thief before me. Brazen. Bold as brass. I'm making history. I hear that same voice behind me suggest that I'm going to get myself killed, and I grin to myself as the cottage opens itself up fully and I take in the peach tree and the veranda, the rusted shell of the car out past the corrugated-iron shed and the chicken coop.

I'm so far inside that I can't hear them, or even feel their presence anymore. And even though I know I'm under no threat, it's still an eerie and intimidating pilgrimage. I start to tread lighter as I get closer. So much so that if Lionel were to come out now, he'd have every reason to be suspicious. I wonder if he's watching me. I hear the short clicks of crickets, little shifts in the grass. I breathe deep.

302

I stomp a path out of the tall grass and make it to the tall, gnarly reach of the peach tree. It smells sweet and musty. But upon looking up into its foliage, my heart sinks and dread spreads. There's not one peach to be picked. It's barren. The season is finished. Of course. *Shit.* Which means I am too. Maybe Warwick Trent knew. Maybe that's why he was so smug and confident. I edge closer, peering into the higher branches, hoping to sight a cluster of late bloomers that might have held on over Christmas. But there's no deep orange, no blush of crimson. I'm in trouble.

I'm fixed so fiercely on the tree that I don't notice Jack Lionel's shadow filling the open window of his living room. He bends and peers out. I'm startled to hear his voice.

"Charlie! How goes it, my boy?"

I jump back. My limbs huddle together.

"Mr. Lionel. Hello. Sorry. I'm sorry."

"Call me Jack, call me Jack." He waves his hand, smiling. "You won't find any good 'uns this late, I'm afraid, mate. Last of em fell about a fortnight ago, I reckon. Too many to pick this year, plus I bin ill, so I just let em fall."

I look down. There's a lumpy carpet of decaying peaches at my feet. It's a windfall, but it does very little to dissolve my worry. Because hovering above them are dozens and dozens of insects. Mostly bees. I follow their flight, and see a hive under a gutter on the house. There are black ants running trails, slaters and worms burrowing into the soft flesh. March flies and blowflies and houseflies. It's the stuff of nightmares. I go stiff and cold. This is no longer straightforward. I shudder and step back. I need to piss.

Lionel props his elbows on the window frame and moves to lean forward through the windowsill, but I stop him before he's visible.

"No! Stay there: they'll see you," I hiss, holding my hand up, still looking down.

"Who?"

"Kids from school," I whisper loudly. "They're watching me. I can't explain now. But I can't let them see that I know you. Jack, I need to take some of these peaches. Is that orright?"

"Be my guest, son," Jack laughs from inside. "You want a satchel, or a paper bag? Or I got a bucket in the laundry. What are you kids up to? Making a pig trap, are youse? They love my peaches, those bastards. Come right up to the house. You hear em rummagin about of a night, drives me spare."

"No. No bags. Thank you, though."

"Suit yerself. But take what you like, mate. They're all yours."

I look down. My breath is short. There's a teeming metropolis of insects down there. It's worse than An Lu's garden, but I don't have Jeffrey here to retrieve the ball. My skin tightens. I feel as though I'm already covered in them. Like they're crawling all over my body, scratching and slithering. I clasp my hands together and grind my palms.

"There's a lot of bees," I say.

Jack Lionel lights a cigarette and shake his head.

"Ah, pay em no mind. They're next to harmless anyway. Look at em. They're half pissed. All over the shop."

"Really?"

"Yair, look at em. Near useless. The fruit's gone rotten and fermented in the heat. So them bees are lickered up to the eyebrows. They won't bother you, mate. Nuthin to be worried about."

"Are you sure?"

"Sure as eggs is eggs."

I stare at the ground. He may be right. They do look sluggish. Dissolute and clumsy. Maybe they really are drunk. Either way, I have no choice. I've got to get brave.

I realize too that I've been standing here too long. This hasn't gone the way I'd imagined. This scene lacks the arrogant ease, the casual swagger that I'd hoped for. And I worry that they're lined up back there, ready to accuse me of being a coward anyway, with an armful of shitty-looking rotten peaches. They'll wonder why I paused for so long after seeing no signs of danger. Or maybe they'll suspect me of knowing something they didn't. Maybe they'll think Lionel wasn't even home, and that I knew all along.

I glance up and beyond him, into his dim living room, right up on the wall, and I think I know what to do. I see a way to immortalize this. I seek out his eye.

"Listen, Jack. I need a little favor. How'd you like me to come round and cook you Sunday dinner?"

He lights up.

*** 

It's destined to become the stuff of legend, and only Jack Lionel and I will ever know the truth. No doubt the tale will grow taller and fatter with age. The events will grow grander and broader and more daring; the story will go its own way, and with it my name. It'll harden into common myth. But what no spectator that day will ever know, or anyone who will later lend their ear to an account, is that it requires more courage for me to tentatively bend and snatch up that rotten fruit from amid that sea of bees. My hands tremble. I can barely work my fingers. But I get them, all five of them, into the crook of my arm, hot and soft and mushy, and it feels incredible, like something has clicked into place, like how you feel when you can finally ride a bike or you trust yourself to swim in the deepest part of the river. I hold them against my thrumming chest. I get brave.

And I turn to leave, to stride victoriously back to the gate and the waiting crowd. But suddenly Jack Lionel bursts through his screen door, hollering to high heaven and waving that big empty rifle like the madman they all believe him to be. I can hear the consternation from the group on the road. Erupting in a single chorus. And I can hear Jeffrey Lu above them all, shrill and panicked, telling me to look out. I turn. I drop my peaches. And I run at Jack Lionel, meeting him on the edge of his veranda, swift and sure, and snatch his rifle with one heroic swipe. It's heavier than I imagined. I throw it aside and I push him in the chest and he grins and winks at me as he staggers back and falls, like I'd shot him in the heart on the set of a Western. It's good theater. And I stand over him, pointing, gesturing furtively as he crawls back, but all I really say is: *Thanks, Jack. I'll see you on Sunday.* And he chuckles and pretends to roll in agony and he farewells me with a single nod.

305

I gather up the fruit, which now has a pelt of dust, and I hurry down the drive. I try to act tough, breathing heavily with my shoulders squared, as though I'd really just been in a scrap and emerged victorious. Jeffrey Lu meets me halfway. He'd run in as soon as he'd seen Lionel, but stopped dead after he'd seen me smite him with that single shove. He can't stand still.

"Holy *shit*! Holy shit! *Chuck!* Holy shit! You killed him!" His eyes are wild. His voice squeaks.

"I didn't kill him, dickhead," I announce calmly. "I just pushed him over. He'll be okay."

"Fucking hell, Chuck! He just came right at you! With a fucking *gun*! That was incredible. Holy shit! Holy *shit*! You should be dead! I don't believe it! I do *not*!"

We walk side by side. And I am met at first with silence and awe. But then they close in. There are exclamations of wonder and shock. Someone independently verifies that I have won the bet, but the story is bigger than that now. I'd been attacked by the man they loved to fear, and they'd seen him in the flesh for the first time. Better yet, they'd seen him just as angry and murderous as they'd been led to believe. They'd had the myth confirmed. It was true. And I'd beat him down. Without a moment of hesitation. I slew the dragon. I was the hero.

The huddle presses closer. Younger kids touch the peaches racked in my arm as though they are round bars of bullion. The rest of them are like a press pack, hounding me for information. What does he look like up close? Does he have a long scar down his face? A tattoo of a skull on his arm?

In truth, it isn't nearly as satisfying as I thought it would be. I finally have a peach, but my victory feels a little hollow. Still, there is real fulfillment in seeing Warwick Trent hang back with his arms folded. He doesn't say a single word. I've beaten him.

And the peaches do feel good. I'm proud to be clutching them, because I know what it took, and it felt as though a weight had shifted as soon as I had them in my hands. I decide to save one pit just for myself, just one single stone to keep for this whole horrid summer. And maybe one for Eliza. Then I'll give the rest to Jeffrey.

The crowd presses for a little while longer before my moment is interrupted by a kid on the edge who suddenly points back toward town and says, simply:

"Look."

We all fall silent and lift our eyes. There is trouble.

A pillar of smoke, dense and dark. A volcano is erupting. It is distant, but not too distant. It looks to be perilously close to the town center. And there is a moment where we all quietly take it in, that single column, climbing and writhing straight up. There isn't a breath of wind. And we pay it due regard. This is a dark spirit with substance. Everyone in Corrigan knows there is something real here, that this is something to truly be afraid of, that this kind of smoke holds fire at its heart.

I squint and try to work out exactly where it is, wondering what could have gone up so quickly. Then I drop the fruit from my arms and I run.

***

I've got a stitch. A jagged piece of iron digging into my side. I try not to picture my muscles tearing away from the bone with every jolt of my feet. I'm hurting, but I keep running anyway, with all the panicked energy of foreboding, close enough now to smell the smoke in the air, close enough to hear the peal of sirens. I hope I'm wrong. Oh God. Oh Jesus Christ, I hope I'm wrong. I'm out of breath, I'm spent, but I will myself further. Past the river, the bridge, the station; through town; past the Miners' Hall, my worry bubbling closer and closer to the surface. My shirt sticks to my chest, and sweat rolls and drips off my jaw. My breathing is raspy and thin. I can't go much further.

I jolt heavily down the slope of the oval, and in the distance I see people moving toward the fire; judging by its location, my suspicions are all but confirmed and my legs almost buckle then and there. But I have to press on. Across the grass, onto the street. My steps are messy now, my arms flailing like they've got no bones. I can hear voices and commotion. I'm on her street now. The peppermint trees cast their umbrella arms. And it's chaos. It's madness. I bolt up the path. I see an ambulance and my throat goes thick. A single fire truck is angled across Eliza's front lawn. Neighbors spray the street with their garden hoses. A chain of folks are passing tin buckets of water to the scene. Less helpful onlookers are being pushed back. And I sprint to meet them, writhing my way to the fore. And there, right in front of me, the Wishart house is crackling furiously from the inside. It's a single box of flames. Ribbons of red and orange lick at broken windows. But

307

they seem to have it contained. It's stifling and hard to breathe. I can't believe it. I am yelled at by a bearded man dressed in khaki, but I stand my ground, scanning the crowd. It's a wall of heat. I have to squint through the smoke to see. But there she is! *There!* Fucking hell, oh God, there she is, and I almost collapse because she's all right. I'm dragged back by somebody who clumps past me toward the blaze. He says something stern over his shoulder, but I don't hear. Eliza stands with her back straight, alongside her mother, who is weeping into a handkerchief. I watch as Mrs. Wishart darts brief glances up at her house, then crumples, turning her face away. Eliza looks on dispassionately, as though it's someone else's home.

And there's the shire president, lying flat on the lawn, attended by ambulance officers. It's clear he's been saved from the house. He has a ventilator mask strapped over his face. I watch as they carefully sit him up. He rests his arms on his knees. There's a bandage covering his right leg. His hair is askew, he has no shirt on. His belly is like a ball. His skin is grimy and sweaty. Someone asks him something and he shakes his head weakly.

There's a loud explosion, and the crowd gasps. I hear the shattering of glass. Everyone flinches except Eliza. The volunteers bark instructions and they move more urgently. More people have turned up to lend a hand or observe. Some are poised like matadors with wet blankets should spot fires erupt, praying the wind doesn't pick up.

My eyes water and I cough into my armpit. It's getting harder to breathe. The sky is red and peppered with flakes of ash. The antipodean snow dome.

I wipe my eyes with my shirt and look back to Eliza Wishart, trying to catch her gaze. But she just stares on ahead. I can't place her face. A lady offers her water and some kind words, but she ignores them, shrugging her hand off her shoulder.

And for some reason I'm reminded of Eric Cooke, haggard and angry, at the moment they finally asked him the question. *I just wanted to hurt somebody,* he replied. But that was never the whole story, was

308

it? Only he could have known that, and he held his secrets tight in his fist, in his chest. And there's always more to know. Always. The mystery just gets covered in history. Or is it the other way around? It gets wrested and wrapped in some other riddle. And I think of Jenny Likens, who also watched her sister die, who said nothing until the end, who got brave too late. Who must have seethed and stung every single day afterward, whose heart must have been crippled worse than her legs, who must have wanted to scratch and burn that word into her own skin like a tattoo. *Sorry*. And I don't doubt she would have wanted to see that horrible house consumed in flames, exorcised and razed, maybe with Gertrude Baniszewski still inside.

The flames are all but tamed in an hour or so. The house is gutted, the roof has collapsed. It's an empty black shell. The smoke thins and the Corrigan dusk is an otherwordly crimson. It feels as though half the town is here. Eliza hasn't moved. She stands alone. Her father has been ferried away by the ambulance. Her mother is being consoled by a group of ladies who crowd her tightly and issue tissues and concern.

The people behind me start murmuring about how it might have started. Stove tops, gas leaks, faulty wires, open hearths, cigarettes. Each one skimmed over and considered with a nod. No one casts even a cursory glance at the hardfaced girl standing on her own, staring at the remains of her house without shock or sorrow.

And then somebody says it, like I knew they would. And they talk about the post office, like I knew they would. And of course it's given more credence than it could possibly deserve. When I hear his name, there's that lump in my throat again and a tug at my raw chest. It makes me want to break down, it really does.

Because I know the truth. I know the exact moment Jasper Jones left Corrigan behind for good. It was a couple of weeks ago. I was on the street, bowling to Jeffrey, walking back to my mark in the dry heat. And I'm not sure how, but I stopped and looked up and knew at that moment that he'd gone. It was confirmed for me later that night, when

I found a bottle of whiskey, a pack of smokes, and a fountain pen on my windowsill. But at that moment, I *felt* him go. I *knew*. And I surveyed the silent street, the ordered lawns and shut doors and the sun shimmering white off windscreens, where the only sound was the cacophony of insects. No spotter planes. No searches. Nothing stirred. Jasper Jones fell out of the world and nobody noticed. Nobody cared. And I understood. I knew just what he'd meant that night. And I had to shut my eyes fast before Jeffrey could see.

And they'll notice now, because something has been burned. Now they'll look for Jasper Jones. But, like Laura Wishart, they'll never find him. He's too smart and too fast for them. He's too clever and canny.

I turn my back and walk away from them. I cross the grass to Eliza, who swivels upon my approach and crimps her lips into a short sad smile as I place my hand on her shoulder. I've finally got the right words in me. And I lean in and whisper them in her ear as flakes of ash settle around us.

# ACKNOWLEDGMENTS

Team Silvey is blessed with a wonderful, loyal, and largely unrewarded membership. So, as a shabby recompense, here's an earnest and loving salute to:

My parents, Rocket and Chris, as generous a partnership as you're ever likely to encounter. This whole enterprise is simply not possible without their readiness to help.

To Dr. Wendy Were, who, for the smartest lady in the world:

a) assured me it would be a fine idea to purchase a 1978 Morris Minor and

b) is yet to discover I'm a complete charlatan.

Thankfully, she continues to exercise her poor judgment by being constantly, judiciously, and wisely supportive.

To Glyn Parry, who has always contorted himself backwardswise to help my scribbling.

To Brooke, who dresses me down and biggens me up the very best of all.

To Jane Palfreyman for her incredible enthusiasm and conviction, and to all the folks at A&U, whose willingness to get behind this book has been sensational.

To Ali Lavau for her very gentle methods of alerting me to when my writing sucked arse.

To Lou and Zoe at Sleepers, thanks for being awesome.

To the booksellers and librarians who support my books, who never seem to get a Guernsey in these things, thank you very much.

To Benytron Goldfield, the patron saint of hardball, whose assurance and belief have been unwavering and fantastic, who can do all the things that I can't. Much obliged, sir.

To my rock, my beloved Nancy Sikes, and to all who have plugged into her sockets.

To Adam Caporn, the Keiffy to my Migget. Well done.

To Miss Michela Faith Cleary, Minister in charge of Botanical Accuracy, for her steady support and stubborn belief and for the Carnac candles lit for exhausted authors.

To W. H. Arnden, who finally became a man in a Hungarian shower after a hot Turkish bath, whose love of Fact is exceeded only by his affection for nonsense.

To anyone foolish enough to bite when I asked The Batman Question.

And finally, thank heavens for Betsy, my brother, for the winter of Getting It Done, for swiping his credit cards to a thin nub to get Jasper across the line, and for being a constant and steady presence for the whole of this ridiculous ride.